To Shar

awesom

- Darren

The Fantabulous Tales of the Frivolous Fox

Darren Emond

Paperback ISBN: 978-1-7387750-0-2

Ebook ISBN: 978-1-7387750-1-9

Contents

Foreword

The Fantabulous Tales of the Frivolous Fox, as a novel, has a very weird origin story. I was living in Montreal at the time- this would be in the early 2000's, though memory is pretty hazy of that point in my life. I had enjoyed a pretty successful career as a commercial artist and a magician up until then, painting murals, working in comics, pulling rabbits out of hats and the like- yet my alcoholism had gotten well and truly out of hand and the tremors in mine were so bad that I could barely hold a pencil, paint brush, or a deck of cards. My girlfriend of eight years had left me and I was reduced to living in an apartment with one article of furniture (a couch I had brought in off the street) that was ridden with bed bugs. I slept on the hardwood floor for years, waiting to be evicted as all of my money had gone towards vodka and I was months behind on the rent.

My life consisted of three rooms. A hospital, the pool hall, and the one with that hardwood floor I actually found comfortable when I passed out on it in regular intervals. I still had a computer in that room, only because it was so old that the pawn shop didn't want it. With no internet, cable, or other amenities, and being unable to draw anymore- yet still with a serviceable computer, I was suddenly hit with a surge of inspiration that I should write a new novel.

In the span of about a month, I worked with vodka-fueled intensity and wrote the entire thing. It was about a hundred and fifty pages from beginning to end. I had no skeletal structure worked out whatsoever and just made the whole thing up as I went along, yet there it sat in the memory banks of that dusty old computer for years. I know it's trendy to say that the characters wrote themselves, and that I was just the spiritual vessel or some other such nonsense, but that's far too pretentious for my taste. (Though I will admit that, as I myself had no idea where the story would take me, it led me down some strange, unexpected roads.) The truth is that I really just wanted to write a story where the protagonist could be as irresponsible as I was and yet still have a great life- full of adventure and romance, yet set in a fantasy world where the rules of reality and accountability did not apply. I myself was clever enough that I was essentially working as a con-man in order to pay for my booze, and retrospectively speaking, Fox's disdain for noblemen and career as a thief was really just a result of my own attempts to somehow justify grifting from those who lived a normal, productive life. Looking back on it, it really was simple wish-fulfillment. I knew where I was going, and it was hardly a fairy-tale.

By 2013, I was given about two months to live by my doctor in Montreal who had been stuffing me full of Ativan to stave off the inevitable. I had developed a pretty serious addiction to that drug by then, which I was eating like candy to compliment my alcohol abuse. I had been kicked out of several apartments and was squatting in a boarding house in the worst neighborhood in the city, yet the old computer still came with me wherever I went. Gran mal seizures were a daily occurrence, and I would often go three weeks without any food, which wasn't missed anyways because my taste buds were burned beyond the ability to taste anything from constantly jamming a magic wand I used to perform with down my throat and vomiting into a waste-paper basket I kept nearby for the purpose.

After one particularly brutal night spent seizing on the floor, I promised myself that if I lived 'til morning that I'd get some help. The next day I called my parents in Sault Ste. Marie Ontario who sent me a bus ticket via the internet. I didn't have anything to pack, but needed to bring a case of beer in my duffle bag to keep from seizing on the greyhound. My buddy Zachariah stored all of my large oil paintings in his basement and helped me get on the bus as I could barely even walk anymore.

Arriving in Sault Ste. Marie, I barely knew where I was, my skin was jaundiced, I was malnourished in the extreme, and my parents did everything in their power to nurse me back to health. Several trips to detox, two rehabs, and one death later (lasted about four and a half minutes before I was resuscitated therefore I am technically a zombie) the tender ministrations of my parents and some good old fashioned grit got me clean and sober enough to start drawing and painting again, and I even set up a modest little apartment/studio in the downtown area. I got to work updating my portfolio and was reacquainted with my old comic-book buddies at several of the conventions around Ontario. Geof Isherwood hooked me up illustrating an Iron Maiden comic book for Acme Ink, and a few local writers hired me to illustrate their books as well. In my free time, struggling to stay clean and still suffering from extreme withdrawal, I brought out the old novel of the Fantabulous Tales of the Frivolous Fox and started self-publishing the story as a comic-book. I didn't remember how the story ended and just started transcribing it as I went along.

At one particular comic-con in Toronto, I showed my portfolio to a prominent Canadian publishing house; which, for the purposes of this foreword, shall remain nameless. I had been sober about two years at that point and had just finished a fully painted graphic novel for a local writer that they were really impressed with. I pitched them the idea of the Fox comic-book, but seeing as how I had a completed novel written already they told me that they wanted to print that first.

Thrilled at the opportunity, I returned to Sault Ste. Marie and got to work with fervor. I had by then transferred the book onto a laptop I had gotten as a Christmas gift from my parents and starting reading it- seemingly for the first time. Unfortunately, what I had been proud of back then was virtually illegible now. It was clearly the work of a frenzied mind, driven insane by alcohol abuse. Whole chunks of the book just didn't make sense, and there was no syntax or sentence structure, therefore I re-wrote the entire thing, basically from scratch, attempting to render a cohesive story whilst still maintaining that initial spark of derangement and sheer lunacy which fueled the entire thing in the first place.

Unfortunately, the publishing house I had intended to go with seemed content to lead me by the bridle for an eternity without ever actually publishing anything. I eventually rage quit, and back into storage the book went.

It was three years later when my buddy- and fellow comic book artist, Christopher Chamberlain invited me over to meet his family. After meeting the two most adorable children on earth, I was introduced to his wife, who is an author with many books under her belt- books that she published through amazon. Sensing an opportunity but not willing to relive the copious amount of stress I went through trying to get Fox published the first time, I gave her all the money in my wallet (I believe it was eighty bucks) and begged her to do the legwork for me. She agreed, though I'm pretty sure I got the better part of the deal. If you are holding this book in your hands, it's her you have to thank.

As this book goes to press, I am currently seven years and change sober. I volunteer throughout the community in Sault Ste. Marie, mostly speaking at high schools and mental health events about the dangers of addiction, have a great relationship with my family, particularly mom and dad, sister Debra whose place I crash at whenever I'm in Toronto, and her daughter MacKenna who can always look forward to finding a potato under the Christmas tree every year from her uncle Darren. Between stints volunteering throughout the community, playing chess at the library, and hitting AA and

NA meetings, I'm currently hard at work adapting the Fantabulous Tales Of The Frivolous Fox into a comic-book, this time with a slightly more salient script to work from. I'd love for the comic to do well, but even if my particular brand of madness doesn't catch on, writing and drawing all day gives me a certain sense of satisfaction that alcohol induced comas and the semi-lucid daily terrors which inevitably followed never could. Visualizing Balthazar and all of the character that inhabit it has me flexing creative muscles I had long believed to be atrophied and I'm loving every day I get to do it!

Rave reviews for The Fantabulous Tales of the Frivolous Fox-

"This is the greatest book ever written. I mean, seriously, it's that good- and I don't even know how to read." –Darren Emond

"Everyone should buy this book. Everyone needs multiple copies of this book!" –Darren Emond

"Amazon was wise to publish this book! You are wise for reading it. You have impeccable taste. You have lost weight. You look great." –Darren Emond

"Ceci est le meilleur livre que jais jamais lue. Et je sais meme pas comment lire en englais." –Darren Emond

"If for some reason you don't care for this book, it's not Darren's fault, it's yours." –Darren Emond

"Only Darren Emond could have illustrated this book!" –Darren Emond

"Darren Emond is the only man genius enough to review this book!" –Darren Emond

"Enough already." –Darren Emond

Prologue

There are few professions known to man in which fame is detrimental to one's success. Of these, the occupation of thief stands paramount. Fox, the reluctant protagonist of our tale, had been the best thief in the vast metropolis of Gemmen since he was a child. This has led many to believe that he was, in fact, much older than in reality. As a small child, Fox was the best thief in all of Gemmen, as a fledgling adult, he was the best thief on all of Balthazar, and as a young man, he was legend. His skills were sought after by rogues and noblemen, wastrels, wantons and wealthy alike. When Fox was commissioned to steal an artifact, one could be assured that the item was as good as purloined the moment the necessary coin crossed his palm. For the right price, the mysterious and elusive Fox could make all of one's problems disappear. In short, the demise- or prosperity of many of those who resided in Gemmen depended on whether or not they curried the favor of the infamous arch-thief.

Gemmen was a vast kingdom whose province canvassed most of the western hemisphere of the mythical realm of Balthazar. The summers were marked by intense heat from the small sun which hung low on the horizon, and the winters, though short, could freeze the bones of the stoutest of men.

Kingdoms the size of Gemmen were largely populated by beggars and cripples who could afford no shelter save for that provided by the monolithic walls which surrounded many of the larger cities, and kept those safely ensconced within from the unrelenting force of nature's fiercest elements. Inside the walls however, these had to contend with dangers equal in their voracity, yet subtler in their execution- that being the wills of bloated and greedy nobles who preyed upon them daily in their never-ending efforts to increase their equally bloated coffers.

The capitol city of Gemmen was one of four seats of powers on Balthazar, each kingdom having the same name as its province, and played host to every type of colorful character one could imagine. The massive outer walls barely held back a rich panoply of art, culture, adventure, excitement, wealth, crime, decadence, perversion, danger, and a plethora of exotic and wonderful terrors. Each new alleyway or turn of the road led one down a winding path to the great unknown. Fortunes were squandered and won at the gambling tables, true love was found and lost, intense tragedies were endured - great passion and pain could all be found if one knew where to look.

Giant, marauding barbarians wearing their scars as medals of honor lumbered through the streets looking to test their skills against all challengers, whilst silk covered whimsical sirens seemingly glided across the cobblestone with promises of even greater dangers evident in the gleam in their eyes and the curved corners of their full lips. Thieves slinked about in the darkness, eyes fixed on the fat purses of even fatter noblemen, both of whom were wary of the nameless dark robed assassin cloaked in the pools of blackness cast by towering ramparts where the sun itself was too frightened to visit.

Beneath the feigned security that the polished ironworks and well swept city streets promised, there was a complex web of basins and bars where true freedom was enjoyed only by those daring enough to seize it. For the right price, anything could be found here, and a man stout of heart, strong of limb, and sound of mind could make his fortune, or be crushed beneath the heel of his own ambition. The seedy underbelly of Gemmen, unseen, unnoticed, and rarely spoken of by the elite castes, was cruel and unforgiving, but for a man like Fox, it was the only place where true freedom, divorced from the laws of men, could be found.

Gemmen was overseen by King Alric, himself a fat noble of middling years who had inherited both his title, and a shock of receding blond hair, now grey at the temples, from his father, the tyrannical King Armin, who had nearly brought Gemmen to the brink of ruin through the decadent indulgences and abuses of power which marked his rule. Though he would never admit it, the wily King Alric had much in common with Fox himself, for both were of the clever sort who understood the value inherent in feigning weakness. Alric was content for his people to think of him much as they did he who sired him- a lazy, slovenly ruler who took little interest in the goings on of his Kingdom beyond the need for collecting taxes and the content of his cups. Indeed, the palace guards, and by extent, the city militia, regularly turned a blind eye to most of the illicit activity in the city, preferring to let the various guilds handle their problems internally, and only stepping in to restore order when things got really out of hand. King Alric himself made regular, clandestine use of Fox's services, and thus, having witnessed the King's machinations first-hand, our hero was one of the few people in Gemmen who was acutely aware that Alric was not so stupid as he allowed himself to be perceived; that he clung to power by hypocritically, frequently, and always covertly, availed himself of the services offered primarily by the thieves' and assassin's guilds which he so thoroughly denounced publicly as blights upon his civilization.

The guilds were what really kept order in Gemmen. Such it had always been. None held any memory of when this was not so. All professions, legal or otherwise, were overseen by the various guilds, and one could not perform one's duties without paying tribute to the leader of their respective orders. From smithies, to merchants, to assassins and thieves, the law of the guilds was absolute.

Fox, as we heretofore may have guessed, was a member of the thieves' guild; though very few members of the guild knew him personally. Only Cammarran, undisputed lord of the thieves' guild and a few of his trusted advisors had ever had any personal contact with Fox himself- that is to say, any contact that they were aware of. Countless men and women regularly passed Fox on the street, and just as many did not afford him a second glance. Even King Alric himself had only ever purloined Fox's services with Cammarran acting as intermediary, and only then at a price which would cripple most wealthy men, for Fox brooked no law but his own, and, save for Cammarran himself, despised those who considered themselves to be in a position of authority over others -particularly King Alric. In fact, Fox's skills were such that he had little need for gold at all, yet he loved charging exorbitant prices for his services for no other reason than to put a strain on the purses of the wealthy echelon of society. In his own way, he enjoyed the poetic justice in which the elite of Gemmen so relied upon the services of those whom they adamantly disavowed. The irony was too delicious for a man such as Fox, who took child-like delight in all of life's mischief, not to relish.

As a fledgling thief only recently inducted into the order, Fox often littered the streets of the beggars quarter with any coin that he might have on his person, yet this proved to have an adverse effect than intended, as those who populated these more desperate environs often fought tooth and nail with each other in their efforts to gather them up. It had since been clear to him that avarice was a virus, and he soon changed tack by leaving small bundles of cloth teeming with riches that he himself had no use for, cleverly hidden about for any desperate soul lucky enough to find them. As such, the labyrinthine collections of back alleys and canals in the more dilapidated quarters of the city still played host to desperate, wandering tatterdemalions who constantly poked and prodded every crag and cranny about them in search of bundles of treasure that they knew the infamous thief had left for them.

Many were the men and women who recited tall tales of having met Fox personally, and amongst these everyone had a thoroughly detailed description of the arch-bandit. He was seven feet tall some would say. Others held claim that he was immortal. Still others claimed that he was half were-beast, trapped in the forests outside the wall and raised like a man.

The truth, unimpressive as it is, was that Fox was the most unassuming individual that one could ever meet. He was somewhat short in stature, and wore generic peasant attire of the blandest variety. He did not possess the hulking muscles characteristic of the barbarian clans, nor the wasted features of the beggars who made up the bulk of the citizenry. His lithe, delineated physique he kept concealed beneath a patched shagreen tunic which held a multitude of hidden pouches, each of which had been graced with untold numbers of illicitly purloined items. His daggers were intricately sewn into the very fabric of his faded deer-skin trousers in such a manner as to keep them from jangling against each other, and his mud-caked boots were mounted upon a base of layered sheep skin which helped to absorb the impact of falls from great heights. The soles of said boots were made from the toughest leathers Gemmen’s tanneries had to offer, their texture much like Fox's rough, calloused hands, equally bronzed by the sun and hard-earned from years of scaling course and dauntingly steep ramparts. Despite this, Fox's fingertips were sensitive enough to distinguish between gold and copper by feel alone, and so supple as to be found pleasing to many a young maiden who writhed under their touch during a fleeting night's encounter.

Herein was the true genius behind the greatest thief of this mythical age. Fox did not seek fame, and did everything in his power to avoid it. However, the more impish of the fates always had means to catch one off guard, and arrogance, as always, was the most potent enemy of all great men. Though many had tried, the only man powerful, cunning, and stupid enough to bring about Fox's ruin, was himself.

A thief in Gemmen did not operate long without the permission of the Thieves' Guild. In fact, any young man or woman who attempted to entertain a solo career in some illicit manner or other inevitably had to contend with the guild, and Fox, despite all of his skills, was no exception. The punishment for disobeying the rules was always death. There was honor among thieves in Gemmen, and the strictest of the three tenets dictated that attacks on other thieves was not permitted without the strict endorsement of Cammarran-when they did happen punishment was swift and severe. Thanks in no small part to Cammarran; the thieves of his guild always took care of their own. There were however, occasional exceptions...

CHAPTER ONE - THE THREE THIEVES

Let us now turn our attention far from the golden panoplies of Gemmen's more respectable quarters. Let our gaze, difficult as it may be, linger only briefly upon the marvels of architecture which distinguish the tallest of Gemmen's spires and polished ironworks, past the crowded marketplace, past the thieves' district, past the squalid huts and ramshackle buildings, further still, to an area where there is little work for burglar or beggar. Let us pause only now, as we gaze down, through a thick veil of unforgiving rain, upon a lone, muddy street made muddier by the unrelenting downpour which is the only frequent visitor this home of the downtrodden ever receives. For most, the rain heralds the newest in an unending series of struggles for survival. For some, it is seen as a means to wash away layers of grime and transgressions best forgotten yet oft to be repeated. Between the huts and lean-to dwellings of those long abandoned by hope, walk three mysterious figures, each clad in a flowing black robe which clings wetly to their surprisingly well-toned and healthy frames.

Even in this dilapidated quarter of Alrics' Kingdom, the streets are far from barren. What were once men and women now scurry about like vermin, their glossy eyes darting about in search of shelter from the storm that most would never find. The three men, now walking single file, brush their way past the half-dead wastrels, sure footed despite the muddy slopes which perhaps had once served as streets. Absent here was the King's militia, as were his tax collectors, for in these desolate wastes, there was nothing to tax.

Upon shoving the last beggar aside, an old crone, still adorned in the shreds of a once-white dress she had worn her entire adult life, and so decrepit that it was quite plausible that this miserable night of unrelenting ferocity would be her last, the three men reach an unmarked door set deep into the wall of a crumbling cobblestone edifice which would have been condemned in any other borough of the city. The building itself is completely unadorned, and only the local dwellers of the slum in which it stands know it to be a tavern -one which is as likely to serve up a pipe-full of white lotus as ale. As the heavy, rotted door opens up to the smoke filled room, none of the patrons inside cast a glance in the direction of the three cloaked figures. These had been conditioned to mind their own affairs long ago, and there are none present in the ramshackle hovel, dust covered and stained with the blood of battles long passed too numerous for anyone to remember, and too frequent for anyone to care, who isn't here on business. In fact, though most of the hard looking menagerie who whisper to each other in darkened corners hold flagons of ale, this is for pretense only. The casks of wine and brew kept beneath an overturned plankard of wood which serves as the bar had long since soured. A single man in a repulsively dirty apron stands behind said bar, with an equally sour expression on his face, and here is the only one who glances in the direction of the trio, nodding slightly and tilting his head to one side. The three cloaked figures take this as the sign they had been expecting and head in the direction thus indicated, halting at a makeshift table held together mostly with twine and spit, yet nevertheless cleaner and more functional than any other present. Though most of the patrons of the unnamed tavern stand about in small clusters, there are three upturned oak barrels at one side of the table which none had dared to avail themselves of; and here the three men plant themselves in front of the only other seated there. This man also wears a cloak, very similar to those worn by the trio, though darker, the kind of darkness which seems to suck one in, especially amid the dull grey, sickly pallor of the environment. It is obvious to those present that a muscular frame and piercing, clever eyes are housed beneath it.

Upon seating themselves, the three men immediately pull back the hoods of their own cloaks, revealing desperate faces which nonetheless seem full of life and spirit compared to those others in the tavern, whose haunted stares and sunken eyes reveal not the slightest acquaintance with hope. Each of the trio bears small, well trimmed beards, the tallest being flecked with white. It is he who speaks now.

"Buoron." he whispers.

Upon hearing his name, the black-robed figure also pulls back his hood, revealing a clean-shaven, young face with lean, hawk-like features set under a mane of raven colored hair, shaven at the sides and tied back with straps of leather so as to keep his vision un-obscured. "Morgut, Maleon, Trigg," he whispers back. "It has been a long time. Of what service can I be to the thieves' guild?"

Morgut, the tall man who had spoken first, and clearly the leader of the others, spoke again." It is best if we keep the thieves guild out of this." he mutters in a hush voice.

Somewhat taken aback, Buoron nevertheless manages to keep his voice down.

"Am I to understand that this clandestine mission of yours is undertaken without Cammarran's permission?" he whispers.

Morgut only nods.

"Well." Buoron sighs. At least now I know why you three insisted that we meet in such..." he hesitates, glancing about, "austere accommodations."

Morgut leans across the table, his voice becoming even lower than the hushed whispers which mark all other conversation taking part about them. "We wish to take out a contract."

"Naturally" Buoron cut him off "Why else would you come to the assassin's guild?"

"We wish to take out a contract..." Morgut repeats. "On Fox."

Upon hearing the name of the legendary bandit, Buoron's eyes widen, disturbing the symmetry of his finely tapered features. When next he speaks, his voice is near inaudible. "Are you mad?"

"No!" hisses the one called Trigg. "We are desperate! The man leaves no work for the rest of us!"

"Hush!" growls Morgut, pressing his arm against the smaller man's chest. "For a thief, you draw far too much attention to yourself!" He takes in a deep breath of flaccid, stale air prior to continuing. When he speaks again, it is in the same low, composed manner he has governed himself with throughout the hushed conversation.

"Trigg speaks true. There are many of us who grow tired with Cammarran's clear bias towards Fox. If he were to be eliminated..." he pauses "You would find yourself earning a fatter purse than you have seen ere now."

"Morgut." replies Buoron. He speaks in careful, measured tone. "We go back a long time. We were once brothers in the thieves' guild before Cammarran dismissed me from the order. As you know, the assassin's guild took me in, as they take in many skilled thieves who cannot abide Cammarran's strict disciplinarian manner. I have less loyalty to the King of thieves than do you. But what you are asking is impossible. No assassin even knows where to find Fox, and even fewer would dare test their steel against him."

"We are not asking you too." replies Trigg. "This is why we came to the assassin's guild with this task. Your order is quite known for more... covert means of disposing of an unwanted individual."

"Nevertheless." Buoron shoots back, barely masking his growing discontent. "There is not one amongst my order who would take on this contract. Not for all the gold in Damaas. I suggest you forget this endeavor and strike whatever terms you can with Cammarran." the assassin pauses momentarily before continuing "However, if you are so malcontent, you will find that the assassin's guild deals more..." he hesitates, allowing a smile to spread across his thin lips for emphasis "favorably with its members." The smile is the first to grace an environment such as this in an age. It's meaning is lost on none."We always have need of new recruits. Perhaps you three might find taking lives more satisfying than purses."

"I told you we were wasting our time." whispers Maleon, the smallest of the trio.

Ignoring him, Morgut leans in closer to the assassin. "Spread the word." he whispers. "If any of your order should be interested in the task, know that his fortune; and reputation... would be assured."

Buoron seems to consider this for a moment, and replies with only the slightest of nods.

CHAPTER TWO - THE FEARSOME FOX OF GEMMEN

Try as he might, Fox could not keep the lids which covered his eyes from prying apart, despite the fact that his long lashes seemed to have glued themselves together the night before in an effort to permanently seal them. The sun rose fast on Balthazar, and within a short period of time it cast the full intensity of its rays upon him, each of which seemed unflinching in their intent to gaze upon the emerald green orbs that were Fox's only distinguishing feature. He squinted futilely, wanting only to remain in darkness until the throbbing in his head subsided. Nevertheless, despite a valiant resistance effort, the penetrating gaze of the sun seemed stubbornly determined to win the contest of wills between these two powerful entities.

Fox was never hung-over for long. No matter how heavily he indulged himself, a good night's sleep seemed to be all he ever needed in order to perform at optimum levels of efficiency upon the morrow. He knew that it would only take a moment for the fog to lift from his swollen brain, but in the interim, in the moments between slumber and wakefulness, he was too befuddled to register where he was.

He felt coarse, irritating sand throughout his breeches. The smell of salt, the strong breeze against his only partially numb face, and the clamor of crashing waves whispered to him that he was on a beach. Reluctantly, he allowed consciousness to emerge. In an instant, it all came back to him. The night before, he had purloined a cask of particularly strong Raimian spirits from a street vendor at the merchant quarters near the eastern wall, and, having nothing whatsoever to do, decided to partake in an evening swim outside of the city.

Despite Gemmen's vast size, it had only four main points of entry in the great wall which surrounded it. This made for exceptionally long delays for travelers coming to and fro the city, but was lucrative for King Alric, for in this way, he ensured that no one escaped having to pay the heavy border taxes he extolled. Nevertheless, the wall contained many secret points of egress that a single man without a mount could squeeze through, provided they knew where to look.

Gemmen was largely surrounded by a great forest where late-night terrors long since abandoned to the realm of superstition, still lurked. To the south, it was butted against a huge range of mountains where savage Hillmen, remnants of a bygone age, would permit no traveller to pass. On its western edge however, lay a great expanse of ocean where trading ships paid even heavier taxes than the caravans who entered the city via the wall. Fox often visited the beach at nightfall, for there were few pleasures that he enjoyed in life more than fighting with the ferocious riptides that were known to smash to splinters anything smaller than a heavily fortified, fully crewed fishing vessel.

Few dared visit the western shoreline after nightfall, and even the great ships, many of which had spent months at sea, remained anchored far out beyond the horizon upon approaching Gemmen after dark, sailing to port only after the bright rays of the day forced the beasts of the night back to their nocturnal lairs.

Fox always had the beach to himself during these times, which was how he preferred it, for he was a solitary man by nature. Despite possessing the silver tongue which his trade necessitated, he had only ever engaged in long bouts of conversation with Cammarran, and even then with great disinterest. His own internal monologue was always vastly more amusing than the concerns of mundane life lamented by others.

Occasionally, during his midnight adventures to the coastline, Fox would have to struggle with the feral predators who, emboldened by the night, would creep out of their homes in the forest in search of exotic new prey proffered from the ocean itself, but this was a small price to pay, for the cooling waters provided the only comfort from the scalding summer heat that one could enjoy -lest they be decadent nobles surrounded by slave girls, incessantly fanning their sweaty, bloated bodies with leafy branches.

Having refreshed himself in the salty, crisp water the night before, Fox had lain in the sand to dry, drink, and read. Few but the noblemen whose ilk Fox so readily despised had ever acquired the skill of literacy, and even Fox himself fought against ever having had to learn it. In his youth, Cammarran had insisted that he study with sword masters and scholars alike. The swordplay Fox thoroughly enjoyed, yet consistently rebelled against any and all studies that were not physical in nature. Once he had mastered the art however, he began to devour the contents of any book he could get his hands on. Philosophy, poetry, history, adventure stories, it all interested him, though he would never admit so to Cammarran.

Slowly, Fox rose to a sitting position and aggressively rubbed his eyes with the palms of his calloused hands. They refused to cooperate however, and allowed him to see the world only though a blurry filter, cheating him of the beautiful view of the sunlight flitting upon the waves. He shook his head from side to side quickly until both his focus, and his sobriety returned.

He entertained the notion of partaking in an early morning swim, but the looming shadow of ships on the horizon convinced him otherwise. Soon the piers would be teeming, and anyone who was seen about not standing on a plank would be subject to questioning by the armed regiment of the King's tax collectors. Fox knew that at any moment, the shoreline would be bustling with the King's men -all locked in a mad, bureaucratic frenzy with angry sailors who had been out to sea for far too long, and wanted nothing more than strong drink and nubile company -neither of which Gemmen's border patrol were particularly famous for.

Rising to his feet, Fox dusted himself of the thin veneer of sand that had dried upon him the night before and now clung to him like a second skin. Having finished his book, an exaggerated account of a traveler's adventures, Fox simply left it lying at his feet. He carried not even a purse upon his person, as he found that it weighed him down unnecessarily. He had plenty of concealed pockets in his thin green tunic and umber-hued leather breaches for whatever he needed, these consisting of little more than his small collection of throwing knives, a sliver of flint, and recently acquired fistfuls of sand. Fox preferred to keep his pockets empty so that he could fill them again throughout the day with whatever trinkets caught his eye, yet even these he found burdensome, and so he would cache whatever he did not redistribute to the poorer citizens in several secret locations throughout the city-none of which he could remember the location of.

The art of acquisition was something Fox never cared to understand. In fact, he was so un-invested in it, that he never cared to understand why he never cared to understand it. Whatever he wanted, he simply took. And he never had to worry about shelter. He had made his lair everywhere from mansions to mangers, and never gave a thought as to where he would spend the night- his only concern that he never lingered in one place overlong. Life was easy, and the longing for a true challenge had been steadily growing within him.

He made his way towards the portion of the great wall which separated the beach from Gemmen and protected the city from the massive tidal waves that the fiercer storms sometimes brought with them whenever they deigned to visit.

Occasionally, he would camp out in the surrounding forests, spending a week or two hunting and fishing and living off the land, but had never ventured particularly far from the capitol. He had always thoroughly enjoyed his life as a thief in Gemmen, only lately, he had begun to become bored. He could endure anything the great western Kingdom had to throw at him, and had survived more than most, yet there was nothing he loathed more than boredom.

The sandy path he had been treading soon sprouted grass which dampened his boots with dew and before long he stood at the foot of the great wall. He steered clear of the main gate which marked the westernmost entry point to the city, and positioned himself further down. He ran his fingers across the great, monolithic surface, stopping at an unmarked stone framed by loose masonry. This he pressed in, and was greeted immediately by the low hum of straining gears and internal clockwork as the mechanisms buried deep within began to move. His actions were rewarded when a giant slab, large enough to admit one man, began to turn slowly inwards, swiveling upon one of the erect metal shafts that ran throughout the wall and ensured it's durability against storms and cannon-fire alike. Such passageways were hidden throughout Gemmen, and only the utmost elite of the thieves' guild knew of them, though even these possessed no knowledge of when, or by whom, they had been constructed. To

Fox and his fellow thieves, the back alleys and rooftops of Gemmen contained an entire world that most who shuffled about in diligently shepherded herds never dreamed existed.

Fox felt his way through the narrow shaft, which funneled the strong wind coming off of the sea, and slipped through the tunnel. The passage sealed shut behind him and he merged into the crowd which wound its way lazily about in well-rehearsed rhythm, too pre-occupied with the drudgery of daily existence to notice his coming.

He was now in one of the busiest merchant's quarters of Gemmen. Portions of the city this close to the western wall depended on availing themselves of foreign trade as quickly as possible, relieving sea-going vessels of their wares before the traders themselves could travel deeper into the city in search of better deals for their goods brought from far-away lands. Balthazar relied heavily on trade, for climate conditions varied greatly from one corner to the next, and as a result, no one city-state was truly self-sustainable, and relied extensively on its neighbors for everything from exotic produce, seeds, spices, and the more illicit of substances native to their respective lands.

Even at this early hour, the streets were bustling with activity, and in no time at all, gliding invisibly through the streets, Fox had filled his pockets with exotic fruits and viands and settled himself into a quiet corner to breakfast.

There was no doubt about it; Fox thought to himself as he gnawed on a strip of salted jerkey- he was restless. He filled his belly and, with no particular destination in mind, began meandering through the city in his never-ending search for adventure.

Cammarran awoke upon a bed of soft, down filled pillows, nestled under a cover of silken sheets. As he did every morning, he quietly scolded himself for the comfort he took in such finery. As a thief, he had endured much hardship in his youth without complaint; but those days were long past. He was never a particularly good thief; he had never been overly strong, or fast, but one thing he always had in abundance was guile. He was so clever in fact; that he managed to become the youngest master of the order the guild had ever known. But that was long ago and he was no longer a young man. He had managed to grow old in a profession not known for its alumni. The notion of sleeping in a horse's stable, or upon a windy, rain soaked rooftop was completely alien to him now. He had grown weak in body, yet remained strong in spirit. Most nights, despite the rigors of responsibility his position entailed, he slept well. Recent events however, weighed so heavily upon him that, despite the comfortable lavishness he surrounded himself with, he found little rest.

The King of thieves had eyes and ears everywhere. His position as leader of the thieves' guild meant that he brokered information as readily as he fenced goods. His spy network was such that he was easily the most well-informed man in all of Gemmen. The city was alive to him. Like a bloated spider at the center of a web, his sensed the vibrations that ran through the streets. He did not simply know;

he felt, everything. His home beneath the Bear's Den tavern was not only the secret headquarters of the thieves' guild, but also a vortex of illicit information with himself at the epicenter.

That the Bear's Den was a front for the thieves' guild was perhaps the worst kept secret in Gemmen however, for most knew that Cammarran ran the order in his home buried deep beneath the sawdust-covered floorboards of the tavern. King Alric maintained the pretense that he had no idea where the guild operated from, yet often sent his runners to and fro the inn on clandestine errands in service of his own political machinations. Occassionally, some citizen outcry would compel the King to raid the inn in symbolic effort to rout the guild, yet Cammarran was always notified well in advance, and such charades were few and far between.

Cammarran held a position of both fear and respect in Gemmen, and the Bear's Den was widely known to be neutral territory, where no untoward behavior was tolerated lest whomever responsible wished to deal with the wrath of their own guild leaders -all of whom owed a debt to Cammarran.

Recently, it had come to his attention that three of his order had approached the assassin's guild in the hopes of having Fox eliminated. Cammarran had raised Fox since he was a boy, the two men would never admit it to each other, but their relationship was much more father and son than mentor and apprentice. The errant thieves had been dealt with rather effortlessly. Their execution had been very public, each one slain, ironically enough, by members of the assassin's guild themselves. Their deaths had been very public, performed in the center of the thieves' district, and served as a warning to any who would defy the thieves' code. Their actions were a mere annoyance, a minor wrinkle, one of many; that had been successfully ironed out. The chain of events the three fools had unwittingly set into motion however; was something else entirely...

The greatest advantage the assassin's guild had over the thieves' was that, through clever manipulation of a loophole in Alric's laws, they were allowed to operate quite openly. Citizens of Gemmen were permitted to enlist the services of bounty hunters so long as whosoever wronged them had broken the King's rule. It was under this pretense that the assassins operated. The fact that none of their targets were ever taken alive meant that Alric kept his dungeons mostly empty and was spared the cost of feeding prisoners, and the fact that many of said targets had not in fact run afoul of any law whatsoever was purely speculative. As such, assassins operating under the guise of bounty hunters enjoyed the King's protection so long as they did so under the scrutiny of their guild leader, a man of iron will and iron thews known as Hergod, who despite his advanced years, was still revered for his swordsmanship. The caste system under which Gemmen operated was only enhanced by the presence of the assassins, for whosoever had the most coin to offer them always had their problems, and the men responsible for them, methodically eliminated. The fact that members of the thieves' guild were, on the surface, in direct violation of the laws of Gemmen meant that arranging the executions of Morgut, Trigg and Maleon was child's play for a man as powerful as Cammarran.

Morgut, Trigg, and Maleon had never been particularly competent thieves, if they had been, they would have known the dangers inherent in being easy to find -for rarely did these three ever leave the quarter, lest they were on an errand for Cammarran himself. The assassin's guild delivered their executions free of any payment, much in the same way that the thieves of Cammarrans' order frequently assisted them in turn.

Cammarran had been alerted to the plot by Hergod himself, who had once been a deadly assassin in his own right, and now clung to power through the fear and intimidation his reputation had garnered him. Cammarran and Hergod had always been allies through necessity, much in the same way that the previous leaders of the assassins and thieves guilds had been throughout every generation. The two men rarely had contact with one another, and even then, never in person. The unspoken rule was that if, while executing a contract, an assassin helped him or herself to whatever they cared to steal, than it was perfectly within their rights to do so. In turn, if a thief of Cammarran's order was forced to take a life during a particularly dangerous mission, such was equally acceptable. In this way the two guilds had managed to maintain a healthy, symbiotic relationship throughout the ages, trading with each other in much the same way as the fisherman's guild traded with the bankers'. The only difference was, on a surface level at least; the assassins and thieves' particular guilds were not licensed or endorsed by the King. In reality however, they were equally, if not more so, essential cogs in the complex machine-work that was Gemmen.

Despite being a man more physical than cerebral, one did not rise to position of leader of the assassins by being stupid, and Hergod knew that should he endorse the contract offered for Fox, that such action would strain the long standing peace between the assassins and thieves guilds by arousing the wrath of Cammarran- perhaps even becoming the catalyst for a war between the two orders.There too was the fact that Hergod, despite being an assassin, considered himself a man of honor. He would not simply accept whatever contract was offered him, but selected his targets carefully, methodically. He believed his guild to be a boon to Gemmen that they offered a service to those who had nowhere else to turn. Cammarran was not sure he could disagree.

According to the emissary that Hergod had sent to the Bear's Den, the assassin Buoron, once a prolific member of the thieves guild itself, had been offered the contract on Fox's life. Buoron had been excommunicated from the guild by Cammarran's decree, for he had proven to be far too bloodthirsty for the delicate work that was required of thieves. Morgut and his two cronies Trigg and Maleon likely assumed that Buoron held much resentment towards the thieves' guild, making him the logical choice to execute their dire plot. What the three thieves could not have known however, was that it was Cammarran who had requested of Hergod that he take Buoron under his tutelage, and that Buoron still held a great deal of loyalty towards him.

Cammarran had believed that Buoron's skills were far more suited towards the profession of assassin rather than thief, and Buoron, in turn, derived much more satisfaction out of his new career path. He had always felt a secret debt of gratitude towards Cammarran for recommending him to Hergod, as he much preferred an environment where his skills at taking lives were appreciated, not frowned upon.

And so it was, that immediately after his meeting with the three thieves, Buoron sought out Hergod directly to inform him of the plot. Hergod, who himself owed much of his rise to power to Cammarran's clever machinations, had not only relayed the information to him, but offered the services of his guild to clean up the mess in his house. The contract on Fox was denied by the master of the assassins, but in its place, three new contracts were forged, sealing the fate of Morgut, Trigg, and Maleon.

Though Cammarran and Hergod interacted only rarely, when aid was asked upon by the other it was always forthcoming. In this respect, Hergod did not fail, for the execution of the three traitorous thieves had been performed with ruthless efficiency, each having their throats slit in broad daylight and in full view of the citizens of the thieves' district. A reminder had been sent for all who knew how to read the unwritten language of thieves. Cammarran was not a man to be outwitted.

There were three rules the thieves guild abided by. Any other transgression, provided the proper amends were made, could be forgiven. Every thief was made aware, upon their induction into the guild, that the penalty for breaking any one of the trinity was death. Two of these rules had been decreed by King Alric's predecessors, had been passed down from King to King, and had been inherited by every leader of the guild since its inception. They were the framework upon which the alliance between the thieves' quarter and the crown was built. That a thief could never steal from the poor was paramount of these. A merchant targeted so often that he went bankrupt meant that he could not pay his taxes to the King, which in turn stunted the overall economy in Gemmen, something that no King could allow. The second tenet decreed that any act of violence towards women and children was strictly prohibited. The thieves' guild was the home for professionals, not butchers, and there were appearances to consider, lest the King himself feel pressure from his subjects to come down hard upon the thieves' district. Inductees to Cammarran's order had to be masters of stealth. Those who did not make the cut, those who attempted a solo career as thief without the sponsorship of the guild, were carefully and methodically eliminated.

The final rule- King Alric, as well as all of the Kings before him, leading back to the powerful warlord Gemmen himself for whom the entire western hemisphere of Balthazar was named, had nothing whatsoever to do with, yet was perhaps the most important of the three for the continuing survival of the guild. Loyalty to one's brothers was essential, and crimes against a fellow thief within the order were not permitted. Cammarran was a strict man. He had always enforced the thieves' code ruthlessly. Despite this, in a city the size of Gemmen, there was always the thief who believed he could outsmart him.

This was not the first time during his tenure that the code had been broken. The result was always the same. No matter how ambitious, no matter how clever, the thief who broke the code was found out, sought out, and destroyed. Nor was this particular turn of events surprising. Dissent towards Fox was inevitable. Not only were the most sought after, as well as most lucrative contracts consistently assigned to him, but his skills were so legendary that the wealthiest of nobles had begun to double their guards at night, had thickened their ramparts, and had built their towers so high that few were the thieves brazen enough to climb them. In short, Fox had been making life very difficult for the other thieves of the order.

The niggling problem that Morgut, Trigg and Maleon presented had been dealt with. All knew the penalty for breaking the thieves' code. There would be no one seeking retribution for their deaths. Cammarran need not concern himself regarding the three thieves again. All members of his order had been reminded what fate awaited them should they cross their master. Nevertheless, fate was oft cruel in equal measurements to those who would seek to wield it. Perhaps it was fate's design to illustrate that it was master of all, that all were slaves against its capricious whim, for the incompetent, traitorous fools now served as the catalyst for a problem infinitely greater in scope- the resurrection of the most powerful foe the Kingdom has ever faced since lo before its very inception; and one whose name Cammarran had secretly hoped never to hear spoken again... Krillian.

When Hergod informed Cammarran of the the plot to assassinate his ward, he brought news which chilled his very blood. Cammarran was a brave man, braver than most, yet the news that Krillian, the deadliest assassin Balthazar has ever known, the most feared man in the four realms, had emerged from self-imposed exile to claim the contract of Fox's life was the culmination of his worst fears materialized. He had never concerned himself overmuch with the safety of the impetuous young thief. E'en when assigning him the most dangerous of tasks, he trusted in his abililty to overcome any obstacle set before him, yet he alone knew Krillian's secret, he alone knew that if there was one sword on all of Balthazar capable of slaying the fearsome Fox of Gemmen, it was Krillian's.

Eight years gone, when Fox was yet but a child, the arch-assassin had mysteriously vanished. Hergod was secretly glad to see him go, for though the guildmaster had inducted him into the order, then nothing more than a street urchin in whom he saw potential, Krillian had long since begun operating without his endorsement. The penalty for such was the same as in any other guild, yet Hergod, even with an army of trained killers at his disposal, would not oppose him. Such was a war he would not win. Upon presenting himself before Hergod to claim the contract on Fox's life, he did not state where he had been, and none dared to ask. That Hergod had annexed the contract was irrelevant. That none now lived who could pay the contract was irrelevant. An assassin had been commissioned to eliminate a target, and Krillian had accepted the contract. He would stop at nothing until his task was completed.

The assassin's guild, much like the thieves, were permitted to operate within the confines of Gemmen so long as protocol was considered. Hergod and Cammarran both proved capable of ensuring their respective guilds continued existance through strict enforcement of their code. Krillian had no such qualms. He believed all to be beneath him. He cared not what lives he took. His willingness to take on whatever contract was offered him, providing one had the coin, garnered him fortune enough that he could have retired for ten lifetimes, spending each surrounded by such luxury as to make a nobleman seem a peasant. Upon his disappearance, many thought that he had done exactly this. Still others believed he had moved his enterprise to the golden city of Damaas, the only Kingdom on Balthazar greater in wealth and scale than Gemmen, but these rumors quickly dissipated. Balthazar was not so large that a man like Krillian could simply disappear. The traders, nomads, vagabonds and rangers who made their livelihood upon the caravan routes brokered information as readily as they did goods, if Krillian had resurfaced ere now, Cammarran, Hergod, and likely all of Balthazar would have known. The truth, Cammarran knew, was that Fox was the only target Krillian felt worthy of his blade. The fates of the thief and the assassin were intertwined, destined to collide. Were they to do so now, Fox would not survive. Fox's own talents had caused the young thief to become overconfident. Should he learn that the grim spectre of death now hunted him, he would likely rush headlong to meet him. He was perhaps the only man brave, and stupid enough to view such as flattery. Quick and decisive action was needed were he to save him.

That Krillian bothered alerting Hergod if his intent was a mystery. Perhaps he had done so knowing that the guildmaster would inform Cammarran, and thus lure his prize out of hiding. Perhaps a lingering thread of loyalty yet tethered him to he who had first set him upon his path. Hergod was the first to see the potential in the boy he discovered upon the streets of Gemmen, much in the same way Cammarran had recruited Fox, yet though Fox grew to thrive within the thieves' guild, Krillian's thirst for blood could never be sated. He became twisted and evil, oft preferring to butcher and dismember his prey when more covert means of elimination were asked for. Long had Cammarran known that he must send Fox away from Gemmen. The time was overdue in fact. He alone knew what awaited him outside of Gemmen's walls. It was selfishness which caused him to delay. No longer; to remain meant death. Word had not yet spread that the legendary thief of Gemmen was now being hunted by the most dangerous man on Balthazar, though Cammarran knew that that very soon, the people of the capitol, as well as the province beyond, would be speaking of little else. Were his plan to succeed, he would need to seize upon the moment. He had known for quite some time that his young ward was becoming increasingly discontent with life in the western Kingdom. Like Krillian before him, Gemmen had increasingly failed to challenge him in his chosen vocation. Cammarran had attained his position as undisputed master of the thieves' guild not by brawn, but through a mixture of deft strategy and shrewd cunning. If he were to save the life of his friend, it was these virtues that he needed to rely upon.

The guild-master rose from his bed and, bare foot across fine carpeting, made his way to the large, gold leaf framed mirror across the room. He barely recognized the man who stared back at him. He had gotten old. He had begun the practice of shaving his head to mask his thinning hair. The black silk robe he wore bulged at the center and strained against the girth of his once slender midsection. Now riddled with anxiety, his profile did not make for an impressive appearance. He had always secretly hoped that, upon achieving his destiny, Fox himself would be the one to replace him as master of the order, yet his young apprentice had never shown even the faintest interest in the task, and even if he had, Fox had proven time and again to be far too ill-equipped for the day to day monotony of fencing stolen goods and negotiating contracts -to say nothing of the strain involved in managing a city-wide network of rogues and outlaws.

For most of his adult life, Cammarran had ruled the thieves' guild here in Gemmen, and the long days had taken their toll. Unlike Hergod, who occasionally joined the ranks of his assassins on a hunt, Cammarran rarely left his extravagant chamber tucked beneath the seedy, un-kept tavern overhead. His days were mostly spent journaling his accounts in the massive leather-bound log book which sat upon the study in the giant, windowless room, or meeting with clients in the adjoining antechamber. He would be doing none of these today. Since hearing the news of Krillian's return, Cammarran had done nothing save revise his plan.

The more Fox wandered about aimlessly the various warrens of Gemmen, the more restless he became. He knew her every secrets, he had raced across her every rooftop and crawled through her every underground passage. He had dined in her finest restaurants and slept in her dirtiest alleyways. Gemmen, with all of her beauty and wonder, nevertheless proved to be a lover who no longer stirred his blood.

More and more, though he himself had not yet come to realize it, the notion of leaving had been percolating in his brain. The thought of new adventure always excited him. In fact, Fox viewed the entirety of life as nothing more than a grand series of adventures. He had lived a hard life, yet never did he abandon his cheery, irreverant disposition. Whether he was sleeping on a stone floor or on silken down, it mattered very little to him. Fox had known no other home but Gemmen. He was barely into adulthood, and already his legend had spread to faraway lands that he himself had yet to visit. The irony was not lost on him.

Often he would pass by huddled crowds in the street, knit closely together that they might share in the warmth of lamp-light, whose flickering torches trapped retreating shadows into each of Gemmen's back alleys where escape was impossible. These he would hear speak of the legendary Fox of Gemmen, and these he would pass by without a glance thrown his way. Fox was the every-man, innocuous, invisible; his ability to blend in to a crowd bordering on the supernatural. He was notorious and faceless, celebrated and alone.

It was late afternoon by the time Fox reached the Bear's Den tavern and the streets were teeming with those who held to a false sense of security beneath the warm gaze of Balthazar's sun. There were few noblemen who dared enter the thieves' district at any time of day, and fewer still who wished it known what business brought them. Fox was unaware that his footsteps led him hither, and was surprised when he arrived. He had visited the tavern countless times in the past, yet, if asked, none of the scheming faces of those who represented regular clientele would have ever marked his passing.

The Bear's Den was a tavern not unlike any other, and any man who entered her doors was either thief, client, or, on rare occasions, a weary traveler seeking to quench their thirst, unaware of the establishment's true purpose. These last never lingered, for the tavern sold sour wine, stale beer, bread so hard that, wielded as a cudgel, one could bludgeon a man to death with it, blue cheese that was never intended to be said color, and meat that needed to be hacked into cud with a rapier before one could ever hope to chew it. Cammarran saw each man and woman who had business with him personally, and there was no way to discern who was a figure of import and who was not. Here, the comings and goings of every breed, class, and character were common.

Fox sat at a table near the back of the tavern, as was his wont, and feigned waiting patiently for a serving wench that he knew would never come. The comely females who worked for Cammarran had abandoned their sense of hospitality, as well as their pretenses to virtue long ago. They knew that a table full of raucous soldiers would afford them a better night's coin than a mere mendicant in peasants clothing ever could- however they had to earn it.

Eventually he received the signal that he had been waiting for. The fat barkeep, his apron so stained that rumor told it had never been cleaned, left his place behind the bar and made his way to a small oil lamp overhanging the only other door in the establishment. The slovenly man proceeded to light it with a fresh piece of kindling plucked from the nearby hearth. This was the signal that Cammarran was free to meet with any who needed to speak with him, either client or thief.

Bowing his head, Fox hurried through the door to a small back room stacked with casks and barrels. The room was lit by a single oil lamp bracketed against the wall. Fox tugged at this and was immediately rewarded with the opening of a hidden panel set squarely in the stonework. He made his way down the winding stairwell it presented until he came to a solid iron door at its foot. Up until now, the sparse metalwork which adorned the tavern had been rust-covered and corroded, but the the reinforced iron slab in front of him seemed to glow by comparison. Fox banged his calloused hand loudly against its surface with the sound of leather smacking steel. Almost immediately, a thin steel bar along the surface slid back to reveal two squinted eyes, weighed heavily with the burden of responsibility; but with the gleam of fierce intelligence etched into their penetrating gaze. The heavy door swung open to reveal the figure of Cammarran.

As per usual, the lord of thieves was clad neck to heel in a flowing black robe woven of the finest Raimien silk. His bald pate gleamed in the lamplight which, in a room completely devoid of the sun, danced eerily across the brightly polished surfaces of heavily varnished wood, chrome and gold plated trinkets that decorated the inside of the antechamber where Cammarran conducted all of his business. The small room had a single door on the other side, identical to the one Fox just entered which in turn led to Cammarran's inner sanctum, but it was this, much smaller room that was the epicenter of Gemmen's criminal underworld. In the middle of the room sat a large oak table so heavy looking that one had to wonder how it made its way down the narrow stairwell the day it was first brought in. In stark contrast to the pristine decor of the rest of the chamber, the large table was littered with assorted papyrus, vials of ink with worn plumes sticking out of them at jagged angles, heavy tomes stacked in erratic fashion, and other tools of Cammarran's trade too numerous to mention. There were no guards present, for any business conducted in the small room beneath the floorboards of the inn was best conducted between as few parties as possible, and none in Gemmen would dare raise a hand to Cammarran.

Fox braced himself for the familiar disappointed, condescending smirk to spread across Cammarran's features which his mentor always chose to wear when greeting him. Instead he was surprised to see the old man's wrinkles converge about an ill-fitting, somewhat forced smile.

"Fox!" he ejaculated happily, before slinging a meaty arm over his shoulder, pulling him inside. "Just the man I wanted to see! How have you been?"

To say that Fox was taken aback was an understatement, for no matter how much coin the young thief brought into the guild, Cammarran had heretofore almost always addressed him as one would a petulant child.

Releasing his arm from Fox's shoulder, Cammarran made his way to the large desk, sat behind it, and signaled for Fox to seat himself upon the adjacent, red sequined chair which was the only other item of furniture present. This Fox did with no small amount of speculation, for he trusted not the recent shift in demeanor, and was on guard for some manner of trick.

"Fine Cammarran." he said in a low voice, through pursed lips, beneath a wrinkled brow. "How are you?"

Cammarran leaned back in his chair and rested the back of his shaven head upon folded arms.

"It has occurred to me recently..." he began, ignoring Fox's question altogether."That I have never truly been able to cure you of your wanderlust, despite my best efforts to coerce you into purchasing a villa and setting down roots."

There was truth in what the thief lord said, yet Fox could not shake the notion that he was being played like an instrument finely tuned by honeyed words.

"Was it not you who said that a sedentary life equaled a dead thief?" he responded, verbally jousting as best he knew how.

Cammarran gasped in exasperation, yet the warm smile never left his countenance.

“Yes Fox” he said. “Though I had always hoped that you would save some of the gold you have made and retire from thievery altogether. Besides, when have you ever listened to my advice anyway?”

“How many times must we have this conversation?” replied Fox. “I am a thief, and a thief I shall always remain. Wasn’t it you who once told me that you never met a retired thief?”

“Perhaps you missed the point of that story.” Cammarran replied, clearly struggling with exasperation, yet never allowing the smile to escape his tenuous grasp. “Nevertheless, I feel as though the time has arrived for you to take your leave of Gemmen."

If Fox was surprised before, it was nothing compared to this moment in time. Never before had he heard Cammarran even hint at the idea that he would ever leave Gemmen.

Cammarran missed nothing, and instantly recognized how his comment had caught his young friend off guard.

"Don't pretend like you haven't thought of it before." he continued, and for the first time, Fox realized that he had.

"Are you not bored here? There is no feat which you have not accomplished. No task to challenge you, no palace or guard tower that you have not raided..."

Cammarran continued to speak for some time, but Fox had stopped paying attention. Normally he would while away the time during one of Cammarran's lectures dreaming of new adventures that awaited him outside the walls of the Bear's Den. Now his mind was alive with ideas of adventures which awaited him outside the very walls of Gemmen itself.

Had he not longed to visit far away kingdoms? Had he not yearned for unknown thrills and exotic new pleasures? He decided that he had.

"You're right!" Fox suddenly interjected. It was perhaps the first time he had so readily agreed with Cammarran. "In fact, it is past time I moved on from here! Why, just think of how much time I have wasted already!"

Fox's mind was utterly consumed by the new notion. He was perhaps the wiliest, most clever young thief Cammarran had ever met, yet despite this, Fox rarely chose to house more than one thought in his head at a time.

This was the moment Cammarran had waited for. He rose heavily from behind his table, wasting not a second. A scroll suddenly materialized in his hand, pulled from an inner pocket of his dark robe. This he rolled into a tube, then, holding a candle flame over a stump of red wax, allowed it to bleed onto the parchment. He picked up a steel cylinder from his desk and pressed it into the wax. Then he prepared a second parchment in like fashion, though this one he did not seal, and pressed them both towards him.

“One of these parchments has been marked with my seal.” he announced “Present it to Ciella, Queen of the thieves’ guild in Damaas. She and I have shared a... history together." his voice trailed off slightly before continuing whilst his internal monologue retreated to times past where it refused to remain “The other contains a map to her location. The guild in Damaas operates out of a tavern called the Tarot. The letter identifies you as a thief named Barnabas who has chosen to relocate in the east. Guard them both well, for your belongings will be searched thoroughly before you are allowed entry to the eastern Kingdom, and the soldiers there do not take kindly to thieves. With the letter, you will be granted license to operate in Damaas under Ciella's endorsement."

At this last comment, Cammarran's gaze shifted slightly. He stared off into a corner of the room, yet his permanently squinted eyes refused to pull focus. "I do envy you the sight of the golden city. I myself would love to see it again." he muttered, more to himself than to Fox.

Fox had not known that Cammarran had ever been outside of Gemmen. The thought that he too was once a younger man, filled with the same wander-lust that now coursed through his veins, had never before occurred to him.

He had no time to entertain these new ideas however, for, having completed his pitch, Cammarran approached him in quite an unexpected manner. Placing the rolled parchments in Fox's outstretched hand, he gripped him in a fierce embrace. Fox tensed. His body became rigid as he awkwardly returned the gesture.

"I shall miss you my friend" Cammarran said. "Be wary on your new adventure. I have taught you everything I know. I doubt not your resourcefulness; it is your stubbornness I fear will be the death of you."

No further words were spoken. For the briefest of moments, it occurred to Fox that this would be the last time he and Cammarran would ever speak; but he found the thought unpleasant, so he shuffled it aside. He slid the parchments into his tunic and, spinning on his heel, raced out of the room.

On some level, Fox had suspected that he had perhaps just been manipulated, but, not caring for the notion, he readily dismissed it as well. He shot out of the tavern with the spring in his step that always spurred him onwards towards new adventure.

Cammarran stood alone in the antechamber. His ploy had worked. With Fox well away from Gemmen, given a new alias, and he the only man who knew of it, the odds of Krillian finding him narrowed. Though he had reasons of his own to believe a confrontation between the assassin and thief was inevitable, he could not allow Fox to face him without first learning of what awaited him in Damaas. For too long had the guildmaster kept him in Gemmen. It was always his intent that the young thief should travel eastward upon a path of self discovery. Perhaps it was selfishness which had kept him from sending him away sooner. Nevertheless, recent events forced his hand. He could not protet his ward from what awaited him forever. He should have been elated. He had known exactly what to say in order to manipulate him. The plan had worked perfectly; yet he could not shake the weight of melancholy which pressed heavily upon his sagging shoulders.

CHAPTER THREE - BOLT

After his meeting with Cammarran, Fox had his mind set on leaving Gemmen immediately. In fact, he had been heading directly to the easternmost border when, as was frequent, he became distracted; for his path coincided with the great Collosseum of the city which buttressed the eastern wall.

Fox had found this to be rather rude, for he had his mind set upon beginning his journey strait away, yet the city of Gemmen had thrown the Collosseum directly in front of his path in a clear effort to waylay him. Nevertheless, he was not one to ignore good fortune, and the Collosseum had always been one of his favorite places to visit.

Next to the palace itself, the Collosseum was the largest structure in all of Gemmen. Alric had it constructed shortly after being crowned King, for gambling had always been a favored pastime of the citizens of not only the capitol city, but the outlying villages and farms that speckled the perimeter of the province. In fact, people came from far and wide to bet on the horse races there, and a large marketplace composed mostly of inns and taverns had sprung up around it to accommodate them. In short order, once the Colloseum had been erected, the eastern section of Gemmen had been transformed into a bustling hub of commerce -all of which was heavily taxed by the King.

As Fox neared the monolithic structure, which stretched the length of several city blocks, the roar of the crowd inside told him that a race was about to begin. He had just stolen a small basket of fruit from one of the local street vendors and decided to take in the show. Concealing himself in the cast shadow of a portion of the towering outer wall of the Collosseum, Fox stuffed the basket into his tunic and began to climb. His fingers and toes, adamant as a sculptor's chisel, pressed themselves into the minute crags offered by the smoothened mortar and, like a spider, he began to scale the imposingly stark incline. Years of practice allowed him to race up sheer stone surfaces such as these as quickly and as easily as a squirrel might a tree. The crowd inside was too heavily distracted to notice as he swung over the apex of the wall and dropped as silently as a falling leaf behind them. The distance between the top of the wall and the uppermost rung of stone benches on its inner side was only a few meters, and the cushioned soles of Fox's boots absorbed the impact effortlessly. In this way, he completely circumvented the exorbitant fee that was charged for entry through the main gate. He had no doubt that he could have easily obtained the necessary coin one needed to pay in order to gain access in a more socially acceptable manner, but this method was for other men, and he had no wish to add to the wily King Alric's already teeming coffers.

The interior of the Collosseum, hidden from view by its thick outer walls, was dominated by a large circular race track at its center, surrounded by rows of stone benches rising in rings; much liked the inner markings of a concave tree stump. The rings broke at intervals leaving large laneways where people could travel from one row to the next. The further and higher of these concentric circles were for the peasants and working class citizens, while the smaller, lower tiered rings were reserved specifically for those who had more coin to wager on the outcome of the races below. Travelling from the center point of this giant, radiating circle outwards to the higher levels, one could actually witness the physical transformation that a man might make after losing his fortune, and his very sanity to the strong vice of gambling. The Collosseum was one of the few places in all of Gemmen where mendicants and merchants, paupers and princes alike, congregated. And with any luck, or lack thereof, one quickly became the other based entirely upon the whims of chance.

Fox made his way through the throngs of people, weaving expertly through the masses that stood pressed shoulder to shoulder, towards the epicenter where the best view could be had. In no time at all he found a seat that he desired. The problem was that a fat nobleman had the discourtesy of squatting himself there before Fox knew that he wanted it.

A casual glance of the scenario was all he needed to ascertain the situation. The man, being a noble, wore fine jewelry. His fat fingers were decorated with amethyst rings which sparkled vainly in the sunlight. Chains of finely wrought gold collected beads of sweat off the rolls of his double-chin, and the fine silk robes that flowed about his ample frame were suited more for a cushioned carriage ride than for the dust covered, cobblestone streets of the district. Men of this type usually tended to surround themselves with the most decadent of elitist entourages, yet this particular noble was alone. His outing that afternoon was clearly a clandestine one. His sweat was palpable. He had wagered greatly.

"Excuse me good sir!" Fox bellowed as he approached the sweaty, anxiety-ridden nobleman.

The noble seemed very startled, and shot a frenetic, irritated look at Fox before he replied. "What is it you want?!" he ejaculated rudely. His half-crazed, manic expression told that he had no time or patience for beggars.

Undaunted, Fox leaned close and whispered in his ear. "I am known as Gorm, agent of the great spy Julius. Your wife has contracted me to have you followed. Clearly gambling upon these races is something that she... disapproves of."

"Wha... what is it you want!" spluttered the man again, though this time with a voice laced with panic, and absent the air of distracted irritation he had heretofore displayed.

"At ease." said Fox "Slip a few coppers into my hand and return home immediately. I'll inform Julius that I never saw you here. If he disbelieves me, you will have the perfect alibi. I suggest that once you get home you pamper your spouse greatly, so that she will not soon forget that you were in her company all afternoon."

The fat man rose to his feet nervously, handed Fox a small satchel filled with copper and, thanking him, ran off towards the gate as fast as he could; jostling, and even knocking members of the assembled throng aside in his haste.

Fox sat down, threw a few dates into his mouth and bit into them. He had a wonderful view of the race. Most thieves were heavy gamblers, Fox was the exception. Better to let others gamble for you and purloin them of their winnings should they get lucky, he thought.

He was awash in a sea of rabid gamblers when the horses shot out of the gate. It was a sight of unparalelled beauty. Most of the cheering crowd he was immersed in was clearly interested in the race solely on its ability to earn them coin, but not Fox; for him, the animals were intoxicating in their splendor. Their tautness of muscle and sinew as they buried their hooves into the ground, only to propel themselves forward as though intending to take flight enthralled him. The track churned like butter beneath their powerful legs in a symphony of strength, beauty and power as knotted muscles danced under leathery flesh.

Through it all, one horse in particular was a vision of pure speed and grace. Her limbs seemed not to touch the ground as she veritably soared across the track, the only evidence of her passing being hoof marks upon the sand that none of the thousands of attentive witnesses ever saw alight. Every thrust of her powerful limbs shot the horse forward as though fired from a canon, so that her rider seemed to be merely clinging for his life, a hindrance rather than a help.

Fox saw a kindred spirit in the animal. He wanted her; and when he saw something that he wanted, he usually got it.

The horse won the race by a clear margin. Fox's keen ears caught enough of the dialogue around him in order to discern that her name was, appropriately enough, Bolt. A smile spread across his lips and his emerald eyes, like encrusted jewels, sparkled.

After the race, most of those present filed towards the exits, there to resume their mundane lives and carefully coordinated roles in the clockwork machinery of Gemmen's echelon, the tiers of which a scattered number had only recently managed to descend. A few lucky ones made their way towards the booths that made up much of the perimeter surrounding the track. Here, winning notes would be exchanged for coin. Each note was stamped with the King's own seal, making forgeries next to impossible, which was fine with Fox, for he had no patience for earning his living by any other means save the instant gratification of thievery.

Fox had no note, yet secured his place in line at one of the booths nonetheless. This was a tactic that he had used many times in the past, and was one of his favorite games to play.

He sidled behind two noblemen of middling age, one slim and short of stature, the other much taller and so grotesquely obese that he took up as much horizontal space in the crowd as he did vertical.

"I knew it!" yelled the fat man. "With a name like Bolt, how can one go wrong?! Ha ha!" He drove his fleshy elbow into the smaller man's chest. The man merely grunted uncomfortably and returned his laughter. The palpable stink which wafted on their breath was the least amongst indicators that both men were inebriated.

The fat man waved his note in front of his slender companion. "Eighty gold coins!" he announced for all to hear. A belch punctuated the end of each of his slurred sentences. "And my wife says I shouldn't gamble! Ha! I think I shall visit a whore's chambers this evening! It will be nice to be properly appreciated by a woman for a change!" Then he threw his head back in laughter. The weasel at his side laughed heartily as well. It was clear to Fox that the small man hoped to be the recipient of some random act of impulsive generosity as a result of his companion's newly aquired fortune.

The fat man wore a small satchel tied to a large strap of leather he used to belt his cotton shirt in place, this was unbuttoned half way down his chest, and ended in a vee just over where the frilly chemise had been forced under the thick leather strap which had been winced so tightly as to accentuate the bulge of his midsection. His bare chest was covered in coarse black hair that he clearly wished for all to see, and clung wetly to the thin, sweat-stained fabric. He slid the winning note into the satchel. It would not remain there for long.

Speed, as always, was the key ingredient to any good theft. Above all the skills that Fox had nurtured over the years, he knew this to be of the utmost import.

The act took place in seconds. Fox sidled past the fat man. Had he wished to do so, he could have done so invisibly. However, he allowed his shoulder to graze the drunken man's own. The action was nearly imperceptible, yet was performed with the skill of an accomplished artist. A good thief is entirely dependent on the crowd that he works in. In environs such as these, one would expect to get jostled by a passing stranger, and it was for this reason that Fox's actions remained entirely unnoticed. He slipped his nimble fingers into the satchel the moment that the two men collided, the larger action concealing the smaller one. The deft fingers, their muscle memory as lucid as that of an accomplished harpsichordist, purloined the note, crumpled it neatly, and folded it inwards, tucked neatly into the crook of his palm. Without slowing his forward momentum, Fox disappeared into the crowd.

A good thief understood that no matter how successfully a lift was performed, it was always a good idea to distance oneself from the crime, yet despite himself, Fox could not help but linger in order to bear witness to what was sure to be a comedy of errors of epic proportions, one which promised to be far more rewarding than the theft itself.

The two men reached the front of the line and presented themselves to the teller. The fat man reached into his satchel, his broad grin transforming into an angry scowl as his fingers darted about the bag's interior in their frantic quest to find the winning note. Upon realizing that he had been robbed, the obnoxious lout spun about in a fit of impotent rage. When he did not receive an immediate admission of guilt from any around him -one that he doubtless believed his angry expression would somehow illicit, he turned his rage upon the nearest available target- this being his sycophantic, fair-weather friend. With a meaty left fist the size of a glazed ham, the big man lashed out and struck him squarely in the jaw. The skinny man was knocked onto his backside by the blow, but, being only momentarily stunned, was immediately up again, swinging his fists madly.

In mere moments, the scene had devolved into utter chaos, punctuated by a cacophony of screams, wails, and shouts of profanity. The Collosseum's own security forces, drawn to the sound of gnashing teeth and cracking ribs like metal to a lodestone, ran headlong into the melee, fire-hardened wooden cudgels raised high. The shrieks of high-strung noblewomen drew their private security escorts into the madness, desperate for a chance to vent their frustrations after a long afternoon of playing nursemaid. Muscle-bound barbarians and honorless mercenaries, who were always spoiling for a fight, seemingly appeared out of nowhere, not caring who they struck down or why, so long as it provided good sport.

In short order, the entire area had degenerated into a symphony of violence, and Fox thought it wise to leave before it could reach its crescendo. He turned on his heel gleefully and slipped away from the ever-escalating riot he himself had instigated, leaving behind a rising swirl of dust that enveloped all unfortunate souls who happened to be near it.

It was a bouncing gait which delivered Fox to one of the booths at the far end of the Collosseum. There was no longer anyone waiting in line by the time he reached it, and the teller, dressed in the dark blue uniform that marked him as a servant of the King, was just making preparations for the next race. Fox presented himself in front of the man, even younger than he, and, grinning ear to ear, presented him with his winning note.

"My!" the young fop cried upon gazing at the small piece of parchment. "We don't usually get winnings this large! You should be congratulated on your good fortune sir!"

"Thank you" replied Fox. "Perchance, can you tell me where I might find this horse's owner?"

"Lord Henry." The man responded with an eager smile, full of youthful exuberance. "I suspect that you can find him at the party tonight. After a win like this one, he'll be sure to be celebrating at the Silver Stallion! You can buy him a drink if you like."

"Thank you." replied Fox, "I believe that I shall."

Fox scooped up his eighty gold coins, placed them into his tunic, and wandered off into the distance in search of a fine bottle of wine and another fruit basket to while away the rest of the afternoon with. If he were to travel to Damaas, he thought, he might as well do so with a capable travelling companion; preferably one who did not talk overly much.

The Silver Stallion was a favored inn near the Colloseum where many of the top jockeys and their masters congregated. Fox had been here before on some errand or other that he could not recollect, yet he remembered disliking very much. He generally cared for no company save his own, but especially despised finding himself in a den of noblemen, preferring instead the more disreputable establishments in the seedier quarters of Gemmen, where the ale was cheap, the women cheaper, and the perfumed air of pretention was nowhere to be found.

The inn was near the stable grounds where the most prized stallions were kept, not far from the Collosseum itself. It stood far enough away from the stables so that the smell of offal that wafted about on the morning breeze did not offend the delicate sensibilities of the noblemen who frequented it, yet close enough to remain in the vortex of the thriving night-time community the Collosseum had brought with it to the area.

The sun had set and Fox made his way unnoticed through the crowd of revelers dancing and singing in the streets, their alcohol-fueled exuberance cutting through class and caste, revealing the carnal desires beneath which united them them all during the nighttime hours and were just as likely to be disavowed upon the morrow when sobriety brought with it the unwelcome visitor of regret. The orphanages upon the outer perimeter of Gemmen teemed with the product of such unions between the privileged and the poor, cast aside that their matrons might return to the heart of the city unburdened and equally unable to break the cycle of pain and punishment in their neverending search for pleasure and reward.

The Silver Stallion was simplicity itself to locate. It was taller than the plethora of somewhat less austere inns which surrounded it, this one being reserved for the company of the wealthiest noblemen of the racing circuit, and stood at the epicenter of debauchery which drew all towards it. Though the building had been erected only recently, the architecture mimicked that of ancient Gemmen. Laticed ironworks, meticulously polished so as to reflect the name of the establishment, were wrought about the entire structure, ornate in the extreme so as to seem gaudy and pretentious to all who did not suffer from these same defects of character. The large wooden door which seperated the entrance to the inn from the garden courtyard where the lesser castes were permitted to congregate, was intricately carved with the images of several horses running in erratic pattern across its surface, and was guarded by two of the largest men Fox had ever seen. The guards did not wear the standard dark blue uniform of the King's soldiers, which led Fox to believe that the Silver Stallion provided its own security, likely chosen for their discresion as much as their other talents. They were garbed in long, flowing pantaloons and leather vests which left their broad, muscular chests and abdomens visible, and despite the few, tipsy young maidens who hung about the entrance vying for their attention, seemed utterly focused on duty.

Fox had busied himself most of the day by filling a small basket with gourmet meats and cheeses which he had availed himself of from the many shops and stalls in the area. With basket in hand, he walked confidently up to the two men, each of whom stood a head taller than he, and had to gaze down to look at him.

"At ease gentlemen!" he cried to the nearest of the two.

"Noblemen only" came the curt, well-rehearsed reply.

"Noble!" Fox answered back with a jubilant grin "I have been called many things, but never noble. No, you have proven yourself as astute as you are wise good sir, for I am but a poor errand-boy sent by the palace with a gift for Lord Henry."

Fox lifted the basket under the nose of one of the rigidly poised guard, letting him smell the rich aroma of the delicacies inside.

"King Alric himself, I am told, though I was hired by retainer only, wishes to congratulate the Lord on his recent victory." Fox continued, still smiling ear to ear.

"Noblemen only." came the reply again, though this time with a slightly more uncertain tone accentuated in its pitch.

"I see." replied Fox, letting his gaze fall to the ground despondently. "Very well then, I shall simply return to the palace. I do hope that our beloved King takes no insult to the fact that his gift was refused."

Fox turned about slowly and began to amble away.

"Wait!" cried the guard. Fox spun about, a look of concerned curiosity upon his face. The two guards exchanged quick, darting glances at one another. Losing none of his air of authority, the one whom he had been conversing sidestepped from the entrance.

"You may deliver your gift to Lord Henry." he said "Provided you do not linger."

"I would." countered Fox, "Yet I have no idea what his Grace looks like."

The second guard, silent up until now chimed in. "You will find him seated at the bar, surrounded by his many well-wishers. He is a somewhat..." he hesitated "girthy man with a red skullcap."

"Thank you!" Fox replied, not caring to demean the guards any further. He patted one on the shoulder, and without waiting for the heavy door to be opened for him, swung it open himself in one fluid motion and boldly made his way in.

Inside, the inn was a thief's paradise. The huge room, crowded to the rafters with drunken revelers, was heavily decorated with ornate tapestries which stretched up to the high ceiling, where a massive chandelier reflected the glow of the valuable gems it was adorned with. A rainbow of multi-colored lights flickered in the firelight of the chandeliers' many branches, and reflected off the spilled wine, each bottle of which cost as much as an average man's daily wages, that lay in puddles upon finely polished tables. Sculptures of geldings crafted from iron and brass by the most skilled of artisans stood upon their hind legs in every corner, trapped forever in full sprint. The tankards of wine each man and woman held in their ringed fingers were spun from the finest ivory, each one of which was being constantly re-filled the moment its contents were libated by the many voluptuous serving wenches who wandered about with crystal jugs of wine, and little else, pressed against their heaving bosoms.

Lord Henry was not difficult to locate. The decadent nobleman in the red skullcap was being hoisted above his peers near the gleaming, ornate bar, and was trying futily to down a flagon of wine whilst simultaneously maintaining his balance atop the self indulgent crowd, who were just drunk enough as to believe that they could hold his massive bulk aloft indefinitely. His white silken robe was now virtually purple from spilled wine, and all were singing bawdy songs as they passed him about. Fox decided that he needed to bide his time before he approached the nobleman. He set his basket of goods carelessly upon the nearest table, and sunk into the darkest corner that he could find.

For a thief, Fox was embarrassingly low on patience, and was relieved when eventually, the time came when Lord Henry was seated at a table alone. Many of his peers had left the party early, some were in line at the outhouse behind the inn, and still others were enjoying more voluptuous company than his own in the upstairs chambers.

Seizing the opportunity, Fox glided across the room, weaving expertly through the many hazards represented by stumbling drunkards, those who hurried to see that their cups could never be drained, and the dizzying array of stimuli which was more disorienting than the libations therein.

"Good evening." he said to the horse owner. "Do you mind if I join you for a moment?"

Lord Henry was startled. He had not heard Fox's approach. "Wha...?" came his drunken reply. His ruby adorned skullcap sat lopsidedly upon his head, revealing what whispishly thin hair he still had glued to his sweaty scalp.

Without waiting for a reply, Fox sat down at the table. "Your horse is an impressive animal." he said "How much would you sell her for?"

Lord Henry seemed genuinely surprised. No doubt he was wondering how a peasant was ever allowed admittance into the inn, while simultaneously marveling at the audacity that such a one might think that he could afford to purchase a nobleman's prized steed. Whether the shabbily attired man before him were mad, or simply some court jester sent to entertain the austere classes, Lord Henry could not know, yet he seemed, for the moment at least, content to play along. “Ha!” he laughed. “That horse stands to make me a lot of coin! She’s the fastest on the circuit! Why, I wouldn’t sell her for less than fifty pieces of gold!”

“Let’s make it eighty.” Fox replied “If I may have her tonight." He reached into his tunic, found the coins there, and splashed them across the table.

Lord Henry's eyes nearly bulged from his rotund face. Seemingly fully recovered from his stupor, the greedy nobleman pawed furiously at the gold, successfully blanketing them under the heavy folds of cloth which swathed his large, flabby arms.

"Are you mad?!" he cried through clenched teeth. "To cavalierly toss such a fortune about! Are you so new to Gemmen that you are unaware that there are thieves everywhere? Why, the legendary Fox himself may well haunt this very room!"

Fox pressed on. "There is one other condition." he said.

The greed in Lord Henry's eyes dulled but a little as he stared down at his arms, seemingly trying to see through them and gaze upon the gold hidden underneath.

"You must allow me to sleep in your stables this night."

Lord Henry stared up at Fox incredulously. "My stables?" he replied. "Why, we are now seated in one of the finest inns in all of Gemmen, surely you would prefer a soft bed with a warm strumpet to share it with?"

"Surely." replied Fox. "Yet how would I hope to pay for such services? I have just given you my every coin."

At this, Fox rose slowly from the table, and, helping himself to a bottle left to sit carelessly nearby, stole out into the night. Lord Henry watched the young man leave, his jaw agape, a stupid look of awe, averice, and incredulity writ upon his features.

CHAPTER FOUR - LAIR OF THE WHITE WORM

Fox was greeted the next morning by the aroma of fresh horse manure and the piercing sensation of slivers of straw in his every orifice. The secret of spending the night in a horses stable, he knew, was to become so blindingly drunk, that any foul odors were readily believed to be one's own, and therefore easier to ignore.

He forced himself to his feet. He had the distinct impression that events following his encounter with Lord Henry were probably best left forgotten. This was convenient, for he had forgotten them. What he had believed to be a bottle of fine wine had been, in actuality, stiff Raimien spirits, and, being completely unfamiliar with the concept of restraint, he had devoured its entire contents before consciousness refused to partake in his exploits any longer and abandoned him in disgust. He could not remember if he had picked any lock in order to access the grounds, or merely vaulted over the gate fencing in the property the night before. All he knew was that, through casual inquiry, he had at some point ascertained the location of the stabling grounds which housed Bolt- though he had seemingly decided it wise to reaquire his faculties before seeking her out.

He gathered his disheveled form from the haystack that had been his bed the night before and with no small amount of effort, made his way towards the blurry outline of an outhouse he spied in the distance. He travelled but half the distance when he dropped his trousers and flooded an ant hill. The horses did not avail themselves of the outhouse, he thought to himself, and if he were going to share accommodations with them, he would afford himself the same privilege. He gazed up into the sky. The sun was just beginning to rise and cast a dazzling cornucopia of colors across the horizon which hurt his eyes, but whose beauty refused him the ability to look away.

A young pony wandered about who gave the impression as though it knew where it was going therefore he decided to follow it. Coming across a nearby troth, he plunged his head into it in an effort to fully restore himself. It wasn't until his breath threatened to give out that he withdrew from the water and was rewarded for doing so by the sight of a small satchel, framed between wisps of his own bangs which clung to his face and sent rivulets of water to collect on his jerkin, slung over a nail protruding from one of the many stalls. In it, he found dried oats mashed into a gruel no doubt reserved for feeding the horse resided within and sat down in the dirt to breakfast. He savored every bite, every swallow with the same zeal that he savored life itself, for pleasures, large and small, existed only in tandem with one's ability to appreciate them. Once taken for granted, e'en Balthazar's greatest gifts would seem as naught but an inconvenience during one's fruitless search for satisfaction amongst the plentiful bounty.

It did not take him long to locate Bolt, for she was housed in the finest stall the stables had to offer. At this early hour, there were no handlers about, and Fox could have ridden off on any one of the horses he chose; but Bolt was by far the finest of the lot, and after all, he had paid eighty gold pieces for her.

Bolt was awake and alert when Fox approached her, prancing about in her pen and scraping the dirt with her hooves restlessly. Had he thought her beautiful before, such visions, gleaned from a distance, proved to be but the merest glimpse of the reality. Like Fox himself, she was lean, and heavily corded with lithe musculature which delineated her every feature. Her leathery flesh was a mixture in color of bronze and gold and her mane was so black that it swallowed the light from the sun. She had long legs and angular facial features; in fact, every inch of the young mare seemed as though it had been engineered for speed by some cosmic sculptor of infinite genius and skill.

Bolt neighed cheerfully when Fox approached. It was almost as though she were expecting him, though perhaps she was simply eager for a morning run. He decided that he would oblige her.

Bolt rose up on her hind legs to greet him as he leapt nimbly over the gate. Upon descending, Fox greeted her by gently pressing his face against hers. Bolt returned the gesture and neighed what seemed like poetry into his ear. For a moment, his cunning, fiery green eyes introduced themselves to her large, doe-shaped amber ones, sparkling with the welcoming intelligence of a kindred soul, a fierce spirit which longed to roam free. Wasting no time, he slung a nearby, highly polished saddle about her back, then, all in the same fluid motion, he kicked open the gate and swung himself up onto his newly acquired partner in crime.

It was evident that the mare wished to make her way to the race track in the distance that she might avail herself of some exercise, for try as he might to steer her towards the front gate separating the grounds from the city streets, his actions resulted in him being flung from the saddle and thrown to the ground. Fox shared in the joy of the horse's accomplishment, for never afore had he been so easily tossed about by man nor beast. Upon picking himself up from the floor, his laughter must certainly have convinced the animal that further mischief lie in wait were she to follow her new companion, for she restrained herself to a cantor during his second attempt and allowed herself to be guided.

Upon arriving at the front entrance to the stable yards, Fox realized that he had not picked the lock the night before as he had surmised, for the large iron gate still remained securely bolted. It took only a moment for his nimble fingers to work the lock with a thin metal filing he found nearby, yet even this simple chore seemed to take an eternity, for both he and Bolt were skittish, and eager to be on their way.

Bolt's gait slowed to an aggravatingly slow pace upon entering the congested streets beyond, and she let Fox know of her discontent by neighing petulantly. In fact, it was all he could do to keep her restrained. She was a racehorse after all, and was not used to the slow, plodding trot that a stroll through the bustling city streets of Gemmen necessitated. Fox felt equally uneasy, for as the pair made their way through the large, well-maintained cobblestone roads about the Collosseum and into the narrower, dirty streets nearer to the eastern border, all eyes seemed to be on him.

The streets of the capitol were always congested, no matter what time of day, or in what borough one visited, though Fox had never been so acutely aware of this fact as he was now. He had spent a lifetime acquiring the skill of moving about unnoticed, yet Bolt was far from the lumbering oxen and pack horses that the people here-about were used to seeing at this hour in the morning, and all eyes were fixated on the new novelty. Most had never seen a mare half as fine as she outside of the Collosseum, and for those who had, it was usually some young nobleman out whoring poised in the saddle. The sight of a raggedly garbed peasant with a tangled mess of uncombed hair upon so fine a steed was as alien a sight as if Fox had hovered past mounted atop a flying apple-cart.

Though he and Bolt were eager to escape the crowded, claustrophobia-inducing streets of Gemmen, Fox had one final errand to perform before taking leave of the city.

Not far from the eastern exit, the great wall which surrounded

Gemmen merged into a steep mountainside that had been carved expertly so as to become part of the wall itself. The cliff led up to a lofty, snow-capped peak which stretched off southward as far as the eye could see; where the Hillmen, fierce warriors who steadfastedly refused the advent of progress and culture, still haunted the crags. The cliff-face was even smoother than the man-made wall which had become an extension of it; save for the mouth of a small cave which had been carelessly boarded up with what were now rotted planks of wood. The cave, known to the locals colloquially as 'Balthazar's Maw', rarely saw any visitors, for on the rare occasions it was spoken of, such tales of warning were articulated by strained voices full of superstition and dread. Occasionally, during the fiercest of winter storms, some desperate vagabond would dare to venture inward in search of shelter, only to be never heard from again.

Fox alone was acutely aware of the fate of these unfortunate souls, for he himself had explored the cave both thoroughly and frequently -it being one of the few haunts where he could always be assured of his privacy. He knew that the horrors within fully eclipsed that of any rumors which surrounded it, for no imagination was deranged enough to conjure up the image of what lie beneath, even if plucked from the depths of a feverish nightmare.

Beyond the small opening of the cave, a short corridor led downwards at a steep angle before branching into a web of tunnels which wound their way in interweaving patterns throughout the entire mountainside. These caverns branched out under Gemmen itself and ran the entire length of the city. Thus the common folk above lived their entire lives without ever knowing that beneath their very feet lay a maze of underground avenues that were, in and of themselves, merely a small portion of an enormous subterranean labyrinth.

Even Fox did not know how far the tunnels extended, or what purpose they served, yet he surmised that the entire mountain was riddled with passageways throughout, each layered deeper than the next. He had never been able to explore as far as he would have liked, for the only source of illumination in the tunnels themselves was the lantern that he always brought with him, and this could not stay lit indefinitely. He had sometimes wondered if the entire mountain itself was hollowed out, like some kind of giant ant-hill. The idea may have seemed impossible to most, but what Fox had already born witness to in these very depths caused him to have a different perspective on what most deemed possible.

Those few who ventured to explore what lie beyond Balthazar's Maw, should they be quick of wit and sword alike, might have been able to contend with the giant, venomous spiders, each the size of a man, who roamed about the passages in clusters -charcoal black with fur like barbed wire sprouting from their lance-like appendages, but none save Fox was handy enough with a sword to face the true terror that lie within.

Gigantic worms, likely as long as entire warrens of the city above, slithered throughout the underground arteries, so engorged that their girth completely filled the tunnels themselves. There were fewer of these than the hordes of spiders, especially nearer to the surface, yet they became ever more prevalent in both number and scale the deeper one descended.

From previous encounters, Fox knew their flesh to be eerily transparent, save for the sickening yellow sheen of a slimy mucous membrane which laminated their entire bodies, and thin, greenish-blue veins that stood out in stark relief and spiraled about their entire, ethereal forms. The mucous seemed to serve as some kind of lubricant, which allowed them to squeeze through the narrow tunnels that their own constant passing helped to give form.

He had not seen a worm from the rear, yet the few he encountered possessed heads nearly as thick around as their bodies. Their squat faces consisted of little more than gaping mouths that were almost completely circular in shape, rimmed with jagged teeth set in layers, which seemed to be designed to slowly pull their prey into the sucking hole of their cavernous maws.

At the top of their heads, and almost comically disproportionate in scale, the worms possessed two lid-less eyes, no larger than pebbles, set deeply into their faces so as to be nearly covered in the folds of the veiny, engorged flesh which surrounded them. Their skin was so translucent, that one could actually see the path these retinas traced back to the miniature brains set deeply behind them. Upon the contours of their bodies several barbs of wiry black hair could be discerned, which rendered the mountain arteries smooth to the touch with their constant stroking of them for traction.

Inside their tubular bodies, internal organs were completely visible as well. Lungs, stomach, intestine, and a tiny throbbing heart seemed to compose the entirety of their anatomy. With each beat of that pulsating organ, rushes of purple-ish blood could be seen coursing along the winding path of veins, which caused the entirety of the creatures to throb like a raw nerve, and in turn caused their ribbed forms to shrink and contract. Being completely devoid of bones, tendons, or musculature of any kind, this constant, pulsating rhythm seemed to provide them with their only means of locomotion.

Only once had Fox seen the stomach of one of the beasts half-full with what remained of a partially digested spider-creature still thrashing about in churning digestive fluids. He counted himself lucky that he had never seen the body of a man in such a state, for such a grotesque, macabre sight would have likely forever burned itself into his psyche and proven a burdensome presence amongst his memories.

Despite their horrifying appearance, Fox had always found the worms to be of little challenge. Their miniaturized eyes were especially sensitive to light, and the sight of his lantern always provoked them into lunging at him madly. To slay them, he merely had to thrust his sword into the gaping chasms of their mouths, positioned at the right angle, and allow their own mandibles to force the blade slowly into their miniscule brains in their efforts to devour him.

On rare occasions, Fox had stumbled across the corpse of one of the worms during his explorations that had become entangled in a cleverly laid snare of webbing the size of a fisherman's net set across its path. These had been fed upon slowly until they had met their agonizing demise. The spiders seemed to feed on naught but fluid however, for once the worm had been sucked dry, its lifeless body was left to clog up the underground passage, so that only the faintest trace of air could make its way past their inert forms as it waited patiently for them to rot away.

Occasionally, the tunnels opened into enormous caverns the size of cathedrals, ceilinged with canine-shaped stalactites made entirely of jade which dripped slime onto the coursing rivers beneath. The rivers themselves reflected the green of the jadestone and transformed into heaving waterfalls as they spilled further down towards the center of Balthazar itself, much like emerald blood being pumped through veins, winding their way back towards some unnatural central nervous system buried deep within the center of the world.

The gigantic rooms, scattered throughout, offered the only source of illumination in the depths of the underground labyrinth, for the jadestone appeared to emit its own lightsource, reflected off the water, bathing all in a dim emerald glow. The atmospheric luminescence clung to the thin layer of moisture which wafted about like a fog, infusing it somehow, lending an eerie ambiance to the entire chamber. Regrettably, there appeared to be no means of harnessing said light, which made further exploration impossible lest he become forever lost in the darkness.

In his more introspective of moments, Fox sometimes wondered if Balthazar itself were some manner of living organism, and that the great cities which sprawled across his surface were naught but infectious wounds, scarring him with razed land used to erect shelters to house the ultimate parasitic organism- that of man. Fox had always considered the primal motivation of his race, this being the acquisition of wealth, to be a plague; one which infected the minds of those who had much and drove them to prey upon those who had little. Perhaps the giant worms and other beasts of myth and legend that he had thus far encountered were merely Balthazar's way of fighting back lest such infection spread internally. Perhaps these creatures of seeming horror had just as much right to live, and even thrive, as did his own, which held a hollow, capricious, and even arrogant claim to be the more civilized and enlightened of the species. Had he himself not consistently lamented the thinly veiled pretenses of what was called civilization? Perhaps this is why he preferred the more honest, wild demeanor of the more overt of nature's predators, who seemed nevertheless content with what Balthazar provided them, as he did the scheming, subtle machinations of his own species which drove them ever to consume more than was needed. Could the giant worms themselves, much like healers who administrated leeches to an infected wound, not be seen as the protectors of some larger immune system? Could their purpose be nothing more than that of staunching the growing reach of man? To keep the parasitic infestation contained upon the surface so that it could not spread to Balthazar's inner organs? Did the worms not, in fact, keep the internal rivers and channels, the very blood and airways of Balthazar sterilized from their corrosive touch?

Fox never dwelled overly long on these complex issues. There was no true way of knowing what his natural place and purpose was in this life, nor did he relish the notion of any predetermined fate save for that dictated by he alone. There was no point in spending hours on end asking questions when there were no readily available answers to be had. Though he possessed a shrewd intellect, he had long ago decided that such musings were best left to scholars, not thieves. His own sense of curiosity was suited more towards discovering wonders, not contemplating them.

There were many such wonders to be had in the realm beneath the mountain, but on this day, Fox was of a singular purpose, and had no intention of going about exploring where he had already been. His sights were set on new adventure, and he longed to uncover what other secrets Balthazar had to share in the lands far from Gemmen. He would have forgone the labyrinth entirely, despite the fact that it was one of his favorite places to visit and was set in such proximity to the eastern point of exit that his path had set him towards, yet if he was truly to take his leave of Gemmen for good, he could not do so without his favorite toy that he had so cleverly hidden within- the one place he knew of where it would remain untouched by any hand save his own.

He lashed Bolt to a tree a fair distance from the cave. The mare did not seem to resent this, for Balthazar's maw was one of the few places within the towering walls of Gemmen one could be assured of their privacy, and she seemed grateful for the respite, having had her patience tested in the extreme by making her way hither plodding through teeming masses of curious onlookers she was far from accustomed to navigating given her life upon the racetrack. With Bolt munching contentedly upon what was perhaps the single patch of grass in all of Gemmen untrodden by countless footsteps, Fox made his way to a small, gnarled bush which sat next to the cliffside. The leafless branches, long dead yet whose limbs, locked in rigermortis, were laden with unbreakable, thorny brambles, scraped against the calloused leather of his hands in their efforts to pierce them, and nearly succeeded in doing so when he came upon the miniature oil lamp that was stashed here upon his last visit. He set the lamp on the ground, felt around in his tunic for the sliver of flint he kept there, and, finding it, began to strike it upon a coarse stone nearby in an attempt to ignite the wick. The cloth was nearly dry from remaining too long untended to, but eventually burst into flame when an errant spark shot towards it remained agitated just long enough to combust what remained of the oil. The enthusiastic burst of light created by the newborn flame immediately dimmed to a warm yellow glow once realization dawned upon it that there was little to feed upon. This was barely visible under the bright morning sun and flitted behind the mud-caked glass of the lantern's chamber. Fox cleaned the lantern as best he could, wiping it on the front of his jerkin, then, hoisting it up to eye level, kicked aside a rotted plankard and made his way down into Balthazar's Maw.

Of the numerous secret caches of wealth that Fox had hoarded in hard to find, secret locations throughout Gemmen, many of which had been stumbled upon by those lucky enough to tread the back-alleys and rooftops of his private world, only here, where the bravest of men feared to tread, did he keep his most valued possession. Hidden underneath the well-travelled roadways, deeply rutted from the mundane passing of ox-carts and carriages, was the one item that Fox never forgot the location of, and the only treasure he had ever cared to keep. It was a weapon nearly as legendary as himself- the sword that had ended the life of many an unlucky soul who dared to challenge it, and which those who had seen the results of its handiwork had given the name Fang. The name had caught on with the locals, fueling their awe of the prowess of the arch-bandit who wielded it, and Fox had always secretly approved.

Fox only ever retrieved Fang from its resting place whenever he suspected that he may have cause to use it, and only then for particularly dangerous late-night raids, trusting instead in his skill with the throwing knives that he kept so cleverly hidden upon his person. Though many men, and some women, walked within the Kingdom's walls with swords upon their hips, it was rare that a peasant, the image of which he worked so diligently to maintain, ever carried arms of any kind. This was not because the plethora of beggars and lotus addicts had no call to defend themselves, far from it, for the misbegotten denizens of the more squalid quarters of Gemmen were amongst those most often called upon to do so- but was simply because they lacked the necessary coin one needed to purchase weapons of any kind. The poorer classes were afflicted with much more pressing needs- that of acquiring food rather than steel, and a warrior was far less likely to be the recipient of charity than a mendicant who wore tattered rags in place of armor, who bore a strand of fraying rope in place of a scabbarded belt.

Fang had been presented to Fox as a gift from Cammarran back before he had fully grown into manhood. The weapon had been forged specifically for him, for despite being little larger than a knife-with its pommel nevertheless tailored for double-handed use, it weighed as much as the heavy broadswords favored by the muscle-bound barbarian clans. The sword was forged from the strongest iron on Balthazar, and had been folded and hammered many times over by the most expert of blacksmiths until it was as dense as the anvil upon which it had been birthed. Cammarran had the blade commissioned upon the advice of one of Fox's early sword-masters, who believed that he needed a smaller weapon to suit his emerging fighting style, yet one strong enough to parry blows from the much larger instruments of war that he would no doubt come to face in his chosen life as a thief. In this regard, the sword had proven to be worthy, for in its time it had halted the full swing of studded maces and duel-bladed battle axes alike, yet was small enough to fence with the light, serrated rapiers favored by the King's soldiery. Fox proved capable of wielding the heavy weapon expertly, even before reaching the full strength that years of training and the full maturity of his body had endowed him with, and in fact, seemed to weigh no more than a willow branch in his hands. Occasionally, Cammarran had hinted as to the reason why Fox was stronger, faster and generally more capable than other men, but Fox never bothered to press him on this.

The fire in Fox's oil lamp was losing a battle to the gently flowing breeze which cooled the subterranean passage he now tread as he made his way deeper into the mountainside. In his free hand, he held multiple knives by the blade, ready for a cast lest he run afoul of any of the giant spiders that roamed beneath, but these rarely travelled so close to the surface, and his short trek had thus far proven to be uneventful. He counted three intersections that he passed upon his left and turned down the fourth. He brushed aside a heavy cob-web the size and thickness of a brothel curtain which framed the make-shift doorway, one which had been spun so long ago that little of the tack which had once coated its surfaced remained. Pushing his way past the heavy yet intricately spun veil, he stepped inside.

The ever-dimming light his lamp gave off wavered slightly, desperately clinging to life, as though the fire itself preferred its own demise over having to face the gloomy ambiance within- when Fox finally came across what he had been searching for. There, propped up against the smooth tunnel wall, still wrapped in the well-oiled leather straps he had bound it with, was his sword. Fox was unsurprised to find that it had not been tampered with, for the spiders had no interest in anything they did not deem to be food, and the worms, to the best of his knowledge, never roamed this close to the surface.

Uncaring of the little fuel he had left in his lamp, and thus, the ever-narrowing window of time he had before being swallowed by total darkness, Fox took the time to unsheathe the blade and give it a few practice swings. He could not recollect having ever oiled the sword since the day it was first presented to him, yet its mirrored surface reflected the lamplight with nary a trace of rust to hinder it, despite being secreted in such a damp, coarse environment. His throwing knives he kept somewhat dulled, for occasionally he had need to use them like daggers in combat, and the small blades were likely to shatter like glass against the edge of a larger weapon were they too finely honed; but the edge of Fang he kept razor sharp. He could hear the swishing noise the sword made as its keen egdge effortlessly carved through the soft breeze as he swung it about his body in the complex maneuvers that he had so thoroughly rehearsed since childhood. Finally satisfied, he replaced the blade back into its dull, unadorned scabbard, lashed it to his hip, and, retrieving his lantern from where he had left it to sputter stubbornly on the cavern floor, made his way towards the cave's exit.

No sooner had he reached the main corridor, when the cavern began to tremble. The tiny flicker in his lantern danced about in excitement at the sudden rush of oncoming air which forced itself into the tunnel. This was no naturally occurring phenomenon, Fox knew, but heralded the arrival of something far more sinister.

In his excitement, he had forgotten to take necessary precautions. He knew from past experience that the worms in the labyrinth were nearly blind, and aside from their own shrill voices- which they used as a type of echo location, depended upon tremors in the ground to sense their prey. Carelessly, he had forgotten to tread silently, and his unmasked footsteps had sent reverberations deeper into the ground where the worms congregated. Clearly infuriated at any trespassers into their domain, one of the worms had chosen to brave the tunnels near the surface in order to seek him out.

Fox was never one to back down from a fight, after all, he had slain the worms before; but something on this day, some unfamiliar emotion which shared no kinship to cowardice, urged him to flee rather than fight.

Forgetting all sense of stealth, he raced up the rocky slope towards the safety that the faint trace of sunlight at its acme promised him. He felt, rather than saw the giant mass of spiky teeth and throbbing exoskeleton as it advanced upon him rapidly, narrowing the distance between them with every thrust of its coil-like body. Arriving at the mouth of the cave, Fox leapt towards the grassy veldt beyond, his powerful thrust carrying him the distance of the entire slope as he dove.

His arms were the first part of his body to pierce through the veil of light, and as they touched the grass beyond, he pulled himself into a roll. Tucking his legs underneath him, Fox re-directed his momentum towards the side. He sprung to his feet, slamming his back against the mouth of the cave as he did so. No sooner had he completed this desperate act of acrobatics, when the globulous, giant head of the worm shot out of the tunnel, clamping its massive jaws shut upon the air where his feet had been mere moments before.

Fox had never before seen one of the worms out in direct sunlight before, nor, he surmised, had any man before him. The sight was even more unbelievable than his fertile imagination could have conceived. Had any other been about, their senses would have likely been unable to process the sight, madness the reward for any attempt at doing so. Seen in full view of the sun, the transparent mass of toothy flesh was even more horrifying than it was from the other side of the portal to the netherworld, where the grotesque details of its pulsating, slime covered form were revealed by the dim flicker of his lamp alone.

Much to his surprise, the worm did not recoil immediately back into the cave as he expected. Instead, it threw its head back and opened it jaws wide, splaying its rows of jagged teeth to the sky.

Fox had heard the piercing cry of the worms before, but never with such intensity as he did now. Without the mucous-stained walls of the tunnels to absorb the sound, the high-pitched shriek -the likes of which cannot here be described, for no man had ever heard anything even remotely akin in order to draw comparison, was so horrible to bear that it forced him to his knees with both hands clamped about his ears. In this position, through watery-eyes, Fox witnessed the sight before him in disbelief. The worm, in its veracious attempt to devour him, had gotten itself stuck.

The giant head thumped off the ground, sending shockwaves which rippled through the grass, but even this uncanny sight was nothing compared to what happened next. Streams of cracks like broken glass began to streak across the surface of the worm's now glowing flesh. Small welts and craters began to appear sporadically, casting dark mars on the phosphorescent skin. Soon, the entire beast was surrounded in acrid smoke, and the pungent stink of charred flesh permeated the air. The constant sonic attack began to escalate as regions of the worm's upper body spontaneously burst into flame.

Fox shook himself from his stupor. His well-honed reflexes utterly refused to allow him to become frozen in place. Instead, he could not help but feel a swelling surge of empathy for the poor creature.

Slowly, he got to his feet. The screams had become so powerful that they pounded his body with their force and distorted the land about him. It took all of the strength in his mighty thews to place one foot in front of the other, for the strain he placed upon his mind in order to maintain consciousness nevertheless caused the world about him to warp and buckle. His own senses fought against him, causing him to see multicolored spinning lights where he knew there could be none. He continued forward through the epicenter of a rapidly spinning kaleidoscope which unrelentingly attempted to hammer him to the ground. Bracing himself for what he was sure would shatter his ear drums; he released his right hand from where it had been protecting his ear, fully exposing himself to the sonic barrage. Seemingly availing itself of this opportunity, the ever-escalating delirium now attempted to shut down his senses entirely. Fox reached for his scabbard and, nearly blacking out from the effort, freed Fang from its housing.

Suddenly, there came a respite from the deafening clamor, as the worm attempted to draw what may well have been its last breath. Wasting no time, Fox brought Fang down with all of the strength in his mighty arms -upon the very rock which pinned the worm in place. Furiously, he hacked away at the mouth of the cave itself, bringing all of the strength and speed he possessed to bear. Shrapnel's of stone shot through the air stinging his face as he labored. A chip in the boulder he had been hammering at turned into a seam. The giant worm itself, unknowingly, was helping Fox in his endeavor to free it from its mooring, for its constant flailing about managed to accomplish what he alone could not. The boulder shattered from the stress inflicted upon it from its two powerful adversaries, and almost instantaneously, the worm pulled it's still smoldering head back into the safety of its lair. No sooner had the retreat been affected, when the shrieking began anew, only this time, the wail faded into the distance as the charred worm descended deeper into the labrynth.

No sooner had the cacophony faded to nothingness, when the entire mouth of the cave began to crumble. A great cloud of dust swirled about the air, and when it had settled, the entrance to the great subterranean Kingdom of monsters was no more. Fox was certain that given the blood curdling screams which had preceded the cave in- the effects of which likely were felt throughout the entire eastern quarter of Gemmen, that no-one would have felt any pressing inclination to unearth it again. Balthazar's Maw had closed, and Fox surmised that this was probably for the best, for those on either side of the mysterious portal to the netherworld.

He fell to the ground, utterly exhausted from the ordeal. There he lay for some time, nursing his throbbing head-ache, the likes of which no excessive amounts of drinking had ever punished him with. Long moments passed in silence, the type of silence Fox had never experienced before. It seemed as though the birds and insects themselves had fled the area, leaving him to lie alone in utter tranquility.

As the haze cleared from his mind, it suddenly dawned on him that Bolt was still nearby, picketed to a tree over the nearby rise. The poor beast must have been in a state of frenzy from the overwhelming assault on her senses. Likely she had either uprooted the tree in her efforts to escape or strangled herself trying.

Leaping to his feet, the pounding in his head completely forgotten, Fox raced over the grassy knoll to where he had her tethered. There, still lashed to the sturdy tree where he had left her, stood a decidedly unhappy Bolt. Physically, she seemed unhurt, yet she snorted at him in derision as he approached. Fox could not help but smile. Clearly he had chosen well, for the horse seemed to have in abundance the fortitude one needed were they were to share in his adventures.

Despite their recent ordeal, the two friends were in decidedly good spirits as they made the short jaunt to the eastern gate. The streets were no longer full of curious onlookers, for Fox's latest adventure had caused most to scurry back into whatever homes or shelters were near to hand. He had no doubt that when these eventually emerged, they would do so with countless new tales to be told, set against the flickering, ambient shadows of firelight, surrounding shrieking specters of long dead anscestors sent to avenge past transgressions, fueling the superstitions of generations to come.

Though Fox had been in the vicinity of all four of the capitol's main gates ample times in the past, never afore had he attempted to take his leave of the city by legal means. On this day, the great eastern gate was a bittersweet reminder that Gemmen, for all of its familiarity, could yet fill one who believed himself inoculated to its charms with wonder and awe. As he and Bolt neared the enormous iron-wrought portcullis, the traffic became ever more congested, and both man and horse, along with all else present, craned their necks in order to fully take in its majesty. The curved arches of the gate stood even taller than the great wall which buttressed it, where a horde of the sturdiest animals in the land were stabled that their combined might could work the complex system of pulleys and gears necessary to shift the massive portal upon its axis. In all of Alric's time as King, he had yet to face any serious revolt against his rule, and the gates had only ever been shut against the fierce storms and nighttime terrors of the untamed wilds of Balthazar. In the time of his father, the savage Hillmen who dwelt upon the slopes of Mount Gemmen would occasionally attempt an incursion, yet these were beat back with such ferocity that, in recent times, they contented themselves with raiding whatever caravans strayed too close to their territory. Alric had never ordered they be routed, for though no noble would admit to the fact, 'twas the hillmen themselves who were responsible for the very creation of the Kingdom long ago, a Kingdom they rejected for a life as pariahs when the society they formed reached its height of decadence. Nevertheless, the giant drums which checkered the surface at regular intervals of the adjoining wall were always kept full with boiling oil, the towers were kept manned with the most keen-eyed of scouts, and rows of archers which lined the battlements kept their bows taut. The canons nestled in every rook were fired at the turn of each season under the pretense of celebration, yet in reality, this was to insure that they were always in proper working order. When seen from this vantage, it was little wonder to those who were here congregated that the Kingdom remained the unchallenged seat of power in the west. It was the duty of every King to ensure that it remained so, for travelers who sought entry to the capitol had no memory of a time when the land itself was wartorn, and each of the great Kingdoms were established that they might subjugate their own feral natures. Conquest was replaced with culture, the strong were made to serve the weak, and the gate, the first glimpse all wayfarers, vagabonds, merchants and immigrants alike saw of the western empire, served not only as a precursor of the many wonders which lie in wait within, but lent no doubt that tyranny and oppression would forever be the laws of the land whose might was ne'er to be challenged.

Gemmen secured its place as the center of power in the west mainly because of the imposing outer wall which encircled it, as well the ancient Kings who were the architects of its construction, dating back to the warlord Gemmen himself- the namesake of the Kingdom as well the entire western hemisphere of the realm. Gemmen, the man, was rumored to have been a savage Hillman who united the scattered tribes under his banner during the great war which razed all of Balthazar, and from the ashes of which the new world emerged, yet Alric and his entire lineage did their best to disavow this, claiming instead that their ancestor had been a nobleman of culture who had the benefits of a more austere pedigree. Despite this clear re-writing of history, Alric has never forgotten that his power is derived from strength, not nobility, and the city's exterior has always remained as durable as the warriors who inspired its creation. The entire concept of nobility in fact, was a farce, entertained by only the most ignorant of those who counted themselves amongst their number. Since the creation of the trade routes between Kingdoms, every race and creed on Balthazar had long since intermingled. Only the southern Kingdom of Raimia and the Hillmen themselves remained xenophobic, and these were rumored to be inbred to the point that, though they retained the characteristics of their ancestors, such came at a heady cost. Alric spent as little coin as possible on the general upkeep of Gemmen, for he relied heavily on the vanity of the noble castes to keep their own properties and fiefdoms in pristine condition. The city's own militia was composed mostly of the offspring of the lords themselves, clad in flashy dark blue uniforms that served poorly as armor, yet drew the gaze of many a comely lass who found the power and prestige associated with the costume appealing. It was the guilds responsibility to keep the criminal elements in check, and these complained not at all of the general incompetence of the local soldiery. Nevertheless, it was clear that the otherwise frugal King spared no expense when it came to his own battlements, as well as the soldiers who manned them.

During the daylight hours, the sun danced playfully upon the rubies and gold embossed house insignias which decorated the pommels of the lordling soldiers' rapiers, but when the sun set, the moon cast a decidedly different pallor on the crimson stained blades of those who garrisoned the wall. These were not the young fops who played at war, but grim men who had been seasoned by hard-fought campaigns- men whose payment was not rendered in false pretenses to glory, nor wine, women and song, but by blood, sweat and honor. Many of these had once been rangers, members of the messenger's guild, kin and ally to gypsies, vagabonds and roaming bandits alike, as well as the only men and women on all of Balthazar permitted to enter each of the four Kingdoms freely without ever a toll being asked of them. As such, they were never fully trusted by the King, for rangers swore no fealty to any but the land, yet a lifetime spent absent the protection of any Lord ensured that they were not to be trifled with. Rangers knew more than most what lie beyond the protection of any city wall. Nomads since birth, it was the duty of these wizards of the forest to keep each Kingdom appraised of the goings on in the world, from the politics of rival Kingdoms and provinces, to the ever looming threat of the untamed wilds, whose denizens bigotry-fueled rumor often told they held truck with. Kings, stewards, and regents alike depended upon rangers in order to communicate with each other, both overtly, and clandestinely, and in this way, their role of brokering information was equally as important to the grand machinery of Balthazar as the caravaneers whose job it was to import and export goods. Those who survived such a life, their efforts unlauded, could look forward to a retirement protecting the borders of one of said Kingdoms from threats real or imagined, often times both, yet most prefered to meet their fates in the forests and plains where they were born, alone and unseen, where their remains would feed and bring new life to Balthazar.

Traffic at the eastern gate was as thick as ever when Fox and Bolt immersed themselves in it- even after the alarming wail which only recently echoed throughout the region- now seemingly forgotten as every type of traveler, from weary merchant to wide-eyed fortune seeker attempted entry and egress through the wall. Frustrations were high. Nevertheless, the day shift was a welcome respite for those who protected the gate, for the frayed tempers of caravaneers were a welcome change in manners compared to those of the feral man-eaters who roamed about the city walls after dark.

The two companions bristled at this new delay. They had been forced to wait for most of the afternoon in what seemed like a fool's parade, all squabbling with the other as personal boundaries were dissolved in a morass of pressed together shoulders and the stink of tightly knitted livestock. Having progressed to the front of the line at last, they were approached by a stern looking soldier whose demeanor told that he had even less inclination of being there as did they. The sentry wore not the crushed blue uniform of Gemmen's militia, but durable armor with no house insignia- merely cold steel which complimented the equally cold gaze of a bastard. His sword was lashed to his hip, and he held but a thin piece of parchment and a quill. He seemed not even to sweat under the intense rays of the summer sun, despite the heavy plating of his armor. Whether the man was once a member of the messenger's guild, Fox couldn't tell, yet that his talents were wasted on such trivialities was evident. Were it not for the traces of grey in his long red mustache, doubtless this one would be roaming the plains still, living off the land and seeking new challenges with which to pit himself.

"State your name and business." he said with rehearsed rhythm.

"My name is Barnabas." Fox replied. "My destination is Damaas."

In direct opposition to Fox, the soldier had hard features, heavily delineated with battle scars that were nearly indistinguishable from the rutted lines which marked his face prematurely. His thin lips, lost in the swell of the mustache which hung to his collarbone, curled into a smirk, and his already squinted eyes narrowed even further with suspicion.

"On that sliver of a thing?" he replied, indicating Bolt. Un-intimidated, she returned his stare and snorted rudely. "The road to Damaas is long and fraught with peril. Where are your supplies?"

The man's keen observational skills confirmed Fox's suspicions that this was indeed a former member of the messengers guild- a ranger who knew the land well and had chosen to live out his twilight years with the promise of a soft bed in place of packed dirt, delivering news to the four corners of Balthazar for little pay and even less comfort.

Despite Fox's admiration for the messenger's guild, for any who did not suffer from the vaunted condescension of nobles, rangers were not city bred, and thus decidedly unequipped at dealing with the cunning of a clever thief.

"The first leg in our journey is but a two days ride to the small village of Baraan. There, we plan to join a caravan which will escort us for the rest of our trip." he smiled magnanimously, depending on his charm lest his credence falter

The look of suspicion faded, replaced by a knowing smirk. "Would that I were going with you." he said whilst waving them past "May your luck fail you that your trip be not a dull one."

Fox flashed a toothy smile and ambled past, leaving the man to deal with the long line of carts filled with rotted produce tethered to unwashed oxen, manned by those equal in both demeanor and prestige. There was no fee for taking one's leave of Gemmen, only for entry, for those who had no coin to spend within the walls were best served outside of them. This was well, for Fox had no coin on his person to pay had he cared to.

He made his ways through the gate and weaved through the heavy traffic beyond. Each measured hoof-beat was excruciatingly boring for both he and Bolt, for the lumbering rows of caravans were both monotonous and difficult to circumnavigate. It was early evening before they finally came upon open road, unburdened by the constant flow of commerce coming to and fro the city. This was the moment they had both been waiting for.

He drove his heels into Bolt's flanks. The horse needed no such coercion.

In an instant, the world about him exploded into a blinding array of furious motion. His eyes filled with tears which further distorted his perception until his entire environs seemed composed of nothing but streaking rays of blurred light. Forest greens and umbers melted into a collage of distorted chaos. He felt like an insect that had wandered carelessly upon the shaft of an arrow moments before it was shot from a taught bow. Such was the utter surrealness of his speed that he could not be certain if he were racing across the land, or if the land were racing past him. Unable to restrain himself any longer, he let loose a scream of delight which was promptly erased by the vortex of white noise at which he was the epicenter. All of his life had Fox sought freedom, yet never before had he felt as close to that ultimate goal as he did in this moment. The wind lashed violently at his face, nearly tearing his hair from his scalp, and he laughed in the face of it. Within what seemed like mere moments, Gemmen was far behind, and the future, whatever it may have in store, lay before him.

As Bolt's hoofs churned the land beneath him, Fox was only dimly aware as to the truest source of his elation. On some level, the internal mechanisms of his mind operated with neither his consent nor his endorsement. He had known that his last night in Gemmen needed to be celebrated with the greatest act of thievery of his career; though he himself remained blissfully unnaware, he had, in fact, achieved this spectacularly. As he raced along the road to Damaas, completely unburdened by any of the trappings of civilization, with no material possessions on his person of any kind save his own sword and the clothes upon his back, he alone had accomplished what no man before him had even dared attempt- he had successfully stolen from himself.

The sun had long since set, and Cammarran was, as per usual, still journaling the day's events in his massive leather-bound log book that sat upon his study. He had grown accustomed to, and even enjoyed his home beneath the Bear's Den, for the lack of any natural light made it difficult for him to resent the late hours that he worked.

He closed the heavy tome and, as he did every night before retiring, uncorked a bottle of stiff Raimian spirits and poured himself a tall glass. Cammarran had gotten used to the long hours he was forced to work, for his network was enormous, and he never relied upon any aides to help him manage it. He sat on the edge of his bed in practiced routine and downed the contents of the glass in one mighty swallow. He had never allowed himself the luxury of getting drunk, but had come to rely on a nightly draught of the potent spirit to help ease the transition to slumber.

He was just about to blow out the nearby candle on his bedside table when the tiny flicker of flame extinguished as if by its own volition. The sleepy fog he had been under the spell of disappeared immediately and, still dimly illuminated by the few remaining candles about the room, his hand shot into the drawer and seized upon the well-maintained dagger he kept there. The feeling of dread he now experienced was certainly unwelcome, yet not unexpected.

"Show yourself assassin!" he shouted "You will find that Cammarran, Lord of thieves has no superstitious fears for you to prey upon!"

The remaining candles about the chamber seemed to dim slightly, as a voice which reverberated about the room, yet seemed to come from nowhere, answered him.

"Where is Fox?"

Cammarran had never heard the voice ere now, yet he knew to whom it belonged. It was a voice unlike any he had ever heard. It was almost sing-song, even soothing in its pitch, yet it carried with it reverberating tremors of nausea and anxiety.

He leapt to his feet, still holding the polished dagger firmly in his grip, yet the candlelight cast flickering shadows where it reflected off the blade which he could not keep from shaking. His eyes darted to each of them, his sweat was palpable. The entire room was eerily silent as he made his way slowly about it, the tip of his steel carving a path through the darkness for each of his wary footsteps to follow.

"Let us not waste time in unmanly deceit!" Cammarran shouted "We both know that I am well aware of Fox's whereabouts. Let us move directly to torture. I welcome it!"

He made his way to the far end of the chamber and set his back firmly against the wall. Even in his prime, he was never a particularly good swordsman- though he knew enough to hold his dagger in reverse position, ready for a defensive repost, the hand which clung to it continued to betray him as it wavered with every rush of adrenaline that shot through him.

He opened his mouth to try to goad his adversary further. Cammarran knew that his true strength lied in his cunning. If he had any hope of surviving this night, it would be through his words, not his might.

The words never came however, for though he stood erect against a pool of shadow in the wall, two hands seemingly materialized from the shadows themselves and choked the words in his throat. Thinking quickly, reason only partially obscured by desperation, the Lord of thieves spun about and slashed at his invisible adversary. His dagger struck sparks against the stonework and his efforts were rewarded with naught but a shredded tapestry.

"Do not toy with me assassin! I am Cammarran, master of the thieves' guild of Gemmen! I demand that you face me!"

For a long moment, silence was his only reply.

"I know you Krillian." Cammarran whispered "I know from whence you came... I know what evil spawned you... You shall not have him..."

"Then you shall take it to your grave..." the voice whispered back melodiously

Suddenly, a flash of steel knocked his dagger to the floor. With speed like lightning, the spiked pommel behind it struck him atop his bald pate, leaving a crimson scar which sent rivulets of blood running down the creases in his forehead. Despite himself, Cammarran fell to his knees. His head felt heavy, yet he was forced to look his opponent in the eye as the tip of a long serrated rapier lifted his chin.

"Krillian." He spat out the name "Do your worst, for I do not fear death."

As Krillian stepped out of the shadows, he seemed to take them with him. Cammarran had never seen the man before; he had only heard the legends. They paled in comparison.

He was the tallest man he had ever seen, his gaunt body was clad head to toe in black leather and cloth. His face was swathed, leaving only his eyes visible. The eyes did not seem human. They were of the purest green; ignoring the candlelight, they appeared to glow as though illuminated from an internal fire. He pressed the tip of his rapier up into Cammarran's neck until it drew blood, and as he did so, the eyes flared in intensity.

"Where is Fox?" he said again. His whimsical voice, no louder than a whisper, was that of Death itself, come to claim him.

Cammarran's eyes rested only briefly upon the cold steel which pressed itself into his throat, then they scanned the room about him, lingering momentarily upon the log book on his study before darting back to face the assassin.

"You will find that true thieves in Gemmen do not so readily betray one another." Cammarran's voice was muted, trapped behind his grimace. His teeth grinded against each other and his lips were drawn taut in readiness to spew out a barage of insults, yet never again would the King of thieves mutter a sound.

With a flick of his wrist, the sword in Krillian's hand etched a thin red line across Cammarran's throat. The once undisputed Lord of the thieves' guild of Gemmen slumped to the floor. He momentarily bore grim witness to his own life leaving his body, reflected in the puddle of blood which pooled beneath him. Then he was no more.

The floorboards refused to creak beneath the assassin's padded footsteps lest they disturb him as he made his way to the study and scanned the pages of the tome. Leaving the book where he found it,

Krillian disappeared back into the shadows.

CHAPTER FIVE - THE DARK CLAW

The trip to Baraan had, rather unfortunately, proven to be quite peaceful. Though the trek was wont to take two days by caravan, Fox had found himself at the border of the village by mid-afternoon of the next day. Bolt proved to be not only the fastest horse in the realm, but the most durable as well, for she seemed never to tire and was in possession of reserves of stamina which rivaled his own.

The pair had set up camp off the main road the night before near a small creek, yet despite keeping the fire low and foregoing the construction of any shelter, they were not attacked by any of the were-beasts who roamed about the woods after dark. Fox chided himself, for he knew that he would likely have had better luck had he not camped so near the village. He hoped that the rest of his journey would prove to be more dangerous if he could but make himself a more tantalizing target.

There was plenty of healthy grass in the small pasture where they found themselves, and though Bolt was perhaps more accustomed to a gruel consisting of mashed vegetables, oats and hay, she nevertheless seemed content with the ample food and water nature provided. Unfortunately for Fox, the young thief had to be somewhat more creative in order to secure his meal as a diet of mulch he did not find overly palatable. With his sliver of flint, he managed to ignite his small blaze using dried moss as kindling; Fang proved as capable as any axe when it came to obtaining firewood, and though he was no ranger, he soon had a serviceable cook fire. With no patience for hunting, he set himself to the task of stripping the coarse bark off of a birch tree, revealing the fresh green skin beneath which he then cut into strips and boiled in a bowl of the tough outer bark itself. The soup he made would have tasted much better had it been salted, yet the sap of the tree made for a broth that was just bitter enough to digest. There were plenty of nearby mushrooms that he could have added to the broth, yet being city bred, he did not know which of these were hallucinogenic, or outright poisonous, and thus deemed discretion as the better part of valor. As he laid his head upon the soft dirt floor that night, his stomach still rumbled, yet they had reached a happy compromise, for Fox promised it a healthy portion of venison lathered in gravy upon reaching Baraan.

The sun had just risen by the time Fox had finished washing himself in the shallow creek. He regretted that it was not deep enough for a morning swim, yet the rumbling in his belly did not agree and urged him onwards in search of a large breakfast.

Soon, the mid-afternoon sun which had been struggling to pierce the veil of trees shun brightly upon a large clearing the path he and Bolt had been travelling transformed into. The duo had stayed off of the main thoroughfare so as not to become waylaid by the heavy caravan traffic, and only now did their path merge with the King's highway which led to the village. Despite this, the pair proved to be the only travelers on what should have been a bustling caravan route. Baraan, Fox knew, was the only stop for traders making their way to Gemmen for days in any direction. He should have been wading through a river of lumbering caravansary and smelly oxen. Contemplating mysteries was usually of little interest to him though, as he preferred an improvised approach to problem solving, and he did not wish to divert any of his faculties away from appreciating the beautiful summer day. He smiled at his good fortune and slowed Bolt to a canter.

The first sign of civilization was a small stable outlying the village and they had no sooner come across it when a raggedy stable boy ran out to greet them. The young boy's hair was the color of straw, much like Fox's own, and hung erratically about his face. He was dressed in tatters, yet Fox could tell that the clothes he wore, despite being torn and patched countless times over, had only recently been cleaned. He deduced immediately that the young man was not simply a stable hand, but the owner and proprietor of the stable itself –an entrepreneur who believed in the importance of appearances.

The stable consisted of a small shack at its center, which was ill-maintained compared to the stables themselves. That the beasts were better housed than the boy did not surprise Fox, for the lad was not paid to look after himself; yet despite the abundace of fresh hay lying about in bales and troths full to brimming, there seemed to be no animals in need of tending.

"Good afternoon sir!" the boy cried enthusiastically. "It's nice to see a traveler again. It's a copper for the night, four for the week."

It was easy to see why the boy was so excited. Clearly, he was in need of the business, and Fox doubted that he had ever laid eyes upon a steed as fine as Bolt.

"Sir?" Fox replied with a grin. "Do you take me for a nobleman?"

"Why yes sir." The boy replied. Clearly he thought that this was the correct answer. "That is to say sir, that your clothing is strange to me, but only a great man would have a horse such as yours sir!"

"Great?!" Fox cried, the wry expression never leaving his face. "Do you believe that a noble birth makes one great?"

"Yes sir." replied the boy. "I mean, no sir." His eyes began to scan the dirt beneath him in hopes that the correct answer would present itself.

Fox decided to end the poor lad's growing uneasiness. "Not 'sir' lad. The name is Barnabas. I thank you for your services, yet I believe that my horse and I shall venture into Baraan together."

Bolt had only just begun to move forward when the boy stepped in front of them, barring their path.

"Begging your pardon si.... Barnabas." he stammered "By the regent's orders, only beasts bearing carts to market are allowed within the village."

Fox stared down at the tatterdemalion with new-found respect.

He knew that the lad would not budge. Bolt did not share his admiration, for she snorted in his direction, striking her front hoof upon the dirt irritably.

Swinging his leg across the saddle, Fox dropped to the ground. He knelt to one knee and placed an arm upon the boy's shoulder.

"I can see that there is no point in trying to deceive one so clever as yourself." he began "I am indeed a nobleman of the highest caste, sent on a secret errand by King Alric himself. I was ambushed by thieves upon my clandestine journey. They managed to rob me of all of my coin, even my nobleman's attire, and I was lucky to escape with my life."

The boy's eyes widened with awe before he spoke. "The Dark Claw..." he said with muted voice "I knew the King would not desert us in our time of need! Was it they who ambushed you upon your journey?"

"Yes indeed." Fox replied, his countenance not registering any of the surprise he felt. "I have come to deal with... the Dark Claw."

"I knew it!" the boy smiled triumphantly

"Nevertheless" Fox continued "I will not, by royal decree, order one of the King's hard-working subjects to shelter my mount for free. Should you be willing to keep my secret, I shall pay you a gold coin once I meet with the regent. But be warned..." Fox's voice shrunk to a whisper and his eyes grew in intensity as he fully threw himself into the role. "My mission is perilous. Should I be killed, you may keep this horse..." he waved a hand towards Bolt who snorted once again in offence "The finest in the King's stables, as payment."

"A gold coin!" the boy ejaculated "Why… I have never even seen one! Fear not Sir Barnabas! I shall have her purring!"

"Not a word of this to anyone, understand?" Fox whispered again, as though the possibility of nearby spies was very real.

"I understand sir. You can count on me."

"I know I can." He patted the boy on the shoulder and began the short walk to the village whose stunted silhouette was visible in the distance. Bolt may have been in no humor to be left behind, yet he was sure that she had found her match in the young peasant boy.

Baraan was much like Fox had expected, a simple town populated by simple, hard working people. The village proper consisted of little more than a central marketplace surrounded by several small homes which clearly belonged to the vendors who tended the market, interspersed with larger estates belonging to the noblemen who in turn employed the merchants. The tiny village was surrounded by farmland which housed most of the citizens whose job it was to keep the market full and to trade with their neighbors. It was a quaint economy of life, a fully sustainable ecosystem which could have remained autonomous were it not for the fact that it lie within the province of Gemmen, and therefore owed fealty to King Alric. Though he had expected the village to be of modest means, Fox was completely unprepared for the stark poverty he encountered. The dirt-stained faces he passed seemed robbed of hope, the garb was tattered, and the shuffling about of the assorted working classes seemed devoid of passion and purpose.

He made his way through the small marketplace in search of the venison he had promised himself, only to find that the market was nearly devoid of goods. It took only a short period of wandering about to discover why.

The more townsfolk he crossed paths with, the more Fox began to realize that the entire village seemed to be populated by desperate men and women who clearly suffered from lack of sleep and nutrition. There were no children playing in the streets, rather the few of these he did encounter clung to the slips of their mother's dresses, wailing incessantly. The quaint village he had been longing to visit had been reduced to the environs one would have expected to see in the most dilapidated squalors of the capitol city. He kept his ears strained as he ambled about. Despite a lifetime spent acquiring the skill of moving unseen however, his presence seemed to draw eyes upon him as though he were the only visitor the locals had seen in some time. His own generic costume and features gave him the look of a man of means amonst the Baraanites- the appearance of which he had always strived diligently to avoid.

In a short while, he had picked up enough snippets of dialogue to deduce the source of the villages' ailment. It seemed a small group of bandits had been raiding the countryside recently, pillaging all but the largest of caravan trains. Were it not for the heavy tithes Baraan owed to the King, the village would likely not have suffered overmuch, yet circumstances dictated that the town be dependent on trade which the series of raids had all but negated. The more distance he covered, the more his brow knitted in consternation, for what Fox knew of King Alric told that little aid for these people would be forthcoming, and that taxes would be levied with no excuses brooked.

There wasn't much in life which perturbed Fox, yet he had been raised to respect the thieves' code, and the thought of fellow thieves stealing from the poor vexed him greatly. Clearly, these bandits were not of any affiliation with the brotherhood in Gemmen and were operating without endorsement from the guild. Such brazenness would eventually draw the attention of Cammarran who could be depended upon to deal with the matter both swiftly and harshly, yet in the interim, with trade having ground to a halt, the people were suffering greatly.

As he continued to tour the small village, he was pleased to note that not all possessed gaunt faces and hollow eyes, for in every flock, no matter how lean, there were always wolves to be found, and Baraan still had its share of noblemen. He had always enjoyed ridding the noble castes of Gemmen of their bloated purses, and distributing said wealth to the poorer quarters had been an almost daily routine of his. It became increasingly clear that the small village of Baraan was in desperate need of a thief, and it was a tremendous stroke of luck that, unbeknownst to them, they now played host to the greatest of any age.

It was all he could do to restrain himself from implementing his vocation straight away, yet though patience had always been the hardest skill set for Fox to master, he was still a thief, and like all thieves, he knew that before he began performing their art in any new place, one needed to establish a den. As he scanned the perimeter for an ideal location, his gaze caught that of an abandoned guard tower in the distance which seemed promising.

In larger cities, such towers were oft found near the outskirts in order to protect the citizens from external dangers, but Baraan was but a small farming town with no outer wall to protect it, and the tower stood within the confines of the general marketplace itself. No doubt it had been erected long ago to serve as a lookout, for prior to the land being transformed into pasture; it would have been butted against by the forest, making Baraan easy prey for the creatures who dwelt there.

His stomach complained at this new delay, and without wasting further time, he made his way thither.

The tower was indeed old, older still than the village which surrounded it. Seen from its base, it appeared to have been un-manned for an age. When he was certain that no eyes were upon him, he began the process of scaling. The tall yet narrow cylindrical edifice had received so little maintenance that it was riddled throughout with deep grooves and crevices, leaving an easy path for one raised in the thieves district of Gemmen to follow, and arriving at the top proved to be of very little challenge. Once there, the flat surface of its acme seemed almost to have been tailored to suit his needs. The small circular roof was by far the tallest point in Baraan, and was ensconced in miniature ramparts which would serve perfectly to conceal him from prying eyes beneath, even if he stood at his full height. In the center of the circle lay a mangled mat of straw that would make for perfect bedding. Also, his privacy was assured, for a quick scan with a trained eye informed him that his new lair had seen naught but truant children and the occasional gull for over an age.

He concealed Fang under the mound of straw, for farmers were even less likely to wander about armed than were beggars and he had no wish to draw even further attention to himself than he already had. The day was bright and clear and Fox briefly entertained the notion of an afternoon nap, but the gnawing hunger that had plagued him since his last sparse meal convinced him otherwise.

He leaned against one of the ramparts, still sturdy despite its lack of use and gazed out at the village below him. There he saw miniature versions of men and women shuffling about their daily lives, each too preoccupied with the roles they had resigned themselves to in order to realize that in so doing they had deprived themselves of the best view in the region. He wondered if these people were even aware that their lot in life was little more than that of a cog in a broken machine. These had worked their entire lives tilling the land, only to see the fruit of their labors go to the lords that they had so willingly sworn allegiance to. Could those beneath him but see from such vantage, perhaps they could share in the perspective held by thief and assassin alike, as well as all of those who dared become citizens of Balthazar's hidden world, so near to hand yet always out of reach for those who could not penetrate the thin veil of what was deemed forbidden.

It was enough that the Baraanites had their labor stolen from them by the truly vilest of all thieves- the noble castes, for such undoing was of one's own volition, yet that they should fall victim to common bandits as well was simply intolerable. The only joy to be found was in the realization that the regent himself would have to explain to Alric why he was unable to pay his usual tribute to Gemmen's treasury. Perhaps then, and only then, help might be forthcoming from the palace, yet if and when the King's guard did arrive- the yoke of oppression would be winched tighter still.

Fox took in a deep breath of fresh air to cleanse his mind from uninvited thoughts. It tasted sweet. The morning breeze carried no hint of sweat and offal this high from the ground, and there was no taint of the poisons of industry he had not e'en realized he had become so accustomed to. Thus far, the quaintness of country life agreed with him. Had he any complaint, it was the lack of any immediate danger to set his blood racing.

As he gazed off into the distance, he espied a rusted water trough which ran down the side of a nearby building far below him. When he was satisfied that the street below was temporarily barren, he leaped up upon the rampart he had been leaning against, and with a broad smile on his face, dove.

The thrill which preceded imminent death elated him. There was no experience quite like it. Fox loved nothing more than cheating that grim specter of what he believed to be her most cherished prize, for often had he proferred himself to her, only to evade her grasp at the final moment. He flew through the air gracefully, tauntingly, arms outstretched like wings, seizing the realm designated to birds as though it were his own. The light breeze now assailed him with a torrent of anger at his audacity in defying it. His eyes welled with tears which further blurred the lines of his own mortality.

With a grip like a smithy's vice, he reached out and grasped the trough. The pipe proved incapable of withstanding the shock to its moorings however as one by one, the bolts which kept it in place ripped out of their cobblestone dwellings. It was a bumpy ride, but Fox held steadfast. Eventually his momentum slowed, and the thin metal bent upon the last bracket which held it in place. Burdened by the weight of its sudden passenger, the trough, which up until this point had only ever escorted rivulets of rainwater to the street below, bent halfway down the building it had been attached to. Fox hung tightly as the thin half-pipe lowered him slowly to the ground, releasing his hold a few meters above the street. Coming down squarely upon the cushioned insoles of his boots, he tucked into a roll to cushion the blow. He came out of the roll with a bounce and continued down the narrow street with a further spring to his step. In Fox's experience, it was impossible to live life to the fullest lest one be consistently reminded that it could come to an end at any moment.

Rounding the corner and emerging into traffic once more, the people completely unaware as to the means of his spectacular arrival amongst them, he noted that his audacity had been rewarded, for among the scattered farmers and their families which dotted the thoroughfare walked two plump noblemen, thoroughly engaged in conversation with one another and doing their devout best to ignore the peasants with whom they were forced to share the dirt roads of Baraan with. Whether such was mere coincidence or if Balthazar himself was impressed with his antics he neither knew nor cared for good fortune was best savored when seized upon.

The two nobles were slightly older than middle age and were clad in the height of Gemmen fashion. The shorter of the two bore a small skull-cap, similar to the one Fox's erstwhile companion Lord Henry seemed to favor, the other wore no hat, but had long, flowing blonde hair tied back with a red leather strap. The top of his head was completely bald and seemed badly burned by the sun. Nevertheless, the decadent nobleman clearly thought this to be his best feature somehow, for the fact that he wore no headdress told Fox that he would rather his pate become scorched 'til his own skin began peeling than protect himself from the heavy western sun by concealing it. The mid-sections of each man were rotund, a common feature of noblemen, and winced back tightly with sequined leather belts which held fat purses and loosely scabbarded rapiers to protect them. Only on the taller man did the belly seem out of place, for his remaining features were lean by comparison, yet both nobles were snobbishly Gemmenites, for nowhere were there traces of audacious Raimian accoutrements, gaudy Damaascian gold, and never had Fox seen a man of wealth who favored the brutish warrior garb and bone plated armor of the Hyrstians from the northern mountains. The frilly chemises each wore were of crushed velvet set over flowing pantaloons that were in turn tucked into knee-high equestrian jackboots which no amount of polish could save from Baraan's streets where nary a trace of cobblestone could be found. Fox's smile spread near to his ears. The fates had thus far proved to be exceedingly kind indeed.

It was well into the evening when Fox returned to his lair. He had spent a small fortune at the marketplace that afternoon and the large glazed hen garnished with raisins which sat plumply before him was one of the few such delicacies Baraan had left to offer and was a testament to just how much coin Fox was able to procure. To drink, he had a bottle of he knew not what, but which tasted like a cross between red wine from the south-eastern valleys whose fermentation had been sped with an infusion of honey, diluted with a more regional liquor fermented with potatoes and grain, and was certain to induce a legendary headache for one with meek constitution. He curled up in his straw bedding and washed down a mouthful of meat with the harsh libation. He had procured one of the few books the village had to offer, this one being an adventure tale about pirates upon the great western seas that were rumored to run off the edge of the world. This he read until the liquor rendered his vision blurred beneath the waning moonlight. He then fell into a deep, contented slumber, dreaming of adventure in undiscovered lands.

Fox spent three days and three nights in Baraan. During that time, he had been single handedly responsible for the massive redistribution of wealth that the townspeople celebrated and the nobles lamented. Though he was thoroughly enjoying himself, he knew that the time had come to take his leave. Baraan was not Gemmen, and it would not be long before the locals began to tell tales of a raggedly garbed man who decended from his lofty tower to spend a daily fortune at market. He longed to be reunited with Bolt that the two might find trouble upon the open road.

He left the bones of his nightly meals upon the tower for the gulls to feed on, lashed Fang to his hip, and set off once more upon his meandering trek towards Damaas.

The distance from his den to the stable which held Bolt was a short one, yet in that time, the faces he saw seemed reinvigorated. Gone were the sour expressions writ with desperation, save for those which adorned the few noblemen that he passed.

He was very much looking forward to seeing the young boy whom he had entrusted with his steed. Perhaps this was because, save for the merchants with whom he bartered, the lad had been the only person he had spoken to during his entire time in the village- but Fox knew that it was something more. He had no inclination towards figuring out why he felt so fondly about the boy, preferring instead to enjoy the feeling rather than spoiling it with any attempt at trying to understand it.

Upon arriving at the stables, the young peasant again came out to greet him, and Fox was surprised to note that the single look of desperation to be found on a pauper's face that day belonged to him alone.

"Good morrow to you sir!" he said, though his face registered none of the jovial greeting Fox's presence elicited.

"Good morrow." Fox replied.

"I knew that your coming was a good omen. The fortune of the village has taken a decidedly good turn of late."

"Then why so dour?" Fox responded. The look of concern he bore did not have to be forced, for it came naturally from he knew not where.

The boy stammered only momentarily before responding. "Not at all sir. I'm sure that your mission was a success, rumor has reached me that the marketplace has been doing swift business. It's just that, there is yet little work for the stable yards." he stammered yet again before continuing "Despite Baraan's recent fortunes, wayfarers are still too afraid to visit, and thus there are no horses to stable. Yours is the only one I've had these last few days."

"And I trust that you have taken good care of her." Fox replied

At this, the boy stood erect and proud. "Yessir, I take good care of all of my charges!"

Fox smiled. "No doubt. You are correct young master. My meeting with the regent went exceptionally well. I have chosen to maintain the costume of a peasant so as to avoid any suspicion despite having been well rewarded by his Lordship."

At this, Fox reached into his tunic, removed a small pouch, and handed it to the boy.

"I never inquired about your name the last time we met."

"It is Cam sir." he replied while accepting the leather pouch. He tentatively undid the drawstrings and reached inside.

"As agreed upon- ten gold pieces." Fox said with a smile.

At this, the small pouch slipped through Cam's fingers and fell to the ground. Ten gold pieces; each marked with the King's seal spilled out upon the dirt.

"Careful." said Fox. "It is ill-advised to toss about such a fortune."

Tears formed in the eyes of the boy before he spoke. "I cannot accept this sir!"

"Nonsense! Once I informed the regent how much help you have been he insisted upon it!"

Fox knelt to one knee and placed a hand on Cam's shoulder. "With this much coin, you can purchase a stable in Gemmen. I have no doubt that one as enterprising as yourself can make swift profit. There is a recently sealed cave near the eastern entrance by the newly erected Colloseum where land can be purchased for a pittance despite the booming economy entirely reliant on fine horses. I have no doubt that with the sealing of said cave; business will soon be in abundance. The area is known for its riders and will be in need of an experienced stablemaster, one with genuine skill and care who did not arise to his position merely by way of noble birth. Doubtless, you will eventually hire hands to aid you. Only do not allow yourself to become infected by the greed of those who dwell there, for doing so will welcome thieves to your table who will reset the balance. Be honest and true, and these will leave you in peace whilst targeting those who would sneer at your humble beginnings. Harken to me Cam, and your future will be charmed."

Without a word, Cam gripped Fox in a fierce hug. Fox had rarely been the recipient of such a gesture, and attempted awkwardly to reciprocate.

As he had expected, Bolt had been incredibly well taken care of. She appeared strong, weel-fed and healthy and, as evidenced by her gleeful neighing, was delighted to see him as he approached. He pressed his face against hers in greeting, then, wasting no more time, threw her saddle about her and set out again toward the open road. As before, Fox had chosen to pack sparingly for this leg of his journey, yet this time, he chose to add a small pouch of salt to his meager belongings.

As the duo put Baraan behind them, Fox was surprised to note that he felt no particular inclination to race along the King's highway as when he left Gemmen. The countryside was beautiful, and neither he nor his steed were in any great rush. Bolt trotted along gleefully, flaring her nostrils that she might take in the energizing country air as Fox in turn took in the view.

They had not gotten far when Fox's unerring sense of danger began to warn him that something was amiss. Bolt snorted in agreement as they rounded a curve. Neither was startled when a small group consisting of four men suddenly thrust themselves across their path from the nearby concealment of some shrubbery along the side of the road.

Fox chided himself, for he should have expected this. No doubt these were the notorious group of bandits who had recently brought much hardship to Baraan. He struggled to remember how this group called themselves. 'The Dark Fist'? No. Fox rolled about several names in his head until he decided upon the 'Black Plague'. He was certain this was it.

"Beware stranger!" cried out their apparent leader. "You would be wise to surrender that fine mount of yours. I warn you not to trifle with us, for now you face the Dark Claw!"

Fox rolled his eyes towards the sky. He wasn't even close.

"The Dark Claw?" he answered back. "Is that not some strain of venereal disease?"

"You dare mock us?!" the man shouted. "Don't you know who we are? We represent the scourge of the west... the fiercest bandits in all of Gemmen whose very name instills terror in the hearts of the bravest of travelers!"

The man Fox had been addressing was the tallest and most muscular of the four. Fox was certain that he was correct when he had assumed him to be the leader. All four were young and in their prime, though slightly older than he. Each man wore pieces of armor cobbled together from the four corners of Balthazar. He could identify breastplates, grieves, and various other bits of armament from Hyrst, Raimia, Damaas and Gemmen as well as every borderland in between. They were clearly reavers playing at being thieves. Had he despised them before, he now looked upon them with unbridled loathing.

Bringing Bolt to a halt, he loosened Fang in its scabbard.

"I have indeed heard the name" he said. "I am known as the fearsome Fox of Gemmen. Perhaps you have heard tell of my name?"

All four men threw their heads back in laughter. "Do not seek to frighten us." The leader spoke again. "It is well known that Fox's domain lies further on in the Kingdom's capitol."

"As well, Fox is a personal friend of mine!" cried another "I myself taught him much of his vaunted swordplay!"

"Do not dare to speak of the Kingdom of Gemmen to me." Fox replied coldly, his eyes aglow with rage, the effect of which superimposed dread upon the laughter of the men when they saw them.

Fox hesitated momentarily before speaking again. Taking advantage of the sudden silence which permeated the air, he allowed his eyes to focus upon those of the reavers. Here he lingered, letting the intensity of his emerald gaze attest to the truth of his words. When he spoke again, his voice was distilled menace which lent no doubt as to the veracity of his claim.

"The shadows have long been my home. Do you wish to know why I reveal myself to a stinking lot of fetal excrement such as yourselves?"

The trace of a smile played across his lips, the chilling effect of which the foursome made no attempt at feigning bravery against. Clearly these had become accustomed to delivering insults, not receiving them. Many were the men, most far better than they, whom Fox had frozen into place with the sheer ferocity and supernatural power of his fiery green eyes. It told these men both that they had erred, and that they would never enjoy the opportunity to do so again.

"It is because you shall not live to tell of it."

Without another word, Fox launched himself from Bolt's saddle-with his hand clutched firmly about Fang's hilt; the blade freed itself from its scabbard as he vaulted through the air. To the leader's credit, he managed to bring his own blade up, attempting to block Fox's downward slash, but this proved to be his undoing. Fox's forward momentum, aided by the velocity of his descent, coupled with the strength of his mighty arms and the sheer weight of his instrument of death brought Fang down with such unbridled power that it drove the defending blade downwards, his movement ending with the reaver's own sword imbedded in his shoulder, nearly severing it in twain. The leader of the motley bandits fell to the ground, still impaled by his own weapon which now stuck out of his chest like a gravestone marker.

A shrill cry alerted Fox to the next attack as two of the three remaining men rushed him. The first man lunged with his double-edged mercenary saber. Fox waited until the last possible moment before beating the blade aside with such ferocity, that the sword flew back to impale itself in the midsection of the man's own comrade who was running alongside him. With the same movement, Fang continued upon its arc and came up perpendicularly to cleave the assailant, his own steel still buried deep within the chest of his comrade, from chin through to the top of his skull. The two men toppled one on top of the other, the gore from each of their wounds puddling about the mass of erratically tangled limbs.

Fox's teeth flashed beneath a grin under his knitted brow. It had been too long since he was in a good fight. His own unique style of swordsmanship he had developed since he was a child, and was based upon the principle of perpetual motion- that attack and parry were not two separate techniques, but one in the same. Every strike was a parry, and every parry a strike.

Fox crouched into a defensive stance as his final adversary rushed him, eyes gone mad, not realizing that he raced headlong towards his doom. This time, Fox chose not to deflect the oncoming blade, but ducked beneath its vertical slash, slamming his shoulder into his attacker's mid-section as he did so. The remaining man, he who claimed to have instructed him in the finer art of swordplay, was sent hurling into the air from the impact and performed a full roll, head over heel, before slamming upon his back on the ground. The fallen adversary still clung to his blade in this position and managed to raise it defensively from where he lay upon the road, but Fox was already in motion. He pivoted upon one foot, bringing the full momentum he had begun with his first movement about, and, aided by the force granted him by the arc of this move, struck the defensive blade with such ferocity that it sent it flying from the still quivering fingers which tried so desperately to hold it. The sword flew into the nearby trees and was lost in the tall grass. Fang ended its own graceful dance with the tip of its razor point pressed against the remaining member of the Dark Claw's throat. There, Fox's legendary sword paused momentarily as its final victim threw his arms up in desperation over his tightly shut eyes and thin-lipped grimace, his face thoroughly contorted in anticipation of the blow he was sure to follow. Fox hesitated, savoring the moment.

"It is not in my nature to kill fellow thieves." he spoke. He did not care to prolong any man's suffering, yet his anger was such that he wished to share his vindication. Fox had abided by the thieves' code for most of his life. It was important to him for this man to understand why he was about to die, despite, or perhaps because of the added anguish it would incur. "You four have broken the code." Fox stared about his environs before he spoke again. "This is quite the enterprise you have here. Baraan is but a small, unprotected village populated by farmers, yet it stands as a necessary port along the trade routes to the Kingdom of Gemmen. I'm sure that this has proven to be a profitable venture. Had you attempted such dishonorable actions nearer to Gemmen, Cammarran himself would have seen to your executions. Now, the task falls to me."

"Cammarran!" cried the man, still attempting to shield himself from the inevitable with arms folded about his face. "Cammarran is dead!"

At this Fox paused. The words had pierced his heart more deeply than any sword ever could. He pressed his weight into Fang's pommel until the tip of the blade tasted blood.

"You lie!"

The prostrate man allowed his arms to fall by his side. He knew now that his life was at an end. Perhaps he saw in this moment his single chance at revenge, for his features softened into a smile as he spoke.

"The fault is yours." he said, his voice barely above a whisper. "Krillian has killed him. He searches for you. Tell me Fox, how long can even you continue to escape death's cold embrace?"

The poetic, ominous words escaped the man's lips like frost carried by a winter's breeze, chilling Fox to his core. They proved to be the last the reaver ever spoke. Without a word, Fox pressed against the pommel of Fang, ending the antagonizing speech and the man who spoke it before either could do more harm. Yet the damage was done. The four men presented no physical threat to him, yet as Fox stared about the battleground and all he had wrought, he knew that he would bear the scars of this battle for the rest of his days.

He stood fixed in the center of the road for some time, hovering over the prostrate forms of his most recently vanquished foes. He first attempted to convince himself that the reaver had been lying, but Fox knew the truth when he heard it. Slowly, he awoke from his stupor as realization, followed by grim acceptance fell over him. He had lingered here too long.

Bolt could sense Fox's emotions as he wordlessly climbed atop her back. She seemed almost empathically to reciprocate the mix of anger, confusion and pain of her rider as the two continued down the road. There was no turning back, Fox knew. Even had he chose to return to Gemmen, the path would be marked by sorrow. For all of his skill, even he could not bring back the dead.

The bodies of those who had been the source of much woe to the land were left to lie upon the road, their own blood turning the ground to mud. The gristly scene would remain as a warning for those who chose to break the thieves' code in the wake of Cammaran's death. Fox could think of no greater gift to bestow upon his posthumous mentor. The trials of Baraan were over, and though the experience had a profound effect, it was one best left on the trail behind him.

As Fox and Bolt continued along the King's highway towards Damaas, the storm clouds which began to take form overhead perfectly framed the scene as no words could. Balthazar wept for him, and the path ahead seemed infinitely darker.

CHAPTER SIX - THE LADY OF THE LAKE

The storm raged for two days and nights before it broke, and Fox had been forced to build shelters out of branches and pine boughs in order to protect both he and Bolt from its veracity. Little ground had been covered, for each shelter needed to be constructed large enough to accommodate the mare lest she fall sick and be unable to continue. The pair set up camp each night at the first sign of twilight that Fox might have the time required to construct leafy domes upon a skeleton of tree limbs large enough to accomedate her. He had kept clear of the main thoroughfare, preferring instead to travel along the winding back roads and forest trails where he could be assured of his privacy. This he did at the expense of sharing accommodations with any passing caravan train. He slept in the nude, allowing his clothes to dry by hanging them from the inside of his shelter, only to have them soaked through again upon the morning. On the second such night, the wind and rain succeeded in collapsing his structure and he was forced to toil by moonlight reconstructing it. He had eaten very little, and had not bothered with a fire, satisfying he and his mount with the fruit from an apple tree he had passed late on the second day. He sacrificed much of his own meal that Bolt might keep up her strength during the arduous journey, and to her credit, one would not have suspected that the mare had enjoyed a lifetime of warmth and security the finest stables in Gemmen afforded her, for the horse continued to prove herself as a hearty travelling companion in possession of fortitude to rival any military steed set upon a long campaign. The weather suited Fox well, for his humor demanded neither warmth nor sustenance.

In times past, whenever Fox was troubled, he simply cast aside whatever had been bothering him, refusing to entertain notions which gave him unease- yet such strategy refused to comply when faced with the reality that his only friend had recently been murdered. He could only console himself with the notion that soon, there would be a reckoning. It was these thoughts which fueled the rage which gave him warmth. The fires of hate he had known once before, and had saved him then as it did now.

All who lived upon Balthazar had heard tales of Krillian. The stories which surrounded the dark lord of assassins had been told around campfires and smoke filled taverns during the late night hours since Fox was a child. He had never given much thought to the man, for the legends which surrounded him were often equally seeped in superstition and dread as were his own and were therefore granted equal credibility. Only now did Krillian, a man whom he had never before seen, seem to haunt his nightmares with various illusions of a dark robed figure in ecstasy as he took the life of his now posthumous mentor. Fox knew that should he be unable to find any distraction, the unrelenting specter could very well consume him.

The sun was an especially welcome visitor on the morning of the third day since his encounter with the Dark Claw, for the murky grim ambiance of the storm had done little to assuage Fox's mood, which proved to be as torrential as the weather. Not only did the break in the storm serve to lift the travelling companion's spirits, but, having made their camp upon the shore of a large river the night before, Fox did not relish the idea of having to ford it during a squall, and the new dawn brought with it a faint trace of hope for both he and his mighty steed. The bright sun was so welcome a sight in fact, that there was little chance of it failing to raise the spirits of even the dourest of travelers.

Even with the constant downpour, he and Bolt had ridden through many a fine meadow, and the horse had enjoyed a steady diet of mulch to compliment Fox's store of apples; but with new optimism came new appetites, and Fox, not being content with the occasional fruit, soon realized that his had come back in earnest. The few remaining sign posts which marked the old trails, those that existed prior to the dawn of civilization which followed the great war and led to the construction of the King's highway which linked the four Kingdoms, indicated that the next civilized outpost- that of Serdia, was still half a week's ride hence, and Fox had decided to take advantage of the break in the weather to do some hunting. The markings of the sign post were difficult to discern, for long ago each region had their own unique dialects. With the rise of the four seats of power, a common tongue had emerged that all but negated the old in every region save for that of the Hillmen who adamantly clung to the old ways. Thankfully, Cammarran had insisted that Fox maintain a passing familiarity with the language of old Gemmen however, and though he had bristled against learning it, the master of the thief guild's wisdom had once again proven its worth. His only regret was that he did not have the foresight to pack a bow, for though he could set up snares for smaller game, it would take an eternity to snare as many squirrels and field mice as were necessary to satisfy his now voracious appetite.

Normally, such hardships as bad weather and lack of food would have bothered him not at all, yet in times past when Fox had chosen to live off the land, he did so with the knowlege that he could return to civilization at a moment's notice to avail himself of whatever he wanted. The life of a thief who had no-one to thieve from, as he was now learning, was not a pleasant one, and he had come to regret that he had not chosen to better prepare for the hardships of his journey. This, coupled with the loss of a dear friend, had made the last two days near to unbearable. For a man like Fox, who had elevated hedonism to an art form- his recent adventures had proven to be entirely unacceptable.

It was possible to fashion a bow and some arrows from what

nature provided, yet such crudely constructed instruments rarely had the tensile strength required to kill larger game. The bows that Fox was accustomed to in Gemmen, even those of far lesser quality than the ones which the King's archers used to defend the great wall- were nearly always made of fire-hardened hickory, multi-layered and glued with resin. A few sticks of wood lashed together with some vine, Fox knew, served perfectly well as a child's toy, but would prove to be of little value in his present situation.

The solution to his current dilemma was self-evident- he needed to fashion himself a spear. He was well trained with the quarterstaff, and he had yet to meet the man who could beat his cast with a well-balanced javelin. In these environs, he knew, a good spear would serve perfectly as both. His own sword Fang was such a unique weapon that those whom it slayed were easily identified by the King's investigators as being victims of the arch-bandit. Fox had no doubt that, having slain the 'Dark Claw', the bodies of those will have sent a clear message that the fearsome Fox of Gemmen had taken his leave of the capital city, and should he need to slay any more roadside bandits upon his journey, he did not wish for his movements to be so easily tracked.

The long-hidden sun, now strong and un-obscured by the dark clouds which seemed to have been following him, baked the fresh spoor lying about, and caused the air to veritably reek with the scent of nearby game. Wasting no further time, he scanned the area until his eyes rested upon a particularly erect young oak tree which grew straight and strong near the riverbed.

He spent much of that morning hacking away at the tree with Fang until he had a strong, nearly perfectly straight shaft. Bolt had watched him work with amused curiosity as she grazed contentedly nearby. He had ceased the practice of tying his mount, for the two had come to share a strong bond, and the horse had shown not e'en the slightest inclination towards abandoning her new friend. There too was the question of defense, for Balthazar was a dangerous world, and a tethered mount was easy prey for the multitude of terrors which roamed the countryside. With the exception of the minor threat presented by the Dark Claw, they had been fortunate in this regard so far, yet Fox was certain that they would have to contend with far greater dangers before they arrived at the golden city of Damaas.

At its full zenith, the sun gazed down upon Fox as he smoothed out a rigid knot in the wood with the point of one of his throwing knives, and was now set upon the task of lashing stones to its base with some grass that he had corded into a tough rope for the purpose. The stones did more than simply give added weight and heft to the weapon; it also provided a studded surface which made for an easier grip when used for a cast. With this phase of his labor complete, all the weapon lacked was a tip. A dagger may have served for this purpose, yet Fox knew that had he used one of his own, he could not be assured that the weight distribution would be properly calibrated to suit his needs. The answer to this conundrum lied in the nearby river, for on all of Balthazar, Fox knew, there was no stronger rock than that which could be found submerged in the fast moving currents of the mighty rivers which raced across her surface. The swift, underwater rapids of rivers such as the one upon whose shore he now visited, served much like the hammer of a blacksmith- beating against the submerged bedrock for centuries until it became finely tempered.

He stripped to his breach-cloth and tucked a dagger into the thin leather of the waistband. The river was still churning violently, for it had yet to slow due to the storm which had so recently agitated it, yet Fox was an expert swimmer and dove into the cool water without any concern. From past experience, he knew that he could hold his breath for an inordinate amount of time, thus he ignored the first submerged rocky outcroppings he encountered and dove deeper, fighting with the vicious rip-tide until he came across a larger deposit deep in the inky depths. This particular river was deeper than most, even this close to the shore, and the light offered by the sun strained through the surface when he came upon what he sought. Sweeping the algae from a solid outcropping that had likely never before felt the touch of a mortal hand; he began to chip away at it with the tip of his dagger. It was hard work, for the rock was as strong as was the metal of his knife, and the tide continually attempted to drag him from his labor. Twice he had to swim to the surface and gain another lungful of air, but eventually his efforts proved fruitful, and when he broke the surface of the river for a third time, he did so with a large chunk of the adamant stone in his possession.

Sitting upon the shore of the river, still clad in his breach-clout, he began to work the stone into the shape of a large arrowhead.

He had nearly worn two of his daggers to the hilt when he brought the task to fruition. He had no doubt that had he immediately set himself upon the trail proffered by the nearby spoor, that he could bring down whatever animal had been responsible for it with his throwing knives, but he was certain that the beast would no doubt suffer greatly had he chosen to attempt this course of action. He was not so desperate that he was prepared to cause unnecessary suffering to any animal when a well placed spear shot served as a far more humane alternative. There too was the possibility that a large animal, such as a buck, struck with multiple knives, would run off deeper into the woods to die alone, thereby requiring Fox to track it a second time.

It was well into the afternoon when he finally completed the construction of his weapon. He wedged his make-shift spearhead into a small split in the shaft, lashing it firmly in place with more of the tough grass he had braided together. Then he sealed the split with some sap from a nearby pine tree. The shaft was erect, and weighted down perfectly with the plethora of stones embedded in the hilt. He spun the spear about his naked torso and was pleased with its balance. It was as fine a weapon as any he could have found at a quality smithy. In the distance, he spotted a knot in a thick oak, and was rewarded when his spear buried itself into the center of it from the force of his practice cast.

Bolt was enjoying a nap nearby under the shade of a leafy evergreen and Fox decided to let her be as he set out upon the trail of his next meal. The mare had endured much and well-deserved a rest.

He was no expert tracker, yet his senses were keen, and he managed to track what he was certain to be a deer to where its trail ended further downstream. This was not surprising, for on a day such as this, with the sun at its full height, most of the nearby game would have likely retreated to the cool waters in order to escape the scathing rays overhead.

He was certain that his prey had no doubt picked up upon his own scent and had therefore chosen to drink much farther down the river in comparative safety. This he minded not at all, for impersonating a log and floating downstream proved to be both a stealthy and cool way of hunting.

He drifted for nearly a league or more, ignoring the smaller game such as rabbits and several types of rodent he was unfamiliar with until he spied a fine young doe lapping at the shore in the distance. She was still too far out of range for him to attempt to bring her down, and he reminded himself of the importance of patience, lest he give in to his own gnawing hunger and strike too soon.

He allowed himself to drift towards the shore where he was sure to get proper footing, and when he had shortened the distance between he and the doe, leapt upwards dramatically from the depths and threw his arm back for a cast of his newly-forged weapon. The water which raced along the shaft had no time to fall back from whence it came when his intended target fell upon the rocky outcropping of the riverside, the tip of a large fletched arrow jutting out if its heart.

Fox stood rooted in place, completely dumbfounded. All about him the birds of the forest scattered towards the safety of the sky, yet

Fox remained stupidly motionless. He tried vainly to make sense of the events which had just transpired. When these failed, he gave up immediately and waded towards the fallen animal.

He had no sooner crouched over the prostrate form of the deer when his keen ears detected running footsteps in the veil of trees beyond. He readied his spear. Perhaps this would be the distraction that he had longed for! He hoped that, at any moment, some terror of the forest, perhaps a were-beast, a bandit, a cannibalistic Hillman on safari, or some other danger equally as exciting and voracious might come crashing through the glade in order to engage him in mortal combat and test his skills with his new weapon.

The foliage spread apart to reveal the most stunningly beautiful woman that Fox had ever seen, instilling within him a sudden sense of vulnerability the likes of which he found eminently disconcerting.

He was dripping wet and nearly naked. He had not shaved in many a day and his long, tousled blonde hair clung wetly to his scruffy face. His spear, cobbled together from the wilderness itself, completed the profile. He resembled nothing less than a wild-man who had never before seen civilization.

The woman by comparison, though she was dressed in simple peasant garb comprised of tight, tanned riding leathers, boots, and a white blouse which was sleeveless and cut above her lithe, muscular abdomen, struck Fox immediately as the most elegant he had ever before laid eyes on.

She had the darkest hair he had ever seen; hair which seemed to swallow the afternoon light, rendering the sun itself powerless against her. It was tied back loosely and left to lie upon her naked shoulders, which, though kissed by the sun, seemed ghostly pale by comparison. In one hand she held a longbow, as long as she was tall, and on her back, winced so tightly that its cord was completely hidden between the swell of her well-rounded breasts- which nevertheless seemed not to crease her form-fitting blouse, was a rawhide quiver brimming with so many fletchings, that it seemed as though she wore a feathered headress where they rose above the top of her ebony mane. Her figure was perfection. Though lean, her hips flared beneath her hardened mid-section. When she moved, it was with pantherish strides, agile, rhythmic and sure-footed, like a dancer, or a fierce and confident predator... or both. She was sultry and deadly all at once. Her full lips would not deny the contrast between her large, dark eyes whose long lashes were as black as the strands which fell about her ivory features. Like a spectre, like a wraith, whose fairness was tethered to this world, she glided towards him. She was no noblewoman, this much was certain, yet moved with more grace than any Fox had ever encountered. Clearly, she was adept with the bow, as the deer at Fox's feet could readily attest.

A long, rather uncomfortable silence followed. Fox's jaw was agape. The woman merely smiled. It was not a complete smile, for merely one side of her mouth curled upwards where the fullness of her lips could not follow, nevertheless, the effect could be read in her eyes which sparkled with beguiling amusement as light dancing playfully upon obsidian.

Suddenly, Fox became acutely aware as to the root of his unease, for his trance was dispelled when he realized that he stood unclothed, unwashed, save for the rivulets of water which raced down his body in their effort to escape, and completely bedraggled. Frantically, he attempted to cover himself, a sight rendered quite comical, for there was nothing about to cover himself with.

"Please don't feel the need to cover yourself on my account." The mysterious woman said. Her voice was simultaneously whimsical, amused, and quite charming despite the circumstances. She nodded to the prostrate deer at Fox's feet. "I don't think he'll mind. My name is Sariss."

Fox struggled momentarily to find his voice. It occurred to him that he had not actually spoken since his departure from Baraan. This delay seemed to amuse the woman even further, for she laughed before she spoke again.

"If you make no effort to introduce yourself, than I shall continue to think of you as I see you. Wild naked man of the woods...."

Fox hesitated again. What was his name? He had momentarily forgotten it. He could clearly not tell her that his name was Fox; for that name carried notoriety that, given the current circumstance, he wished greatly to avoid. He opened his mouth with every intention of answering her query with the name Barnabas.

"Costa!" he shot back.

It was the first time since childhood that the legendary Fox of Gemmen had ever told anyone his true name.

CHAPTER SEVEN - THE FANTABULOUS ORIGIN OF THE FEARSOME FOX

There was nothing special about the name. It had never held any meaning for Fox. It was simply the name assigned to him during his interlude at the North Gemmen Home for Wayward Children. Prostitution was a booming trade in Gemmen, and, like him, many newborn infants were left at the doorstep of the orphanage- unwanted castaways and victims of a society which held no place for them. He was one of a long list of Gemmen's bastards, cast aside and forgotten. Few of these children ever lived to see adulthood, those who did oft found the gallows marking the end of their careers as beggars, killers, or worse. A hastily scribbled logbook entry marked the only evidence that they had ever existed at all.

A child without a mother was like a plant without water and often bore bitter fruit; yet Fox was unique amongst the homogenized coterie of misfits in that his caretakers, despite their best efforts, failed utterly in their frequent attempts to beat the insolence out of him. There were many amongst these charges who displayed an initial obstinance, yet in time, all were eventually brought to heel, domesticated and tamed. In the case of Fox, stubbornness was the nomenclature given to sheer will personified, which the strongest cudgel could not break.

A collection of scrapes and bruises, Fox had seen but eight of Gemmen's harsh winters when he was discovered stealing food from the kitchens- this proved to be his first lesson in thievery, for he learned at far too young an age what lie in store for thieves who allowed themselves to be caught. That night, the headmaster's chief enforcer, a globulous, sweaty man named Gorblut, who had clearly retained much of the kitchen's supplies for himself during his tenure- had laid into Fox with a particularly savage beating. At this stage in his development, Fox was completely unaware as to how great his emerging strength truly was, and he had managed to kill Gorblut with a savage blow to the side of the head from a piece of dowel that he had taken to concealing upon his person.

That night, Fox was locked in a small pantry that the caretakers of the North Gemmen Home for Wayward Children oft used as a make-shift prison. The city guard had been alerted to the crime, and he spent much of that evening in quiet contemplation of the executioner's axe that he knew awaited him in the morning.

Fox had never seen anything of Gemmen outside of the orphanage save for the majestic silhouette of the palace oft spied in the distance. His emotions were like that of a boiling cauldron, for the ironic cruelty of his situation was not lost on him. His long awaited escape from his militant surroundings was finally assured; he was to see the vaunted Kingdom at last, whose dim outline was given life upon the fertile landscape of his imagination, yet his much anticipated visit to the sprawling city proper was ill-fated to be his last. He had heard, and believed the rumors that King Alric had a special place in the bowels of his dungeons where children faced the same fate as full grown men and women who were commonly executed in the square under full view of the citizenry. Were any to be sympathetic to his plight, he could rest assured that ignorance as to the true machinations of the palace would prevail. Had he been the son of a nobleman, or even a recognized citizen of Gemmen itself accused of the murder, the penalty would have been far less severe, yet caring for the plethora of orphans that Gemmen spat out on a daily basis strained the coffers of King Alric, then a younger man who had recently inherited both the Kingship of Gemmen, and a substantial debt to his neighbors from his spendthrift father. The solution to the financial burden of caring for Gemmen's bastards was not altogether inhumane for a man like Alric who believed himself more cunning than cruel, for it was a simple thing to deny a future to those who could hope for none.

That final, desperate evening, keenly delineated by despair and anxiety, marked the first time that Fox had ever picked a lock. The effort was exceedingly frustrating, for he had not yet developed the practiced hand which would serve him so well later in life, but while he struggled at first with the bolt which held the singular window of the room in place, he soon found that the innards of the lock were much easier to manipulate than its reinforced exterior. This he managed to do by shuffling about the housing with a thin iron filing that he found lying upon the floor, painstakingly sliding the bolt from its mooring beneath the strike plate, each increment a victory, until his tireless efforts succeeded in releasing the latch.

The winters in Gemmen were fierce, and the night Fox escaped his erstwhile home was colder than most. Though he had successfully affected his escape, he made it only as far as the abandoned stables located nearby. The stables had been vacant the entirety of the time Fox had spent at the home, for the gruel he and his fellow orphans were forced to subside upon was not ample enough for any extra mouths. Those caretakers who resided within Gemmen commuted upon simple mounts, yet these were always tethered to posts in the courtyard and had long since returned to the city.

The young child came to know of the vast reserves of stamina that he was in possession of under the most grueling of circumstances for the thin cotton of his drawstring pants and patchwork chemise offered little protection from the fierce cold, and there was not so much as a bundle of hay that he could have collected for warmth- yet he had no choice but to make the best of his circumstances, for the abandoned stable was the only shelter for leagues other than the orphanage where certain death awaited. It wasn't until the sun arose the next morning that Fox could see enough of his environs that he chose to brave the massive snowdrifts and make his way towards the inner city.

As he crawled across the mountainous banks of snow, it occurred to the young Fox that his passage would have been very easy to track, for his hands and feet left easy markings in the soft, white powder. Had anyone bothered to make an attempt at finding him, they would have found it easy to do so. The notion gave him strength. Had his recent caretakers believed that recovering their lost charge would have been as easy as scooping up his body off the ground once the snows had melted, then Fox was content to leave them a disappointed lot.

The morning that Fox left the home for wayward children was a desperate one, yet not without wonder. When he finally came to a large cobblestone road, he followed it for miles, not knowing where it would take him, content enough that his movement gave warmth to his limbs. He had assumed, of course, that the path he was travelling led towards the shelter that the city promised, but he never would have guessed that his chosen route would taken him directly in front of the palace itself.

For one whose entire world was naught but the quarters and common rooms of the orphanage, the sight of King Alric's palace was so awe-inspiring as to encapsulate all of his senses. The street had become congested with people, growing in number and pooling at the foot of the palace, drawn to it as he was, yet Fox ignored them as readily as he did the gnawing hunger in his belly. That such a structure could be sculpted by the hands of men was beyond his reasoning. He had heard speak of Alric's castle during his time at the orphanage, yet the image he had formed in his mind's eye failed utterly in their attempts to describe it. The towers and ramparts stretched so far into the clouds that Fox could only assume that gods sat atop of them. Surely, nothing but the hand of a god could have shaped the ornate metalwork that the monolithic structure itself was adorned with; the iron bridges which linked each of the towers so that those who dwelt within could traverse the sky without ever the need to alight. No mortal hand could have spun such finely wrought lattrices the like of which graced each of the untold number of balconies jutting outwards in perfect symmetry that the members of Alric's house might stare down upon those so far beneath them. Surely, such audacity, such verve, was beyond the arrogance of men.

Despite being so transfixed however, the need for food and shelter soon overtook him. It was here, at the foot of such abundance, where Fox did try his hand at begging. In the looming shadow of excess he did ask for little, only to find the citizens of Gemmen to be as cold and distant as the palace itself; when he did receive aid in the form of a few morsels of food, his endeavors to obtain them stung at his pride. In time, he would scale these towers. Given time, he would conquer them.

And so he moved on; a young pup, a mongrel, veraciously hungry and shivering from the cold, his indomitable spirit his only companion. He was then much like the piece of iron filing which he had used to affect his erstwhile escape- small and insignificant; cast aside, assigned no value, yet still hardened by forge-fire whom destiny assigned greater purpose than did man.

Even at this early stage in his life, the young Fox had proven himself to be extraordinarily resourceful, yet even he would not have survived the unrelenting winter without the help of a little luck. He had taken to wandering about the streets after dark, stealing whatever he could to survive, ducking into alleyways in order to sidestep the marauding ruffians, lotus addicts, and the criminally insane element who haunted the streets after dark, their nocturnal activities and the shame inherrant therein hidden from the judgement of the sun whilst embraced by the shadows, neither offering them absolvement. He slept during the day in whatever shelters he could find, frequently being chased off by angry shop owners and slumlords at which time the cycle began anew.

It was on one such evening that he found shelter in Gemmen's Temple of Light. Such temples were found across all of Balthazar and were older still than the formation of the great Kingdoms of north, east, south and west; though their architecture was beyond the skill of any who lived at that time. Such temples were said to be places of great healing, and the only power on Balthazar not subject to the laws of the ruling class, as the monks within claimed to worship the goddess Meridian and lived solely by her divine law. Prior to the rise of the Kings of old, the authority of the temple was absolute. Though still afforded status denied to all but the elite,

Balthazar's nobles, save for the more devout members of their echelon, had long since turned to modern means of medicine to treat their ailments, whilst those to whom this option was denied oft found themselves no recourse but the white lotus, whose healing properties were naught but hollow promises set to precipitate any ailment. By chance of fate, the massive temple door had been barred rather sloppily the night before and Fox was able to squeeze his thin frame through the slight opening thus presented.

The temple interior was by far the largest chamber Fox had ever seen. Its high vaulted ceiling was held in place by a multitude of spiraled columns which were laced with gold leaf and ironworks similar to those which graced the palace itself. Surrounding the large central chamber was an intricate web of corridors and side-rooms, and it was during his exploration of the labyrinthine hallways that he chanced to stumble across a small storage room which had seen so little use, that Fox was certain the monks themselves had forgotten about it.

The storage room was sparse and the floor was littered with hay. Fox collected as much of the hay as he could into one corner, making himself a bed. On the first night in his new den, he fell fast asleep, feeling like a King in his own private palace.

On the morrow, he explored his new home further and found a small cellar door which led to the street overhead. The cellar was covered with a veritable mountain of snow, and it took him most of the day to tunnel through it using nothing but his bare hands as implements. When he was done, he had his own private entrance to his new home in the form of a tunnel, well hidden within the bank of the snow overhead.

Fox was thoroughly content. Surely, one could ask for nothing more. He had a dwelling where he could stay rent-free. The city militia gave the temple a wide berth, and even during the daylight hours visitors were scarce, for whatever powers of healing the monks within once claimed to have had long since faded, their ministrations replaced by modern poultices that numbed the senses even as they numbed pain.

The best part of Fox's new home was the small marketplace nearby. He had learned how to steal out of desperation, and he had gotten good at it. So good in fact, that he had nearly pillaged the small market into bankruptcy by the time the snows had melted. Little did he known then that his actions were to draw the gaze of the all-seeing eye of the Lord of the thieves' guild.

The shop-keeps of the small market could tolerate a certain amount of thievery, for such was the nature of life in Gemmen, but when the actions of the heretofore undiscovered thief began to place a serious crimp in profit margins, decisive action was needed.

And so it was that at the end of a particularly hard day's work, the small band of merchants which Fox had been pillaging from bandied together with their respective guild leader in order to voice their plight at the Bear's Den tavern. Cammarran was a man not yet into his twilight then- still adjusting to his new position as head of the order, yet he held true to the rule of law which had been passed down to him from all who proceeded his position. Thieves did not steal from the poor. The penalty for those who did was death.

It took a great deal of convincing to assure the merchants guild that the errant thief operated without his endorsement, and Cammarran did not take the news lightly. The possibility that a band of thieves who resented his appointment had decided to rebel against his authority was very real, and if such was indeed the case, a display of strength via swift and decisive action was necessary. It was a great stroke of luck for the young Fox that the new head of the guild wished to prove himself, for Cammarran did not immediately order his execution, preferring instead the option of ferreting out any possible revolt in order that he might determine the number of malcontents.

The arrival of spring had brought with it a cornucopia of fresh fruits and vegetables which lined the stalls of every vendor. Though the soil in Gemmen had not yet produced its bounty, the influx of caravans the warm weather brought with it carried with them exotic produce from faraway lands, and Fox had taken a strong liking to the many strange foods that the change in climate offered him. The merchant's stall he now visited took no heed of him as he stuffed his thin shirt with a handful of berries, for he had grown far too clever to be discovered by those who were so easily distracted in their attempts to peddle their wares. He had by this time mastered the art of misdirection. He could move about the small marketplace like a ghost, unseen yet ever present. His skills had become great- though not so great as to fool the four master thieves who, posing as paupers, had infiltrated the market on that day.

Julius- then sword-master of the thieves guild and one of Cammarran's most trusted lieutenants, noted that the boy's technique, though still in its infancy, was nevertheless impressive. He was at first quite certain that this small child could not have been solely responsible for the rash of theft that the marketplace had become infected with, yet having shadowed his every movement that afternoon in the hopes that he might discover the boy's mentor, he began to be convinced otherwise.

Fox knew enough of the machinations of Gemmen at this point that he was aware that a thieves' guild existed. His humility told him that he was beneath their their notice. His hubris told him that he had nothing to fear from them. For all of his skill, he was still untrained, and had yet to learn the lesson that a thief should never keep to one den overlong lest the chance of his being discovered multiply exponentially. The sun was low on the horizon when Fox eventually returned to the temple, and unbeknownst to him, his own shadow was not the only one which followed him on that day.

Previous to this, the only time Fox had ever gotten caught during his neophyte career as thief was also the first time he had ever tried his hand at pick-pocketing. This attempt had been clumsy at best, yet he nevertheless was able to avail himself of a small dagger clipped to the belt of a passing serf. The serf had felt the dagger release from its mooring, and had given him a merry chase, yet Fox was familiar with the territory and managed to elude him. Perhaps it was his need to feel as though he were properly armed in the midst of such dangerous environs, or perhaps it was because the dagger had been so difficult to acquire; whatever the reason, the small blade was easily the most valued of Fox's meager possessions, and as such, he never took it off. It was this unadorned, rather insignificant looking knife which was set to change the course of his life forever.

He had just fallen asleep on his bed of straw that evening, when his home was infiltrated by three very unwelcome visitors. He awoke with the tip of a long rapier pressed against his throat.

"Good morning young master!" Julius said, fully rousing Fox from his slumber. Behind where he stood, his four compatriots laughed and Julius turned to face them.

"Well men!" he said "It seems as though we have trapped our master thief in his lair."

The one called Julius leaned low to where Fox lay and spoke again, this time in a hushed tone.

"Cammarran wishes greatly to meet you."

Without a word, Fox rolled under the outstretched blade, removing his tiny dagger in the same movement from where he had it lashed to the waistband of his threadbare pants. Such was the speed of his attack that Julius was taken completely off guard. Fox came out of the roll and slashed at the thieves' exposed shin. His strike proved to be so fierce that it opened a vicious wound and caused Julius to fall to the floor screaming in agony. Instantly, Fox was upon him, snarling like a wild animal. He leapt atop the prostrate form of the sword-master, and would have ended his life there and then were it not for the swift action of one of the other thieves. The man brought the pommel of his heavy rapier down hard upon the back of Fox's head, and his world exploded into a blinding flash of light, followed immediately by the darkness of oblivion.

The four members of the guild returned to the Bear's Den with their prize intact. Julius was informed that, with the proper treatment, his wound would heal in time. His ego however, never would.

The heavy burlap sack he was thrust into was dropped at Cammarran's feet. The young Fox had regained consciousness for some time, and had been struggling to break free of his binding ever since-when the bag hit the floor, the drawstrings came loose just enough for him to claw his way out. He emerged from the sack and stared at the man who sat before him, wishing nothing more than to leap towards his new adversary in order to avenge his own wounded pride. Having escaped captivity once before, he would do anything to do so again. Freedom had been to his liking. Never again would he allow himself to be caged. He gritted his teeth into a feral snarl.

Cammarran merely smiled in amusement. "I sent you to catch me a thief..." he began "Though it looks as though you have snared me a Fox."

CHAPTER EIGHT - THE FARMER'S DAUGHTER

"Costa!" Fox said again, though this time louder, as though he were trying to convince himself of the truth of his words as much as this woman.

"Costa." she repeated, smiling. The smile itself seemed born of sorcery, for he seemed utterly caught in its beguiling spell.

"I prefer that to 'wild naked man of the woods.' Tell me Costa, what brings you to such a state?" she allowed herself a small chuckle as she stared him up and down appreciatively, fully taking in his nakedness. He was hard pressed to recall having ever felt so vulnerable. Thinking quickly, he relied on his years of well-rehearsed subterfuge.

"I was travelling with a caravan. We were attacked by bandits. I was lucky to escape with my life. I now travel with naught but my mount who is tethered nearby. As I have not eaten, I thought that I would try my hand at hunting."

Fox had seen nearly all of the great plays at the grand theatre in Gemmen, and, though rushed, believed his performance as good as any.

"Ah." replied Sariss, raising her eyes to the sky "No doubt the 'Dark Claw.'"

The manner in which she spoke the name convinced Fox that this woman was well aware of how silly the title sounded when spoken aloud.

"Well, worry not Costa. Word has just reached us that that band of thieves has been dispatched outside of Baraan."

"Truly?" replied Fox. His face was a mask of pure innocence.

"Indeed. It is said that all four members of the band were dispatched by a single swordsman, though I fear that we fellow travelers have much more to worry about. Some have speculated that their wounds seem like the handy-work of that master thief Fox from out of Gemmen."

"I have heard of this man." Fox replied "Word has it that he has never left the capitol. How can one be so sure that he is the one responsible?"

"A caravan that my family and I recently came into contact with spoke of little else. Apparently, some of the King's most experienced men had been sent to investigate. They reported back that the wounds inflicted upon the band were reminiscent of that thief which they had been tracking."

This surprised Fox greatly, though he took great care not to allow the emotion to play upon his features. Alric was a wily man, it was certainly feasible that he had been tracking him for some time- yet the King himself often proved to be one of Fox's most frequent retainers. It made little sense that he should suddenly change tack and try to have him apprehended. He could only conclude that, with the death of Cammarran, Alric sought to pursue him more aggressively. Perhaps he had been unaware as to how much and how often Cammarran intervened on his behalf in order to keep him out of the city guard's clutches.

The prospect of ever returning to Gemmen proved to be less and less desirable. Despite his attempts at living an anonymous life, his legend, it would seem, had caught up with him. No doubt that without the protection of Cammarran himself, the noble castes of Gemmen had been putting additional pressure on the King to capture the one who had made life so difficult for them. The thought shamed Fox, for he decided then that he had never truly appreciated how much easier Cammarran had made life for him.

"Family?" Fox enquired, trying to change the subject

"Yes." responded Sariss. I travel with my father and brother. We have made camp just over yonder rise." she waved her hand in the direction that she had come "No doubt you might care to join us for dinner."

"Dinner?" Fox replied

Sariss laughed her melodious laugh once more, her demeanor rendering him incredibly comfortable and ill at ease all at once.

"Why yes. Lest I miss my guess, it was I who fell the animal; therefore the spoils of the hunt are mine. Don't worry though, we may have little, but my family is not above... charity."

Fox smiled at the insult. He admired a worthy foe.

"Why don't you gather your mount and meet us to sup? Don't worry about the doe; I can carry it just fine on my own."

Then, as if to prove her point, and with strength that belied her slim form, she slung the deer over her shoulder. She cast him a backward glance as she made her way over the rise.

"Oh, and Costa?" she added "Do try and wear something a little more... formal to dinner will you?"

The small camp was not hard to find. He merely had to follow the trail of smoke from the family's cooking fire. He was unaccustomed to accepting charity from strangers, and as he and Bolt crested the small mound which rimmed the camp, his pride told him to turn back- his hunger urged him forward.

He had taken the time to cleverly conceal the letter and map he had received from Cammarran into the weave of his saddlebag. He did not expect to be searched before entering the camp, yet it would not do for his newly adopted alias to be compromised by a parchment which identified him as a thief dubbed Barnabas. Likewise, he kept his sword far from hand and left his spear behind lest he appear threatening.

The symbiotic bond he now shared with Bolt proved to be uncanny, for though the horse was completely unaware of his recent encounter with the woman at the riverside, she seemed positively jovial in her gait, as though she had found the entire situation she had not born witness to thoroughly amusing.

As the pair came into sight of the clearing where Sariss and her family had settled, Fox took in the scene with the same level of scrutiny that his lifetime spent as a thief demanded of him. The camp was strategically located, near to the river. There was a patch of healthy grass at the rear where two large oxen were grazing contentedly next to the small wagon which was their charge. The oxen were enormous, much larger than those Fox was familiar seeing at the marketplaces in Gemmen. They were clearly well-fed and well tended to, slow moving to be sure, yet strong and durable. The wagon had a heavy canvas tied to its frame which could be removed as the weather warranted. Fox deduced immediately that the family owned little, for the wagon was much smaller than one would expect when carrying the material possessions of three people. He decided immediately that he would be comfortable in their company.

Sariss herself stood off to one side, stoking the small cooking fire with a long pine branch which had been stripped of its needles. Near to her, flaying the deer with a rather old and worn looking hunting knife was one of the largest men Fox had ever seen. He looked like a barbarian, though Fox knew instantly by his bearing that this was not so. The man had the hulking musculature of those, and the manner in which he skinned the deer told that he was sure-footed and confident with a blade- also his general disposition seemed to be as gruff and calloused as the fiercest warrior, yet Fox recognized instantly that his giant frame had been acquired by the lifetime of hard work and toil that was demanded of a farmer. His skin was bronzed by the sun. His fingers were thick and calloused. He had long blonde hair, much like Fox's own, though graying somewhat at the temples. His long locks fell over his bull-like shoulders where they were tied back with a thin leather strap. He was cleanly shaven, despite being somewhat road-weary and covered with dust. He wore no shirt and only thin, airy cotton pants. His boots were of tough rawhide, heavily patched, and Fox had to wonder if the man had ever owned another pair. The muscles which lined his upper body were heavily delineated and moved gracefully as he worked. His enormous chest flared like a bellows every time he drew breath. He deduced immediately both that this was Sariss's father, and that he was a capable man not to be underestimated.

He allowed himself the luxury of approaching the pair rather clumsily to announce his arrival. He and Bolt made so much noise as they cleared the foliage which lined the encampment that Sariss was alerted to their presence immediately.

"Welcome to our camp Mr. Costa." she said, hailing him. Then she pointed her firebrand in the big man's direction. "This is my father, Aron."

Without slowing his labor, the big man merely gave Fox a slight nod and grunted in acknowledgement.

"You must forgive my father." Sariss said. "He is not renowned for his hospitality, yet I choose to keep him around because he knows how to skin a deer. Please, won't you join us?"

Fox made his way to the wagon and left Bolt to graze with the oxen. One of the beasts glared at him and snorted, and Fox could not help but be amused as to how the ox was so like Aron in both size and demeanor.

"My thanks again for allowing me the comforts of your hospitality" he said as he approached Sariss and began to help her with the fire.

"Nonsense!" she replied "It is a travelers duty to look out for one another. Now go and fetch me some wood that we might rekindle these embers."

Fox was impressed. The woman's tone would have seemed almost demeaning in her ability to give orders, yet she followed every one with such a radiant smile that even one such as he, who had stead-fastedly refused any authority save his own, could not possibly take offence.

The blaze was no sooner coaxed into health by the tender ministrations of the pair when a rather exuberant young man clumsily bounded through the nearby tree-line. Fox had heard him coming well before his arrival. He was certain that Sariss did as well. In one hand, he waved a splendid rapier about, one which would doubtlessly earn more coin at market then nearly the entirety of their possessions, stained with leaves and sap where it had been used to hack through the foliage.

"Isn't that venison ready yet?" he cried. "I'm half starved!"

Fox took the young man's bearing immediately. He gave an impression similar to that of Sariss herself. He had the same jet-black hair and somewhat pale complexion, though his long locks were wild and free and hung in wispish strands about his face where it was not blown back by the wind. Like Aron, he was cleanly shaven, though there the resemblances ended. He had the same well defined musculature of the farmer, yet his physique was lean and wiry. He was tall, and bore the same wicked grin as Sariss. A sleeveless jerkin and peasant's ensemble similar to Fox's own completed the profile. He decided instantly that he liked the young man, for his roguish charisma was undeniable. It reminded him of himself.

He bounded down the hill and placed a gentle kiss on Sariss's cheek.

"The work would go much faster if you decided to help!" she replied with a grin that mirrored his own. Fox was certain that the verbal jousting between the pair was one they had both become quite accustomed to.

The young man's smile merely broadened in reply as he turned his attention to Fox himself.

"You must be Costa. My sister has told us about you." He extended a hand and Fox shook it, playing his role as desperate vagabond as best he could. "My name is Erik. Glad to have another set of hands, for my father has been working mine to the bone."

Fox smiled. He detected no malice whatsoever in the boy. He seemed the very picture of naïve innocence- care-free and bold. He gave the impression of one much younger than his sister, yet physically, Fox could not immediately discern who the eldest of the two was.

The afternoon played out into evening. The fire was allowed to ebb so that the meat could cook more thoroughly over its coals. Fox spent his time erecting a small horizontal crossbeam set between a pair of saplings where the deer carcass could be hung and cured. Aron set himself to building a small lean-to from the tarpaulin of the wagon; Sariss was in charge of roasting the meat and feeding the oxen, and even spared a few carrots for Bolt herself who had taken an instant liking to her, while Erik had taken the opportunity to wander off.

Eventually, they all sat next to the fire to sup. With the meat fully cooked, Sariss had thrown more wood onto the small blaze. They no longer had need of the coals, and night was fast approaching where a larger flame would be needed to compete with the darkness. There was little conversation throughout the meal as everyone seemed content to satisfy their appetites. The venison had been seasoned to perfection, and Fox could not help but admire how, though prepared by modest means, the meat was as delicious as any served upon the silver plate of the most distinguished tavern in Gemmen. What remained of the deer had been heavily salted so as to aid in preserving the meat, yet the flank which they now enjoyed, enriched as it was by his own neglected appetite, was amongst the better meals he had ever been served. To drink, they had river water which Aron had collected in a small bucket. Each took turn drinking out of the bucket itself, and there was a comfortable familiarity in sharing not just a meal, but the same utensils as well, for the meat itself was carved and set out upon a thin slab of wood which served as a communal plate. When the supper was over, idle conversation began, and even the reticent Aron began to ask him questions.

"Where is it you are you headed?" he inquired

There was no point in trying to deceive the man, Fox thought, for the cleverest of lies was always couched in the truth. "I ride for Damaas. And you?"

"Damaas!" Erik jumped in "We also ride for Damaas. Tell me, are you a citizen there?"

"Forgive my brother's enthusiasm" Sariss interrupted. "He has known little but farmland our entire lives and has been prattling non-stop of his desire to see the golden city since our departure."

"No." replied Fox, laughing. "My home is in the capitol of Gemmen."

"We too are from Gemmen!" Erik replied. He caught a surprised look from Sariss and amended his story. "That is too say, we are from the province. Up until recently we owned a small farm on the pasture lands outside of the capital city. We just recently sold the property to finance our trip."

"I see." Fox replied. He chose not to pry any farther, nevertheless Sariss continued with the story.

"Our younger sister Veronica has been a student at the Temple of Light in Damaas this past year. We recently received word from her stating that she has designs towards marriage. We go there now so that her suitor may formally ask my father for her hand; and what of you Mr. Costa? What errand brings you to Damaas?"

"My brother and I own a small smithy shop in the merchant district of the Kingdom." Fox replied "I go to Damaas to collect on some credit and to purchase some gold inlay for the shop." It was as good a story as any, he thought to himself.

"I hope you do not intent to carry it back on that thing." Aron said as he pointed to Bolt with the tip of his hunting knife.

"No." laughed Fox. "She is merely my mount until I arrive in Damaas, then I plan to join a caravan for the return trip."

"Your steed is truly a magnificent animal!" Erik interjected, seemingly enjoying contradicting his father "I would have taken you for a travelling nobleman of some sort."

"No noble I!" Fox replied, clearly dismayed by the comment. Out of the corner of his eye, he saw Aron smile for the first time since their meeting.

"If you both will excuse me." the big man said "It has been a long day."

He stuffed a large piece of the venison in his mouth, using the same knife with which he flayed it, then made his way to the lean-to which served as their shelter for the evening. He turned to face his son before crawling inside.

"There will be no wandering about after dark!" he said gruffly

The young man folded his arms across his chest from where he sat near the fire and frowned petulantly.

"We don't know if the entirety of those roadside bandits have been accounted for."

Without looking back, the big man disappeared into the nook.

Fox smiled. He was quite sure that Aron had come to rely heavily on his daughter's ability to keep Erik in line.

The three remaining companions were not so tired as Aron however, and after engaging in some banal conversation, they soon took their party to the river's edge. They were still within ample view of the firelight, which competed madly with the overhead moon in what proved to be a beautiful dance of light upon the water. Far from the heavy torrents that Fox had to contend with earlier, the river was now quiet and still, save for a few ripples which a soft breeze stirred upon its surface and whispered through the tall, untamed grass beyond where Bolt continued to fill her belly. It was an evening of resounding splendor and beauty such as Balthazar was wont to grace travelers with who braved the wilds far from the security of the King's highway.

Fox sprawled himself out on the rocky shore. Sariss rolled up her pant legs, removed her boots and waded into the river, while Erik danced about the water's edge practicing his swordplay.

Fox watched the youth practice his routines and was greatly impressed. He had initially assumed the lad to be unworthy of so fine a blade and could not fathom how it was that a farmer's son had grown to be so familiar with a sword. The complicated maneuvers he executed were clearly taught to him by a sword-master, for Fox recognized both the techniques and their various origins. Since the end of the great war in which the Kingdom of Raimia nearly conquered all of Balthazar, much of the fencing arts which had been unique to each region had become widely spread, yet most swordsmen were still purists, and tended to adhere to the styles of their particular regions. This was something Fox could never understand, for his own sword-masters had conveyed in him the importance of being adept in a variety of techniques. Erik too, seemed to share this conviction, for his movements were a seemless blend of double-handed strikes honed by the barbarians of Hyrst, mixed with the nimble footwork of the culture-obsessed Raimians.

As the young man spun about in maneuver after maneuver, slashing at the water occasionally as he did so, Fox came to appreciate that swordplay was something that the otherwise whimsical young lad took very seriously indeed. The only flaw in his technique was that he had mastered the sword too well. Fox knew that true combat rarely fell within the parameters of well-choreographed attacks and parries. There was too much energy wasted in the complex spins, thrusts, and rolls. A true sword-master did not feel the need to so arrogantly display his skill. He wished that he could instruct the boy properly, yet to do so would betray his carefully laid-out charade.

"He really is quite good isn't he?" Sariss suddenly interjected, breaking the stillness. She waded closer towards him as she spoke again. "Erik and I are twins. Our sister Veronica was but a child when our mother was slain, and father put aside what little coin we ever had in order to hire sword-masters to train him. Up until then, I don't think he ever put much importance on sword-play. Father is very overprotective of us, and his overbearing nature only got worse after mother's death. I always insisted that I should learn as well, but father forbade it. It is not that he believes the sword to be beyond a woman's ken... father has always treated us as equals, only my own talents were always with the bow and it was in this direction that he encouraged me."

"I too believe that it is wise for all citizens of Balthazar to be capable of defending themselves." Fox replied "Though I myself have never been called upon to do so."

The fledgling conversation was interrupted by Erik, who, having finished his work-out, now made his way to where Fox and Sariss relaxed upon the river-bed.

"It truly is a shame that the arch-thief Fox dispatched of those roadside bandits." he said, swinging his blade in circular fashion, and allowing the water that still clung to it to splash his sister. "I would have liked to have dispatched of them myself!"

Despite his boasting, Fox had seen the skill, or lack thereof, of those who had called themselves the 'Dark Claw,' and he was not completely unsure as to whether or not the boy might have been able to accomplish this feat. Nevertheless, Fox had long prided himself on his ability to size up an adversary, and he was certain that Erik had never before killed a man. Regardless of one's skill with a blade, all of the training on Balthazar did not prepare one for such an endeavor.

"A shame indeed!" Sariss replied, shaking herself from the water her brother had splashed her with. "It certainly would be nice to have one less mouth to feed on this journey."

Erik accepted the rebuke with a characteristic smirk before replying.

"Well, as father has forbidden me to do anymore hunting this evening, I believe that I shall retire as well."

He swung his sword a final time in complicated rhythm before replacing it back into its scabbard and Fox had to suppress a smile. Despite the boy's boisterous, indifferent attitude, he was certain that this last movement was for his own benefit. Though the two had taken an instant liking to each other, if Erik was to leave his sister alone with a stranger, he no doubt thought it prudent that he know of his competency with a sword.

"Costa. There is safety in numbers." he said smiling "I do hope that you choose to travel with us a while longer!"

"Sleep well!" Sariss cried out after him as he made his way back towards the fire. Rising to her feet, she waded back into the water. Despite himself, Fox could not help but admire her voluptuous silhouette as framed by the moonlight.

"Veronica's suitor is a nobleman named Edward." Sariss continued as she drew her arms through her hair and tilted her head back in what was perhaps not intended to be a seductive manner, but which produced the same results. "He is a bard of some note. We are even told that he plays at court."

"And what of your husband," Fox asked, "does he not travel with you?"

It was unclear to him why he was asking such personal questions of this woman, and his seeming need to do so troubled him greatly. First, he had revealed his true name to her, and now he was astounded at the sound of his own voice as it continued to ask questions which were none of his affair. For a man who prided himself on being a loner, his recent behavior was uncharacteristic to say the least... Though he had never bothered to truly learn the art of conversation, his recent attempts at doing so revealed a mystery with no easy solution.

"Husband!" Sariss exclaimed. "I am no prize to be won!"

"I see." responded Fox. "So you object to the marriage of your sister then?"

"Why no!" said Sariss. "I find the whole thing to be very romantic. Don't you?"

"Why yes." responded Fox. The mind of a woman was yet another riddle which he resigned himself to never fully understanding.

"You are welcome to travel with us if you like." Sariss said whilst spinning her arms about in a circle in effort to keep her balance upon the river floor "My brother was right when he said that there is safety in numbers. The forest is rife with danger, and you did indicate that you have no real skill with a sword."

"I shall think on it." responded Fox

"You must really forgive my father for his poor manners." Sariss continued, wading deeper into the stream. "Our family has worked hard our entire lives that we could send Veronica to the Temple of Light. She is probably the first farmer's daughter ever to be accepted amongst their ranks. The temple in Damaas is the largest, most well respected on all of Balthazar. Father sent her thither to become a healer, not to engage in dalliances with some bard. Our farm may not have been much, but selling it in order to afford this trip was one of the hardest things that he has ever had to do."

"And what of all of your belongings?" inquired Fox, again betraying his own reticence

"A condition of the sale was that they shall remain at the farm until such time as we return."

"Then where shall you live?" He seemed utterly incapable of ceasing his probing line of questioning. Luckily, Sariss did not seem to mind.

"We have come to an arrangement with King Alric's solicitor." she said "Upon our return, my father and I shall be given a small cabin on fertile land. In return, we are to use the land and our farming expertise to raise cattle for the King. Though Erik has not informed us of his intentions, father and I are well aware that he has eyes towards a career at sea. Very soon now he will leave us and book passage on a ship. He does little but dream of swashbuckling adventures in foreign lands and has proven time and again to be ill-suited as a farm hand."

Fox nodded at this, for he understood the sentiment all too well. Life as a thief had its own hardships, which only the stoutest of men and women could endure, yet at least an outlaw answered to no authority save his or her own. It was true that the thieves' guild in Gemmen did have an appointed leader, yet unlike nobility, which one was born to, the leaders of the various guilds of Balthazar, much like the Captains of sea-going vessels, earned their respected ranks and positions.

Sariss paused in her soliloquy momentarily. She ceased splashing about in the waves and stared up at the moonlight before continuing.

"In a way, I envy my brother. Since our mother's death, the task has fallen on me to care for our family. With Veronica to be wed and Erik far too ill-equipped for the task, it falls on me to care for my father. I know much about raising cattle, yet never have I done so for another man's profits."

At this, Fox could not help but feel chagrined. Sariss struck him as a competent, strong woman. She would have made a good thief. It was a shame that the machinations of her life seemed to have her so trapped. He had always valued his own freedom above all. Her story only added volition to his own belief that a life of isolation, free from attachment, was the most desirable.

The farmer's daughter wrapped her arms about her for warmth as she spoke, despite the fact that the warm weather did not necessitate this.

"I can tell you that father is not thrilled about Veronica marrying into nobility. Edward is the nephew of King Marcus of Raimia, and once Veronica marries into that family, she will never have to worry about wealth ever again."

Fox hid his surprise at hearing this. That a noble from the vainest of the four realms should wed a peasant girl was unheard of. All on Balthazar knew the role Raimia played during the great war, and despite generations of peace, many still viewed the southern Kingdom with inherent distrust.

Once, long ago, when all of Balthazar consisted of little more than tribes who all warred with the other, Raimia was the first to coalesce their power. It was their attempt at conquering all other lands that forced the various factions of the remaining three corners of the world into powerful alliances which existed to this day. It was largely due to the Hillmen of his own provice who united their strength with the barbarous warriors who descended from their mountain in the northlands of Hyrst that drove the enemy back. When the Raimian armies returned southward to lick their wounds, the great civil wars began, ending with the amalgamation of local cultures and peoples into what were now the four nexus's of power- Hyrst, Raimia, Gemmen, and Damaas. Nevertheless, there still remained many remnants of the old times. In Fox's own corner of the world, there yet lingered many clans who refused to abandon the teachings of Gemmen himself. The King would have men believe these tribes extinct, yet most know these savage, uncivilized people still roam about the southern mountains of the west, refusing to abandon their primitive ways and viewing civilization as a weakness.

"You would think that this would make my father happy." Sariss continued with her story. "But he despises noblemen. 'Like wolves to the lambing,' he says of them."

Fox smiled. He knew there was a reason that he liked the man.

"There was an incident that occurred at our farm many years ago." Sariss continued, now quite despondently "Three young noblemen were making their way through our pasture unannounced. It seems that they were taking a shortcut to the capitol and cared not a whit that they were trespassing upon our land. I was but a girl at the time and was taking my morning bath in the lake when they came upon me. They tried to have their fun, but I escaped and ran back to the house. They pursued me the entire way. My father was tilling the land when he saw me running towards him followed by the three men. He ran into the house and found his old broadsword before meeting the nobles outside of our home. I had never afore seen my father wield the blade, and had long suspected that it was kept merely as an heirloom of some sort, yet he managed to beat them all back with a skill and ferocity I knew not he possessed."

There was an air of unrestrained pride in Sariss's voice as she spoke the latter. Despite the somber nature of her story, Fox was forced to smile. He knew a warrior when he saw one, and did not share in Sariss's surprise.

“My mother and Erik were away at the time. My father had warned me to stay near the house, as he always did; yet that day I had chosen to disobey him.” Sariss lowered her head and buried her face into her hands before continuing. The moonlight momentarily ignored the river and reflected solely upon her tears.

“I sat there powerless as I watched the duel." she continued "The tide of the fray had shifted once the young nobles had surrounded my father and began using their long rapiers to stick him like a pig. He was bleeding heavily from all sides, yet each time he struck, his massive broadsword smashed through the noblemen's defenses and inflicted mighty wounds. Eventually they ran off. We heard later that they had barely survived the attack. Father nearly perished that day as well. The young noblemen received the care of the best clerics in Gemmen, shunning those of the Temple of Light whose ranks my sister is so eager to join. My father was tended to at first by me, then by my mother when she returned. Like Veronica, mother always had a gift for healing. Were it not for her, father's wounds would have claimed him.

Mother doubled our chores whilst he rested. Eventually he recovered and life seemed to return to normal. The noblemen however, refused to let the matter lie. When the palace denied their claims that father be brought to justice, the noble fops turned to the assassin's guild, only to find that they themselves refused to accept a contract involving a humble farmer and his kin. With no other option afforded them, they pooled their fortunes and hired Krillian, the greatest assassin in all of Gemmen to exact their revenge. I remember that day well, for it was I who found her... Father was working the land like always, and Veronica, being no more than a babe, was asleep in her crib. I had just finished my morning chores and had come into the kitchen to toast some bread upon the hearth when I saw her lying there. My mother, on the floor, her white dress stained with blood. Erik had tried to defend her. Krillian had let him live... He never speaks about that day, yet I know that he thinks of it often, for nothing else could explain his obsession with learning the sword."

"How old were you?" Fox responded. His concern was genuine, for he too had suffered great loss at the hand Krillian.

"Eric and I had seen but eight summers." she replied "My father changed after that. He used to smile often. The bodies of the three nobles were found washed up upon the sea shore soon after. Inquisitors from the palace came to our farm to question father, yet could bring no evidence to bear. Word had reached the palace that father was skilled with a sword, yet there was little pressure upon the city guard to persue the matter any further. Perhaps the inquisitors themselves believed justice had been done. We have spoken little of it since..."

Sariss turned about and began to wade back to shore. She wiped the tears from her face and forced a smile.

"I'm sorry. I must be suffering from road fatigue. It is said that two travelers who meet upon a long journey often confide in each other that which they would normally not share with another."

"Please do not apologize." Fox said consolingly

"I believe it is time for me to retire as well." she said. "I do hope that you are still here in the morning."

Without another word, Sariss came out of the water and made her way towards the distant firelight. Fox could not bear to look at her. His own emotions were in turmoil yet he could not understand why. Sariss's story was not unique; even as he sat there contemplating, some fierce injustice was happening somewhere within the walls of Gemmen which he had no power to rectify. Likely, Hergod, ruler of the assassins guild had felt the matter settled, forbiding any retaliation upon the family. It was the task of the guilds to keep order in Gemmen after all, despite the palace's claims to the contrary; yet the lingering presence of Krillian refused to leave his mind.

He shook his head free of the thoughts. The assassin was a threat made of flesh and blood. He would not allow mere thoughts of the man plague him, lest he grant victory to one he had not yet met in combat. There was nothing he could do to help these people upon the instant, and it was not his responsibility to try. Their problems were not his own. He was reminded again of the value of keeping to his own affairs. If he were incapable of solving the world's problems, than what was the point of becoming cognizant of them? He hardened his heart and set his mind to resolution. Upon the morrow, he would abandon his new companions and continue upon his adventures alone.

The notion gave him comfort. He made his way back towards Bolt and ran his hand through her mane. She was clearly the only company he needed, for her mind was not awash with the myriad complexity of human emotions and the concerns that accompanied them. Like Fox, all she needed was food, drink, and adventure; anything else was an unwelcome distraction.

Bolt had chosen to remain near the grassy patch where Fox had left her and was still munching gleefully, untroubled and care-free. Fox longed to rest in the small meadow at her feet, yet he knew that if he did so, he would awake with clothes wet with morning dew.

He made his way instead to a mound of dirt near to the still smoldering fire and fell into it. There he made every attempt to forget his recent conversation with Sariss that he might rest. He was nearly successful in this endeavor when his senses, fading to the realm of sleep, returned to him in a flush. He had heard nothing, yet knew that something was amiss. He cast a glance at Bolt that she might confirm his heightened awareness with her own. She rested near the pair of oxen, and all three of the beasts displayed their uneasiness by shifting about uncomfortably and striking at the dirt with their hooves.

He crossed the distance to Bolt and put a calming hand upon her before retrieving Fang from its place of conceilment. He unsheathed the blade. He felt powerful, strong as he did so. Keeping it well in front of him, he stalked off towards the nearby veil of trees hoping to find an enemy that he might slay. His blood raced within him. This he understood. Problems which could be met with steel were problems whose shadow did not linger.

The forest was disappointingly tranquil as he made his way through the underbrush, yet for reasons that he never cared to understand, he knew that he was heading towards danger. He used Fang to push aside the curtain of foliage as he travelled, moving as quietly as possible. It took his eyes mere moments to adjust to the night, for though he had travelled now a good distance from the firelight, and the moon strained to pierce through the thick ceiling of needles and leaves which lined the branches overhead, he had little problem seeing. It had always been this way. His ability to see clearly in near total darkness was one of many assets which made him the greatest, most feared thief in the four realms. Despite this uncanny ability, he allowed his eyes to close momentarily that he might reach out with his other senses. Long ago he had learned that no matter how perceptive ones eyes, they were nevertheless limited in their ability to perceive naught but what was in front of them, and in his experience, this was rarely where danger lie. The plethora of woodland noises made by the creatures of the wild focused his attention on the bushes to his left which, he noted, had only now begun to rustle.

The bushes exploded in a whirlwind of bramble and leaves, followed immediately by the talons of an enormous were-beast which stretched out to claim him, yet Fox succeeded in throwing himself into a backwards roll, successfully putting distance between he and the threat. Alighting on his feet, the two adversaries glared at each other momentarily, each assessing the other. Fox met the anticipatory snarl of the beast with one of his own.

The were-beast stood erect on its hind legs with arms oustretched like a man, yet there the resemblances ended. The creature had the head of a wolf, though bigger, and with two red eyes that smoldered like fire and drew one's gaze from its charcoal pelt. Its fingers were hooked inwards and had raking talons at the end of each. That it was was intelligent was clear in the fact that it refrained from commiting immediately to another charge. No doubt Fox's ability to evade its initial assault informed it that here was prey more dangerous than most. The were-beast paced about in a circle, scraping lines into the ground, perhaps preparing for a charge; perhaps in the hope that its horrifying appearance would cause its adversary to flee in terror, thus making for an easy kill. Fox mimicked the movements precisely, arching his back, allowing his gaze to compete with that of the beasts' openly. He stood only as high as the creature's midsection. His fingers twitched upon Fang's hilt with anticipation, sending tremors through the blade that longed for a kill.

Unsurprisingly, the creature was the first to break the stalemate.

With speed like lightning, its steely claws raked outwards, each hooked talon seeking to rend flesh from bone. As fast as it was, Fox was, in this moment, faster. Though nature had granted the animal greater speed than he, Fox's own cunning allowed him to anticipate the initial attack. He tucked himself into a roll once more, only this time his motion brought him towards the slavering maw of his adversary. It remained only to capitalize on his initial gambit- were he to be victorious, such victory needed to be quick and decisive.

Having closed the distance, Fox swung upwards with a mighty stroke of his own, sending the oustetched, unnaturally elongated forearm of the monster flying into the trees. A fountain of blood rained down upon the battlefield. The creature staggered momentarily until, driven mad by its own pain and fury, pressed forward once more with even greater feral intensity.

Blinded by its own rage, the were-beast's adrenalyne betrayed it, for the fresh surge of blood soaked the nearby foliage in a pool of morass. Unaware that every movement weakened it, that each attack precipitated its demise, the beast began to slow, and Fox was able to side step each of its feral attacks.

Faced with its own inevitable demise, as well as the ensuing panic, born of incredulity that its erstwhile meal could itself somehow have become predator, the were-beast attempted to ensnare Fox into its mighty jaws that it might, with final effort, end the life of he who had taken its own. Unwilling to prolong the creature's suffering;

Fox deftly sidestepped the slavering maw and planted Fang deep into the skull behind it, embedding the sword deep into the fleshy tissue of its brain. The monstrous collection of tooth, claw and glowing red eyes fell upon the gore-stained underbrush, its steely appendages twitching; the hilt of Fang still jutting from out the side of its shattered temple. For a moment, Fox fully took in the nightmarish appearance of the terror he had just slain, allowing himself the privilege of reveling in his victory. The green fire emitted from his own eyes cooled to a soft glow. With the thrill of combat thus ended, his limbs, now weary, began to register the great strain he had put them under. He slumped to the ground beside his most recent conquest. There he slept, thoroughly contented, his head resting comfortably against the pelt of his kill.

CHAPTER NINE - THE SEA OF SERDIA

Fox awoke feeling fully refreshed. The sun was set to wash the inky darkness from the sky. This was just as well, for whilst his new companions yet slumbered nearby, he busied himself with dragging the corpse of the recently slain were-beast to be swallowed by the density of the foliage. He covered the blood-stained ground with fresh dirt and carefully cleaned Fang with a handful of leaves before re-sheathing it. Were his companions to stumble across his recent activities, he would no doubt be forced to face many questions for which no ready answers were available.

He had every intention of leaping atop Bolt and rushing off to continue his adventures alone, abandoning his new friends there and then, save for one lingering thought which held him at bay. Were-beasts the like he had just destroyed rarely attacked any encampment of men, for of all the species on Balthazar, these alone held mastery of that most feared element of all such creatures who dwelt within darkness, that of fire. Perhaps such beasts were more brazen this far from Gemmen's borders. In any event, and despite his mastery of solitude, he very much disliked the idea of Aron and his family being eviscerated in their sleep were he not there to protect them. Besides, Sariss was a brilliant shot with the longbow, and the next village was yet three days hence. If the deer meat he had enjoyed the night before was any indication, Fox was certain that she would be good company... if only for her skills as a hunter.

He made his way to the river and gave himself a morning bath, and, for no reason which he was aware of, a thorough shave as well. He used his sharpest dagger for the job, yet still found the process to be painful and irritating. He stripped himself to his breechclout and draped his clothes over a nearby tree branch. With a hastily-made broom made of springy pine needles he beat the dust from them as best he could before donning them again. As he had no comb, he scraped his hair back with his fingernails and tied it back neatly with fringe that he cut from his saddle.

He gazed at his reflection in the water. He cared as little for appearances as he did for company. Had he cared for either, he was certain that his new companions would be as impressed with his appearance as he was.

He made his way to the still-smoldering fire that he might breakfast. He threw a few sticks and branches atop the coals and blew on them until the flame was resurrected. As the fire gained new purchase on life, he made his way to where the deer carcass was set to cure and cut a long strip. Perhaps his battle the night before had awoken within him a stronger appetite than he had surmised, for he cut three more. Then he placed a netting of fir branches across the hearth and laid the meat atop it. The branches were run through with sap, and, stripped of their needles, would not burn easily. Nevertheless, placing the meat so near the flame in this manner would cause it to char rather than cook, which was common practice for travelers, for it was wise to make as much use of daylight as possible when covering large distances. It was certainly for this reason that he chose to salt and season his repast with Sariss's nearby stores that it might prove more palatable.

Erik was the first to emerge from the shelter. The sun was still low on the horizon and as the camp was soaked with dew, made gemstones of each blade of grass it touched.

"Good morning Costa!" he cried, not seeming to care if he woke those inside "That smells incredible! I'm hungry enough to eat that deer live!"

The pair were joined by Sariss and Aron who seemed imminently grateful that such a meal was waiting for them. Each filled their bellies before breaking camp, which was deconstructed in such time and efficiency as to make any military captain proud. Soon, they were on the path to Damaas once more, and as they were all of them heading in the same direction with plenty of venison left within the wagon, Fox chose to remain in their company. He rode astride Bolt unhindered, for her saddle was stored within the wagon as well as all of his meager supplies. Sariss kept her bow strung should they come across any game; therefore Fox chose to leave his spear behind. There was wisdom in travelling with a wagon and oxen, for though the pace was plodding, he enjoyed a state of comfort which had cleverly evaded him since taking his leave of Baraan. The massive horned beasts could make no greater time across the overgrown path as did their masters, yet though Fox alone was mounted, none seemed to show the slightest sign of weariness as they continued eastward across the untamed landscape.

As they progressed, Fox's spirits lifted. They were within view of the great southern mountains which marked the borders of Gemmen, far in the distance yet seemingly near to the touch. Beyond their veil lie the Kingdom of Raimia, whose beauty and architecture were said to be unrivaled in each of the four realms. The swells and peaks were breathtaking. Entire forests seemed like swaths of green painted by the mighty brush of some cosmic artisan, followed by icy grays whose gradation to the purest white of the snowy alps was flawless in its execution; yet even at their highest Fox knew that these failed to compete with the mighty zeniths of the Kingdom of Hyrst in the north. Balthazar held such wonders that he longed to travel for a lifetime that he might see them all.

There was no conversation amongst them as each seemed as enamored with their surroundings as was Fox. Erik took point, sword in hand, though more for practice as all was docile and serene and danger was nowhere to be found as he lead the party across what had now become wetlands. Shallow marshes and crystal springs reflected the cloudless sky so that it was difficult to discern where one ended and the other began save when said reflections rippled upon a multitude of miniature isles seemingly set in a grid-like pattern. Fox's nostrils flared at the influx of oxygen created by such abundance of life. He enjoyed renewed health and vigor, a gift of the land, the water, and the myriad creatures who took to the skies to flit playfully about them. Erik seemed at least to take this new chore seriously. He drove a hard pace, for though such moments were to be enjoyed to their fullest extent, travelling without the protection of a caravan was dangerous business on Balthazar, and the safety of the forest where one was not so fully exposed was desired before nightfall-provided the farmer's son might find a serviceable path into the wall of trees far in the distance.

Aron took up the rear and it was Sariss's duty to drive the oxen, yet rather than sit comfterably in the wagon where her boots might remain dry, she chose instead to walk beside them, leading the beasts by their tethered bridle. Soon, a slight spring which had been meandering about them grew in scale until it became a mighty river, barring their path. It was fed by numerous such springs which ran southward from a lake which no doubt resided upon the plateau to the north and in turn now drove them southward. Erik brought them to a halt and the three were met up by his father.

"We shall follow the river down towards the King's highway." the farmer began "To my knowledge, there are no bridges upon the thoroughfare this close to Gemmen, therefore doubtless it shall become narrow enough to ford yonder."

"Really father." Sariss exclaimed "Had we simply taken the King's highway since leaving the capitol we would have made far better time 'ere now."

"Aye, and likely been bled of all of our coin as well." Aron responded with characteristic irritability "The old pilgrim trails served well enough before the construction of that blasted highway that Alric might charge peasants as much as noblemen and fully manned caravans for passage, and until they make a law which forbids a man and his family from traveling cross-country, I'll not divest myelf of so much as a copper!"

"Besides sister!" Erik suddenly interjected "We don't need the King's guard! Should we cross paths with gypsy, nomad or ranger you have my sword to protect us! Why, it's a shame that we have not yet encountered any bandits, for I would have found such a welcome distraction!"

"Be not so quick to denounce the ranger's boy!" Aron chided "It is precisely because of their guild that men such as we can yet use these lands for travel and hunting. Merely be thankful that we have not been attacked by were-beasts of the night whose ilk those nomads thanklessly dispatch that you might not have need to wield your sword."

"Perhaps age breeds superstition." Erik smiled "There are no such creatures beyond the pages of storybooks."

"And when was it you learned to read brother?" Sariss retorted

"Aye." Aron added "And I am old enough to have seen a thing or two that might send you running back to the farmstead, your smugness with you; bad enough that we must make this journey without you wishing it more difficult." he turned his attention to Fox and his demeanor softened "Costa. Will you volunteer to ford the river first? Should there be any undercurrent, t'would be best that you be the one to discover it lest we lose our wagon and our supplies with it."

Fox nodded his enthusiasm. Despite the wetlands they travelled, the air itself was scalding and the idea of cooling himself in the water appealed to him greatly. The weather was made hotter by his refusal to remove his jerkin, as Aron and Erik had done. As his entire torso was traced with thin scars that ran the contours of his body, the product of a lifetime of exploits which, if penned, would each tell a tale fit to thrill the most experienced adventurer, such was a tale he nonetheless wished to avoid the telling.

"Sariss." Aaron continued, capitalizing on the fact that all had now congregated close enough to hear "While we drive the wagon, I want you to fill every spare canteen and bucket with water from the river. We'll need it when we cross the sea of Serdia."

"The sea?" Erik responded excitedly

The big man smiled before speaking and Fox was thoroughly amused. Perhaps it was because Aron smiled so rarely; likely it was simply because he had come to enjoy the constant verbal jousting the family engaged in. Travelling with his new companions had proven to be a much more interesting experience than he had at first counted on. He appreciated the dichotomy of their relationship. They continued to spar and argue, yet underneath the pretence of hostility, he knew that each was utterly devoted to the other. Fox had witnessed such inter-personal dynamics before, yet never before was he so directly involved.

"The sea of Serdia is a desert son, a vast sea with nothing but sand in any direction. At its far end sits the city the desert was named after and the final outpost denoting the province of Gemmen. Serdia is a port town which shares its border with Damaas, the largest city in Gemmen next to the capitol, home to thieves, cut-throats and scoundrels. We must be careful to conserve our water supply, for it will take three days to cross and we cannot have our wits dulled lest we be easy prey for the vultures, both man and beast."

"Hmph!" Erik snorted "If we had bothered to purchase horses we could have done so in half the time!"

"Bad enough that I have to feed you!" Aron retorted "Perhaps you would have preferred it had I purchased an entire caravan to escort us to Damaas! We would save much time if you stopped arguing with me and got on about your duties."

At this last comment from her father, Sariss laughed mightily and, sitting atop the wagon, availed herself of the reigns.

"Come. Should we ford the river by mid-afternoon we will find wood aplenty that we might cook what remains of our venison. I have no desire to sup on dried salted jerkey and our reserves of even dryer oats and meal."

They had not travelled far when, as predicted, the river did indeed narrow greatly. Fox recognized that Aron was correct. Further downstream, it was likely dammed in order to divert its course into smaller streams, effectively circumnavigating the highway, whilst here at its apex; the river had been chiseled into a much narrower path where fording seemed possible. It was here Aron called the party to a halt. In the distance, beyond the river, a line of trees could be seen where one could be assured of eastward footpaths and serviceable wagon trails.

Fox and Bolt immediately set to the fording, while Aron and his family busied themselves with battening the wagon. It was clear the old farmer did not relish being this close to the main thoroughfare, for he worked diligently as with great haste. Bolt was quite content for the opportunity to cool herself in the calm waters which, at its deepest, rose only to Fox's thighs where he sat in the saddle. She paused momentarily at the centermost point to drink and gleefully spat a long stream of water like a fountain out in front of her.

Balthazar was not fit to reward those with its splendor without first proving themselves worthy however, for no sooner had they set upon their way again, when a vicious current, not seen from the surface, and coming from seemingly nowhere, hit Bolt with such fury that it knocked the legs from out of her. For a brief moment, both rider and mount were completely submerged, and, unable to right themselves, sent tumbling downstream, dragged against the coarse rocks of the riverbed.

Thinking quickly, Fox planted his boots firmly against a jagged stone and slammed his shoulder against Bolt's flank. With a supreme effort, he managed to brace himself against both the weight of the animal, and the strong undertow, which churned violently beneath while leaving the mirror-like surface completely undisturbed.

The iron muscles in Fox's legs screamed at the effort as he pushed both himself and Bolt into a standing position where their heads broke the water's surface and they were able to draw breath. Drawing on his reserves of strength, Fox gripped Bolt by her mane, holding her aloft, and for a brief moment, both were locked in deadly struggle with the submerged tide which threatened to drag them off, battered and broken, to where the water ran deeper and they would certainly be drowned.

He risked a quick glance over his shoulder. Aron and his family had not yet noticed his plight. As Bolt could find no purchase for footing, it was left to him to drag her through the underwater current.

The effort was excruciating, for the riptide whose deadly embrace they had become trapped in was so strong that the panicked mare thrashed about violently- yet in this way, the river actually helped Fox in his labor, for, being unable to right herself, he was able to take advantage of the horse's own buoyancy to drag her along.

The going was perilous, for the underwater current slammed into Fox's steel-hard calve muscles and threatened to knock him down with each step he took, His biceps bulged under the strain of having to pull his cherished mount after him. It was a slow, desperate battle, but eventually, the narrow riptide ended and they were in calm waters once more. Bolt succeeded in righting herself, and the two walked side by side to the safety of the far shore.

Fox had faced the onslaught of such hidden riptides before. These always began in shallow water and seemed to exist for the sole purpose of dragging unsuspecting prey who dared to trust in the safety of the shallows, off to where they could be claimed by the depths. Caravaneers familiar with these regions told that the riptides emanated from underwater caves, for the trapped air within would, at random intervals, jet towards the surface to cleanse the river of intrepids. The riptides appeared randomly, without warning, and were yet another example of the many traps and hazards an adventurer had to face on Balthazar if they dared to ever let their guard down.

He rested his hands upon his knees and caught his breath. Once again, his own strength and resourcefulness had allowed him to defy the many perils which Balthazar continually threw in his path. He glanced up at his companions, now in the distance. To his relief, they seemed completely unaware as to the inhuman feat of strength by which he was able to drag his own horse through the concealed current.

"Aron, Sariss, Erik!" he shouted "Undertow! I scarcely made it across!"

The big man turned. He was so far away that he barely heard him. He nodded in Fox's direction to show that he understood.

The thought of swimming across to aid his companions occurred to Fox, yet he instantly dismissed the idea, for a humble steel merchant, having so narrowly escaped drowning himself, would not readily cast himself back into the very waters which nearly claimed him as trophy. Despite himself, he could not help but worry that the simple peasant family would prove to be far too unaccustomed to the dangers of Balthazar to face such a hazard.

Fox watched from a distance as Aron made preparations to face the undertow. The big man looped the length of rope which served to tie down their tarpaulin about a large riverstone. The other end of the rope he ran through the yoke and the axel of the wagon. Fox believed that he knew what was intended, yet remained skeptical that the farmer was capable of such a colossal feat of strength.

He gazed in wonder as Aron, gripping the heavy rock in one meaty hand, ran three steps to the edge of the river bank and hurled the stone.

The rippling muscles of the farmer's heavily delineated physique could be seen even from Fox's distant vantage point as they shifted their momentum one to the other, straining under the taut skin of his heavily bronzed hide. Each interlocking muscle gave their strength to the other, twisting and cording as they worked in perfect concert, ending in the swing of one mighty arm. The powerful display reminded Fox of the stallions at the Coliseum, whose every ligament danced in perfect harmony, all with the unified purpose of achieving maximum velocity; and just as those powerful animals filled him with a sense of awe, so too did the giant peasant farmer, who seemed to be in possession of extraordinary levels of strength which he had grossly underestimated.

The stone seemed the size of a pebble at first, yet radically took on new dimension as it sailed across the river, trailing the thick rope behind it. It landed with a thud at Fox's feet, leaving a deep crevice in the soft grass and sandy underbelly of the riverbed. Seen from up close, the stone was even larger than Fox had surmised, and was nothing less than a small boulder. Aron's giant form was clearly well-earned through a lifetime of intense physical labor. Instantly he had new respect for the man, respect that, until recently, he had reserved for none but his posthumous mentor Cammarran and scant others of the thieves' guild in Gemmen. There remained yet much to learn of those who lived outside the Kingdom's great walls.

It took him a moment to untie the stone, for Aron had used a sturdy fisherman's knot that he was unfamiliar with, but having finally succeeded, he lashed the cord securely about the trunk of the sturdiest tree in his vicinity.

The rope was secured to a tree on the opposite shore in much the same fashion, yet still looped through the yoke of the oxen lest the peasant family be carried downstream upon fording. With the thick cable in place, Fox's new companions began to drive the oxen into the river.

Fox watched intently as they made swift progress. They had not yet hit the invisible riptide which lie in wait for them. Sariss took the lead. With one arm, she yanked the bridle, coaxing the oxen through the water, while with the other, she held tightly to the rope. The water rose to a level just beneath her breasts, causing the thin filament of her chemise to cling to her firm body, and Fox found that he could not tear his eyes away from the form thus revealed through the wetness. He chided himself for this at first, only to remind himself that there was nothing vulgar about the appreciation of beauty. He had no such qualms about admiring the form of Aron as the big man took his cast, and Sariss, likewise, was a beautiful creature to behold; perhaps the most beauteous he had ever encountered. Seen through the blouse, her form was both supple and firm. Even with the current, now growing in intensity, battering her long legs where they plunged beneath the water under the swell of her well-rounded hips, she moved defiantly with cat-like agility and grace. Taken in its entirety, her beauty was sublime. There was strength and grace in her every movement. She was supple yet firm, curvaceous yet lithe and tawny- a vision of perfection. Even amongst nature's bounty, she was here, at this moment, with the sun glistening on her pale skin, the darkness of her hair, her eyes, the redness of her full lips, stark by comparison, the most beauteous of all of Balththazar's creations. Despite its most recent failed attempt, Balthazar, it would seem, had now succeeded in stealing his breath from him. He was only grateful that the family was far too preoccupied in this moment to notice his overt gaze.

Behind Sariss, Aron maintained a position next to the wagon. He leaned against it with one heavy shoulder and, like his daughter, clung to the rope tightly with his free hand. Fox could not see Erik, but assumed that the lad was behind the wagon pushing it from the rear.

Sariss, being on point, was the first to encounter the undertow, which up until now had been churning beneath the surface as though in anticipation of her arrival. The current hit her hard, and Fox was momentarily riddled with anxiety, yet she stoically clung to the rope. Her face registered no surprise when the vicious riptide hit, and he could detect a look of grim determination on her porcelain features.

Instantly, she turned about and began tugging on the horns of the lead ox. The animals were accustomed to the plow, not fording rivers, yet remained strong and surefooted as they merged into the hazardous current with the stubbornness and tenacity oft attributed to their kind. The wagon buckled against the pressure, yet Aron leaned into it with his heavy frame, making capsizing impossible.

The peasant family clearly had reserves of fortitude those who lived within Gemmen's walls lacked. Each of them clung to the rope thus stretched across the river, pulling themselves through the strong current with great tenacity and without complaint until the riptide itself was forced to bow to their superior will and allow them passage.

Upon successfully reaching the far bank, both Aron and Sariss placed their hands on their knees as Fox had and drew deep breaths. Erik, who until now had been concealed by the wagon, threw himself into the soft grass and lay on his back, sighing contentedly.

"A hard day's work that!" Aron said as acknowledgement of his offspring's laudable efforts.

"How is it that you were able to cross Costa?" Sariss queried, catching her breath "You had no rope to brace yourself against, and your mount is not so sturdy as trained pack animals."

"The current was much milder when I crossed." Fox replied "Had I known it would pick up with such intensity, I would have dove in to help you."

Both Sariss and Erik seemed satisfied with the explanation. His instincts told him that Aron was not.

"As well you did not!" Erik ejaculated "That riptide would have turned your bones to jelly!"

Fox smiled.

The family did not pause for additional accolades, but began immediately to prepare for the next leg of their journey. Erik and Aron tended to the wagon, while Fox helped Sariss fill their numerous canteens at the river's edge. In short order they were on their way again. They did not pause that they might build a fire to cook what remained of their venison as Sariss had earlier suggested, but made a meal out of their stores of jerky and dried oats and fruits. Even Erik did not complain at this, for fording the river had cost them time and all were anxious to cover more ground before nightfall. They shared what they had freely with Fox who was forced to remind himself that such was not charity, for he had twice now aided the expedition in secret.

The morning had shifted into afternoon when Erik, who had re-assumed his post at the head of the party, began to drive a faster pace. He had previously been slowed from doing so due to the many bogs and marshes which marked the terrain, yet now, the land had opened into wide plains. The landscape continued to shift the further east they travelled, and vegetation grew more and more sparsely as they neared the dunes which marked the desert of Serdia. Balthazar was mercurial in temperament, and its climate varied greatly over relatively minute distances. In part, this is why the caravan trains were such a necessary part of life for its citizens, for amongst other commodities, caravans could deliver fresh produce from tropical lands to areas still blanketed with snow without risk of spoiling. Fox greatly anticipated encountering such a caravan now that they had come upon open plains, for he reveled in the solitude that can only be obtained when surrounded by others. There was much to be learned in a crowd, and secrets were oft given freely to one who is ignored.

The caravan trains were undoubtedly the life-blood of Balthazar, for their well-worn routes lay like a network of veins across her surface, delivering goods necessary for the survival of each individual province; but the caravaneers themselves were often unscrupulous, colorful characters with little in the way of morality. In short, they were the sort of company that Fox very much preferred, and would no doubt offer a refreshing change from the stoic, and oft implacably stern demeanor of Aron.

The slight sand dunes they had been traversing soon grew in size and dramatic intensity, and as they made their way further, became more and more sparse of any vegetation whatsoever. Soon they were in the belly of the massive sea of Serdia. The desert welcomed them into its womb, for the breeze was soft and pleasant under the scalding, unrelenting gaze of the sun with no canopy to shield it. It wasn't until they were firmly ensconced between the mighty dunes that the winds picked up, and miniature dust devils began to lap at their ankles impishly. The tiny swirls of sand began to grow in intensity however, and it wasn't long before they were spitting coarse pebbles into the faces of the entire party. It was here that Aron called the expedition to a halt, waving at his son in the distance to re-join them.

"We must batten down here for the night." he announced

"But Father!" Sariss cried "It's barely past mid-day!"

Erik and Fox shared Sariss's reaction, though Fox gave leave to the former to voice it.

"Really father!" he said "The sooner we get out of this accursed desert, the sooner I can help myself to a flagon of ale in yonder Serdia! Why stop now when we have barely just begun?"

"Aye, and how do you plan on satisfying your debaucheries once your bones are bleached?!" Aron grunted in reply "I wasn't always a farmer son. There was a time when I too travelled these lands. Mark my words, this breeze exists simply to catch the uninitiated, such as yourself, off-guard. I estimate that we have less than a turn of the glass before we are caught in a full sand-storm."

"Nonsense!" Erik retorted, now clearly irritated at the unjustifiable delay "Even if what you say is true, I for one am brave enough to face it!"

"Silence your tongue or I'll flay your hide myself and spare the carrion the trouble! We make our preparations here or you'll never taste a pint of ale again!"

For a moment, Aron scowled at his son, yet the moment was brief, for Erik soon cowed under the menacing gaze of his father.

Fox was unaccustomed to making preparations when it came to facing danger. Even as the greatest thief in all of Gemmen, he preferred to charge in to any situation, trusting only on his strength and cunning to save him. Occasionally, when he was commissioned to purloin an item from a particularly daunting local, such as the palace itself, Cammarran would spend days drawing up plans and devising strategies for him, yet Fox often ignored these completely, preferring the fun and spontaneity of improvisation.

The desert was unknown to him however, and if the were-beast he had slain the previous night was any indication, he knew that his new companions would need his help ere long as they continued to pit themselves against the many terrors Balthazar threw their way. Aron's plan was sound, and Fox was forced to swallow his pride and aid in its execution.

The wagon was divested of all of its contents which were left to sit upon the desert floor. It was then upended with the solid undercarriage braced against the wind, which, as Aron had predicted, began to grow in intensity. The tarpaulin was driven into the ground with long wooden pegs that Aron had thought to bring -it would seem, specifically for such an emergency.

The inside of the jerry-rigged shelter was small, yet Aron insisted on stacking all of the wagon's meager contents up against its base, so as to brace the upturned carriage in order to keep it from tipping over and crushing them. When they had completed, the interior of the shelter was so tiny that Fox had to wonder how they would all fit inside of it if the vicious storm ever came to pass.

The Oxen were tethered to the desert floor itself. The strong rope which bridled them was driven into the sand with more of the wooden pegs. Bolt was tethered in the same manner, yet she was situated behind the oxen so that they could act as a shield for her. Aron had assured Fox that the massive pack animals would be able to weather the oncoming storm, yet without them forming a wall for Bolt, the slender horse would not.

Fox remained doubtful that such a storm was truly brewing, despite the growing intensity of the wind, and that even if it were, that it would be as fierce as Aron was predicting, yet he and his fellow travelers had no sooner finished their labor when the savage ferocity of the storm became undeniable.

Here, Aron ordered everyone into the shelter, and it was at this command that Fox bristled with thinly concealed rage.

For the entirety of his life, Fox had always been next to incapable of taking orders. What was the point of being a thief if one had to live their lives upon another's whim, he often told himself. Fox had always considered this aspect of his personality to be a strength of character, despite Cammarran's insistence that it was a weakness. Even when he had begun his career as a fledgling thief under the tutelage of Cammarran himself, he had always insisted that he do things his way, often refusing to accept lucrative contracts altogether when he believed that too much control was being exerted over him by the client. It wasn't until his reputation as the best thief Gemmen had to offer was widespread that he was given the freedom to operate as he saw fit. He began to wonder if he had not perhaps erred when he had assumed the guise of steel merchant, for were it not for his utter disdain of noblemen, he would have proffered himself as a lord-one who was accustomed to giving orders, not taking them.

The only means Fox could have employed in order to obey Aron in this situation, he knew, was to convince himself that the farmer's plan was his own. And this he did, asserting to himself that all efforts in preparing for the storm had followed the route of his own carefully constructed scheme. He congratulated himself on the wisdom of it. It was a contented, even smug young Fox who entered the lean-to shelter upon the sea of Serdia, to share his clever accommodations with the ignorant peasants he had been forced to care for. The enclosure was so tight that all four were forced to press against the other, as well as the wall, here presented by the upturned wagon, in order to help brace it. Sariss was wedged so tightly against him that Fox was certain that, were the circumstances different, he would have been forced to face her protective father in a duel for her honor. The rays of the sun which bathed the sea of Serdia had proven to be so intense that their clothes had long since dried from their perilous encounter with the river, yet now each became soaked in sweat, for the small enclosure, with the added warmth of their bodies knit so closely together, channeled heat like a stone kiln.

Fox could feel the warmth emanating from Sariss's body, just as he could feel her heart race beneath her breasts. His own blood raced in rhythm with hers, for her every perfect curve swelled against him. He worried that should the heat reach a fever pitch, that he may well go mad being so near her. He could not know for certain if Sariss shared his torment, for her face was buried into his chest, yet her rapidly escaping breath told him that this was so.

Fox had, of course, lain with women before. The pursuit of life's various pleasures had always been his highest priority. He had seldom ever lain with a woman who was not a concubine however, and on those rare occasions, though he had not paid for the privilege, the act bore not a trace of the intense feeling of intimacy he now shared with another. Though Sariss, as those before her had done, did indeed bring his blood to a fevered pitch, lying next to her upon the desert floor had stirred in him a sensation which was altogether new to him. Sariss was the closest thing to perfection he had ever seen, and as he lie next to her, he knew in that instance that he wished nothing more than to preserve it. The young thief had born witness to horrors and monstrosities the like most could never imagine. His will was Balthazar's own, for only those brave enough to challenge the evils of this world were rewarded with its greatest beauty.

The four companions lay huddled beneath the tarpaulin for many an hour. The storm that Fox was now convinced that he himself had anticipated did indeed rage about them with unmitigated fury. Several times they had to throw the entirety of their weight and strength of limb into the floor of the wagon to keep it braced against the violent frenzy which threatened to overturn it. The planks of the wagon groaned and creaked in protest as they continued to be battered by wave after wave of pelting sand, yet the strong wood held steadfast as the people it housed, refusing to be broken by nature's will.

Night had fallen by the time the sandstorm had fully ceased, and Fox's companions had fallen into an exhausted slumber, for the storm had taken a heavy toll on their reserves of stamina. He gazed down at the serene face of Sariss as she slept, her face still pressed tightly against his shoulder. The emotions she stirred in him were those of peace and serenity, yet intermingled with a deep sadness which made no sense, for never before had he know joy and despondency to share simultaneous space in his mind. Silently, so as not to awake the family, he crept out of the hovel and went to check on Bolt.

The light of the moon was dim and the dunes offered little reflection. Despite his superhuman ability to see in near total darkness, it wasn't until Fox neared her that he was able to ascertain her condition. The storm was even more intense than predicted. He knew for certain that any other mare would have no doubt surrendered to it, yet though she appeared to be covered head to toe in a thin veneer of sand, she nevertheless appeared to be unharmed. He walked up to his cherished mount and patted her gently on the top of her head. Bolt cooed at his touch, and once again, his emerald eyes gazed into her amber ones. As before, when he had first acquired her as companion, he felt as though they were kindred spirits. Both shared strength and stubbornness in abundance, as well as the belief that, should one possess the fortitude, life was not merely a storm to be weathered.

Though she complained not at all, Fox was able to see intermittent welts upon her hide. The banks of sand now climbed the length of her legs and kissed the underside of her belly. The oxen had it much worse, for where they had shielded Bolt from the storm, the sand rose nearly half way up their midsections. Fox had no doubt that, having been buried so deeply, the animals would never be able to free themselves without aid. As he did not wish to rouse the peasant family who slumbered next to any implements he might use for the purpose, he descended to his knees and began scooping away the sand with his hands. It was dawn before he completed.

CHAPTER TEN - METROPOLIS, THE SAND SNAKE OF SERDIA

By the time the unforgiving sun had fully made its return and now presented itself in wavy, dischorded hues of dizzying intensity upon the horizon, Fox had managed to sleep little over an hour. His labor the night before had been grueling, and had demanded of him nearly all of his reserves of stamina. The small mountains of sand he had displaced made for comfortable bedding, and having accomplished his goal of freeing the animals from its clutches, he had fallen into one of them and allowed his own exhaustion to claim him. The soft breeze roused the gentle banks he had thus disturbed the night before and the thin powdered dust flitted about him as he rose, tickling his nose. The effect was beautiful, for Balthazar always rewarded those who survived its cruel tests. The thin effervescent swirl surrounded him in a cascade of brilliant light reflected from the sun. Colors danced about him in a dazzling array filtered through his still-sleepy eyes, and Fox dared not to wake fully, lest he spoil the haunting beauty of the illusion.

Tilting his head back, Fox closed his eyes again to keep his retinas from being scorched. When he reopened them, he knew that he yet had work to do. He rose wearily and made his way back to the oxen.

The beasts seemed content to be able to move about freely again, yet were so covered in a thick layer of dust that one could not see the burnt umber hue of their pelts beneath it. He began the task of shaking the sand free of their shaggy coats, but as his efforts bore little fruit, he eventually gave up. The still-befuddled animals seemed not to care one whit as to the extra layer of grit they had accumulated the night before, therefore Fox could not think of any reason why he should either. The oxen were bred for power, not beauty, and there was no room in their brains for any consideration of vanity. The thought patterns of such beasts centered about food, water, and defecation; and Fox could not help but envy them in this, for such was often his life's ambition as well. He gazed down at his own disheveled form and realized that he too was covered head to toe with a thin veneer of sand which seemed glued in place from the sweat of his labor the night before. Immediately, he decided that he did not care either.

Sariss was the first to emerge from the improvised hut and she sidled up beside him. She too was dusty from the night before, yet nowhere near to the same extent, and the layer of grime did not seem to diminish her beauty a whit.

"How are Luther and Lola?" She said smiling.

"Who?" replied Fox

"The oxen of course."

"You named them?"

"Certainly. Have you not given your horse a name?"

"Yes." Fox stammered "That is to say, I have not named her myself, though her name is Bolt."

"A fine name that. Why does it surprise you that I have named Luther and Lola?"

"I have never heard of anyone naming their beasts of burden before." he stammered

"Beasts of burden they may be. Yet they are part of the family." At this, Sariss left her place at Fox's side and made her way to the lead ox, the male, who, he reminded himself, should perhaps now be thought of as Luther, and began to pat him affectionately between his massive, ribbed horns. She looked over her shoulder at him enticingly and laughed.

"Worry not Costa. My father and brother refuse to call them by their names either."

She walked over to Bolt and placed a hand on her back, which caused the mare to snort gleefully.

"She really is beautiful. I've never seen her equal. You must be a wealthy merchant to ride one as fine as she."

"Ha. No. No, I won her at a game of chance; that is all. I could never afford a stallion so fine."

Sariss shuffled nearer to Fox before she spoke again. "Perhaps you can take me riding. I have never had the occasion to ride one so fine."

For a moment Fox and Sariss shared a smile, like a secret from the lips of close friends. It was a moment encapsulated by the beauty of the day; the calm breeze, and the overhead sun which now seemed to smile upon them. Fox could not help but be amazed. He was reminded once again how well Balthazar rewarded tenacity.

"Good morning sister! Costa!" came the voice of a fully rejuvenated Erik, shattering the moment in its entirety "Quite the storm last night wasn't it?!"

Fox and Sariss turned about to face the young man, who was now lumbering up the swell of the nearby dune, his father trailing behind him.

Sariss spun on her heel to face her brother "Quite." she responded with much agitation "If you two will excuse me, I have many chores to attend to."

Sariss stalked off angrily, nearly bumping into her father as she passed him.

"What?" questioned Erik, seemingly quite perplexed

From a distance, Fox was quite sure that he had seen Aron laugh.

Luther snorted and spat in response.

The company breakfasted quickly. They ate naught but standard traveler's fare once again, consisting of their stock of dried jerky and fruit. Aron did not need to warn them of the necessity of conserving their water, for they had wasted half a day already and all knew of the vital importance of preserving the precious liquid. Nevertheless, having apparently crossed these dunes once before, and being intimately aware of its dangers, Aron drank more sparingly than the rest.

They had taken down their make-shift tent and loaded the wagon in record time, for, though Fox had only recently joined them, they all knew of the importance of setting out early and each went about their duties with the utmost precision and efficiency. None had commented on their seeming good fortune that the animals had not been buried the night before, though once again, Fox began to suspect that the ever reticent Aron, having experienced such storms before, knew more than he alluded to.

The party travelled in silence to conserve their energy, each with a bandage of swath wrapped about their faces that might filter the sand from the air. Despite this, the weather remained quite pleasant. The sun seemed lower here, and much bigger about than when seen over Gemmen, yet though it radiated intense heat upon the travelers, this was alleviated by a cool and invigorating breeze which raced across the desert floor causing the sand to shoot up in spirals and flit about them. Fox marveled at this, for no matter where his footsteps took him, each aspect of Balthazar, be it river, the forest, and even the cities themselves, seemed to dance and play as though imbued with mischievous life all their own.

They had been traveling merely a short while when Fox, who had been keeping a close watch of the horizon, spied a small dust cloud in the distance. He took care not to mention this, yet it wasn't long before Erik returned from his position a fair distance ahead in order to confirm the discovery.

"Caravan!" he shouted

Aron had kept close to the wagon, and as they came to a halt, all four of them were within hearing distance from the other.

"How large?" he demanded

"Judging from the distance and the size of the dust cloud in its wake, I would dare to say that were these not times of peace, I would have mistaken it for an army sent to conquer Serdia!"

The large man frowned "Then we shall give it a wide berth."

"But father!" Erik whined "Would it not be safer to travel with a caravan train? You have oft said yourself that there is safety in numbers!"

"You don't know caravaneers the way that I do!" Aron retorted "They are an unscrupulous lot. Out here in the desert, such a beast could swallow us whole without anyone to know of it!"

Fox's attention was on Sariss. Her expression told him that she shared her brother's sentiments.

"Please father! It might be nice to meet new people!"

"People that would just as likely skin you and rob you of everything you own!" Aron shot back "We have made it this far on our own and we shall continue to do so! Erik, resume the lead. Be sure that our path does not cross with any unscrupulous nomads or I'll have your guts for garters!"

Despondently, Erik obeyed his father and resumed his place at the front of the line. Once again Fox was forced to consider abandoning his new companions, for he sensed a great deal of trouble associated with the caravan, and he longed to inflict such upon himself.

Erik was a dutiful son, yet no matter how hard he tried to avoid the caravan, their path seemed to continually align with that giant cloud of dust in the distance. Several times they tried to divert themselves and assume a new route, but the caravan train was so enormous that they were consistently driven back into its swath. Fox could not shake the sensation that they were being herded like cattle, for the giant trench the caravan carved with its passing made it near to impossible not to be swallowed up by it.

Finally, Aron ordered that they should come to a halt, for the dust cloud had become so thick that visibility itself was nil. Each coughed spasmodically despite the swaths they bore about their faces, for the enormous train had disturbed and agitated the environment to near the same extent as the storm which preceded it.

"I suppose we must break camp once again." Erik admonished "At this rate of travel, we shall be lucky to reach Damaas before the snows fall."

"Aye." Aron replied "I will admit that we've had a bad run of it. Be grateful that I had the foresight to alot both time and supplies for such eventualities. Travel across Balthazar is never an easy matter. The lesson here is patience and preparation." The big man's words were rife with stoicism, yet here at last Fox espied the first cracks in his demeanor. Despite himself, he could see that Aron had now become as frustrated as his children. Were it not for his desire to set an example for them, he was sure that the farmer would have succumbed to a fit of impotent rage equal to that of his son's. "Hopefully this caravan will have put some leagues between us by morning. We can then travel without this thrice accursed dust in our faces. We will have need to gather our strength, for if we do not drive a hard pace upon the morrow our stores of water will not last."

The news did not suit Fox's palette. Suddenly, he felt torn. He was here determined to take his leave of the peasant family, yet his steps inexplicably faltered. He had not the time to contemplate this sudden reluctance when the sound of padded hoof beats in the distance broke his concentration.

The great swirl of sand which enveloped them seemed to part as a lone rider was suddenly birthed from its womb. The rider cast a dim, umber-hued silhouette at first, but soon the wavy dark lines which delineated the distorted shape coalesced to reveal the form of a man. Far from what one expected of caravansary, and much to both the surprise, and chagrin of all, the rider was adorned in the expensive accoutrements that denoted a nobleman. His steed was a small, prancing roan which was well-groomed and whose mane was braided with frilly blue lace. The man was thin and wore clothing of crushed cardinal adorned throughout with ribbons of the same blue, and which seemed impossibly clean in the rough environment. His hair was platinum blonde, nearly white, short, and held back with some type of grease, like boiled fat residue, which shun brilliantly under the hot summer sun as though it were encrusted with jewels.

He had a long mustache curled up at the ends and held in place with the same greasy substance. Under the rather extravagant mustache, he wore a broad smile whose teeth gleamed as brightly as his coif, and which announced to even the most naïve traveler that he was not to be trusted. Attached to the lapel of his frilly chemise was a pink pomander, which he held pressed under his nose and which fell neatly into place between his razor-thin mustache and the pointed line of his up-turned septum- though whether this was to breathe in the expensive perfume or to shield himself from the sandstorm, Fox could not be sure. Either way, the pretention was clear. The slight vermillion hue of his skin, similar to that of the roan, spoke of a man that had spent a lifetime in such environments, though his home was far to the south where the sun scorched the dunes, and the flesh, with far greater intensity. Though Gemmen was home to travelers of every nation and creed, never afore had Fox encountered a Raimian.

"Good day fellow travelers!" he announced in a frilly, sing-song voice which nevertheless seemed as loud as his costume and was heard clearly through the sand swirl. Without dismounting, the man gave a bow which seemed thoroughly rehearsed. "I am known as Felix, loyal retainer to the valiant Captain Darus!"

Aron shuffled his way past his son and stood at the head of the group before he spoke. "Good day." he replied though not without trepidation. "I am Aron of Gemmen, this is my daughter Sariss, my son Erik and our friend Costa."

Fox was stunned. He was quite certain that no one had ever addressed him as 'friend' before.

Felix nodded a near-feminine curtsy "It is an unparalleled pleasure to make your aquaintance. We have been aware of your presence for quite some time now, and believe that you would find travel aboard our caravan to be infinitely more pleasurable than having sand blown in your eyes for the rest of your voyage. We go as far as Serdia. Captain Darus extends the invitation personally."

Aron exchanged a glance with Fox briefly before responding, and in that instance Fox saw a look of distrust equal to his own. The people of Raimia rarely travelled so far north. Neither could be sure of what this did portend, yet both men could be sure that such was not a good omen. Little was known of Raimia, and ignorance did not breed confidence. Once, long ago, the southern Kingdom existed in rumor only, before the days of the great war in which their armies advanced upon all of Balthazar. It was said that Raimia was surrounded by an expanse of desert which dwarfed the one they now found themselves in the midst of. Unlike the remainder of Balthazar, whose Kingdoms were merely the capitol cities who shared the same name as their provinces, which in turn held a vast assortment of cities, villages, farmsteads and ports; the entire Kingdom of Raimia was said to consist of the city state itself. Like a shining jewel in a vast desert, there were no outlying settlements where a traveler might take refuge. As such, few were daunting enough to brave the ocean of desert which separated it from the rest of Balthazar, and none could be assured if the reports given by scant caravansary and rangers were rumor, conjecture, or fact. That Raimia was technologically superior was well known, and if the man before him was any indication, the noble castes to the south were doubly as insufferable.

"We would be delighted." Aron replied

Fox was not the least bit surprised at this response. If the caravan truly was as large as Erik was boasting, then it was extremely prudent to be polite. Caravaneers were not to be trifled with, and even the slightest offence was known to lead to bloody battle. Though this man Felix was far from what one expected of a caravaneer, for both Aron and Fox knew that caravan trains were generally comprised of hard men living hard lives. For the moment at least, it was best to comply, and though Erik, Sariss, and even Fox himself were delighted at the invitation, Fox had no doubt that Aron would take full advantage of any opportunity in order to part company.

"Excellent!" Felix replied clapping his hands together. Please feel free to leave your belongings here. They will be attended to."

The more Felix spoke, the more Fox disliked him, for the smile he wore never left his face. In fact, his features seemed as though they had been cast in a perpetual, unalterable, and thoroughly condescending grin. For all of his hatred of noblemen, the smooth-talking diplomat variety of the breed was his least favorite. How a fop such as this came to exist amid the rough-and-tumble lifestyle of a caravaneer was a mystery he was suddenly anxious to solve.

"Your pardon" Aron began "Might our friend Costa perhaps not wait with the wagon? We mean no offense, yet our visit must, by necessity be a short one, and I fear that an untended wagon might be easy prey for thieves."

Fox understood the comment. He was even flattered that Aron

had placed such trust in him, yet still his spirit of adventure bristled at the suggestion.

"Nonsense!" Felix retorted "Captain Darus would have my head should his invitation be refused! Do not fret. There are no thieves upon all of Balthazar who would challenge the might of our valiant Captain! Your belongings will be tended to."

There was little choice in the matter, Fox knew. As a thief, he had lived his life free of such authority. He felt a great swell of pity for Aron in this moment, for he knew that this was not the first time the man had been forced to capitulate to the might of those who considered themselves his betters. Though Felix himself was far from threatening, for the moment, it was best to go along with him lest he arouse the wrath of the remaining caravansary. The desert would, after all, be a convenient place to bury the bodies of four peasant travelers with no one ever being the wiser for the effort. Aron smiled in acknowledgement of this fact and bowed his head in grim reluctance.

As they crested the nearest rise, Fox was greeted to his first glimpse of the caravan. He had assumed it to be large, yet nothing could have prepared him for the sheer scope of what he now bore witness to. Viewed from this distance, the train was so enormous as to be nothing less than a giant snake, winding its way through the dunes. It was only when they neared it that he was able to truly appreciate its scale. His own reasoning buckled in the face of it. Far from being a mere collection of wagons, it seemed nothing less than a giant, moving city. Buildings made of stone and mortar, some several stories high, were mounted on enormous wheels and pulled along by a legion of pack animals the like Fox could not recognize and hadn't even known existed. Some of these were covered in coarse hair like oxen, yet were twice the size of those with massive, ribbed horns growing out of their faces rather than the tops of their heads. Others were taller still, yet with smaller bodies which sat atop incredibly long bird-like legs. The entirety of the moving citadel was harnessed to such esoteric creatures, yet even these were dwarfed by the peaks and towers which jutted out intermittently along the serpentine body, like scales upon the back of an enormous predator set to devour all in its path.

As the party got nearer still, Fox was stunned by the realization that every structure, from the smallest trailer to the largest building, seemed to be interconnected- like a giant, moving hive. The genius of the construction could not be underestimated- for in this way, never would a section of the caravan train fall behind, nor would one get too far ahead. The band of outlaws did not exist that would dare to challenge such a juggernaut.

The clouds of sand it kicked up no longer impeded one's vision of its base, yet the tops of the largest parapets were still obfuscated from sight, though this time by steam, which whistled out of metal pipes like chimneys which lined the tops of the tallest structures. It reminded Fox of the pipes which protruded from the organ in the temple he first called home, for they were quite alike in their construction, though in this instance, he could not begin to glean the purpose of the metal-work tubing, nor could he even guess at what produced the steam, or what function it could possibly serve. Beneath the pipes was a veritable clockwork of machinery which seemed to move of its own volition. Every facet of the caravan train seemed to shift as though it were a living being and not a construction of men.

"Magnificent isn't it?"

The voice came from Felix who had to shout through the sound of the wind and the grinding of machinery to be heard, and had the effect of breaking Fox's reverie. He looked about him and saw that Erik, Sariss and Aron were all trapped in a similar state of awe.

"We call it Metropolis." Felix announced proudly "It was commissioned in Raimia through the brilliant actions of our great King Marcus. Since the great wars have passed, most of the lineage of engineers of the Kingdom's great war machines had grown frustrated with lack of work, this miracle represents our King's efforts in re-directing that energy into something a little more... constructive. You four have the honor of joining us on our maiden voyage. I foresee a future where all of Balthazar is united by moving citadels such as this one!"

Sariss's voice was strained and unheard by all save Fox who stood beside her. "It's...it's unbelievable..."

Fox could not judge the reactions of the rest of his party, for he himself found it impossible to tear his eyes away.

They had, at this point, reached the back of the rear-most trailer. It stood three times as high as Aron himself and was so wide across that it had wheels mounted upon its center axel to keep it from buckling.

The end was comprised entirely of a single massive door which lowered itself like a drawbridge as they approached it. Casually, Felix made his way inside and the others followed. As the door closed behind them, Fox could not help but feel as though they had just been swallowed by some massive, unnatural beast.

What they found within was even more incredible to behold, for the interior seemed much larger than from without. It had every appearance of a stable, though this one housed the same exotic variety of beasts whose comical proportions seemed more at home in a child's drawing than in reality. To one end stood a corridor, and to his utter astonishment, he realized that this must lead to an adjacent wagon; that somehow the wagons themselves were not merely linked from without, but from within as well. It was the only explanation as to how the interior of the stable seemed larger here than when seen from the desert floor.

There were several men milling about, tending to the livestock, and Fox was relieved to note that these wore the raiment's of the poorer, working classes. Each man went about his duty with rigid dicipline, not casting so much as a glance in the direction of Fox and his friends. Felix chose to ignore the men completely and did not bother to make introductions. Perhaps this was because he did not wish to divert their attention from their labor, or perhaps it was because they were simply beneath his notice.

"Welcome to our stables." Felix said "It is here that we keep our pack animals between shifts."

"Shifts?" Sariss responded quizzically

"Yes." Felix responded. He refused to register anything but the smile which seemed permanently etched upon his features, and Fox had to wonder if the man were capable of any other facial expression. He positively glowed with pride as he continued to speak of the mechanical marvel, as though he himself were single-handedly responsible for its creation.

"We do not stop for any reason, for it slows down commerce, which is, after-all, the very mission of our vessel. You four should feel honored that we have slowed to accept you."

Fox was certain that the man's words were couched in lies, though the nature and purpose of which he could not immediately discern. The word 'vessel' however did not seem hyperbolic, for he too had come to see the caravan as such.

"We allow our animals to rest here at regular intervals so that each is refreshed when they resume their task of aiding in Metropolis's locomotion. Even as we speak, our stable hands are escorting your animals hither. Shall we view the rest of the city? Captain Darus is eager to meet you."

"Thank you." replied Aron diplomatically. "Yet I feel as though it would take an eternity to visit such a wonder. Should it not offend you, I believe that my family and I would like to resume our voyage."

"Nonsense!" Felix replied "Captain Darus would have my head were I to allow our guests to travel in such undignified fashion!" The insult was not intended, yet was clear to all save Felix himself. "There are many wonders to see, and as I have been retained as official guide, I would be entirely remiss in my duty were I not to escort you. Lest I miss my guess, you are headed towards Serdia. You must allow us to deliver you there in comfort! Besides, the tour will not take as long as you think, for Metropolis is not merely connected by couplings as you may have already surmised, despite being perhaps ignorant in such matters as engineering, but each individual structure opens into the other so that one can travel from one quarter to the other without ever having to set foot upon the filthy desert floor!"

As he listened to Felix speak, it took great force of will for Fox not to grasp the man and strangle the life out of him. He was certain that Aron shared this sentiment, yet the patron farmer had clearly grown accustomed to living under the yoke of noblemen in a way that Fox never had, and he continued to impress him with his silver-tongued diplomacy.

"We should be honored." Aron said through gritted teeth. Felix either could not sense the big man's reticence, or cared not. Through the corner of his eye, Fox could tell from the expression on their faces that Erik and Sariss were thrilled with the idea.

"This way." Felix said as he waved them in the direction of the nearby corridor.

As they followed him through it, Fox was amazed by the realization that they were, in actuality, passing from trailer to trailer. It was scarcely possible to believe, for it seemed as though he were simply walking from room to room in what might have been any building in Gemmen. Fox had seen many wonders which were the creation of Balthazar itself, yet it seemed as though the progress of man now rose to challenge the very marvels of nature. He could not help but feel as though he was making his way through the bowels and very intestines of an enormous creature, throbbing and swaying as it crawled along its route. He was reminded of the giant worms that existed in the caverns underneath Gemmen and this disturbed him, for he should not have felt as though he had been swallowed by such a menacing beast when he was amongst the company of his own kind, and rare was the situation Fox had ever found himself in where he was not confident in his ability to overcome it. Of what value and worth was a single man when faced with such achievement?

Fox scanned his companions. Erik, he knew, was seething with excitement and anxiety, for his lifetime spent tilling the land at his father's farm could scant have prepared him for anything the like of which he now encountered. Sariss had made it clear to him that her brother longed for a life at sea. It would seem as though the lad had at last realized his life's ambition, for the vessel they now travelled upon was very much like a sea-going ship in all respects, though much larger, and the ocean of sand they sailed, with its vicious storms, roaming bandits, and predatory creatures, was just as perilous as any sea. He felt certain that, as Erik made his way down the corridors between inter-locking trailers, the young man fancied himself as a pirate walking the decks of a great marauder. Standing shoulder to shoulder with him, one could sense his palpable excitement.

Aron's expression was a mix of awe and terror, and Fox was sure that the farmer must have felt akin to a fly trapped by a spider. Sariss looked very much like a young woman taking her first steps into a larger world.

The tour lasted for much of the day. As they made their way through the web of intersecting corridors, they were introduced to gambling rooms, taverns, a bestiary, a cleric's room, a library, and even a small school where a number of children were being taught the rudiments of reading, writing, and navigation. Fox guessed quite correctly at this time that they had still not seen half of what the wondrous city on wheels had to offer.

The magnificence of Metropolis ranked high amongst all of the wonders Fox had ever seen, and he had seen more than most; yet there was something which perturbed him, a feeling which followed him from room to room. Of all of the many people they had encountered within the city, all of whom were peasants much like he and his companions, none had deigned to address them. None had even dared to look in their direction. This was no doubt enforced by the army of sentries which stood stationed at every corridor, all of whom bore the curved scimitars and wore the gold and silver armor of knights of Raimia.

Felix proved to be a wealth of information regarding the city. He spoke boastfully throughout the tour of its many accomplishments and wonders, yet continued to ignore all those they passed, nor did any make any effort to acknowledge his presence in return.

At the end of a particularly long-winded speech as to the ingenuity of their cold storage units, Sariss was the first to broach the question they all had been wondering.

"Where do you find all of the people to work such a venture?" her voice was one of great temerity, yet one which nevertheless refused to be denied

"Why, from Raimia's own prison cells, of course." Felix replied rather nonchalantly, as though the answer itself was obvious

Despite himself, Fox could not help but find his voice... "Slaves."

"Yes." continued Felix "I can see how one might make that error in judgment...Costa wasn't it?" Fox merely nodded. "Not slaves to be sure, but prisoners of war. Rest assured that each man and woman volunteered for service upon Metropolis. Many had been condemned to life sentences at our penal colonies. There a lifetime spent in the sands, digging trenches that we might expand our glorious Kingdom awaits them. Each gladly consented to having their penalties reduced in order to serve Captain Darus."

"And what was their crime?" Fox continued, refusing to let the matter drop

"Why, crimes of war of course." responded Felix as though such an explanation should suffice

"But, Raimia has not been at war for ages" cried Sariss. She opened her mouth to protest further, but was silenced when her father rested a large, meaty hand on her shoulder.

"There are many kinds of war young maiden." Felix replied, bending himself into a bow to face her "And there are equally as many war crimes. Come, we should not dawdle any further. Soon we shall be linking up for the grand event. Metropolis as you see her now is still merely a portion of her true size, for we only join fully when we are destined to arrive at larger ports, and then only at those which sit upon wide open spaces, such as plains, or the sea of Serdia."

"Link up?" Erik inquired

"Indeed." replied Felix "Many of the trading routes along the King's highway are far too narrow for Metropolis. It is common practice therefore that the city disassemble before docking at smaller ports. The city you visit now is still only partially complete, for many of our smaller wagons are still trading in Gemmen and Baraan, as well as the numerous farmsteads in between."

The notion of a swarm of trailers and wagons returning to the whole struck Fox with the image of ants crawling through the desert, only to re-join their commune. In fact, he continued to draw parallels between Metropolis and the marvels of Balthazar itself. There was something perverse in the relationship. He knew not what, but the notion disturbed him. Like insects themselves, each man and woman who comprised the city served a function and a purpose, each operated as though of one mind in order to benefit the whole. It was chilling in its splendor... cruel in its ingenuity. More than the sacrifice of freedom and individuality upon the altar of progress, there was something terrifying and wholly unnatural about the encroachment of man into what has always been the dominion of nature.

He was anxious to meet the oft-mentioned Captain Darus, for only a man of extraordinary strength and will could possibly be responsible for the coordination and execution of such an ambitious and functional enterprise.

"But, what is to keep those from escaping into Gemmen permanently?" Erik inquired, ignoring his father's suggestive look that they should let the matter drop. "It is well known that the thieves and assassins guilds there are well adept at avoiding the long arm of the King's guardsmen. Should any man curry their favor, they would be offered protection as well."

"Not all are criminals." Felix replied, still maintaining the pleasant façade he had kept throughout "We allow only our most trusted noblemen to handle commerce; nobles selected personally by the King. These have been honored above all others, for there is no greater ambition in life than to serve Raimia. We keep the lesser classes about for the simple man-power they are good for. Metropolis cannot survive without it. Our sister ships are, even as we speak, heading towards us on an intercept course that they might join us for the festivities..." Felix paused momentarily before resuming "Yet I have said too much. I shall not rob our Captain of his desire to tell you of that himself. Come, the next stop on our tour is the Inn."

"Inn?" inquired Sariss "But if the caravan does not stop, how do you feed such a compliment of men, women and children?"

"We have many stone kilns used to cook for all of our workers. We also have stores of food in reserve, and at any time of day, dozens of hunters and trackers roam about our perimeter searching for fresh game."

"Like bees and pollen." Fox muttered somewhat under his breath

"Your pardon?" Felix replied

"Nothing."

"Brilliant!" interjected Erik, who seemed to be having the time of his life upon his new adventure and clearly did not share Fox's own paranoid musings

Sariss's eyes were wide with incredulity "It's amazing!" she agreed

Even Aron himself seemed impressed with what the Kingdom of Raimia had accomplished, for Fox could sense the wonder emanating from the man.

"Thank you" replied Felix. Yet it does prove weary at times. Often Metropolis passes by some beautiful oasis or other that many of the men would like to explore, but Darus will not stop for any reason. It is quite a stroke of luck that you have found us on this night."

"And why is that?" said Aron.

"I believe that the Captain himself should be the one to answer that question."

The companions made their way down yet another of the many corridors which linked the various parts of Metropolis. The corridor they found themselves in was somewhat longer than the others, and they had not travelled half its distance when the smell of food and ale filled Fox's nostrils, causing his mouth to water. Soon the corridor opened into its mate and Fox was elated for the first time since they had set foot inside the city, for he recognized immediately what was clearly a den of thieves. The music was raucous, the ale was poured freely, and the men and women who libated within had none of the despondent air of prisoners who had been robbed of their freedom.

Here, hook nosed barbarians cavorted openly with scantily clad dancing girls who waved their silken handkerchiefs in front of their noses tauntingly. Many of the men, dirt stained and heavily muscled were passed out upon crude wooden benches with only a moist trail of vomit to tell of where they had been. There was a single minstrel who sung bawdy songs which all present seemed to know the words to, for the lyrics were belted out on a wave of foul smelling, beer soaked voices. A low-born mendicant, covered in wounds from battles long passed and whose reasons were long forgotten, arm wrestled with a one-eyed Hillman, each pitting all they had ever come to depend on in their hard lives against the other, that being their strength of limb and a pint of ale. Long-legged courtesans flirted openly with all who caught their eye, wearing nothing but whispishly thin strands of satin and caring not a whit about the delicate sensibilities of prudish, sexually repressed high society who would otherwise enforce their vaulted moral standards of chastity upon them, whilst secretly envying their youth and beauty. Many of these engaged in games of strength themselves, refusing to accept their oppressive lot as delicate maidens forced to obey the will of bloated husbands. Completely absent was the rigid self control and militant efficiency which crushed the spirit of those they had encountered previously. In its stead was the care-free exuberance one expected of free men, unbound by the rules of those who cared only about appearances and the noble status it afforded them. The tankards had no emblems or ornamentation, the walls had no tapestries to cover them, and the floor was strewn with naught but sawdust, blood and beer. The meat was raw and the wine was sour, but the air was sweet.

Fox longed to join them, for this was the sort of company he had much yearned for since his initial departure from Gemmen. He was weary of playing the role of steel merchant, for never before had he assumed a false persona for so long a time. He had even begun to empathize with the lifetime of pretense which was thrusted upon the noble castes.

Erik too seemed to share in Fox's desire to join the party, and the young man had none of the reservations Fox was forced to exhibit. His wondering eyes lingered momentarily upon one scantily clad concubine after the other. Nevertheless, his inherent dread of his father seemed to have the practiced effect of keeping him in line. Fox smiled inwardly at this, for he could well imagine the debaucherous extent Erik would have driven himself too were it not for the daunting presence of the giant man behind him.

Even Sariss seemed view the tavern with a broad, inviting smile, though her gaze lingered upon the hard bodies of those of a different gender.

The ever stern Aron however, snorted in derision, and Felix smiled in his direction, for clearly he felt as though this was the appropriate response.

"You have my apologies if you are offended." Felix spoke, and Fox was amazed to note that the man had suddenly lost the smile which had, up until now, seemed a permanent fixture of his synthetic personality. In its place was a sneer, full of revulsion and contempt. Fox enjoyed the role reversal, for he himself was now sporting a broad, infectious grin.

Felix seemed genuinely surprised and embarrassed as to what was happening in the Inn. Fox had no doubt that had he been aware, the foppish noble would have circumvented this leg of the tour altogether.

"It would seem as though, despite my council, Captain Darus has allowed the party to begin early." he said with a contemptuous sigh

"Party?" Sariss enquired

It took a moment for her question to register, for Felix continued to scowl disdainfully at the orgy of decadence his senses had been thus assaulted with. He nevertheless slid back into his role as diplomat and donned his false smile once again before addressing the query. "Come. We have lingered here too long. Let us find our company amongst those of a more distinguished pedigree, with more...discerning taste. The Captain's quarters are just ahead."

Despite himself, Fox could not stop smiling. He had been in the presence of drunken noblemen many times, most recently at the Silver Stallion in Gemmen. He knew that the inherent decadence of the so called 'noble classes', for all of their virtuous pretenses, was a vile thing to behold. The peasant classes, at the very least, cavorted about openly, and Fox was all too familiar with the degradations that noblemen engaged in behind closed doors, for never had he met a courtesan who did not tell tales of the most vicious perversions which took place behind the palace walls of Gemmen, and he had learned long ago that those who were the most concerned with appearances always had the most to hide.

Reluctantly, they followed Felix past the tavern a short distance until they came upon an enormous wooden door that was completely unadorned, save for a large brass knocker bolted into place at one side.

"We have arrived at Captain Darus's personal cabin!" Felix ejaculated. He rapped the knocker which made a baritone thud indicating that the door was thick and made of solid oak.

The door was opened by a giant dressed head to toe in full Raimian battle armor. Upon closer inspection, the guard bore a striking resemblance to the door whose post he was assigned. Up 'til this point, Aron was perhaps the largest man Fox had ever seen, yet the brute stood a full head taller than he. His very presence had the ominous effect of catching the breath in the throats of the entire party. Were he a descendant of a race of mythical ogres, Fox could not be certain, yet there was something clearly unnatural about the sheer size of the man. Aside from his enormity, his entire physique made little sense. His arms were thick as tree trunks and just as knotted and coarse. His forearms were covered in thick hair with veins which stood in stark relief seen clearly through it, like rivers running through a forest on a topographical map- yet for all of the rigid delineation of those arms, his mid-section was soft and flabby. It was a strange dichotomy, for he seemed both to be in excellent shape, yet at the same time fat and slovenly. His bulk was so great that he was nearly as wide around as he was tall. He filled the entire space which the door had just occupied, and seemed just as solid. In his left arm he held the standard helmet of Raimian soldiery, though this one was as large as a well-bucket and was pressed against a strap of leather which served as his belt and must have been as long as the entire corridor they had just walked. In place of the standard scimitars of Raimian calvary, a broarsword such as was favored by the warriors of Hyrst hung from his belt. This was so large, that the heretofore mentioned belt was, by necessity, winced tightly in place in order to support it and had the effect of squeezing his enormous belly outwards so that it overlapped the buckles. His chest-plate was made of copper, and had the standard of the Kingdom of Raimia embossed on its surface, that of a snake coiled about a crown, yet was not large enough to accommodate his mid-section which seemed to act as a bracer which kept it in place. Even the giant's features seemed unnatural, for his nose sat squat and flat on his face and seemed unnaturally large beneath his tiny, beady eyes. His lips were equally squat, as though he had been hit squarely in the face with a flat pan as a child and never fully recovered. He had no hair upon his head, or face, yet a thin purple scar travelled from the top of his bald pate and ended at his upper lip, which was permanently curled into a snarl as a result.

The sight of the man had the effect of silencing the entire party save Felix, who seemed utterly unaffected. "Lieutenant Barratus, may we enter?" he said, while maintaining his characteristically pleasant smile

In response, the mountain of muscle and flesh thus named Barratus curled his upturned lip further into what proved to be an even more menacing sneer and extended his gigantic, calloused hand towards them. With a voice that echoed the staccato of a rockslide crashing down the cliffs of mount Gemmen he replied... "Your weapons."

The party had left their weapons with the rest of their meager possessions back at the wagon, yet none had the chance to tell him this, for a voice which came from behind settled the matter immediately. The voice was as strong as it was succinct, and brooked no room for disobedience.

"That won't be necessary Barratus."

Immediately Barratus stepped aside to allow them entry, swiveling on one mighty thew like a portcullis. As the foursome entered the chamber, Barratus glared menacingly at Fox. Fox returned the glare with an intense, piercing gaze of his own. For a moment, the two men seemed locked in place, for Fox returned the stare with the look of his namesake stalking its prey. Soldier and thief were nature's natural enemies, and though Fox had entered the belly of this particular beast camouflaged, the two men were instantly locked in a courtship of death. He had played the role of meek steel merchant for far too long. His mask was slipping...

"Felix, Barratus, please leave us." came the voice again.

Fox could clearly see the room in its entirety now that the solid wall of flesh, like a slab of muscle and fat had swiveled aside. He could feel beady eyes burning into him momentarily, before the lumbering sound of the padding of giant feet indicated that Barratus had left the cabin. Fox was quite certain that Felix would have graced his Captain with an extravagant, flowery bow before taking his leave, yet he did not care to turn about to look, he was far too busy taking the measure of both the Captain, and his lair.

The Captain's quarters were not what Fox was expecting of a man from Raimia, for it was small and sparsely decorated. In place of expensive satin paintings and tapestries, the walls were adorned with a plethora of weapons from the various Kingdoms of Balthazar. Everything from the crude double-handed battle axes, maces and broadswords of the type favored by northlanders, to the elegant cavalry swords and rapiers favored by guardsmen and thieves alike-were present. To one side, a collection of ranged weapons such as reflex and longbows were mounted atop a glass case bolted into the wall which contained every known type of dagger, dart and throwing knife. Next to these were assortments of small, hooked weapons the like Fox had never seen and whose purpose he could only guess at. Clearly the Captain was well travelled, and seemed to have a predilection for combat. There was no furniture to speak of, merely a collection of crude wooden chairs placed in front of a solid oak table where Captain Darus himself sat.

Fox was pleased to note that he was quite correct when he assumed the Captain to be a man of extraordinary make, for much like the room in which he sat, Captain Darus was clad in the adornments of a warrior-born. His thick forearms bore copper studded bands which rested beneath the chiseled musculature of his exposed biceps. In place of a uniform denoting Raimian nobility, he wore a chest plate made of simple steel, lightweight and durable. The crest of the Kingdom of Raimia which adorned it remained unpolished. Fox could not see his legs where he sat behind the large oak desk, yet felt certain that the Captain wore heavy cavalry boots and greaves. There wasn't a trace of vanity about him in fact, for his entire dress was of a type that was functional, not decorative.

What truly surprised Fox was the look of the man himself, for what had seemed at first glance to be the bronzed skin one expected to see on one who had been so long in the desert, was actually an indication of his lineage. The strong features, square-set jaw and short hair of the deepest black completed the picture. Captain Darus was the descendant of that savage tribe of Hillmen who sired the warlord Gemmen and aided him in beating back the forces of Raimia itself, before utter disdain for the civilization which rose thereafter caused them to retreat back to the mountains. How such a man, the offspring of Raimia's greatest foe could have ascended to the rank of Captain amongst their armies seemed beyond reckoning. Clearly, iron will and competence set him apart from his peers. Were he not a soldier, Fox was certain that he would have liked him.

Captain Darus lifted his head from the pile of papyrus he had been studying with the pointed metal implements native to a navigator, and when he looked the companions in the eye, his steely blue orbs bore no false, diplomatic smile, but conveyed instead a look of overt honesty which told all that he was indeed glad of their arrival.

"You four are headed towards Serdia." he began, his voice earnest and direct "How is it that you have chosen to brave the desert and not taken the King's highway?"

Aron seemed to bristle before he spoke, yet Darus's demeanor nevertheless had the effect of illiciting honesty "King Alric exacts an expensive toll along that route." he said "Until such a time as free men are not allowed to travel as they see fit, we choose to keep what little coin we have."

Fox was surprised at Aron's candor. It seemed he too felt as though Captain Darus was one who respected honesty. He was pleased when Darus threw his head back in laughter.

"Very true my friend and well-said! In fact, this is one of the reasons, besides the vanity of King Marcus of course that we link-up at all. Did you know that the entire city of Metropolis is charged the same toll for travelling the King's highway as a single peasant's wagon? Think on it! Hundreds of men and women charged the same for passage as you and your three companions! It is highway robbery to be sure! King Alric the wily may not be able to force those such as yourselves to travel with a caravan train for fear of breaking trade agreements with his neighbors, yet he all but accomplishes exactly this through sheer sinister duplicity and guile!"

Fox was amazed. Here was mystery wrapped in a riddle! A captain of the vainest of the four Kingdoms who spoke like a commoner-that a man of rank in a Kingdom known for its pretention spoke ill of duplicity was astonishing. He could even feel Aron, Sariss and Erik begin to relax in his company.

Fox knew little of Raimia; only that it was much smaller than either Gemmen or Damaas and had always been quite secretive and isolated in the south. Despite its small size, it was a place rich in culture, innovation, and above all, decadence. It was only through the sheer force of numbers who had resisted it long ago, coupled with the leadership of Gemmen himself that the Kingdom was defeated in battle and denied its rule over all of Balthazar. Were it not for the peace treaties signed in the wake of that great war which spared what remained of the Raimian forces, provided they engage in acts of commerce with the Kingdoms who had risen to oppose it, it was likely Raimia would have remained independent and autonomous. Even now, caravaneers and rangers were the only men who braved the voyage through the unforgiving desert to that mysterious land, and these were doubtless shown little. Though all of Balthazar now enjoyed the fruits of Raimian culture, particularly art, music, and cuisine, the lands to the south were always viewed with skepticism, suspicion, and were granted near-superstitious levels of fear. Even in modern times, the means with which Raimia utilizes in order to adapt to the desert wastelands remain known only to them.

"It is indeed fortunate that you have come across us when you have." Captain Darus continued, breaking Fox's train of thought "Our mission was to travel the entire expanse of Balthazar before returning to Raimia, yet we have just received word from courier that Marcus requires the presence of Felix in order to help advise him at the council of war. We have been ordered to return forthwith. Were the King not so dependent on my army keep him in power, we could have rid ourselves of that sniveling sycophant altogether, yet recent events require my sword once more."

Fox was puzzled. "Council of war? But these are times of peace between the great Kingdoms."

"War is where you find it lad." responded Darus. He seemed quick to change the subject, for he was clearly a soldier, not a politician, and lacked the forked tongue necessary when it came to restraining his candor. "Like as not the King's bed has simply gotten cold without the presence of his favorite concubine."

"Then, you are saying that she travels with you?" questioned Erik

"No lad, what I am saying is that Felix's council directly involves Marcus buggering him on a nightly basis. Nevertheless, it has always been my policy to halt progress the night before entering any large port, such as Gemmen, Serdia, or Damaas, and I would not break with tradition now just to satisfy the depravities of the King. I set a hard pace for those under my command and like to give them a taste of freedom before any earnest trading begins. I have found that allowing such aids in motivation and loyalty. Barratus, whom you have met, is a harsh disciplinarian, and were it not for the occasional festival, I have no doubt that I would have a revolt of my own to quell. Soon, we will be making a full-stop a day's ride from Serdia. Preparations for the festival, as you have seen in our inn, have already begun. I would, of course, be honored if you four would join us."

Aron gazed upon the eager expressions of his children before he responded. "I too have learned the value of rewarding hard work." he said after a moment's pause "We should be honored to attend. May we be pemitted to break camp outside of the confines of your caravan?"

Darus smiled "Certainly. You would be surprised to know, I'd wager, that Metropolis has covered near the entire expanse of the sea of Serdia whilst we have been entertaining you. We now approach a large oasis which we plan to use for our festival grounds. I'm certain that if you venture inward, you would find a convenient spot with a small stream to water your animals. I shall have a security escort deliver you there forthwith."

"Our thanks." responded Aron. "Though I am certain that such an escort will not be necessary."

Darus merely smiled "I shall have a security escort deliver you there forthwith." he said again

Aron bowed low before the Captain and indicated his children to follow suit, which they did with aplomb. Fox hesitated. He looked Darus in the eye and returned his smile. Never had the fearsome Fox of Gemmen bowed to any man, and never would he do so. As he made his way from the chamber, he could not help but wonder how long he could keep his own feral nature at bay.

CHAPTER ELEVEN - THE FOX BARES HIS TEETH

Metropolis had come to a full stop when Fox and his companions were escorted to a nearby grove by a single soldier in full battle armor. Fox's inherent paranoia waned, for they had been reunited with the family's wagon and their beasts, and a cursory glance told him that these had been un-tampered with.

The young man who accompanied them to the nearby oasis was so stoic in demeanor that he complained not at all of the harsh heat, which caused him to sweat visibly under the weight of his full complement of gear.

The oasis housed a small stream at its edge and was so large around that it was nothing less than a small forest set within the barren dunes of the sea of Serdia. There were no mountains about for miles, and the river appeared to have no apparent source- it simply ran a circular pattern about the circumference of the oasis. To others, this would have seemed to be a mystery shrouded in supernatural origins, yet Fox could only marvel when he speculated that the underground tunnels he had become acquainted with ran this far across Balthazar- delivering the boon of water when needed and birthing the vegetation about it.

All were amazed at how much ground the enormous city on wheels had covered, for before entering the patchwork collection of moving citadels Fox had not been able to see anything but endless swells of sand in any direction, and he had not met the man who could compete with his eagle-like vision. The fact that they now stood amongst evergreens which clawed at the sky with their barbed appendages told that Metropolis was capable of speed which defied even his vivid imagination.

Erik had pleaded with his father that they be allowed to quell their hunger at the inn within Metropolis itself, yet Aron had once again exerted his authority over his impulsive son and demanded that they make camp forthwith. It took a great deal of effort on Aron's part to ensure that they had taken the time to water the animals before succumbing to his children's wishes to rush off and join the festival. Erik and Sariss had even gone so far as to refuse to sup on their stores of food, insisting that there would be plenty of fare to be had once they joined the revelry and that there was no need to delve into their own meager supplies. The night was clear and warm, and they had foregone the construction of a shelter as it was common for travelers to sleep out under the stars on such nights when the atmosphere did not portend of rain.

The sun had begun its slow descent beneath the horizon, causing the dunes to radiate as though imbued by an inner fire, and the otherwise hard working family had accomplished very little as well as expended much energy achieving it. Aron, who until now had always demanded a grueling pace, finally gave in to his children's youthful exuberance and announced that it was time to join the party. Fox thought it wise to leave Fang with the wagon, yet took the time to line the hidden pockets of his jerkin with his daggers. To all concerned, he was very much unarmed and unimposing, yet never did the fearsome Fox of Gemmen go out into the night without his claws, cleverly sheathed or no.

As they made their way through the tree-line, the sound of flutes and whistles and cries of drunken revelry told all that the festivities were well underway.

Upon emerging from the veil of trees, Fox was amazed to see that the city had transformed itself entirely during the short period of time they had been away; the center-most tower which he had noted earlier due to its strange assortment of pipes and gears still remained linked with its adjoining structures, yet the multitude of wagons and trailers which had once been lashed about it were now fully detached. These stretched outwards, forming a large circular perimeter around this central hub. The manner in which Metropolis could adapt and morph itself into whatever shape suited its current purpose seemed unreal. It boggled the mind as well as the senses of the young thief. More than anything, he wished to explore such a marvel fully.

Strands of ribbons were stretched from trailer to trailer and there were so many lanterns about, each emanating a radiant glow which ran the gamut of every hue in the spectrum due to their colorful paper shells, that the effect was dizzying. The desert itself seemed to be on fire- for the dunes were bathed in color, as though embers from forge-fire rested in the womb of each. The warm glow the festival emanated was visible on the faces of each jubilant man and woman, once sullen and mute, now alive with mirth and laughter.

They had only just entered the perimeter when a throng of bodies, each of whom rejoicing in their single night's freedom and determined to make the most of it, surrounded them, drawing them into the infectious merriment of the occasion.

Food and wine were passed about freely and dancing was everywhere. Acrobats and jugglers flitted about, demanding no payment for their performances, but simply reveling in the opportunity to share their art- oft dismissed as frivolous and decadent by the noble castes; now celebrated for its beauty, dexterity and grace. Fox had not yet taken the opportunity to imbibe any of the droughts which flowed through the crowds, yet found that the very air itself was intoxicating. Even such a man as Aron could not help but revel in the celebration of freedom that these had waited so long for. Gone now were both jailers and nobles alike, replaced instead by a carnal, primal sense of joy and unrestrained exuberance.

They passed by a ring of upturned oak barrels where peasants much like Aron himself in terms of size and class were downing tankards of ale, and these waved at the friends to join them. Erik planted himself in the middle of the gathering and downed the contents of an entire jar of crude baked clay which was handed to him. Not willing to be upstaged by his son, Aron joined the group and downed his own tankard in one swallow, much to the amusement of the throng.

Fox made his way towards the group, for he himself had been thirsting for an ale since having left Baraan, and he had every intention of defiling himself in a manner of legendary proportions. He had made no fewer than two steps in that direction however when Sariss tugged at his jerkin, pulling him away.

"Leave the lads to their drinking and dicing!" she said laughing "I have a desire to view every offering of this party and my escort is near to hand!"

"You had better join her Costa!" Erik shouted over the din. "For my sister, the expression 'near to hand' means 'under thumb!'"

Erik's jest was met with roaring laughter from those about, and Fox, taking no insult whatsoever, joined them. There were many young men nearby who had been drinking in the voluptuous form of Sariss's figure more deeply than that of their draughts, and Fox had no need to ask for Aron's council to know that he approved of the idea of an escort.

As he allowed himself to be dragged away, he was immediately certain that he had made the right decision, for Sariss began to spin about gracefully to the sound of the pan flutes and presented him with a vision of grace and beauty that he was quite certain the scarred visages and blunt demeanors of those whose company he had just left could not adequately compete with.

He continued to follow Sariss through the festival. She remained ever before him, a whirling dervish of ethereal beauty who seemed ever out of reach. Like a siren she called him, past the stalls, fiddles, flutes, and mobs of gleeful dancers, reveling in their one night's freedom. Though there were some soldiers about, these too seemed to be thoroughly lost in the moment, and no trace of Felix and his ilk could be seen. The more Fox was drawn in, the more grateful he was for allowing himself to be so ensnared.

Soon, they came upon a small clearing which seemed to be the epicenter from which the very spirit of the festivities emanated. Here games of chance and skill were being enjoyed by all, egged on by improvised carnival barkers of every race and stripe. Spun copper cups were set on upturned barrels, one of which concealed a pea, which were shuffled about so that the punters could wager as to which cup held the tiny orb. Fox laughed inwardly, for he was very familiar with the game and knew that the pea itself was secreted into the palm of the performer, and that the only real 'winners' were those who would meet in shadow at a later interval to divvy up their coin. Though he steered Sariss away from such games of preordained luck, he had no wish to begrudge anyone a living, for he had always believed that those whose coin was cast about so liberally on such 'games' did not deserve to keep it.

Nearby, two brutish men, each shirtless and covered in grease no doubt purloined in secret from the kitchens in anticipation of just such a contest, pitted their strength against the other in brutal wrestling matches that were sure to administer aches and pains such as no hangover could possibly compete with. With no thought of the morrow, the giant men seemingly cobbled together with naught but muscle encased in leather, paced about the circular battlefield as marked by a thick rope set into the sand, gritted their teeth and struggled to pin each other to the floor, regardless of how many broken bones and torn ligaments this took to accomplish. All about them men shouted challenges, stoking the egos of those easily gulled into tests of strength, skill and cunning.

For no reason save for the whim of chance, Fox and his nubile companion gravitated towards a dagger tossing competition. The pair now had their arms linked about the other, for Sariss had chosen to slow her pace in order to fully take in her surroundings and had no wish to lose him in the crowd. Here they saw a small gathering of disgruntled men each trying vainly to dethrone the champion. The champion in question seemed not only to be the most skilled amongst the lot, but also the host of the event. The man was thin and tawny, with long ebon hair and mustache that seemed to accentuate his gauntness. He stood a head above those about him, and his eyes spoke of a canniness which belied the broad, toothy grin which rested beneath them. Set up nearby was a wagon wheel braced against one of the many trailers strewn about which served as a target, and having witnessed his most recent cast, Fox was certain that he had spent a lifetime training with daggers and was not about to let the easy opportunity to earn some coin that this festival presented him with to pass him by.

"Come!" bellowed the man "Is there not a man about you who can beat my cast?" he hesitated briefly and laughed before he spoke again. "Is there not a man about you at all?!"

He splayed his long arms and circled about grinning before his steely orbs rested on Sariss, as they clearly found her a tempting target for their stare.

"I believe that mine can!" she shouted, as much in response to the question as to the penetrating, lascivious gaze.

Fox was flabbergasted. He spun about and glared at Sariss with his jaw agape. "No!" he cried, but it was too late, for he was already being drawn into the crowd like a fisherman's boat caught in a whirlpool.

It was a rare thing when the legendary Fox of Gemmen was taken off guard, yet this was exactly what happened, for seemingly before he could protest any further, or properly articulate a viable rebuttal, five throwing knives were placed into his hand and he was being shoved towards the front of the crowd. If Cammarran could see him now, Fox was certain that the old man would have excommunicated him from the guild on the spot. Fox, the most invisible of all thieves, he who had elevated the art of innocuousness to a level never afore heard of, once again found himself the focal point of a host of lurid gawkers.

To back out now, he realized, would draw even more attention; better to lose quickly and be forgotten as yet another unworthy challenger; an unremembered face amongst many. Begrudgingly, he felt the weight of the daggers in his hand. Immediately he realized the ruse. A proper throwing knife was balanced at the fulcrum where the handle met the blade, yet each of these had an uneven weight distribution towards the haft that he was certain those of the champion did not share. Regardless, under other circumstances, Fox was sure that he could compensate. He shuffled towards his mark, here represented by a small groove scratched into the dirt a fair distance from the aforementioned wagon wheel/target. Grinning sheepishly, and with an excited Sariss looking on with hands clasped in anticipation, Fox took his first cast.

The dagger flew clumsily across the expanse, missing the wheel entirely and clanging off the trailer itself where it struck hilt-first upon its broad surface. Immediately, the raucous crowd burst into laughter.

"Perhaps you should find yourself a new champion milady!" shouted the tall man, bowing towards her at the waist "Should you like, I can provide you with my services. I am sure, based upon your chosen company; you might be in need of a man for several reasons!"

Had the crowd been laughing before, the jeering comment had the effect of eliciting a loud staccato of roaring which eclipsed their former efforts.

Despite himself, Fox could not help but focus on Sariss. He had expected her to respond angrily to the slander. The young woman had proven herself to be in possession of reserves of grit and stubbornness which should have caused her to bristle at the comment.

Instead, he was surprised to see that she had taken the insult poorly. Even more surprising was when he realized that she was not embarrassed for herself, but for him- for having been responsible for goading him into the competition, for letting her own merriment and happiness get the better of her.

The thought angered Fox. His emerald green eyes burned with ethereal fury as he took position for his next cast. The remaining four daggers he still held sailed through the air in unison- each piercing through the same slit in the the wagon wheel at its centermost point, driven so deep that the cross guards abutted the wood.

Immediately, the laughter died. The silence which followed was as palpable as the clamor which preceded it. It was as though time itself had stood still in order to allow those congregated to fully appreciate the moment. It wasn't until time itself resumed and several of its increments had passed that the air erupted in a thunderclap of applause. Through it all, and perhaps because it was he alone who spoke, the former champion's voice was audible.

"In legends only have I heard of such a cast."

Fox himself was speechless, therefore he merely shrugged and pushed his way past the crowd, each with jaws agape, resuming his place next to Sariss.

"Costa!" she shrieked "That was amazing!"

"Aye." responded Fox, who had since gathered his wits "Now perhaps we should take our leave before this crowd asks to see it once more. Had I a lifetime to try, I could never get so lucky again."

Sariss laughed merrily and linked her arm through his once again before they took their leave. Fox could not stop his internal monologue from spinning thoughts in his mind. "What have I done?" he repeated to himself as they shuffled away.

The pair had no sooner made good their escape when the former champion came running towards them, his long black hair and flowing mustache trailing upon the wind behind him.

"Hold!" he cried "I will not allow you to leave without partaking of your winnings."

He placed a heavy drawstring purse in Fox's hands. From the weight of it, he could tell that it was laden with coppers. A nobleman might have balked at such wealth, yet he was certain that the satchel represented all of the man's earnings. Fox accepted the purse with seeming enthusiasm.

"My thanks!" he said whilst patting the man on the back and secretly replacing the purse onto the drawstring of his belt. He and Sariss then spun about and made their way off into the night, leaving him there, feet firmly planted as though he were incapable of following.

In some small way, Fox knew, he had just earned the posthumous forgiveness of his mentor. He recalled how the daggers he had been given had been gimmicked. In life, Cammarran had always been strict when it came to upholding the thieves code- and according to that code's tenets, one did not steal from a fellow thief.

CHAPTER TWELVE - A MURDER IN THE NIGHT

Eventually, Fox and Sariss, having toured the fair grounds for some time, meandered back towards where they had left Aron and Erik earlier in the evening. Erik had long since parted ways with his father- off to enjoy an evening's debauchery without the supervision of his soon-to-be disapproving patron. Aron however, was exactly where they had left him, still with tankard in hand and laughing heartily in the company of his new friends. Fox was amused to note that there was another side to the man beyond his usual strict and conservative manner. He had clearly imbibed several tankards since they had parted company, and this no doubt played a large role in freeing Aron from the self-imposed shackles of his own dour personality.

Upon seeing Fox and his daughter, Aron rose and placed a massive arm around them both. "Costa! Daughter!" he bellowed "Allow me to buy you a drink!"

"Only one?" replied Sariss.

Aron threw his head back and roared. Fox realized immediately that he had never 'til this night heard the big man laugh. He decided that he approved of the change. Rarely had he ever taken the time to get to know anyone in his young life, and he always allowed his first impression of people to define them. Had he not seen it himself, he would have, perhaps, thought the big man to be incapable of laughter. It would seem as though there were more layers to Aron than he had first surmised. At the very least, there was mirth to the man which could, under the proper circumstances, be coaxed to the surface, cracking his stern façade like an eggshell.

The three friends drank and feasted late into the night. Erik was nowhere to be seen, and Sariss had alluded that they should not expect to until morning. Likely his nocturnal proclivities involved drinking, fighting and whoring, and Fox understood that some pleasures in life were sweeter when left unsupervised.

Fox had never known camaraderie before. The closest thing he ever had to a friend was Cammarran, and rarely did he spend time in the old man's presence that wasn't consumed with grueling training sessions and long-winded lectures about responsibility. Aron may have been a father figure, yet he treated him as an equal, with respect. Fox found that he could not help but reciprocate. Perhaps it was the ale, yet he had begrudgingly come to admit that he was enjoying the company of this family. Aron was not above making bawdy jokes, and Sariss, not to be undone, displayed a sense of humor and lust for life that was as far removed from the delicate sensibilities and fragile nature of the common noblewoman as was possible. Despite himself, he regretted that he was amongst them under false pretenses. As Fox, the legendary thief of Gemmen, he had not allowed himself the luxury of friends; yet as Costa, humble steel merchant, he could allow himself, perhaps, for the first time, this long eluded privilege. It was a strange mix of bubbling emotions which threatened to overwhelm him, for Fox was nothing if not hedonistic, and pleasure was to be pursued at any cost, yet there was a great resistance in him, one who relished new experiences, to truly surrender to this one. He pushed the turmoil of his thoughts to the back of his mind, choosing instead to experience the moment free of such concerns. This was not a night for introspection, nor was any night for that matter. Better to live in the moment lest one miss the opportunity to fully immerse oneself in their surroundings. Given the zeal that his newfound friends laughed and drank- he was certain that they would agree.

"You gentlemen will have to excuse me" Sariss suddenly interjected upon draining another tankard "This abundance of ale forces me to visit nature." She rose to her feet, kissed her father lovingly on the cheek and said "I'll return shortly." Then she made her way towards the small forest that separated their camp from the caravan.

As she slowly faded from the firelight, Fox's keen gaze was able to pierce the veil of darkness beyond as they followed her. Unseen by any but him, he spied a group of men heading in her direction. Though he could not ascertain their motives, he nevertheless feared the worst and stalked off to follow her.

"And you Costa?" came the voice of Aron behind him "Can you, like my daughter, not hold your ale?"

Fox decided not to inform Aron as to what he had seen. With so many men and women coming to and fro the trees, he could not be certain if the group he had seen were even aware that they were headed in the same direction as Sariss. The man was weighed with so many responsibilities, especially where his family was concerned, that he felt it better to allow him the luxury of sloughing them off for an evening. Likely he was set on naught but a fool's errand.

"Indeed!" he responded "Keep the ale flowing lads, I go only to make room for more."

He followed Sariss's path as best he could, yet the forest was dense, and the moon appeared ever more distant than was normal, thus the night was blanketed in inky darkness which tasked even his ability to see in such environs without the aid of lamplight. When he was certain that he himself was invisible to prying eyes, he placed an outstretched hand on a low hanging branch in front of him and used it to swing himself up into the trees.

Bounding from branch to branch, his sight now completely acclimated, Fox ascended to nature's rooftop. Here the dim outline of the moon was stronger, yet the leafy canopy it delineated was layered such as to be impenetrable and he was forced to depend on his other senses to target Sariss. He knew that he had followed her path carefully- that she was nearby. Clinging to a thin branch and with both feet braced against a thick tree trunk, he leaned out over the veil. Here he attempted to filter out the myriad voices of the wilderness. He concentrated on one after the other, dismissing each in turn and blocking them out lest they distract him further from his goal. The screeching of a nearby murder of crows was not a good omen, for such birds were not native to the desert and the presense of such oft boded ill. Finally, he zeroed in on the sound of rustling branches and unsteady footsteps as they trod upon dry twigs and fallen leaves. He had found the girl, yet Fox was no voyeur, and fully intended to grant her privacy as long as he could be certain that others intended to afford her the same privilege. For a moment he rested there, quiet and still, letting his senses describe his environment. It wasn't long before, having focused himself entirely upon this single area in the small forest; his keen ears detected the footsteps of drunken, clumsy, and rushed footsteps heading in the girl's direction.

Wasting not a moment, he raced across the treeline, somersaulting and vaulting himself from branch to branch with skill that would shame the most accomplished of tumblers. As he veritably flew through the air, he knew that even his unmatched speed would not be enough, for he had much distance to cover and would never reach the young girl before her assailants. Recklessly he allowed his arms and face to become viciously lacerated, for his breakneck pace meant that every passing tree branch was a lance and every leaf a razor. He had yet covered half the necessary distance when his worst fears were realized. A short, high pitched shriek was instantly muffled. This was followed by visions of a clammy hand which must have stifled it. The ensuing laughter confirmed the image in his mind's eye. As he hurled himself down through an opening in the trees where a small clearing could be seen, he reached into his jerkin and removed a handful of daggers. Here, there was no need for him to conceal his skill, for he intended to leave none alive who could attest to it.

Every second wasted felt like an eternity, yet his efforts had not been in vain; for as he plummeted to the forest floor like some errant missile, he could see that Sariss yet struggled with her attackers- that she was not yet harmed. Falling from the sky to descend upon his prey, now fully sober due to a surge in adrenaline, the entire scene was analyzed in the span of a swift intake of breath. Five men formed a circle about the panicked girl. She was held firmly in place by a massive arm, heavily corded with muscle, the hand of which was so enormous that it covered near the entirety of her pale visage. The man who held her did so with little effort, for he was the largest such man that Fox had ever encountered. His bald pate and purple scar which lent malice to his sneer were equally recognizable, for there was something in their first meeting which informed Fox to the core of his being that he would be the one to kill him.

His rapid descent was preceded by a shower of daggers that fell upon the men with unerring accuracy, as though the sky itself rained deadly steel. No sooner had each blade found their mark when Fox himself crashed down into the clearing. His padded boots absorbed much of the impact when he struck the ground, and his heavily muscled legs were kept from breaking under the strain as he immediately threw himself into a roll. His shoulder took most of the impact, striking the ground with such force that the recoil planted him firmly back onto his feet- crouched in defensive stance. For a moment he stood there, snarling at his adversaries, his two remaining blades held one in each hand, a trail of green fire still lingering in the air, tracing the path of his descent and smoldering in his fiery gaze.

For a moment all was still. The shock of the sudden appearance of what seemed to be nothing less than a vengeful forest spirit had stunned all those present into momentary silence. It wasn't until the uncanny scene was accepted by his prey that realization dawned. Four of the men fell to the ground, shrieking and clawing at the hilts of the daggers impaled in their shoulders. Such was the angle of Fox's cast that, were it not for the protection of their armor, each blade would have likely shattered their collarbones. He had not risked targeting Sariss's nearest assailant, for fear that he might have harmed her, and the giant who still held her in his grip was the first to break the silence.

"You!" shouted Barratus "It would seem the peasant boy fancies himself a fighter!" he spat the final word upon the ground, punctuating the sentiment further by tossing Sariss there as well. In one smooth motion, Barratus unsheathed his blade. The heavy iron broadsword was so large that Fox doubted if another man could have wielded it. Sizing up the situation, he realized that his daggers would prove to be less than ineffectual against such an enormous weapon. The thin metal blades would shatter like glass should they attempt to parry a swing from Barratus's own. He would have to rely on his speed if he were to defeat such an adversary. Likewise, the curved scimitars of the rest of the soldiery, though not so massive as that of their Captain's still held Fox at an extreme disadvantage- if he allowed them time to unsheathe them.

Without wasting a moment, Fox spun about the clearing, hacking and slashing with his two remaining daggers, intent on finishing the work their mates had started. So fast was he, that no blade was raised in resistance against him as the soldiers fell like shorn wheat beneath the scythe. Blood canvassed every surface of the battleground when the hurricane fury of Fox's attack had ceased. Four bodies lay at his feet, each with their throats slit, two of whom still gurgled mouthfuls of blood as they futily clung to life- the rising dust in the wake of the storm still swirling about them. Through it all, Sariss, still prostrate upon the leafy floor, looked on with fearful eyes nevertheless churning with wonder and amazement.

Barratus placed his massive sword in ready position. Despite having himself born witness to the superhuman display of ferocity, he stubbornly refused to fear a man he thought so far beneath him.

"It would seem as though you are not whom you claim to be young pup." Barratus growled. The big man was smiling in anticipation. "Some ghost from my past perhaps, sent hither on some great revenge quest?"

"You think too highly of yourself you sweaty mountain of lard." Fox responded. He had fully intended to savor his kill, and was preparing more insults when his keen ears detected a distant crashing through the underbrush. It would seem as though the noise of the battle had netted attention from the nearby festival. The time for verbal jousting was over. He crouched low in preparation to spring. Each of his small blades held in reverse position and dripping blood upon the ground, yet still with thirst unquenched.

"You are indeed adept with those toys." Barratus sneered "Yet do you truly believe you can face my sword with knives fit for naught but buttering my bread?"

Wordlessly, Fox pounced. He feigned attacking the high ground and leaped for the big man's head. Barratus swung his massive sword in response to the bluff. Fox spun about in mid-air, allowing the double-handed broadsword to cleave through the night where his own head had been mere moments before. Once again tucking himself into a roll, this time ending behind his adversary, Fox sliced at the tendons at the back of Barratus's ankles, cutting through his calvary boots to sever them in twain. Howling in pain, Barratus's engorged fingers let loose the giant sword which fell to the ground with a thud. The giant attempted to turn about that he might face his tiny adversary, yet his wounds forbade such an action, for his severed arches refused to support the enormity of his frame. Like a falling tree he thudded to the ground, the impact of his fall causing all the nearby leaves to rustle in agitation.

Fox stood over the prostrate form of his fallen foe. He momentarily savored the moment, not caring that the rushing footsteps of those in the distance grew nearer. He stalked about his fallen enemy with pantherish grace, teeth bared; allowing the knowledge that he was about to die fully grip the captain of the guard. He paced about a moment longer, then, with savage eyes wide with bloodlust and alit with emerald fire, he stepped in for the kill.

"Halt!" came a voice, ruining the moment. Fox recognized it instantly as the commanding voice of Captain Darus. He spun about to see the Captain crash through the nearby thicket. Instantly, Fox sprung backwards into a shroud of leaves, disappearing fully into the forest.

Darus materialized with Aron and a full compliment of soldiers on his heels, each wielding lanterns which lit the clearing like a wildfire. Sariss was in a sitting position at this time and had regained much of her composure. Her father dashed to her side, throwing himself upon the ground and placing a comforting arm about her.

"Daughter!" he cried. "Are you all right?!"

The regiment had formed a tight perimeter about the scene, and with military precision formed a solid wall about Darus as well, their scimitars unsheathed and at the ready. For a moment all was still, the piercing eyes of the Captain, red with the blood of his savage ancestry scanned about the nearby trees. Barratus, thoroughly defeated and humiliated, managed nevertheless to rise to his knees.

"Captain..." he began

Darus's eyes hovered momentarily upon Sariss, now in the protective embrace of her father. They rested momentarily on the corpes of the soldiers that lay about before setting their gaze on Barratus.

"Men." He growled "Leave these bodies to feed the crows.... and somebody fetch me a noose."

Fox had long since made his way back to Metropolis by the time the news had spread. The scouting party with Darus at its head had not yet returned, yet somehow the camp was already abuzz with rumors about their late night encounter. Evidently a vengeful spirit of the forest had seemingly laid claim to the lives of those who had attempted to trespass upon its domain. There seemed to be no great regret evidenced in the voices of those who told the tale as they passed tankards about. Captain Barratus and his lieutenants were clearly not a popular presence among the caravansary. Many of the aforementioned tankards were raised in celebration, and not in mourning, of their untimely demise.

Fox was sitting alone sipping a cup of spiced wine when the military party returned. The forest was now a great source of supernatural dread, and none dared to go near it. There were murmurs of shock and awe when Darus emerged through the trees and set foot upon the sand. Closely behind him were his men, who walked astride a large black warhorse burdened with the weight of Barratus himself. The Captain of the guard was being dragged across the dunes where he lay upon a bed of branches lashed together with twine. At the rear, with a soldier on each side of them, walked Aron and Sariss, both of whom bore grim looks of fiery vengeance in their eyes.

Fox could not know what had transpired in his absence. He was certain that he had remained unseen. He was also reasonably sure that Barratus would not had betrayed him, for such men were slaves to their pride, and this one would never have revealed that he and his men, fully armed, had met their match in the form of a single peasant boy armed only with daggers. He was nevertheless seething with inner turmoil, for though he cared for the woman, he could not be certain of Sariss's account. Had she informed Darus that her savior was not, as rumor spoke of, some ghostly forest elemental, but the nebbish steel merchant they had been travelling with, then Fox was certain that he would have to answer many questions for which he had no readily available answers.

Hiding in the crowd, he watched intently as Darus cleared a circle. There was much shuffling about, and Fox weaved his way through the people carefully, so as not to be seen. He could see Darus barking at his men, and briefly he suspected that the Captain had been issuing orders for his capture, but his fears were quelled when he saw a rope being strung across the eave of the tallest of the encircling wagons. He entertained the notion of disappearing into the night. He could have easily slipped away and made good his escape through the forest. He had, after-all, intended to make the journey to Damaas alone. Though the idea was sound, Fox entertained it only briefly, for he felt a great pull within him to bear witness to the fate of Barratus. Fox was, after all, a master of the art of hiding in plain sight. With this in mind, he continued to shuffle through the crowd until he was within sight and hearing range of what appeared to be a firelight execution.

From his vantage point, Fox could now see clearly as Barratus was placed atop a small stool. Darus himself corded the noose about his neck. The sight was gristly comical, for the large man had to balance upon his severed arches lest he stumble and hang himself. The firelight itself described a keen juxtapose between Darus and Barratus, for it seemed to rest gently upon the features of the Captain of Metropolis, painting the portrait of a handsome, stoic, and almost serene man in its amber hues, whilst simultaneously flickering agitatedly upon those of the Captain of the guard, highlighting his grotesque and hideous visage and causing his monstrous scar to glow ominously.

"Captain Barratus" Though Darus did not deign to raise his voice, such was his commanding presence that all gathered about heard him clearly- like an ominous whisper meant for them alone. "You are charged with the attempted violation of one who has been offered the protection of Metropolis. As Captain of this caravan, I am responsible for the safety of all those in my charge; therefore it falls to me to declare your life forfeit. Do you continue to deny this accusation?"

Faced with the grim reality of his own dire circumstances, here at last, Barratus appeared to realize that his fate was now fully in the hands of a man who knew the truth when he heard it "Very well!" he shouted in defiant admonishment "Yet who among you would deny me my fun? She is but a peasant girl! We are Raimian! I name you hypocrites! The lot of you! Is not the entire purpose of this campaign to bring such peasants to heel?! These are but the spoils of war!"

"Silence!" Darus shouted "You dare?! You would add treason to your crimes?"

Fox was alarmed. It would seem as though the giant had alluded to a plot with layers of complexity far more sinister than even the gruesome circumstances he now found himself in. He had no time to contemplate this however, for upon hearing the words, Aron lunged. Immediately, all of Fox's attention was on the patron farmer. His efforts to claim the giant's life himself were halted as quickly as they had begun however, for the guards who stood at either side of him, with great effort, managed to restrain him. Fox sympathized greatly with the man. He knew of the passion which drove Aron. This was not the first time he had found himself defending his family from those who thought themselves his betters. It had cost him his wife. He would, Fox knew, gladly sacrifice his own life in protection of his daughter.

"Will these then, be you final words Captain?" interjected Darus "I would advise you to choose them well. There is yet time to reclaim some semblance of honor."

"Halt!" Came a sudden cry, interrupting the proceedings. All eyes turned in the direction of this upstart only to find that the voice emanated from the slight form of the King's advisor, Felix. Like a strutting peacock come to peck, the audaciously garbed lickspittle ran into the clearing, panting vainly in attempt to catch his breath.

"Captain Darus!" he shouted "I must protest! The King will not be pleased! Barratus is one of our finest generals! He is to be instrumental in what is to come!"

Murmurs of disapproval shot through the assembled gathering, and Fox was certain that this was not simply due to the bloodlust which often enveloped such a crowd at public hangings- there was more here than could be so easily explained. Barratus was guilty, he had admitted to the crime, and the resentment felt by those who had lived their entire lives the victims of such injustices was not so easily quelled.

"Tell the King what you will!" Darus shouted back, and Fox was amazed to see that the usually stoic Captain had now well and truly lost his temper. He turned to face the assembly before speaking again.

"Let it be known. Though peasants they may be, these were guests upon my vessel. No man; be he Lord, wastrel, or one who shares my own rank in Marcus's great army, shall be granted leave to harm those I protect. This was not merely an attack on the girl, but upon mine honor! Raimian or no, a man who forfeits his honor has no claim to life."

With these words Darus turned to face Barratus who met his fury with a mask of pure hatred. With a hard kick, he knocked the stool out from under him. A sickening thud could be heard as the giant's neck, a victim of his own enormous size, snapped. His eye bulged from atop his scar whilst the permanent sneer it etched into his face became frozen in place. Though the scene was a ghoulish one to behold, Fox noticed from where he stood in the distance that neither Aron nor Sariss averted their gaze.

The crowd had long since dispersed and Sariss and her father had made their way back to their camp in the small forest. None had dared enter after them, for fear of the vengeful wraith which would now forever haunt these woods in the imaginations of all who heard tell the tale. Fox had returned to his cup of spiced wine, and was in the process of once again trying to befuddle his senses when he was approached by the same young man who had escorted he and his friends to their camp earlier in the day. The youth still wore his full complement of armor. The snake and crown emblem upon his breastplate was highly polished and reflected the firelight like a beacon. His demeanor told that he had not partaken in any of the libations of the evening. Clearly, this one was utterly devoted to duty.

"Costa." he announced "I have been searching for you. Captain Darus requests your presence."

"No more orders from the Captain." he responded, his demeanor matching his temperament "I suggest you leave me to my cups, lest you have failed to notice that I wear not the crest of Raimia."

Surprisingly, the youth's sterness softened, as though he was not at all surprised by the reaction. "Perhaps you believe all soldiers lack the will to think for themselves. I follow Darus not because he is my Captain, but because he is a man of honor. Lest I miss my guess, he has done you a great service on this day, or perhaps you are a man with whom honor holds no meaning."

Fox rose and cast the full weight of his penetrating gaze at the young soldier. His eyes began to smolder. Faced with the smoky fire of those eyes, the youth flinched as his body began to quiver with restrained tremors. Nevertheless, he stood his ground.

"Very well." Fox smiled. Despite himself, he could not help but admire courage, even when such was displayed by a soldier. There too was his own curiosity, which could always be depended upon to get him into trouble. "Lead on."

The two men made their way back to the Captain's quarters which now rested at the foot of the tower which marked the hub of the festival. So devoted to duty was the soldier that Fox doubted if he could engage him in conversation even if he cared to, which was well, for he was in no humor. As they walked in silence, the revelers about them, Fox was pleased to note, had thrust themselves back into the festivities with a vigor which suggested that they had either forgotten about, or were celebrating the recent hanging. Either way, they paid the duo no mind; so eager were they to make the most of their one night's merriment.

They arrived in front of the enormous wooden door once manned by Barratus himself, which now separated the Captain's quarters from the night, and the guard rapped loudly upon it with the metal knuckles of his gauntlet. Fox had scanned his escort as they made their way hither, yet he betrayed no knowledge as to why Fox were being summoned.

"Enter." came the strong voice of Darus upon the other side. The sentry left without a word as Fox made his way through the doorway.

The scene played out exactly as it had before. Once again the Captain sat at his large oak table, pouring over his navigational charts as though the dramatic events of the evening had not transpired. Without raising his head from his work, he spoke.

"Costa wasn't it? Thank you for coming."

Fox remained silent

At last, Darus broke from the rehearsed pattern. He rose from behind the desk and began to pace about the chamber. He eyed an assortment of weapons mounted against the wall before he spoke again.

"I understand you are a steel merchant who operates out of Gemmen. Tell me Costa, have your travels ever taken you as far as Raimia?"

"No" responded Fox. He wasn't so much uneasy as he was angry. Though his work often forced him to assume various aliases, he was never forced to justify one for so long a period. It had not escaped his notice that the Captain appeared to be well informed. He was clearly attempting to ensnare him with perceived superior intellect. Perhaps he felt as though Fox would some how betray himself. Either way, the condescention was clear. Soon, this man would learn that he was no marionette who would dance upon the whim of another he told himself.

Darus turned and looked at him before he spoke again. As ever, the man's implacable nature and finely chiseled features betrayed no malignant intent.

"That is a shame. It is the most beautiful Kingdom on all of Balthazar; a place where art, culture and technology have been cultivated to a degree which eclipses all others. Though I have dedicated my life to her service, I must admit, it hasn't been easy. I am a proud father of two sons, and rarely get to see my family. My duties often keep me away for a season or more, and I have little opportunity to see them grow.

"I estimate that a barbarous Hillman would indeed face many challenges amongst such cultured elite." Fox retorted

Darus merely smiled, refusing to acknowledge the blow. "Quite. Though if Barratus is any indication, such is not always the case. Do you know why such a brute was assigned to this post?"

"I do not." responded Fox who now seethed internally. He had indeed betrayed himself he realized, for calling into question a man's low-born status ran contrary to everything he believed in. In doing so, he had unwittingly surrendered the moral high ground.

"He was assigned here because he was rumored to be one of the best swordsmen in all of Raimia."

"It would seem as though he fell somewhat short of his reputation." Fox retorted

"Indeed." Darus made his way back to his table and sat behind it before he spoke again

"Congratulations are in order I am told. Your proficiency at the dagger throwing competition is still being lauded by my men."

Fox chose not to respond.

"Before departing Raimia I was granted leave to spend some quality time with my family. The boys and I often play a game called

'Soldiers and the Fox'. Have you heard of it?"

"I have not." Fox responded, betraying no emotion

"One boy takes on the role of the Fox, that legendary bandit from out of Gemmen, the rest of the children are the city guard. The Fox's job is to hide from the guard. Whosoever finds him gets to become the Fox, and the game begins anew. I will admit; being a Captain myself, I was taken aback by the fact that the Fox was the hero in this game."

"No doubt."

"Well." Darus clasped his hands together. "I must confess that I was not entirely honest with you earlier. In fact, I am overjoyed at having to cut our maiden voyage short, for I greatly look forward to being reunited with my sons... However, if your travels ever take you as far as my home.... It would be my pleasure to introduce you to the game."

"I look forward to it." Fox replied smiling

"You did say that your destination was Damaas did you not?"

"I did."

"Then safe journey to you." The Captain returned the smile.

Fox spun on his heel and left the room. Despite himself, he could not help but feel ill at ease. In the past, he would simply have shed such a state of mind as easily as one might old clothes. On this day however, copious amounts of ale were called for in order to aid the transition.

He made his way as far from the Captain's caravan as possible, availing himself of a bottle of Raimian spirits as he did so. Upon arriving at one of the many wagons which crested the edge of the forest, Fox burrowed his way underneath it and uncorked the bottle. He did not wish to think about what events the morrow might bring, and was determined to imbibe enough of the draught to keep himself from doing so.

CHAPTER THIRTEEN - THE POOL OF MIST

Fox awoke with a stiff chill that ran throughout his entire body. He had spent but one night in the desert previously, and on that occasion, he found warmth next to the firm body of the peasant girl. Such was his haste at finding solitude during this occasion that he underestimated how cold the desert sands could become when denied the rays of the sun, especially when compared to the scalding heat they absorbed during the day. His humor proved to be as mercurial as the weather as he looked down at the now empty bottle of Raimian spirits which lay pressed uncomfterably beneath his pelvis and marveled that he had imbibed so much as to keep him from waking. The sun had not yet fully risen from behind the dunes and he felt a sudden urge to stretch him limbs so as to resuscitate the circulation within them.

Darus was not so cruel a leader as to rouse his men upon the epilogue of such a legendary night of debauchery. Better to let the men recover so that the machine of Metropolis could operate at full capacity rather than be helmed by men dead on their feet. As such, the camp was quiet and still. Fox had no desire to wait about until the area swelled with activity, for having much experience in the matter, he was always keenly aware as to the best time to take his leave of an environment which no longer tolerated his presence. He crawled out from under the wagon, dusted himself off, and ambled off towards the nearby forest.

Upon cresting the tree-line, he came to the small river which ran about the oasis. Wasting no time, he fell to his knees and dunked his head into the cool water. He had not yet shaken the chill which lingered on his bones and the added cold had the effect of jolting him fully to wakefulness. He could not help but lament that no matter how many libations he partook in, he always seemed to recollect whatever trouble he had gotten himself into the night before. Now lying prostrate upon his belly, his head still fully submerged in the stream, he lay motionless whilst attempting to organize his frenzied mind into a semblance of cohesion. The swirling water continued to assault him, both aiding and impeding this effort. Fox had never found success when it came to organizing his thoughts, and his brain, still racing at manic pace, dismissed each idea he cobbled together outright. He had never been able to agree with himself on much, and wasn't particularly fond of his own mind on the best of days, for despite many offerings of friendship, the two could never seem to reach an accord. Doubtless he would run out of breath and drown himself before he was able to decide on a proper course of action. One thing he and his still swollen brain could agree on was that he had not taken the time to acquire the finest horse in Gemmen merely to abandon the mare now. If only she were tethered a fair distance from the peasant family where he could secure her whilst simultaneously avoiding them. His persona of Costa the steel merchant was now well and truly compromised, and Fox had no inclination to explain his actions to anyone, much less an overbearing father and his nettling spawn whom he owed no allegiance.

His lungs were on the verge of collapse when the solution suddenly presented itself. If he but waited long enough, hidden from prying eyes within the trees, he was certain that the family would leave without him, leaving his horse behind. The notion brought him so much joy that he ran off at breakneck speed in their direction that he might share with his new friends his elation at having thus eluded them.

As he burst into the clearing, he saw that Aron, unlike Captain Darus, had not afforded his party the luxury of sleeping in. He and a weathered-looking Erik, whose battered and bruised face told that nursing his hangover in the presence of his stern father was yet a better idea than the company he had been keeping the night before, were busy securing the wagon. Nearby, Luther and Lola were munching happily, blissfully unaware that the oasis was now haunted. His eyes drifted to Bolt and found that Sariss was patting her lovingly upon her flank. Fox could not help but feel the sting of betrayal.

"Costa!" Aron bellowed upon seeing him. He bounded over to his side and Fox momentarily feared what the big man's intentions towards him might be. He was taken completely off-guard when he placed a meaty hand on each of his shoulders and gripped him in an enthusiastic embrace.

"It is good to see you lad! When you did not return, we feared the worst!"

Out of the corner of his eye, Fox scanned the rest of the group. Erik hung his head pensively, as though Fox's presence somehow shamed him. Sariss refused to cast a glance in his direction. Luthor and Lola continued to munch away at the grass.

Aron's voice took on somber pitch as he proceeded to relate to him the events of the night before, and Fox was pleased to note that he himself was not mentioned in the telling of it. He feigned surprise and horror at regular intervals, and, for his part, informed Aron that he had spent the night dicing and was completely unaware of what had transpired in his absence. The two men were still conversing when Sariss approached.

"Come father." she said "The wagon will not pack itself."

"Indeed daughter." he replied, smiling at the rebuke before turning his attention back to Fox "Costa, will you be joining us? The road ahead is perilous, and though you claim to be no fighter, we could always use another set of hands. Those of a friend would be most welcome!"

Fox merely nodded. His attention was focused entirely on Sariss, who was already making her way back towards Bolt.

"Costa." Aron whispered so that none but he could hear "Should you feel so inclined, I would appreciate you joining Erik to fetch water from the river. We have yet a full day's march before we reach Serdia, and I am worried about my daughter. Though she complains not at all, I fear that her recent experience has left her shaken. I would like some time alone that I might attempt to console her."

"Of course." replied Fox, genuinely understanding

Aron gave him a smile full of warmth and went off to speak to his son. For a moment, Fox stood alone. He could not help but stare openly at Sariss, who seemed content to completely ignore him and was once again doting upon Bolt. The mix of several emotions which assaulted him were all of them unknown. The horse, having seen Fox staring at them, returned the affection with all the zeal of an unrepentant traitor. Slowly, like a man burdened with a great weight, Erik approached him with their stores of empty canteens in hand.

The pair made their way to the stream in silence. There was clearly something bothering the boy beyond the general sense of despondency which now hung about the air. The trek to Damaas had taken a decidedly dark turn, yet all had worked out in the end, and Fox could not understand why such gloom had gripped him. Fox always enjoyed silence, and as a whole, felt as though Erik spoke far too much, yet this drastic change in demeanor began to unnerve him. By the time they had reached the river, and Erik had not yet muttered a word, Fox decided that were someone to break the silence the task need fall to him.

"That's quite a bruise you're sporting lad!" he said, indicating one of the many purplish welts on Erik's cheek "A jealous husband perhaps?" Fox could only hope that the jest would make him smile. Though it did not have the intended effect, he was nevertheless rewarded with a reply.

"Aye. It would seem as though the gypsy girl I met who proffered herself to me was not entirely honest. She had been sworn to another and I was ambushed by her promised and several of his friends."

"I see." replied Fox, who by this time was filling his canteen in an effort to make the conversation as casual as possible

"Perhaps you do not." The boy responded, now gazing at the sky as though he had something important held at bay which now threatened to spill forward

"The group was no trouble." he began, and Fox could tell outright that he was, for once, not being boastful "Since the death of my mother, I have trained everyday in the art of swordplay. Even without my steel, I was able to make short work of my attackers. One by one they fell before my strength, speed and skill. Many such brawls have I engaged in whenever my family traded in Gemmen. In truth, despite being the recipient of a few errant blows, I thoroughly enjoyed the thrashing I gave them... When I was finished I took the gypsy girl back to her bed and we made love 'til morning. I had only just returned with little sleep prior to your arrival."

Fox was generally perplexed. He ceased his chore and turned to face the boy before speaking.

"Then why so dour? It would seem as though you had a rather enjoyable evening."

Suddenly, Erik plopped himself down upon a moss covered boulder and buried his face into his hands. For a moment, all was still. When he raised his head, his face was streaming with tears.

"Because I wasn't there!" he cried "I should have been there! What good all of my training if I cannot even protect the ones I love?!"

Fox was stunned. For a moment, all was still. He knew that the boy was in need of consoling, but having never been in such a position before, he had no idea how to go about doing so.

"Though father will not admit it, I am sure that he is ashamed of me."

"I do not believe that is so." Fox replied, finding his voice

"You do not know him Costa. Never has one met a man more devoted to duty...to his family... Night after night I would see father come in from the fields, his hands bleeding; his back arched, driven to the brink of exhaustion. It was not just to provide for us that he worked so hard... Never afore has a farmer paid the enormous sum charged by swordmasters to train a peasant. Season after season he would hire the greatest warriors in Gemmen to make the trip to our homestead that they may train me in the art of fencing and combat... Though it was never his intention that I join Alric's army... He did not want me to become a soldier... merely a protector- someone who did not turn his back on his family when they needed him."

Suddenly, Erik stood up straight. As he rose to his full height, it seemed a transformation took place. When he stood fully erect, the transformation was complete.

"Never again." he whispered to the breeze

Erik turned about slowly and stalked off towards the camp. Fox stayed behind to fill the canteens alone. Clearly, there were amends to be made, ones which the farmer's son intended not to shirk. The irresponsible boy who was once Erik was left abandoned upon the river's edge. Fox could only hope that he himself would ever be spared such a fate.

Fox returned to the campsite laden with water. He was not at all surprised to note that all was in readiness for their departure. Nonetheless, Erik was pacing about the site diligently, seemingly intent on proving his newfound devotion to duty. Aron and Sariss stood side by side next to the wagon, and though he could not hear their conversation, he was pleased to note that the big man's attempt to further bond with his daughter had apparently been successful, for each bore a smile which stood in stark defiance to their recent troubles and spoke strongly to the fortitude and perseverance of the hard working men and women of Balthazar that was their stock.

Aron had wisely chosen to waste little time and the party set to immediately in an effort to distance themselves from the still slumbering city on wheels. Sariss, as per usual, rode atop the wagon, manning the oxen, with Erik once again on point. Aron walked astride his daughter, and Fox and Bolt made up the rear. Fox decided to make this leg of the trek on foot for he had never before ridden horseback for so long and lacked the bowed legs which the plainsmen were known to possess from so long in the saddle. This agreed with Bolt as well, for being a racehorse, she was accustomed to sprinting relatively short distances, and was not bred to carry a man at a slow pace over long periods. Of the entire party, only she seemed jovial in her gait, and Fox was certain that the attention she received from Sariss that morning no doubt included a healthy breakfast. Should Sariss feel so inclined to tend to his horse as well as she did the oxen, Fox had no doubt she would remain well-fed.

They emerged from the oasis and were once again upon the dunes of the sea of Serdia, though this time the faded outline of a city whose towers peaked above an expanse of forest could be seen upon the distant horizon. The sun washed all detail from sight, yet e'en from his vantage point Fox was impressed at its sheer size. The forest itself encapsulated the entirety of his peripheral vision, yet each time he believed that it had swallowed the city; he craned his head to see yet another tower rising from its expanse. Serdia had a reputation for degeneracy which equaled that of the capitol. Being a port town with with all of the notoriety inherent therein, the promise of unknown dangers and high adventure was rekindled by its sight.

As they progressed towards the looming presense of the city of nomads and neerdowells, Fox's anticipation, as well as the vegetation about them, grew in direct correlation. By midday, the trees had risen high enough so as to fully embrace them, yet it wasn't until they were completely ensconced within the forest that Erik returned to the wagon. With the composure of a trained military scout addressing his captain, he informed his father that he had discovered an old trail in the forest, which, though closer to the main thoroughfare than the patron might have cared for, was still serviceable for their needs. The city itself could no longer be seen from their vantage point, yet with Erik in the lead, hacking and slashing a way through the overgrown path with his rapier, all were confident that they made swift progress.

Being intimately familiar with the woods which surround the capitol city, Fox had assumed all such areas to be more or less the same. Though it was rare that he took any pleasure in being mistaken, and often succeeded in convincing himself that he never was, he was here overwhelmed by such beauty and splendor as he had never before encountered. This was difficult for him to discern, for the fir trees still grew close together, their barbed branches intermingling and acting as netting to protect their saplings, the birch and maples stood tall and erect whilst the poplars bent and swayed in the shadow of the mighty oaks that towered above them all. The forest floor was colored with the same ochres, greens and umber hues of fallen leaves and needles which rested beneath the reds, purples and blues of the flora, adding to their rich aroma- yet there was something alien in these marvels which he had difficulty articulating into thought. The cry of the myriad woodland creatures was of a different intonation, as though here the animals spoke to each other through the trees in a different language, and the landscape appeared as though some artisan, utilizing the same color scheme and palette as those who came before, had nevertheless succeeded in painting an altogether new and innovative canvas. The rest of the party seemed as awestruck as he by the stunning visceral, still wet with dew and surrounded by a veil of mist which lingered from the morning despite it being past midday, for the rays of the sun could not penetrate roof the of trees here lest it be at its full zenith. The canopy now sparkled joyfully at its touch, lending a harmony and accord between each living thing. Soon they arrived upon a small clearing, at the center of which lay a pool whose crystals waters were so clear that one could see to its base. Unlike the dunes they had recently escaped from, there was no sand about the bank; instead, the tall grass which bent inwards to drink marked the sole delineation. Fox smiled in response to the warm sun as it kissed his face. Once again, Balthazar had proffered its reward to those who survived its cruelty. Only now did Fox begin to realize that the tests, and the rewards, grew in intensity the closer they arrived to their goal. What lie in wait for him beond the misty pool he could not know, nor for the moment did he care, so lost was he in the beauty of the moment.

It was here that Aron called them to a halt.

"Well." he began "If I am not mistaken, Serdia lies at the center of these woods not half a day's trek. I believe that we can all agree that it is never wise to attempt entry into such a large city after nightfall. I doubt very much that we shall find a better place to camp than this glen, and we all deserve a rest. Let us set up here. We shall make leave at sunup and arrive before midday upon the morrow. As Serdia is the largest port between Gemmen and Damaas, we can make use of the rest of the afternoon within the safety of her walls to refresh our supplies before pressing further eastward."

"But father." Erik said "Should we press on now, we would arrive in Serdia well before nightfall."

It was hardly a comment either Sariss or Fox expected from him. Aron merely smiled at his son before replying.

"Look about you son. Rarely have I seen such splendor. Rarely, I'd wager, has anyone. We have been gifted in this moment. I would hazard that we have earned it." With these words, Aron inhaled deeply and closed his eyes, smiling as the sun warmed his face. When he opened them again, he seemed disappointed to note that his smile was not reciprocated.

Their experience in Metropolis had ended in heartache for all. Perhaps Aron believed that such a dour lot surrounded by such beauty could not be tolerated, for without another word he stripped himself to his undergarments and, completely ignoring the shocked expressions of those about him, ran headlong into the pool.

Fox was stunned. Momentarily he felt as though the big man had taken leave of his senses. Of their entire party, Aron had been the sternest of the lot. It wasn't until, despite himself, he began laughing uncontrollably at the sight that he understood.

"Come!" the patron farmer cried, now floating on his back and grinning broadly "The lot of you smell like a boar's arse!"

The transformation was staggering. The sight of the muscle-bound giant thrashing about the bath with all of the enthusiasm of a child was felt instantly. Almost immediately, the air of despondency which had followed Fox like a dark shroud was cast asunder. Forgetting all pretence to shame, Sariss threw off her boots and peeled off her tight riding leathers, leaving them to lie upon the ground next to the wagon, which Fox could not help but note, was still unpacked and tethered to the oxen. As she ran towards the pool, now clad in naught but her blouse and a breechclout which left little to the imagination, Fox made every attempt at modesty and forced himself to avert his gaze, only to fail at this completely. Seen in nothing but her undergarments, the lithe, yet rounded figure of the peasant girl set his blood to boil and dried the moisture in his throat. By the time she reached the pool and dove in, he realized that he must have been staring at her rather overtly and finally succeeded in his attempt to look away. He turned his attention instead to Erik who had thankfully not seemed to notice he had been ogling his sister, for his concentration seemed to be affixed on unpacking the wagon.

"Will you not join us?" Fox asked, and was pleased somewhat to note that though the young man was still intent on his duty, he yet sported a broad grin which told that he was not beyond being caught up in the mirth of the moment.

"Not as yet." he said warmly "I'll stay behind for the nonce. Once I have properly set up camp and ensured that the beasts are grazed and watered, I shall join you."

Fox merely shrugged. Sariss had already seen him in his loincloth at their first encounter, and if she was to be brave enough to bare all, than he would not disappoint. He left his clothes in the same pile as both hers and Aron's and ran laughing to meet them.

None commented on his torso, which played host to more scars than most. Never afore had he felt so comfterable in the presence of others. Never afore had he let down his guard so completely. The soft mist which hung about the pool filled each of them with life, just as it did the fauna about them.

They splashed about playfully for a time. This subsided as each entered into a state of deep relaxation and tranquility, yet never did the elation of the moment subside. For what seemed like an eternity the three friends allowed the soothing calmness of the water ease their burdens. Aron was the first to break the stillness.

"If you will excuse me, I believe that I will assist Erik in breaking camp. You two remain here, we shant be long, and once done, I will throw the lad into the water if I am forced to."

The big man crawled out of the pool and lumbered off, tossing his head from side to side, his long hair whipping about his face as he did so. The moisture yet clung to his steely physique which glistened between the patch-work of shadow cast by the canopy of leaves where the rays of the sun pierced it. The shoreline itself was bathed in ambient light, carried upon the mist; ensuring the privacy of those within.

It was in this moment that Sariss waded towards him. The presense of the peasant girl elevated the splendor of the scene to one of sheer ecstacy. Never had a vision of beauty been so complete; never afore so perfectly framed. The water, still and serene, rose as high as her waist where she waded, reflecting her lean, hardened midsection. Her abdomen traced a thin line across its center from her navel to the swell of her breasts where her long dark hair rested, contrasting sharply with the white of her chemise- each clinging wetly to her. The paleness of her face seemed to radiate with a light of its own so that only the darkness of her eyes and the redness of her full lips could be seen through the mist. Beneath the water and magnified by its mirror-like surface, her hips swelled as they wove gracefully towards him, her long, naked legs weaving their spell to great effect. Fox was ensorcelled... spellbound. The spell was broken only when the girl reached him and slapped him viciously across the face.

"Who are you?!" she demanded, her features still beautiful thus contorted with rage. "You who sup at my family's table... you who has shared our confidence... ***my*** confidence... only to be met with lies and deceit?! I shall tolerate such insult no longer! Are you a soldier sent on some secret errand by Alric? A spy? Are we but pawns to be employed in some covert mission? Are you an assassin? Like he who slew my mother?!"

She drew in a lungful of air that she might assault him further. Fox intercepted the blow, holding her hand in the gentlest of grip lest she attempt to pull away. For the moment, she did not. She simply stared at him with an expression he had never before seen and did not understand. Suddenly, and without warning, she pressed her body, and her lips against him. Unthinking, Fox returned the kiss with passion equal to her own. His heart beat against his chest as though it were trying to escape. Once again he let down his guard. As suddenly as it occured, she pulled away and slapped him again.

"Stop that!" He cried, immediately regretting the words as she pulled away further in compliance. His mind raced to come up with an answer to her aggressive line of questioning. He had not accounted for this, nor indeed had he planned on having to ever explain his actions to anyone. Fox was accountable to none. It had always been this way, and he had not thought that this would ever change. Though he had never before considered this a weakness, he knew in this instant that he was mistaken, for this girl had managed to accomplish what many before her had tried and which none had succeeded... she had caught him completely off guard. For a moment his mind raced, stumbled, got its footing- then stumbled again.

"I am known as Fox." he heard himself say rather earnestly "Many have called me the fearsome Fox of Gemmen. I am a thief."

Only twice had Fox found himself incapable of lying. Both involved the peasant girl. He knew not why. It was as though some mysterious force guided his actions. He was powerless against it. He knew not the reaction his admonition would garner him, for until he said the words aloud; he was unnaware that his confession was forthcoming. The silence which followed was maddening. He found himself wishing that she would strike him again that she might end it. He could not read her expression, for her head was bowed. Despite this, her hand yet remained in his.

"I see." she murmured after a time "Yet it explains so much..."

She lifted her head. Once again, Fox was unable to read her. The notion that he might have caused her pain guided his hand as it rested upon her lower back. He told himself that he wished only to console her, yet the fire within him would not be denied. Once again they met in passionate embrace. The mist which swirled about concealed them from any prying eyes save those of a single man whose giant silhouette cut a swath through the veil. Aron, who had just then been returning to the pool, paused only to smile, content in the knowlege that his beloved daughter had found the joy that he too had once known in youth. Such was their stubborness; he had feared that these two might never have figured it out. He stalked away that he might grant them their privacy.

CHAPTER FOURTEEN - THE SLUMS OF SERDIA

The afternoon had transitioned to evening by the time Fox and Sariss made their way back from the pool. Such was the beauty of the day that the sun itself seemed stubbornly reluctant to retire. The mist was yet infused with light, carpeting the landscape with an ambient, ethereal glow which soothed all in its warm embrace. The small cooking fire at the center of the encampment only added to the brilliance. Next to the fire was a veritable mountain of freshly chopped birch and maple wood.

Fox had assumed that, given the small pocket of paradise Balthazar had here rewarded them with, they would simply sleep out under the stars, yet a meticulously put together shelter, nearly a log cabin in its own right, had been masterfully constructed near to the fire, yet still far enough away so that the pine boughs which comprised its roof would not be set ablaze from an errant spark. The cabin had a door made from the wagon's own tarpaulin; thatch made from course birch bark, and was large enough to accommodate all four of them comfortably with room to spare. Fox marveled that many of the citizens of Gemmen itself lived an entire lifetime without ever having such austere accommodations. Aron sat next to the small fire, now dressed in trousers only, the remainder of his clothing hung neatly on a nearby tree limb which had been bent for the purpose. He was busy roasting a hare upon a long poplar branch. Next to where he sat were the bodies of five more rabbits, each plumper than the last.

"Why?!" Sariss ejaculated "Have we decided to stop our voyage here and set up permanent residency?"

Aron looked up at the pair of them and smiled. "Aye." he said, laughing "If someone doesn't put a stop to him, I have no doubt that your brother intends to construct a plow next and begin tilling the land. The lad is still out amongst the forest, this time foraging for berries which he says will make for a pleasant dessert to go with our supper."

Sariss sat cross legged next to her father, while Fox grabbed one of the rabbits and began to skin it with Aron's hunting knife he had set next to the game.

"What has come over him I wonder?" Sariss said

The big man smiled again and seemed about to reply when Erik emerged from the tree-line with a large handkerchief tied to a pole rested upon his shoulder. Inside, Fox could see that the handkerchief was teeming with berries.

"I hope everyone is hungry." he said as he plopped the berries next to his father "This forest is absolutely teeming with food. I found a small field nearby which has enough fruit in it to fill a marketplace. I only came back because I could carry no more. Perhaps Sariss can crush these into a jam. We yet have a loaf of stone-ground flax bread in our stores of food from the homestead lest I miss my guess. I'm going to go back so that we have more for the road ahead. Who knows when we'll encounter such a bounty again."

"No lad!" interjected Aron "You'll do naught but give yourself a bath before we eat. Then you'll sit down, shut up, and get your strength back lest you work yourself so hard that you will not be fit enough for the road ahead."

"But father..." Erik protested

"Enough lad! Do as I say. The meat will be ready by the time you return."

"You are right father. I shall return shortly." Without another word, Erik made his way in petulant fashion towards the pool, shoulders bowed not from being chastised, Fox discerned, but from exhaustion.

Sariss did not comment again about her brother's queer behavior, nor did she and Fox deign to reveal the current state of their relationship. The valley was far too beautiful to waste over such heady concerns, and all seemed to be in silent agreement that, as Balthazar was quite sparing in its generosity, evenings such as this were meant to be enjoyed.

By the time Erik returned from his bath, the rabbits had been seasoned and cooked to perfection. Given the opportunity to fully restock their stores of food in nearby Serdia, Sariss had been quite liberal with their own supply of sundries to accompany the meat. Once again, a rich assortment had been placed upon a large communal plate and a refreshing drink of spiced wine, river water and crushed raspberries had been prepared in a large wooden bowl which was passed about freely. The wine Aron had reserved for a special occasion and he announced to all that he felt this was it. Fox had come to understand the man. He realized that the paradigm shift in his behavior was calculated. Above all, Aron would do anything for his family, and if the smiles upon the faces of those who sat about the campfire that evening were indication, he had succeeded in this endeavor.

The four friends ate and drank until the sun was well and truly set, telling bawdy jokes and embarrassing stories about the other. Fox continued to marvel at the charm of the peasant folk, for being unbound by the constraints of decorum the noble classes caged themselves in, there was no offense given, nor taken, as each laughed heartily at barbs that were aimed directly at the other. Even the despondent Erik joined in on the laughter, revealing traces of his old self, particularly when Sariss regaled the camp with tales of how he refused to wear clothing as a child, and how their father used to have her closely monitor the behavior of her twin when they went to market for fear that the lad would streak down the streets of Gemmen, thereby rending the sensibilities of the noble ladies into catatonic shock.

It was nothing less than a perfect evening; set in perfect surroundings; enjoyed by friends. With bellies full of food, drink and mirth, each retired to the safety of the enclosure grateful for the memories that they would forever hold of that brief moment in time.

Aron and his son fell asleep quickly that evening, yet Fox and Sariss, refusing to let go of the moment, crawled out of the enclosure that they might partake in a midnight swim. Their faces and bodies aglow under the light of the full moon, yet still unseen by any eyes, they made the most of their privacy.

Upon the morning, the party was loathe to leave the glen. Aron in particular was not a man who cared for cities, and Serdia, being the largest of these on the road to Damaas, was not a place he wished to spend more time in than was necessary. The plan was to acquire what supplies they needed, and, as they had little coin for an inn, leave the city as far behind them as possible before making their camp once more- as far from the King's highway as possible.

As Aron had predicted, the journey from the misty pool to Serdia was a short one, and with Erik's newfound enthusiasm and vigor as trailblazer they had arrived at the outer wall before it was yet midday. The companions' path, marked by splendid greens and leafy foliage, soon gave way to the grit and offal of rutted trenches, for each road, even the old trails, joined with the King's highway as they snaked their way towards this final outpost of western civilization. This was expected, for, like Gemmen, Serdia had few points of entry so as to ensure that no traveler could enter her walls without paying the King's toll. The beauty of the misty pool was now but a memory; a pleasant dream contrasted by a nightmare in which every manner of wayfarer imaginable fought with the other in their attempt to make inroads. The sights and sounds seemed to demand of Aron and his family that they turn back. For Fox, they appeared as a balm; an old friend welcoming him home.

Seen from a distance, the wall appeared as long, wide, tall, and likewise impressive as that which surrounded the capitol itself; Fox craned his neck and saw that each rampart was manned by archers, just as each rook held canons within its busom. He suddenly realized that he had underestimated Alric's power. Cammarran had insisted that he learn of the geography and history of Balthazar. As such, he was well informed as to the nature and evolution of Serdia, yet until this moment he never truly believed there existed a city in the west that could compete with that of his home. Serdia represented the final outpost marking the delineation between the provinces of Gemmen and Damaas. For those travelers whose path did not lead further westward, the port was all they would see of Gemmen. Clearly the King had chosen this local to make his might known.

Cammarran himself had told him the tale of Serdia; one not mentioned in the history books; for in truth, the city had grown so large in so short a span that no scribe had yet documented its ascension. According to the Lord of thieves, King Alric's father had shown little interest in Serdia; nor indeed any of the cities which lay within his territory, preferring instead to concentrate all of his attention on the capitol whilst leaving the surrounding province to its own devices and the will of its regents. It wasn't until Alric inherited the throne that the palace tightened its grip on the coin which spilled into Gemmen from its neighbors and scooped it into coffers then drained near to empty. Alric was well aware that Serdia was the most strategically located city in his province, for the paths of most who travelled in any direction upon Balthazar often intersected here. During his reign, the walls and battlements had been expanded and fortified, the marketplace had grown, and inns had been erected on every corner to cater to the transient. The farmsteads which dotted the landscape grew with the economy as demand for meats and produce swelled. The livelihood of those who called Serdia home had become entirely dependent on tourism and trade. Serdia had grown so large during Alric's time that it was now easier for most to pay the exorbitant entry fee than it was to circumvent the port town entirely.

Though the Kingdom of Gemmen was yet smaller than that of Damaas, the province itself was the largest on Balthazar, and by increasing his stranglehold upon all of his fiefdoms, Alric had secured his place in the annals of history as the chief strategist of the four powers. The regent in Serdia had been replaced by one fiercely loyal to the crown, and under his rule, the eastern wall of Serdia was expanded and rebuilt so that it rested directly upon the border of Damaas. In this way, those who chose to enter the east were nevertheless forced to pay tolls to the west. If greed was, as prophecy foretold, the downfall of all great men, then the prophets themselves had failed to impart this wisdom to Alric.

Fox, in his standing position next to Bolt, was forced to grip her reigns tightly, for despite being city bred, such a dizzying array of commotion and the bustle of such a large assortment of irritated pilgrims, merchants and scoundrels, made her nervous and skittish. This was a sentiment fully shared by the rest of the party who, having spent so recent an evening in the comfort of nature's belly, were reminded all too soon of the frustrations inherent in being amongst the populace once again. Luther and Lola, as always, remained completely unaffected.

The highway was so wide across that a minimum of five caravans stood next to each other at any point, and every manner of cart and class, as far as Fox's eyes could see in either direction, were all wedged tightly together as none were eager let another pass as they were funneled forwards. At either side, the massive roadway was lined by rows of veteran soldiers, for the frayed tempers of many a barbarian or mercenary meant that a sword, pike or battleaxe was always precariously close to being drawn, and many skulls had been cleaved by those in days past who had allowed their irritability get the better of them. Next to the soldiers, many of whom had swords drawn, were paupers armed only with shovels, who continuously ran onto the roadway every time one of the larger pack animals defecated in order to scoop up their scat and deposit it in the surrounding woods. Children ran about with pitchers of water and spun copper cups in order to collect payment from any who had not taken the time to pack their own stores. The overall smell and sounds set the tone for what was clearly going to be a long, frustrating experience amidst the gridlock.

Only shortly after merging onto the highway however, Fox became surprised at how quickly they were moving. What had seemed to be an unsurpassable wall of men, women and beast, much to his relief, began to flow like water towards the western gate. In the capitol city of Gemmen, the coming and going of traffic through the great wall had always been slow and monotonous, yet here expediency seemed to be favored above all. A moment's contemplation told the tale... The city of his birth was buttressed by the great western ocean and represented the furthest one could travel in that direction by land, therefore there was no need to fast track entry or egress- all would eventually be admitted, and as they could travel no further without booking passage on a ship, whatever business had brought them thither could be counted upon to be carried out. Here in Serdia however, Alric had clearly set up a much more practical means of expediency, for the longer one waited without, the less time one lingered within, and Serdia was nothing if not a clever snare set in place to net as much coin as possible from the four corners of Balthazar.

Among the extravagant carriages which concealed lords and ladies behind their velvet curtains, drawn by silver stallions themselves draped in like material, and the long trains of mud-caked caravans whose beasts of burden, equally caked in mud, were selected not for their grace, but endurance- there were many smaller wagons belonging to the peasant classes and Fox and his companions soon found themselves in familiar company. A patron farmer, somewhat smaller in stature than Aron himself but with the same bull shoulders and hardened musculature, was escorting his son and daughter into Serdia, and his wagon, laden with the produce of his trade, had become sidled next to their own. The children were much younger than Erik and Sariss, and though they did not seem to be twins, were clearly near in age themselves. The farmer walked in front of the wagon with his hand on the yoke binding two oxen, roughly the same size and demeanor as Luthor and Lola, and his children sat in the wagon itself as they laughed and played. It was not long before the kindred spirits became engaged in conversation with the other.

"Ho brother!" said the young farmer as he addressed Aron. "First time in Serdia, is it?" The children atop the wagon completely ignored the conversation and seemed intent to continue laughing and playing which, Fox was quick to note, no doubt reminded Sariss of days gone by, for she looked upon them with that radiant smile of hers which always seemed to have the effect of breaking through any gloom. It was not difficult to surmise that this family maintained a farm nearby, and were visiting Serdia to sell their wares at market. Aron himself looked upon the children with fond memories of days gone past, when he and his own children made their way into Gemmen in much the same fashion.

"Well met friend!" he replied, struggling to be heard over the bleating of the many pack animals and the ongoing chatter of their owners which had become indistinguishable from the other "It has been a long while for myself, though my children have never been this far from the capitol. Do we truly look so out of place?"

"Ha!" the man laughed "Not at all friend. I know a man who works the land when I see him. Yet you have no wares for market."

"Indeed." replied Aron "Our farmstead lies just outside the Kingdom. I myself spent a lifetime bringing my own children to assist me at market," he waved his hand in the general direction of Erik and Sariss who smiled amicably "though had I known that a man would not have to rouse himself before dawn in order to compensate for the long wait outside the walls, I would have perhaps relocated hither long ago." As if to prove his point, the line shifted once again as they continued to move forward.

"Indeed." said the man smiling "Serdia is a port town entirely dependent on commerce. The entire city is akin to one giant marketplace. Though I can assure you this presents its own challenges, for there is much competition amongst close quarters and I am oft forced to sell my wares at such low prices that it is a wonder I have been able to feed my family."

"Aye." responded Aron "The life of a farmer is fit for naught but the stoutest of men. I am known as Aron. "These are my children, Erik and Sariss, and our travelling companion Costa. 'Twas only recently that you and I were brothers in the same trade, for I have sold our land that we might travel to Damaas."

"I am known as Hiram." he replied pleasantly. The two men gripped each other by the forearm in a manner Fox had never before seen. There were many secret handshakes amongst the thieves guild, particularly, when a thief was casing a property, they would often greet others about that they might discern if these were there for the same purpose, yet it had never occurred to him that the farmers guild would have a means of recognizing their own. "No great land for a farmer in Damaas. What brings you hither?"

"My youngest." Aron beamed with pride as he spoke "Veronica, much like my late wife, has always shown a gift for healing. She has been accepted as acolyte in the Temple of Light in Damaas, the largest such temple in all the four Kingdoms!"

"A great honor that!" Hiram replied "My poor wife spends half of her time patching up my son from the countless scrapes and bruises he always seems to inexplicably come home with. T'would be a boon to have a healer about."

"Aye." responded Aron. "T'was much the same with Erik; though I fear that Veronica was so occupied with tending to the aches and pains of our livestock that she, like her brother, had little time for chores."

Both Erik and Sariss laughed at the jibe. Hiram's children continued to completely ignore the conversation. Fox alone was enthralled, for he had never taken the time to observe how peasants interacted with each other. There wasn't the slightest hint of the type of duplicity and guile which underlined the parlance of the thieves and killers he was familiar with, and though they had just met, the two men seemed to share a genuine friendship such as Fox had never known before he himself came into such company.

"We have received word that she intends to marry into nobility."

Aron continued "The dictates of that class demand that her suitor formally ask me for her hand in marriage. As Veronica's studies forbid her from making the trip, I have used the opportunity to sell our farm to Alric so as to finance our voyage. It is time that Erik and Sariss see more of Balthazar than our small homestead can provide."

"Aye." responded Hiram, gazing back at his own children "One cannot keep them on the farm forever. Balthazar is full of perils that we cannot eternally blind them to. Only be wary, we have made this trek countless times, yet never has the situation here in Serdia been more precarious."

"How so?" responded Aron, genuinely concerned

"The thieves and assassins are currently at war within. Recently their feud has spilled out onto the streets, taking many innocent lives as well as their own. You'll find that the farmers who live hereabouts will not linger after dark."

The words hit Fox like a cudgel. Never before had the pact between thief and assassin been broken. He realized immediately that this, no doubt, had to do with Cammarran's passing.

"The land is rife with the news that the leader of the thieves' guild has himself been assassinated." Hiram continued, as if to confirm Fox's own thoughts "Though order has been maintained in the capitol whilst a successor can be named, the news that their leader is no more has caused many of the thieves this far eastward to begin taking on assassination contracts of their own. Such action has led to all out war between the two guilds. 'Tis no fit place for common folk like ourselves anymore. The criers here have warned the locals that a regiment of soldiers from the Kingdom has been dispatched to deal with the problem, yet those of us who are familiar with Alric and his ways are well aware that the King likely intends to let matters sort out on their own."

"How awful." Sariss replied. Though Fox had informed her who and what he was, he had not told her of Cammarran, nor the bond they once shared, nevertheless, she seemed to display great sympathy which, left unchecked, might betray him. "How was he murdered?"

"It would appear that Krillian, the arch-assassin disappeared these many years, has killed the thief-lord in order to gain information on his newest target- the fearsome Fox of Gemmen himself!"

"Krillian!" Erik suddenly shouted. He took two steps towards Hiram and unsheathed his rapier. "He has returned?! Quickly man, tell me where he might be found, that I may slay him!"

At Erik's sudden outburst, Hiram's own children ceased playing and spun about to look at him. At the sight of the young man who, by all appearances, was threatening their father, they began to wail. Hiram himself, momentarily startled, shifted his hand to his own small dagger which was sheathed upon his belt. All eyes seemed to be now centered on the abrupt commotion on the road. Aron, who had managed to keep his composure despite the alarming revelation, placed a giant arm in front of his son, holding him at bay.

"Peace lad!" he shouted "You draw far too much attention to yourself!"

As the big man shouted, and as though to echo his point, a nearby soldier who had witnessed the outburst came rushing forward.

"What is the commotion here?!" he demanded, his air of authority worn upon his sleeve

"All is well." responded Aron diplomatically

"Indeed." Hiram chimed in "I was... I was just asking the lad if I might see that fine weapon of his."

The soldier cast a glance in Erik's direction, stopping at the rapier in his hand

"It is indeed a fine weapon." he snorted "Too fine for a commoner like yourself. Nevertheless, we do not allow weapons of any kind to be drawn on the highway."

Fox had to admire the way in which Erik suddenly restrained himself. For a moment, he had thought that perhaps he would have to retrieve Fang from where the sword rested in the wagon in an effort to save the boy. Erik gained his composure instantly and re-sheathed the blade.

"My apologies." he said through gritted teeth. The soldier merely snorted in derision once more before returning to his post.

"My apologies as well." said Aron to Hiram "My late wife Esmera was murdered by the assassin Krillian. Until now..." he bowed his head "We had hoped that he had perished."

Hiram seemed genuinely aghast. He walked a few paces towards his children and placed a comforting arm on his daughter's lap, quieting her and his son in the same gesture. He stared into their eyes for some time before he spoke again.

"Then I am deeply troubled to have to be the one to tell you this news. Even now, it is said that Krillian stalks these lands in pursuit of that most notorious of thieves, curse all of their lot! These are troubled times my friend. My own wife Miriam is currently back on our farm tending to our youngest. I could not imagine what it would be like to have to walk through this world without her."

The words cut Fox deeply. Though he himself was but an infant when Krillian murdered Aron's wife, he could not help but feel, as the fates had so inexplicably intertwined his destiny with that of the assassin's, their trouble was somehow of his doing.

Aron did not respond and none had expected him to. Fox's own thoughts were in utter turmoil. He had until now successfully avoided thinking upon the arch-assassin. This man's words had brought him to the forefront of his mind once again. Since he first heard from the bandits he had slain outside of Baraan that he himself was responsible for Cammarran's death at the hands of Krillian, Fox had suppressed his desire to hunt him, choosing instead to pursue his own hedonistic campaign towards the golden city. Upon hearing the rage in Erik's voice that the man who killed his mother had emerged from obscurity, Fox's own rage at having lost a loved one to Krillian's blade would no longer be denied. It was clear to him now that all of his recent troubles were the result of one man's actions. Krillian. It was in this moment Fox understood that he would never know peace whilst haunted by the specter of the assassin.

As the pair of wagons progressed closer to the western gate of Serdia, Fox could think of nothing else. Since he was a boy he had heard tales of Krillian. The assassin was oft referred to as the grim specter of death- the dark lord. Cammarran had often reminded him that he must avoid crossing his path at all costs; that Hergod himself was unable to control him- that if Krillian chose to wage war on the thieves that not even the pact which bound the two guilds would hold him at bay. By the time Fox had reached maturity however, little was spoken of Krillian. The thieves' guild, unlike the local populace, did not hold to the belief that Krillian was dead, for they knew not of any blade which could have performed the task. Krillian had faded from the light, unseen and unheard of, yet remained ever a lingering threat. Now it seemed that Fox had inherited both the threat, and the responsibility which accompanied it. How many lives needed to be destroyed? Krillian was a blight upon all of Balthazar, and though Fox had always forged his own destiny, he began to realize that his blade must eventually cross Krillian's own.

His thoughts were interrupted suddenly, for so consumed by them was he that he failed to notice they had arrived at the gate. Hiram and his wagon were waved past immediately without any demand of payment, for the guard who manned the entrance was clearly familiar with the farmer's comings and goings. As he and his family made their way into the city, he turned to face them.

"Fare thee well my friends! Serdia is a large place and it is doubtful we shall see each other again. However, I am well known at the central marketplace. Linger not about the wall, for this is but a clever trap set to snare the uninitiated! Tell any you see that we are friends and they will treat you fairly!"

"Safety to you friend!" Aron cried back "Take good care of your family!"

The rest of the party merely waved as Hiram disappeared on the other side of the wall.

"Name and purpose of your visit?"

Fox spun about to stare at the guard. The man spoke the words in such a manner that it was obvious his entire job consisted of reciting it. He was an older soldier, still of fighting age, but clearly with enough experience to warrant the position of chief sentry. He wore the standard blue dress of the Gemmen infantry and had a hint of grey in his beard which was un-kept and matted over his dull, unpolished breastplate. Like most soldiers who garrisoned the wall, he was not of noble birth, and was likely granted his post as both reward, and punishment for having been, at some point in his career, a competent soldier. Fox had anticipated the apathetic disposition. He had no doubt that this man found his responsibilities as sentry somewhat less satisfying than the honor, thrill, and brotherhood of the battlefield. It was much the same for the soldiers who garrisoned the wall of the capitol, save for one imminently discernable difference. This man's frustration seemed not to be born of the monotony of his post, but of anticipation of what was to come. Fox stared about and noticed that each and every sentry was animated by the same undercurrent of joyful anxiety. It would seem as though the war between the assassins and thieves had reminded the commonfolk here in Serdia of the importance of men such as these. For those oft ignored and underappreciated, it was important to feel as though one was of some value. On this day, when the sun set, the city militia was all which kept those within the wall from becoming casualties of a war they wished no truck with. Fox had no doubt that these guardsmen, looked upon as naught but an inconvenience, an impediment to commerce useful only for breaking up the occasional skirmish, were granted new respect and admiration from those whom they were honor-bound to protect. It was during these times when their mortality was thus threatened that men such as these felt most alive.

Aron introduced himself and his children and told yet again the reason for their voyage to Damaas. The guard merely scribed what was said with an air of complete disinterest.

"And you?" he said, his gaze affixed upon Fox. For a moment, Fox hesitated. So overcome was he with his own thoughts centered about Krillian that he momentarily forgot his cover story. Was he Barnabas? Costa? He began to stammer.

"He is my husband!" Sariss suddenly interjected, and the rest of the party did well in their attempt to cover their surprise.

"Indeed." Aron replied with a grin "After the wedding I hired my son-in-law to help us with the farm."

"Very well." replied the soldier as he hastily described the information on his scroll. The wagon was briefly searched for contraband, yet this was done so sloppily that Fox laughed inwardly. He knew that Alric secretly approved of contraband being brought into his Kingdom, for in this way, much of the culture of the other powers on Balthazar would be his for the taking, all without breaking any trade agreements himself. Bolt was given an appreciative look yet searched not at all. For this Fox was grateful, for of all of their number, the horse proved the least capable of feigning subordination. The search was conducted swiftly. The toll demanded was a silver coin for each of them and here Fox was himself riddled with anxiety. Doubtless Aron would expect him to have the necessary coin. He was relieved when the farmer reached into his purse and paid for all. They were waved through swiftly, as though the sentry believed that he could somehow bring about the onset of night if he could but rush the day.

"Husband?" Erik chided as they entered the city. Fox was relieved at the jibe, for it drew attention away from the fact that he had no coin. He set his mind immediately to acquiring some lest his cover as steel merchant be called into question.

"It's easier to explain." Sariss responded, seemingly irritated. Despite the bitter news of Krillian's re-emergence, Erik and his father both managed a smile. Fox too, could not help but reciprocate. It seemed that no matter what befell his newfound comrades, nothing could dampen the spirits of those who had long ago made peace with turmoil. The nobility of Balthazar could feel secure in their false sense of superiority, for Fox knew that the peasant classes, those who had known nothing but hard work and toil their entire lives, were truly the more resilient and by far the most noble.

The western gate opened up into a huge marketplace just within the wall and Aron immediately brought them together to confer. Though each was familiar with the heady environs of the markets in the capitol, these were sporadic, separated by burroughs where one could find peace from the overwhelming sights and sounds.

Here, the market seemed to expand beyond one's field of vision so as to be disorienting to the senses. All of the trademarks were here, the hawkers, the traders, the bombastic nobles shouting from carriages they refused to dismount, the commoners haggling over useless trinkets and crude soapstone carvings to be put on display as souvenirs of their voyage- all of this was familiar, yet there was a genuine air of malice about the place which was unsettling even by the cut-throat standards of Gemmen. Here, those caught unawares by a clever swindler would likely never have the opportunity for retribution, for Fox did not need Hiram's council in order to discern that the peddlers hereabout were intent upon grifting the gullible.

"I need not tell you" Aron began, echoing Fox's own thoughts "this market is but a snare for eager rabbits with too much coin and too little sense. We shall heed Hiram's warning and attempt to locate the central marketplace he spoke of. I have no doubt that it lies near the Golden Tower yonder." He pointed off towards the distance. Following him in this direction, Fox's eyes fell upon a large tower which stood above all else and seemed to be situated near the centermost point of the city. Even from this vantage, it drew the eye like a beacon, for it reflected the touch of the sun outwards, beckoning and drawing all towards it. "The Golden Tower is the finest inn in the district and has been here in Serdia for as long as the city has been standing. Many come hither from lands far and wide simply to dine there. I believe we will make better time if we split up. I have a list of items we will need to aquire. We can reconvene at the tower before continuing upon our journey.

"Then we shall meet within its tavern?" Erik inquired

"No lad!" Aron replied, tilting his head back in laughter "Should you be granted entry into such an establishment than you would be the first peasant ever to be afforded the privilege in the generations it has been standing. The Golden Tower makes for a convenient place to reconvene; that is all. Commoners such as ourselves are permitted to visit the garden in the courtyard. It is there we shall meet when we have completed our errands. Given what Hiram has told us about this town's recent troubles, I would like for us all to work quickly so that we might be well and truly gone by the time this place becomes a battleground. If you stick to the items I have outlined we should still have plenty of time to accomplish all and meet up again by late afternoon. I wish to exit the western wall as soon as possible so do not dawdle. If you work swiftly, we should have plenty of time to leave Serdia behind us before making camp as far from the highway as possible."

Erik reached out a hand to grab the thin slip of parchment Aron handed to him only to have it plucked from his fingertips by Sariss.

"If I recall." she said "You spent a great deal more time studying fencing than learning your letters. Best leave this list to someone who knows how to read it." Erik took the rebuke with a warm smile, characteristic of the familiar jousting he and his twin sister so readily engaged in.

"Aye." he responded "I have always maintained that a man need not learn how to read when he has servants so readily available."

Sariss merely laughed in response. Aron too, was smiling when he addressed Fox directly.

"Costa. Should you be willing, there are a few lightweight items that you might obtain for us. Erik and Sariss can take the wagon, the oxen and your horse. Best you bring your sword, for I'll wager that even peasants hereabouts are walking the streets armed if Hiram's story is to be believed. I have little coin remaining, yet you are welcome to it."

Fox puffed out his chest pridefully before replying. It had been far too long since he practiced his art. Perhaps the guild here in Serdia were traitors to the order, yet here at last there was a true thief amongst them. "My thanks friend Aron; though you have paid my passage and shared the food off your table. I relish the opportunity to reciprocate. You need not worry about coin."

Aron smiled in response. "Would that were true. Let us part here. I am set to an errand which, if successful, might just pay for the remainder of our trip."

At this, Aron turned about and rummaged through the wagon until his fingers came upon a tiny satchel buried within the hay. The quizzical expression on the faces of Erik and Sariss told Fox that he was not alone in his ignorance as to the satchel, or its contents.

"And what errand might that be?" inquired Sariss with a furrowed brow "What is it you have there and why have we not been made aware of it?"

"Never you mind!" responded Aron rather harshly "Well enough to know that this trip has nearly bankrupted us already and that there may still be a few men here in Serdia who owe me a favor or two."

Aron strapped the pouch to his belt and turned his attention to Fox. He pressed a thin parchment into his hands which contained a list of supplies, and the thief in him felt electricity in its touch. A contract! Fox could scarcely contain his excitement. He had a contract once again! Often in Gemmen he would take breaks from his life as a thief, choosing to camp outside the walls, or to spend days at a time dicing and drinking, but such intervals always found him back at the Bear's Den in search of some new mission to undertake. Cammarran never complained about his absences, and was always there with contract in hand whenever he wandered back. There was always a wealthy nobleman, or some desperate diplomat willing to pay the highest possible price for the guaranteed services of the fearsome Fox of Gemmen, and, acting as fence, Cammarran had always paid him fairly –though the truth of the matter, both men knew, was that Fox cared not a whit about gold, preferring instead to leave his earnings in cleverly concealed bundles hidden throughout the poorer quarters of the city in order to be found by some ragged vagabond who could make more use of it than he. Fox took on jobs simply for the thrill and challenge of completing them. The list in his hand may not have inscribed upon it some mysterious relic from a hidden tomb in the caves of Mount Gemmen, nor evidence of an illicit activity against a corrupt politician, yet it was a contract all the same! Serdia was perhaps smaller than the capitol, yet still her architecture was familiar, still were there rooftops to haunt and back alleys to explore... He took the slip from Aron with trembling fingers, the result of a heart drumming its excitement.

"Are you entirely certain you need no extra coin?" Aron began

"I believe I shall manage!" Fox cut him off "Have no fear! I shall meet you all at the Golden Tower shortly. You shall find that your trust in me has not been misplaced!"

Fox paused only long enough to pat Bolt lovingly on her flank and retrieve Fang from the wagon. Having done so, he spun about like a top and disappeared into the crowd- leaving his companions decidedly puzzled as to his palpable excitement over being handed a shopping list. Their friend was indeed a strange man. There was little chance of ever becoming accustomed to him.

Fox slipped through the crowd until he was well and sure that he had become completely invisible amongst the throng. Though Aron had counseled him to obtain his goods at the central marketplace, Fox had other plans, for it was in such corrupt environs that he thrived.

Within no time, moving like a wraith through the crowd, he had filled the hidden pockets of his tunic with each and every item his mission demanded of him. With time to spare, he set his sights on the plump noblemen who, confident in their security due to the many patrols of soldiery who clustered about the gate, bullied their way through the masses. Should a nobleman of note be assaulted by the general populace on any given day, then whosoever was posted as guard during that time would be lucky to receive a demotion, yet more likely to be placed in stocks, and it was painful to watch the nobles shove their way past hard men of the working class, many of whom, like Aron himself, had the strength of limb which attested to their long years of grueling physical labor which the nobles themselves so heavily relied upon in order to sate their own material cravings, and left unsupervised, could easily repay such ungratefulness with a savage beating.

It was an amusing game which Fox now enjoyed; one he had played many times in the past and stood as testament to his skills. He wandered about the marketplace, helping himself to the pockets and purses of noblemen, whilst avoiding the cardinal blue soldiers who shadowed them and using the crowd as cover. Whatever he managed to fill his own pockets with was the manner in which he kept score. As he darted about helping himself to whatever he liked, he was pleased to note that his skills had not become atrophied from so long a time spent on the road. With the meager goods Aron had entrusted him with thus acquired, and with no means of locating a fence, he set his sights on netting whatever coin he could.

Serdia was, like the village of Baraan before it, completely unprepared for a thief of his caliber, and Fox soon found that he was so laden with wealth that he could simply carry no more. He set about to find a dark alleyway the downtrodden called home in order to deposit a hidden bundle of riches that he might challenge himself to another game. It was a pleasing way to while away the afternoon and one which he had not realized how greatly he had longed for.

Such dwellings of the lost were never difficult to locate in the capitol- he would simply scan his environment for the most dilapidated buildings he could find. Here in Serdia however his efforts proved to be a chore, for there was little of the city that was set aside for dwellings. Eventually he managed to clear the marketplace and wandered into a rural area that seemed run-down enough to suit his purpose. Such areas never played host to the King's soldiers and represented a safe haven for the destitute and the insane where they could rest without fear of molestation. Having found the alleyway he was searching for, he was not surprised to note that it opened into a maze of streets which led nowhere, both in reality, and metaphorically. Once out of sight, he leaped onto the high arching eave of a doorway which stood perpetually ajar, for few had shown any interest in what might lay on the other side. Here he perched and began to fill one of the many crags with the fruits of his work.

All about him, men and women were cradled in such arches, yet these were far too lost in the smoke of the white lotus to notice him. Many of these had once been noblemen themselves, now forever lost to the allure of that evil plant, which of all the assassins and bandits of Balthazar stood high and above the rest as the greatest thief of both wealth and lives. Cammarran himself had excommunicated many a thief who had succumbed to its allure. It was he who had told him of its origins... The white lotus was a weed which grew sparsely on the plains primarily in Gemmen itself, and though King Alric would never admit so publicly, was one of the chief resources and exports of his Kingdom. Healthy crops were often nurtured by enterprising farmers who owned their own parcels of land and wished to capitalize on the heady demand of the hallucinogen. In ancient times, the various warrior tribes who dwelt upon the plains used the weed in ritualistic ceremonies prior to battle, for one of the side effects of inhaling the smoke of the plant once set ablaze was that it numbed pain, and the trance-like state induced upon those ancient warriors was seen as a bridge- connecting them to the spirits of warriors past. Such ceremonies of noble origin had long since been replaced by sheer indulgence fueled by cowardly designs towards escapism. Perhaps the way of the plainsmen represented the intent of Balthazar itself, though now, with modern horticultural techniques, new strains had been developed with increased potency, and addictive properties, resulting in vile hybrids which fed upon the spirits, rather than enhancing them- of those who inhaled the noxious vapors it produced.

It was during these moments of quiet contemplation where Fox felt the most powerless. Should he shower coin upon these people in an attempt to help them, he would only precipitate their demise, for any alms he bestowed would simply go towards another pipe-full. The sole reason men and women such as these, with hollow, lifeless eyes, yet clung to life, many of them, was simply because they could not afford the lethal dose necessary to end their desperate existence.

His musings were suddenly interrupted by the sound of softly padded footsteps upon the shattered cobblestone. The steps were measured and sure, and decidedly out of place in these environs. From his vantage point, crouched like some stone gargoyle, Fox bore witness to a decidedly healthy looking man as he entered the periphery. With measured stride, he weaved his way down the alleyway; his clothing so generic as to be suspicious. The wasted folk hovelled in the crotches of dilapidated doorframes seemed to be somewhat rejuvenated by his presence and greeted him excitedly. Fox watched as a small crowd formed about him, each more eager than the last. He was not the least surprised to see the man distribute satchels of leafy herbs to all who pawed at him desperately.

Of all those who made their livelihood predicating upon the misery of others, lotus pushers Fox despised the most. These had no guild, much less guild leaders to keep them in check, and thus were comprised of the most immoral men and women on Balthazar. Fox had seen thieves of his own guild, competent men and women, fighters who feared no soldier- laid to waste by the hollow promises of joy and freedom from life's woes that was the stock and trade of such men. Many times in the past he witnessed such transactions taking place in Gemmen, perched high above some dilapidated square in much the same manner as he was now, and always did he intervene with his own brand of harsh, vigilante justice. He was just about to leap into the scene below him, his every intent set upon crippling this peddler of lies and empty promises when something held him at bay. A new actor had entered the stage of the play which unfolded beneath him. A large man, healthy and strong, approached the younger, quiet and determined. He handed him a small satchel full of the same herbs and Fox watched in utter horror as he was met with both a warm greeting, and with a satchel of similar size, this one teeming with coin. The large man was one he had come to know, one he had come to admire, and even, despite his best efforts, to respect. He knew this man was driven by his desire to provide for his family, yet never could he have guessed as to what extent. As the exchange took place, Fox could not halt the momentum of the singular thought which raced through his mind... Aron... What have you done?

CHAPTER FIFTEEN - THE LORD AND LADY OF THIEVES

Balthazar had never before played host to a war the like of which now waged inside of Fox. Two armies faced each other across the threshold of his mindscape, the soldiers of grim truth and those of denial, and though truth was allotted the smaller force- denied any arms with which to defend themselves by a reticent god who clearly favored the other, Fox knew that in the end, they must be allowed to prevail.

His entire life had been defined by the forces of corruption. It was naïve of him to suspect that, having chosen to leave the predatory streets of the Kingdom behind, he would have found anything different, that anything else was possible. He chided himself for a fool.

Aron had both the land and the skills to cultivate and sell crops of white lotus. He had not bothered to contemplate how it was a mere farmer possessed the wherewithal to teach his children how to read, how it was that Veronica was the first peasant ever to be admitted as acolyte into the Temple of Light, nor how it was that Erik had been trained by the finest swordmasters in all of Gemmen. It had not occurred to him that such gifts would come at a cost; that for some to prosper others must suffer. Such was the nature of Balthazar. So it had always been. So it would always be. Had Aron been but a nameless face, yet another player in a game that was rigged; a system poisoned to its core, where the rich lived off of the toil of the poor and all were the puppets of decadent regimes, he would not have cared a whit... The penalty for letting down his guard; for allowing himself the luxury of friends... was the sting of bitter betrayal. The price he found heavier than all of the gold on Balthazar.

Despite himself, he had thought the family to be a beacon of purity in a world gone dark. He had always viewed himself as the hero in his own story, yet he was a thief; a villain in a world populated entirely by villains. He could stand in judgement of no man. There were none who could. The corrosive touch of Balthazar extended across its entire surface. The well was poisoned. None were immune.

With head bowed, with purpose forgotten, he leapt to the alley floor and stalked off in the direction of the Golden Tower, shoulders slumped in bitter defeat. Aron, his clandestine transaction complete, had long since taken his leave, unaware that he whom he believed to be a humble steel merchant had been perched high above him as silent witness to his iniquity. Theirs was a relationship now fortified by deceit. His concentration turned to Sariss. Upon all of Balthazar, it was she alone with whom he shared the bonds of honesty; she alone who remained untainted by the evils of this world which Fox had only now come to realize he was exhausted by fighting. She was as ignorant as he as to the contents of the satchel Aron plucked from the wagon earlier in the day. He could not, would not share this secret with her, even if it meant that there were none with whom he was entirely honest, even if it meant that he become silent accomplice to Aron's betrayal.

The day was young and there was time yet before they were set to reconvene, though Fox found that his newly acquired enthusiasm for exploring and exploiting Serdia had lost its luster. He marched in a straight line towards the tower of gold, a decadent altar to vanity at the foot of which slaves to their basest desires gathered to worship. He did not think, nor care how he might go about whiling away what remained of the afternoon. He was of a single purpose- that of finding the peasant girl, that the very sight of her might remind him that there yet remained something worth fighting for. The wanderlust and thirst for adventure which had always been the hallmarks of his character had fully receded. The trek to the Golden Tower was much longer than he had anticipated however, and despite himself, he proved not to be immune to distractions upon the route. Unlike the capitol, the constant flow and ebb of travelers meant that the culture and ambiance here was in constant flux. It shifted from one man to the next, and Fox soon found that his progress through the city streets was akin to visiting the four corners of Balthazar. Though the Kingdom of Gemmen played host to a plethora of cultures itself, never before had he seen such a variety so tightly cloistered. The explorer within him could not help but be aroused. Slowly, his spirits grew. Once again, he began to take pride in his vocation, for the single commonality most cultures he chanced to come across reminded him of who and what he was. Save for the skulking barbarians of Hyrst who valued a man based solely upon his skill as a warrior, all believed their own value to be inherent in the trifling material goods they spent their lives accumulating- that this was somehow the metric to judge a man's worth, forever to be valued over honor and decency. Only thieves challenged this insanity- that one should loathe he who had more until such time as they themselves could be loathed by those who had less. He and his guild would forever exist as a reminder that should any subscribe to this philosophy, than all that they were could be taken from them in the night.

The closer he got to the tower, the more wealth he encountered, as though the tower itself acted as a loadstone for vainglorious elitism. He began to fill his pockets, already full to brimming as he was too distracted earlier to deposit his riches.

As the tower grew in scale, his environment transformed itself into the central marketplace proper. Here was the home of the more honest of traders. Though the prices were steeper, one could at least be assured of quality and legally obtained merchandise by those who called Serdia home, even though Fox could not guess in which domiciles these actually lived. Perhaps their apartments, those who did not farm the land upon the plains east of the great desert sea, were kept apart from Serdia, so that travelers would never lack an opportunity to spend their coin for want of shop, tavern or inn.

Here Serdia teemed with all that one could desire, fueling the envy of those who had not the means to aquire it. He had no doubt that he was now in the most congested quarter of the city, as well as the most diverse, for unlike the rest of Gemmen, whose ecosystem depended upon the separation of the classes, here, the rule of caste seemed not to apply as noblemen and pauper alike intermingled upon the large open square, every inch of which was teeming with wheeled kiosks, wagons, beasts, soldiers, and every type of colorful character plucked from the four corners of Balthazar. Raimian nobility turned their noses at the local noblemen and women, who in turn turned their noses at the working classes, as all vied for the wares of every type of merchant imaginable. The best Gemmen steel could be found here, the finest casks of wine from Raimia, pelts and furs of unknown beasts from Hyrst, many of which had been cobbled together by mad taxidermists and hucksters, as well as jewelry of spun silver and gold from out of Damaas. How Alric, so far away in his palace to the west managed to maintain control of such an environment, much less insure that he received a percentage of every coin exchanged was a mystery, yet if any were clever, or greedy enough to do so, it was he.

Like some throbbing heart at the center of a gaudy circulatory system stood the Golden Tower. Completely encased in gold leaf, gold trim, and intricate golden carvings, and encircled by the lush garden courtyard at its feet, the tower seemed to emanate its own light source as it radiated outwards and bathed the market in a warm yellow glow. So tall was the tower that the pointed needle at its top seemed to pierce the sun, draining its light and drawing it to its base in a manner that assaulted him with its sheer audacity. Once again he felt as though it fell to him to feel Balthazar's rage. He knew not why. That man should encroach upon the glory of nature in such perverse fashion continued to plague him. Throughout the entirety of his journey he had marveled at the achievements of nature whilst simultaneously revolting at those of man. He seemed unable to cease drawing distinctions between the two. Perhaps one day he would understand why.

The entire structure had the look of a multi-barbed spear, and Fox was here given an inclination as to what the golden city of Damaas itself must look like. If the tower was any indication, the eastern Kingdom was indeed, as all save the braggarts of Raimia claimed it to be, the most majestic upon the surface of Balthazar.

He ignored every barker, every crier, every assurance of the finest quality items available as he made his way towards it, his pockets now jingling with gold, rubies and amethyst. The crowd thinned as he made his way through the latticed gate. Soon he stood in the glorious garden courtyard at the foot of the tower. Had this been the capitol, the courtyard itself would never have permitted the presence of any save nobility. Here in Serdia, the lifeblood of the city was its diversity, and exceptions which threatened the delicate sensibilities of lords and ladies were tolerated. Nevertheless, as no peasant could possibly have business here, the only commoners about were those who had come to glimpse at a world which would forever remain out of their reach. It was astonishing to a man like Fox that such beauty was set in such close proximity to as vulgar a display of greed as he had ever seen and yet all congregated about the latter. It was a quintessential example of everything he knew to be wrong about Balthazar and framed his mood perfectly.

As he roamed about the garden paths in his search for Sariss, he attempted to allow the breathtaking scenery the opportunity to overwhelm his troubles. This was difficult due to the uncomfortable presence of the King's soldiers who silently shadowed his every step, for despite the enchantment and splendor all were invited to gaze upon, these marched about in such numbers that the exotic garden could easily have been mistaken for a barracks. The laws in Serdia may have permitted peasants to wander about the garden freely, yet the sentries who followed their path whilst simultaneously leaving the noblemen and women to their own devices, told of a different, unwelcoming reality. Should any commoner need a painful reminder as to their station in life, the garden, and the elusive tower beyond it, served this purpose well. He was conscious of the sword strapped to his belt and momentarily courted the notion that perhaps it was his weapon which caused such consternation, yet he dismissed the idea outright, for Aron had been correct in his original assumption- most of the peasants Fox had encountered in Serdia had been armed as well, and Fang, being a short-sword, did not appear overly menacing in its worn shagreen scabbard.

The garden was beauty caged by ugliness. The mixture of flowers and fauna from every corner of Balthazar was staggering. Water ran through stone kilns held by meticulously carved sculptures into pools that were decorated with purple lotus petals, kin to the white lotus yet with none of the intoxicating properties and more beauteous by far, and the smell of offal from the market beyond was completely replaced by fragrant, intoxicating aromas. The heady oxygen produced by such an assortment of Balthazar's children lent vigor and fire to Fox's blood in a manner he had never before experienced. Flowers he could not recognize called to him like the voice of an old friend. Expertly wrought benches of iron and brass sat beneath the shade of tall elms, yet still afforded no privacy for lovers due to the many patrols who stalked about the perimeter menacingly. Once, long ago, such flowers bloomed across the entirety of Balthazar, yet here, one might weep that their beauty was both preserved, and tainted by the ignomity of man.

Fox ambled along a meticulously swept cobblestone walkway which wound its way towards the gates of the Golden Tower itself. Each polished stone was so finely set into the other that not a single blade of grass grew within the confines of the interlocking joints. The path arced slightly and Fox could not help but feel as though he were cresting a rainbow, such was the plethora of colors which swirled about him. He remained under constant scrutiny beneath the watchful eye of the suspicious security forces whose rounds on this day seemed to coincide with every step he took. It felt obscene to be wandering a forested path so juxtaposed by the controlling arm of civilization, yet were it not for the diligence of the King's soldiers; he knew that the tower would have been stripped of its wealth long ago.

It was these thoughts which finally succeeded in lifting his spirits. The irony was too delicious to be ignored; for on this day, the Lord of Thieves, the greatest of all threats these guards had trained a lifetime to ward against, wandered about freely in the very midst of the tower of untold riches they were sworn to protect. The entirety of their military training hinged upon keeping one such as he as far from this place as possible, yet every step he had taken in his life led him to this point, to this moment. He wondered if news of the recent war between assassin and thief and the rumors of his own departure from the capitol had resulted in such a large security presence, or if intimidating the locals was simply a favored pastime. Whatever the reason, the knowledge that those whose sworn duty was to guard against bandits now bore the presence of the greatest of any age, open and defiant, was what had finally succeeded in conquering the insurmountable melancholy his other musings had garnered him.

The path he had been following came to an end at yet another iron gate, this one separating the entrance of the tower from the courtyard, and it was here he found Sariss. She stood in the shade of a giant oak tree which was so majestic and ancient that it must have overseen the construction of the tower itself. Her back was pressed against the trunk, and it did not take long for her darting eyes, which had been searching for her companions, to locate him.

"Costa!" she cried

Fox was pleased to note that despite the unrestrained, carefree joy she displayed at reuniting with him, she nevertheless remembered to address him by his alias. He almost wished that she had forgotten; if only to bear witness to the shock and panic of the soldiers that would no doubt ensue. She ran up to him and threw her arms about his neck, and it was as though all of his recent worries recoiled at her touch.

"Is not this place wonderful?!" she said, her smile radiating the light from her eyes as she gazed about in wonder. It wasn't until those umber-hued crystal orbs returned to stare into his emerald ones that he replied.

"Indeed. Has there been any sign of your father and brother?"

"Not as yet. I doubt we shall be seeing them for some time. Erik insisted on taking the wagon and Bolt leaving me to find a few scant items that I could carry on my person. I surmise that he is struggling to read his list of items without me there to help him, and father is still about on his mysterious errand."

With her words, the memory of recent events escaped from the recesses of Fox's mind where he had banished them and threatened to sour his humor once again if left unchecked. The only solace he took was that with Erik's newfound bent towards responsibility, he was certain that his horse was in good hands.

"I tried to smell the flowers, but was driven back immediately by the butt of a soldiers spear..." she began, and the anger which Fox had been struggling to keep at bay came back in a rush, flushing his face red.

"Truly?" he whispered as though unaffected by her words "With his spear?"

Fox paused momentarily to draw breath lest his anger consume him entirely. Struck by a sudden wave of inspiration, he placed a delicate arm across Sariss's pale shoulders and smiled.

"Come! As we are the first to arrive, and have an afternoon unburdened by work, perhaps we can partake in a drink!"

"A drink?" Sariss responded quizzically

"Why yes. Unless I miss my guess, the finest ale for a thousand leagues can be found within!"

With a sweeping motion, he gestured to the Golden Tower. Without waiting for her to reply, he guided her towards the gate, manned by two sentries, only to have their steps interrupted when the haft of a spear was placed across his chest. Such was the reception he had enjoyed innumerable times in the past, yet the thought that his lady had herself recently endured such indignity caused the taut muscles beneath his jerkin to knot together tightly in retaliation.

The guard locked eyes with his, and in an instant, his expression told that he saw death there, for he nearly dropped his spear and shuffled backwards beneath Fox's smoldering visage, ablaze with green fire.

The pair who manned the gate were attired in a manner which suggested that they were not of the King's guard, but private security for the Golden Tower itself. Their long, flowing robes, colored gold with gold trim at the seams and lapels, seemed more at home in a palace than a military station. Contrary to the calloused palms, scarred faces and un-kept beards of the soldiers about them, they sported young, handsome features and well trimmed, curved moustaches. Their fingernails where they gripped their ornate weapons were not blackened by dirt, but well-manicured, and what wrinkles they had upon their delicate features touched their eyes so as to suggest a sycophantic career spent smiling, not scowling. Even the manner in which the guard held his spear spoke to Fox that he had not the slightest idea how to use the weapon effectively, and the ornamentation on its surface he knew to be as useless as the window dressing on his flowery robe.

The second guard, perhaps puzzled by his partner's sudden shift in pallor, crossed the distance between them quickly.

"Halt!" he bellowed with a decidedly unearned air of authority "What business have you here?" Fox could feel Sariss's blood race with anxiety where she was linked to his arm.

"What impudence!" cried Fox, assuming his most aristocratic accent "Do you not know to whom you speak? You have the honor of addressing none other but the distinguished Lord and Lady of King Alric's own house! I shall forgive your ignorance based on our appearance, for we have chosen to travel as commoners in order to provide less tempting targets to the many bandits hereabout upon our journey, yet can you fault us for wishing to refresh ourselves before visiting the King's private tailor here in Serdia? Perhaps this satchel of coin will speak for the veracity of my words!"

With this, Fox tossed a small pouch, teeming with gold at the first of the two guards "Now, open this gate lest I forget my own charitable nature and personally inform the King as to how badly the standards of hospitality at the Golden Tower have fallen!"

The sentry's eyed bulged from over his meticulously coiffed moustache as he gazed in open avarice at the contents of the purse.

"My apologies my lord!" he stammered. He bowed low and stared at the ground before speaking again. "I beg your forgiveness for my lack of decorum!"

No sooner had the sentry thus prostrated himself when his comrade raced back to his post and inserted his spear into a large crank which sat at the foot of the gate. Acting as a lever, the spear was worked in a circle. The gates creaked in welcome as chains attached to pulleys began to swivel them open. Like a veil separating one world from the next, the iron gates parted before them.

Fox, having made a career analyzing and mimicking the body language of others, particularly that of nobles; had no trouble whatsoever slipping into the role he had assigned himself. He strode past the guards, Sariss in arm, with such authority that much of it spilled over into Sariss herself; their linked arms acting as a conduit, channeling his courage, audacity and defiance into her. His complete and utter confidence both comforted, and thrilled her; and she could not help but suppress an inaudible giggle as excitement came over her in waves. With eyes wide as saucers, she placed all of her trust in him, surrendering herself completely, and allowed him to guide her into a world she had only ever heard whispered of.

Arm in arm, thief and peasant strode into the tavern at the base of the tower. So majestic was the inn that even the Silver Stallion in the Kingdom paled by comparison, for there, every polished surface reflected the soft, metallic blue of its namesake, yet here, all was bathed in that unique hue of purest avarice. Every article of furniture, every chandelier, every frame of every masterful painting was plated with gold, from the large, gilded tables, woven tapestries on the walls, to the sculptures of bathers so life-like that they seemed to splash about in the fountains. Golden goblets, inlaid with precious stones, sparkled and played under the brilliant, golden rays, which danced about the room, emboldened by a thousand candles and reflected off of every mirrored surface, so that even the patrons within who stared in open shock as two peasants strode into their midst, seemed to glow as though illuminated by an internal golden fire.

Nowhere was this more evident than on the nubile bodies of the strapping male servants, rippling with taut muscles, whose job it was to operate the pulleys of the lifts which ran through the center shaft of the tower, and whose oiled, glistening bodies drew the gaze of many a noblewoman, whose frustrations at being granted admittance into such a world based solely upon the whim of their fat, slovenly husbands, was fully evident by the appreciative gleam in their eyes and their lustful, pouting lips.

In much the same manner, each scantily clad serving wench appeared as golden, erotic idols as the yellow rays danced upon their every tawny and well-rounded curve where they poured rivers of wine from golden goblets. Even the food itself seemed to have been selected to further enhance this ambience, for glazed hams and meats, rich with sauces, gave the illusion of having been carved from the hinds of mythical golden creatures as they sparkled in their beds of olives and dates. What other colors there were seemed to have been selected to enhance this effect as well, for the red sequined cushions of every chair fully complimented the luster of the jewels ensconced in the intricate weaves of kneaded golden leaves and ivy that wove organically about the table legs and bar copings in interlacing patterns. The spiced mead and honeyed ales lent their mouth-watering aromas to the atmosphere just as the soft, orchestral music of the surrounding minstrels gave it voice.

Seen from the outside, it was easy to see how the Golden Tower got its name, yet when one bore witness to the interior, the effect was so dizzying that Sariss had become completely overwhelmed. Such an orgy of avarice and greed was so terrifying in its beauty that she could not help but momentarily place her forearm across her eyes to shield herself. Fox led her to a table in the center of the circular room and all eyes followed their movement. There he made his presence know by adding to the brilliance as a river of coin fell from his fingers onto his reflection upon its mirrored surface. Sariss closed her eyes momentarily in order to filter the dazzling cornucopia which assaulted her senses, and Fox could not help but marvel as he gazed upon her, for even in such surroundings, her beauty was yet the most radiant of all. Her every pale, soft feature, completely unadorned by pretentious baubles, was proof that the fully realized ambitions of man could yet not compete with the beauty of nature.

Even by noblemen standards, the tavern was a collection of the wealthiest elite on Balthazar. It was near mid-day, and full to teeming with aristocratic blood from the four corners of Balthazar. If there were any doubt as to Fox and Sariss's place amongst them, this was easily remedied.

"A bottle of the finest mead in Balthazar for all of the lords and ladies in this house!" Fox cried to the jubilation of the crowd. He kept his eyes fixed on Sariss. If ever there was any deserving of every indulgence on Balthazar, it was she. For the first time in his life, Fox minded not a bit being the center of attention. A lifetime's worth of training on how to remain innocuous he cast aside like a wet cloak one discarded when coming in out of the rain. Cammarran was gone, he had come to accept that, and though his actions now were cathartic to the guild master's teachings, he could only hope that, were he still alive, the old man would smile upon the happiness that had long since eluded his troublesome ward.

In his lifetime, Fox's skillful hands had touched more gold then any in this illustrious room, yet, unbeknownst to him, he had always been chasing something more. As he focused upon the peasant girl, completely ignoring the fortune of material wealth he was surrounded by, he came to believe that he had at last found it.

Within moments, their table was laden with delicacies from the four corners of Balthazar, and Sariss leaned across to look at him. "How is it you have come into such wealth?" she whispered

"Let not your conscience trouble you." Fox replied in dulcet tone "Think you that you are less deserving than any here? These riches predicate upon the lives of men and women such as yourself."

"It seems wrong somehow." she replied uncertainly, chewing on her lower lip and staring in wonder about the room

"That is what they wish you to believe- that it is wrong to question the caste system which, without your consent, has been thrust upon you. What is wrong is that men and women such as these hoard their undeserved wealth whilst people such as you and your family slave and toil upon the land in order to fill their coffers. It is only us- the thieves, who have dared to challenge this."

"Fo... Costa." she corrected herself "I am truly honored, but perhaps it is time we returned to the courtyard to see if my father and brother have returned."

Fox could not keep himself from smiling. Like he, Sariss cared not for the vanity of men, the only treasure she cared for was her family. The thought of seeing Aron again however, knowing how the man had betrayed such devotion, cast a dark cloud across his thoughts.

"Indeed, you are right."

Fox waved to the serving girl who had been hosting their table. She scurried across the room at his beckon, eager to seek his favor. She was similar in age to Sariss herself, only she bore blonde locks in place of Sariss's raven ones. This, along with her voluptuous figure, no doubt being the primary reason she was allowed her placement at the inn, for the sheen of her hair glowed in the soft golden light of the room where it cascaded in waves down to her naked mid-section.

"What is thy favor my lord?" she inquired

Fox placed a shinning ruby into her hand and closed it over the gem. "Only to inform you that you are more deserving of this than any noblewoman here present." he whispered so that none about could hear "Tell me, do you have a family?"

It took a moment for the girl to reply, so overcome by shock was she at having received such a gift. "A... a husband, and a daughter." she gushed, her eyes glassy with tears "Please sire, I beg of you. I cannot accept this payment, for I honor my husband. If you like, I can have another escort you to quarters above."

"No payment." Fox retorted "Tell me, do you wish your child a better lot in life than what has been afforded you?"

"I do sire."

"Then raise her well. Teach her that any on Balthazar, should they be both cunning and strong, can have all that they desire should they be willing to persevere."

The girl's eyes, now wet with tears, centered upon Sariss who retuned the stare with a warm and sympathetic smile.

"I will lord, and thank you." she sobbed, clinging to the ruby so tightly that her knuckles turned white beneath their golden sheen.

Fox leaned close to the girl and whispered again "A lord is a thief who takes from the poor, and I am no such man."

The girl stared at him in surprise, smiled and, bowing low, retreated to her duties. Fox had no doubt that the ruby, plucked from the purse of a nobleman earlier in the day, would be much better served in the possession of one who cared more about her loved ones than the sparkle of any bauble. He had not given her the gift for Sariss's benefit, nor did he wish her to think of him as a braggart, yet from the corner of his eye, he saw writ in her expression that she approved.

"Why did you bring me here?" she asked

Rising from his seat, Fox placed his hand in Sariss's. "Come. Before we take our leave, there is something I wish to show you."

Leaving their feast untouched, the pair crossed the room as Fox guided her to the lift at the center of the spire. The mechanics of the lift were similar to those of dumbwaiters such as were used in many of Gemmen's estates, yet never before had either Fox or Sariss seen one meant to transport people from one level to the next. Fox guided Sariss onto the platform and addressed the loincloth clad giants who manned it. "To the top." he said

The rippling back muscles and bulging triceps of the servants worked in perfect symmetry to the drumming of the orchestra as the workers began to pull the thick chains which ran via a pulley system. Soon, they were lost in sight as the platform began to rise. Sariss threw her arms about Fox in fear and delight; intoxicated by the thrill that they might drop to their imminent deaths at any moment should those below not be up to the task of hoisting them. Higher and higher they rose. Sariss kept her eyes fixed to the top of the tunnel in nervous anticipation. Fox shared in her elation. Doubless the peasant girl had spent many a day upon the farmstead gazing up at the snowy peaks of mount Gemmen. Perhaps she had longed to ascend so high at to touch the horizon. Fox imagined her as a child, playing with her brother in the hayloft whilst her mother chastised them, just as he, during his own childhood, was scaling the tallest buildings in the thieves' district of his home under the watchful eye of Cammarran. Such childlike wonder was shared by all in the days before such dreams were deemed impractical by the dictates of a society which demanded one remain forever grounded. As a thief, Fox's daring was lauded. Here, he was given an opportunity to share what he had been so freely given.

Higher and higher they climbed. With each new level ascended, she clung to him tighter, her excitement palpable. He could feel the beat of her heart beneath her breast pressed so firmly against him. Finally they came to a stop. Fox slid aside the thin metal grating of the gate and they stepped out into a world known only to those daring enough to seize it. Here at the peak, the tower tapered to a point, and the platform they stood upon was but a few breadths wide. They walked out onto the circular balcony at the base of the needle, now blanketed by whispish clouds which lingered upon the atmosphere, and breathed in deeply. Unlike the levels beneath them, there was no rooftop here save for that which was shared by all the lands of Balthazar. The wind lashed at them fiercely, filling their nostrils with sobering vitality as it whipped their hair about their faces. They placed their hands on the outer railing and gazed outwards. For a brief moment which yet lingered, for she was determined not to release it, Sariss stared out across the plains, settling on the ochre blanket that was the sea of Serdia. Its crossing had been an ordeal, yet now seemed but an insignificant speck on the horizon.

Fox placed an arm across her shoulders whilst pointing with the other. "Look below." he beckoned.

Sariss did as he asked and gasped audibly.

"Do you see?" Fox's voice was a whisper, barely audible over the howling winds which continued to cause her hair to dance about her porcelain features, pausing only to cling upon her lips. "This is the world as I see it. Many times have I scaled towers the like of this one, a single faulty grip or crumbling ledge all that separated me from death, and looked down upon the world beneath me. Only here have I gained perspective; a sense of clarity ultimately lost on most. Gaze upon the forms below. See how they scurry about, driven by the capricious whims of men who would see themselves as gods."

"It's beautiful" Sariss gasped; her voice inaubible yet read clearly in the swelling curvature of her lips "I never would have realized."

"Look to the northern mountains." Fox continued, tracing across the horizon with his finger "Of what value the walls of men; of what worth our petty borders when pitted against the gates of the world? What wonders lie beyond, limited only by our imagination and our will to discover them? Look to the oceans, so calm that one whose imagination knew no bounds could not begin to guess as to what might live beneath, nor to which depths they descend. It is only from here that the crashing waves are still and serene, beckoning us to it. Look to the forests. See how they blanket the land, hiding from view what only the plains deign give us a glimpse of? We who know so little of its bounty and yet call ourselves lords? Look to the deserts in the south, how even from here they seem without end. What mysteries undiscovered beyond its scorched surface? Should we who now stand so near to the sun fear its touch? What adventure awaits those who deny the lies and false promises of those who now gorge themselves beneath us? What would become of them if all saw the world as we do now? It is we who lay claim to the world... we whom Balthazar favors should we only be willing to seize it!

Sariss turned her attention eastward and her breath caught in her throat. Fox followed her gaze towards where the land sparkled like jewels in the sunlight. "Damaas."

"Indeed." replied Fox "Long have I wished to see it. Though the eastern lands cover less territory than Gemmen, there are no surrounding villages or fiefdoms. The Kingdom itself spreads across the entire territory, making it the largest civilization on Balthazar... the city of gold."

"It's beautiful." Tears ran down Sariss's soft cheeks as she spoke, and Fox could not know whether this was from the wind which she refused to shut her eyes against, or the plethora of emotions, never before experienced, all assailing her body at once.

"We are allotted one life to see and experience it all." Fox continued "Far too short a time when weighed against such infinity."

"Perhaps you are right." Sariss began "We are the wealthiest of all, for across this great expanse, and against all odds, we have found each other."

Ignoring all else, Fox allowed her to encompass the entirety of his vision. She threw herself into his arms, uncaring of the world below, as they locked in passionate embrace.

Fox wished the moment could have lasted forever, but eventually he pulled upon the long rope near to the platform, whose reverberations signaled to those below that they were prepared to return. Making their way through the tavern once more, this time slower and on steps made uncertain due to the lingering effects of vertigo, they returned to the courtyard.

Hand in hand, the pair strolled about the grounds. Their presence there was not met with such open hostility as before, for the King's soldiers had seen them emerge from the tower and they were left to enjoy the afternoon in peace. The unwanted attention once afforded them was now afforded others. Such was the price of perfidy. One could alleviate ones burden only by casting its weight upon the shoulders of others. Balthazar's malice was a constant. It shifted from one to the next. Many were those, such as the nobles who dined within, who were given freely and unearned all of the riches of Balthazar, yet somewhere, perhaps in the far reaches of the world, unseen and unheeded, the price was paid in full.

Nevertheless, Fox was happy; happier than he had been in a long time. Despite himself, he had found something he had not known he was looking for. It was a happiness whose roots were not set in the suffering of others, for it was born of a symbiosis that was grown and nurtured in perfect tandem with another. Two had come together, pooling all of their love, joy and trust. Together, they had in abundance what none had alone. On this day, a thief had found joy not from taking it from another, but by sharing it. It was the best any could hope for. As they walked through the exotic garden, their arms linked, surrounded by the beauty of the world, Fox felt certain that Balthazar smiled upon them.

"I don't see them." Sariss said after a time.

"Worry not." replied Fox "I'm sure that they are still haggling with the local vendors in order to secure as good a deal as possible."

They completed a tour of the perimeter and had come full circle back to the gate of the Golden Tower, yet still they had seen no trace of Sariss's father and brother. Fox waved to the guard he had so humbled earlier. As the man rushed to his side, he turned to Sariss and spoke.

"I shall go and look for them."

"But the marketplace is enormous, how will you ever find them?" Sariss protested

Fox merely smiled in response. "My lady, I have scoured the deepest, darkest dungeons of Gemmen in search of hidden items of lore. Trust that if any can find Aron and Erik, it is I."

Sariss laughed in response. "I believe you can." she smiled

"Lord and Lady of Gemmen!" said the guard, announcing his arrival "How might I serve you?"

Fox turned to face the man. "I am pressed into an errand of some importance. See to it that my lady wants for nothing whilst I am away."

The guard aligned himself erectly before replying. "I shall see to it personally that the finest page in Serdia is sent to her forthwith!"

"My thanks!" replied Fox. He placed his lips softly to Sariss's before making his way out of the courtyard.

The worry in Sariss's tone perturbed him. He had chosen not

to inform her of her father's illicit dealings. Now that he parted company with her and stalked the streets alone once more, he could not shake himself of the notion of how the big man had so betrayed her innocence. He had believed his world alien to that of the peasant family's, yet even as he attempted to show Sariss the beauty of it, he was reminded of its darker corners. The knowledge that he had seen Aron himself slinking about them caused his hands to knot into fists as he walked. His was a mood which could only be assuaged by an act of wanton irresponsibility. He was primed for a fight, fueled by an urge to do something stupid.

CHAPTER SIXTEEN - THE WAR OF THE GUILDS

Day had turned to dusk and the fearsom Fox of Gemmen had scoured half the city. He found no trace of the two he had been looking for, nor had he found a viable candidate with whom he could vent his frustrations. The people appeared docile and frightened. There were no bullies about to incur his wrath. He was set to return to the Golden Tower and was walking along the main thoroughfare when the streets became noticably less congested- seemingly in direct proportion to the lowering sun and the coming of twilight.

"Best to find shelter friend."

The voice came from a nearby peasant man, much the same in appearance as Hiram and Aron themselves, who was hastily escorting his family through the doors of a nearby inn. "The assassins and thieves are embroiled in a bitter war that runs the streets red after dark. Even the King's soldiers are staying out of the fray until it gets resolved. Serdia at night is no fit place for honest travelers these days. Even the markets close early, as the local farmers here are eager to leave the city behind them afore the sun goes down."

Fox ignored the warning and slowed his gait. The news suited his humor fine. Should he encounter any thief in Serdia who felt as though the thieves' code no longer held authority in the wake of Cammarran's death, they would find that there was still one amongst them who would face such impunity with steel. He rested his hand upon the pommel of his sword. His eyes narrowed, causing them to smolder with that same eerie glow which always signaled trouble.

He was nearing the central marketplace once again; now a lone traveler in what was once an avenue bustling with activity, when the familiar sound of clashing steel rang in his ears. With none of the clamor of the heady mix of traffic to intervene, the welcoming sound, still several blocks distant, rang clearly like the siren song of a familiar lover, whispering to him that trouble was nearby and sending him an open invitation.

Seeking the high ground, Fox scurried up a nearby building, using the sills as one might the rungs of a ladder. Gaining momentum, he raced across the plankards of wood and awnings that served as the roadways of a world known only to those brave enough to live there. When travelling in this manner, thieves could be assured that their passage would go unseen, for it was a truism that most citizens, even the local constabulary, never looked up. Many thieves had theories on this. Some suggested that men feared the vastness of the blanketed stars overhead, for it reminded them of their own mortality. Others posited that this was because their lives were defined by the trappings of their immediate surroundings, always busy running to and fro in narrow-minded pursuits caged by their limited scope of vision, content with the warrens and roadways that their lot in life afforded them, and believing the high balconies and spiraled towers to be the domain of their betters. Occasionally, the children of these attempted to scale the daunting scaffolding of some newly erected edifice or other, but the dreams of those who could yet be stifled by adult authority figures were quickly quelled as they were indoctrined to the dangers such a world presented- their ambitions dissolved into a life of servitude which would never satisfy one destined to rise the ranks of the thieves guild, for when one had nothing, not humility, nor pride or restraint... everything was available for the taking. Though these avenues had been employed by countless members of the thieves guild of Serdia before him, never had they been graced with such speed, dexterity and accomplish as on this night. He was in his element now. Gone was Costa, the humble steel merchant. In his place, the fearsome Fox of Gemmen was on the hunt.

Heeding the call to battle, Fox soared across the rooftops, diving and rolling along the hidden paths of strategically placed scaffolding, banners and ledges laid out before him in days gone past by now traitorous members of his own guild. He had been nurtured in such environments, succored by them. He defied Serdia's protestations at his audacity. Shuttered windows rattled irritably at his passing, nesting bird screamed in anger at his sudden presence in their sanctuaries, and gusts of wind that aggitated the torch-lights marking the corners far beneath him attempted to knock him off balance as punishment for his invasion of their once intimate reality. Fox smiled as he ran, closing the distance with a brazenness that had earned him his reputation as the greatest thief in the realm.

His ever-ascending trek came to an end high above a narrow inroad just to the west of the central marketplace which had become the staging ground of a fierce battle between thieves and assassins. Beneath him, Fox could see the bodies of both sects littered amongst the garbage and offal, remnants of peddlers too eager to depart Serdia to clean up after themselves. The blood and gore resulting from this unseen carnage would likely be cleaned with the rest upon the morrow and life in Serdia would begin anew. On this night however, those who still drew breath were engaged in a desperate fight for survival against adversaries with whom, until recently, they had maintained an uneasy pact of peace. Cammarran, master of thieves, was gone. Hergod, master of assassins, was far to the west in the capitol. Perhaps the old assassin would have honored the memory of his erstwhile ally. Perhaps he would have respected the pact until a successor could be named. Perhaps he would have sought punishment for those thieves who tread upon his domain, as well as the memory of Cammarran by accepting assassination contracts without his endorsement. Fox could not know... neither did he care.

It fell to him to avenge his mentor's legacy. Allies... foes... all had become muddled. All was chaos. Assassin and thief alike would learn of the folly in wakening his wrath.

He let his anger fuel his strength and resolve as he bore witness to the war. Perched high above the combatants, he scanned the entire scene. All attempts at stealth and artfulness which had been the hallmark of both guilds had been abandoned, and it was easy to discern who the players were. Despite his recent disgust at the comport of his own guild in the power vacuum Cammarran had left, Fox could not help but feel pleased when he saw that the assassins had clearly walked into a trap, and were fighting a losing, desperate battle.

What little conversation he could hear over the clashing of steel and the wails of men in their death throes told a story which brought a smile to his lips. The clan of assassins beneath him had pilfered a local smithy shop earlier in the week, killing those within and claiming what treasure they could- for many a local fence had begun dealing with any who would sell illicitly obtained goods cheaply to the local markets near to the western wall, regardless of any endorsement of the thieves guild. The gang of thieves these were engaged with had bottlenecked the assassins into this alleyway, snaring them like flies in a web, and set to the grim task of butchering them like cattle. Had Cammarran been alive, such barbarity would never have been tolerated. Such was his wisdom and power that no conflict between denizens of the underworld would have ever spilled out onto the streets. Regardless; Fox took some measure of comfort that the thieves, in this instant, remained his allies, for he did not relish the thought of having to face his brethren in combat.

The transformation was now complete. The upturned corners of his mouth revealed the glint of his canines. His eyes, radiating green fire like deep-set coals smoldering beneath a knotted brow, was a sight that would cause the bravest of men to quake. His was an anticipation fueled by moral outrage; an ignomity instilled in him since his induction into the thieves guild. That a hard-working family of the merchant class should become the target of elite assassins for no other reason than the coin their lifetimes worth of toil had earned them was an insult to everything the thieves and assassins once stood for. The outlaw guilds of Gemmen existed during Cammarran's reign, and the reign of all of the guild-masters before him, as something grand... something worth fighting for; to challenge the power and control of noblemen- to offer a way of life to those born in the gutters; to give the misfits and cast-offs the means to strike back by carving out their destinies in the only manner afforded them. Now, in his absence, they were reduced to what the noble castes had always accused them of being- dogs fighting for scraps in the street.

Had he the time, Fox would have perhaps succumbed to melancholy. He now realized that he had never truly appreciated the role Cammarran played. He never understood the vast scope of his responsibilities. That all had fallen to such chaos in the wake of his demise was a testament to the will and resolve he had in life. As each assassin trod their padded boots upon the blood soaked cobblestone, pacing about their adversaries, so too did they tread upon the memory of the man who raised him; the man who inducted him into the guild and showed him a better way of life. He could bear witness to such impunity no longer. The time to act was now.

He leapt from his perch, bounding from one building to the next, ever in descending fashion, narrowing the distance between himself and the street below. Fang was unsheathed mid-leap and buried itself into the shoulder of the nearest assassin. Much as before, in the oasis of the great desert sea, men about him became stunned into inactivity by the sudden appearance of a vengeful wraith in their midst.

Taking full advantage of the terror and uncertainty his presence wrought, Fox raced about the battleground, dancing about the long rapiers whose polished steel pierced the night, leaving a bloody trail of assassins acting as cairns to mark his passing. Never before had these born witness to such speed, agility and grace. Many foes he cut down who had not the time to raise their weapons in defence against him. Many were simply too stunned to do so. Those who did not fall before Fang were skewered by his daggers, thrown in the same furious motion with which his sword carved its deadly arc. In the moments between thought and action, the street had become a charnel house with himself as the butcher.

With Fox's presence, the battle was well and truly won. The jaws of his fellow thieves were agape, momentarily frozen in silence. This was broken when a multitude of screams alerted him that a new foe had entered the fray. Feigning a jab to the hooded head of his last remaining adversary, Fox ducked beneath the counter swing, burying Fang into his midsection, spilling guts and gore out onto the street. Only then did he spin about that he might address this new threat. The breath caught in his throat as he did so. Littered amongst the corpses of those he had just slain lay the bodies of each and every thief whose aid he had come to.

Two adversaries now remained. The street was strewn with the bodies of the fallen. Towering over them stood one of the tallest men Fox had ever seen. He was at least as tall as Aron himself, yet thin as a wraith; his slender, nearly gaunt physique being evident despite the shadows he seemed to carry with him as he stepped from out of their depths. Clad head to toe in black, he wore an assassins cloak, yet what could be discerned from the strange armament, lost in the swell of darkness, was akin to nothing found within the four realms. The collection of plated pauldrons, greaves, sabatons, gauntlets and cuirass, each embedded into the very fabric of the uniform, were a picture of macabre beauty, as though some mad smithy with a penchant for implements of torture and malice had been granted the skill of the most accomplished of artisans. The man stood still and calm; his bearing one of imposing control, so that it was imposible to assign to him the speed necessary for such a massacre. Only his cloak appeared to move with any volition, for it wafted upon the slight breeze as though animated with a life of its own. Droplets of blood hung from every barb of his serrated rapier, gripped loosely at his side, as long and thin as he, disturbing his unnatural reflection in the pool where they fell. Though his face was swathed in black cloth, Fox was certain that he was smiling. When he spoke, it was with an almost soothing, sing-song voice, uttered in a whisper, yet reverberated off the walls with such menace and intensity as to chill him to his core.

"You draw far too much attention to yourself young thief. 'Til now, I'll admit, the old man's lessons served you well, for it was difficult, even for me, to track you. It's a pity you did not heed his lessons here in Serdia."

"Krillian." Fox replied, the word dripping with hate "This was a trap set for me alone... one which you orchestrated..."

"One which you are both clever enough to realize and stupid enough to fall for." the melodious voice replied "Which of the two pains you more, son of Balthazar?"

Fox took a moment to look about him, his eyes settling upon one body after the next. "All of this... simply to net a single man." He addressed only himself; yet the assassin saw fit to use his words against him.

"It is a lesson Cammarran himself taught you is it not? A larger action conceals the smaller? It is a wise maxim. Cammarran was an impressive man, one who has seen glimpses of a world most do not know exists... one which he managed to survive through a wisdom and tenacity worthy of his betters. I'll admit I was pleased when I learned that he, above all others, was selected to seek you out, to train you. I believed the guild would make you strong. It seems as though I have done the old man a favor, for he shall never know the shame in how readily his pupil has forgotten his lessons."

"Selected?" Fox began

"The fortune you spent at the Golden Tower in order to show the farmer girl such a good time is still being spoken of." Krillian continued, ignoring the question "That one so attired would wantonly cast such wealth about was a sight never before seen in these lands. Sloppy... really, I am quite disappointed. I believe that, as punishment for your indiscretion, I shall slay the girl as well when I am done with you."

The assassin's words were carried upon a wave of confusion. It was as though every woe, every bitter, traumatic event in his life, long since banished from his consciousness was now resurrected-centered about this single foe. Somehow the hypnotic voice carried with it pain he knew not he possessed. Had his care-free persona been a façade- if there truly was a monster that dwelt behind the walls he had built up in order to protect himself- than this man was it. Suddenly, he was consumed with the insane belief that should he destroy Krillian, he who haunted his every footstep- a lifetimes worth of injustice and cruelty would end along with him. Not merely his own, but that of of Sariss's, of Aron and Erik's, of every life the grim spector of death darkened with its touch. He was a plague, his very existence bane to all who lived upon Balthazar. Fox could never be rid of pain, of uncertainty; never be free to live and love whilst his presence loomed upon the periphery.

Blinded by a rage hitherto unknown, he lunged, the point of his sword thirsting for Krillian's heart. His eyes burned and his canines flashed, each an awesome reflection of unbridled savagery. Much to his surprise, the assassin did not attempt a parry, but merely side-stepped the attack, his speed so blinding as to render his movements a blur. Fox was incredulous. Never before had Fang failed him. It cleaved through the air where the assassin once was. Immediately, he fell; his calf severed, unable to support his weight, unknowing of the stroke that cut him down. He rolled onto his back, Fang raised in defense, only to see that his opponent remained as still and erect as when he first glimpsed him. The hilt of the rapier and the gloved hand which gripped it were lost in shadow, yet his blood was now added to the length of steel which emerged from it. With a flick of his wrist, the sword arced upwards, drawing sparks from the cobblestone. Immediately Fang was sent hurling from his grip. The rapier remained, its tip pressed against his throat.

"Slow." Krillian's voice sang, simultaneously dissaproving and patriarchal

The fire in Fox's eyes began to dim. Before him stood a black void, the focal point of a rage born from each misfortune unknowingly nurtured during his lifetime. He had not conquered it. He had fought with all of his strength, speed and hate, and he had failed.

"Your time amongst these savages has taught you nothing. The task, therefore, falls to me."

The words were followed by a flurry of motion. Suddenly, his body was ripped asunder; blood from countless lacerations soaked his clothing. His strength flowed from him. Darkness began to encompass the entirety of his vision, save for two glowing green orbs at the center... Then darkness claimed all.

CHAPTER SEVENTEEN - BORN AGAIN

He did not know how long he lay there. In the fleeting moments of consciousness he was forced to endure, his delirium played tricks on his mind- told him that he was once again that same child who had escaped the Gemmen school for wayward children, now struggling for warmth, huddled within the ice-caked hay of the orphanages' stable yards.

Like that youth he had known so long ago, the fire within him refused to be snuffed. It burned with ethereal fury, stoking his strength, strength which, though dimmed to embers, could still be kindled to flame. With lifeless arms, he dragged himself across the alley floor. His many wounds had scabbed over, the tattered remnants of his clothing set as a tourniquet, and his still-beating heart pumped fresh blood into his veins. Born of sheer will, it coursed through his entire system, spike by adrenaline, passion, fury and pain.

He had no idea how much distance he covered, for both time and space had become abstract concepts, dimly lit entities hidden beneath a veil of red mist. His lucid vision centered upon a boarded up building which had clearly been his destination before the darkness claimed him. He had no idea how many times he lost consciousness. For reasons unknown to him, the building became his only chance at life. Clawing at the cobblestone, he dragged himself towards it.

The well-maintained exterior told him that the building was not abandoned. The slats which covered the window had been cobbled together hastily, a stop-gap measure to protect what lie within from the war that waged about after nightfall. He loosened one of the plankards and nearly passed out again from the effort, this time refusing to succumb as the rage in him added fresh fuel to the fire that drove him. Had the board been more securely attached, he would perhaps not have succeeded, yet the fixture was only the illusion of a bulwark, a deterent, and was nailed in place in such haphazard manner that a child could have loosened it. Fox clung to the wood, adding the fullness of his weight to his efforts. The slat creaked in protest as it buckled and he tumbled though the small opening which presented itself; falling into a heap on the floor within.

Steam wafted about the interior of the building, warming the ice in his veins and giving him comfort. His eyes fluttered momentarily as he attempted to take in his surroundings. He was dimly aware that he was in a bath-house, for the steam emanated from a large pool which spanned most of the room, yet at his hour, whatever hot coals had been placed into the water should have cooled.

The struggle to comprehend this new riddle, coupled with the effort he had undertaken to loosen the exterior board proved too much for Fox, and once again his own fading consciousness left him.

When he awoke, time had lost all meaning. Somehow, he was once again within a chamber in the underground labyrinth which ran far beneath Gemmen. His mind screamed in protest at this notion. Had the strange adventure which had taken him so far from his home been naught but a dream? Images of the desert, a city on wheels, a golden tower and more came to him in waves- scattered details of a picture not yet made whole and too fragmented to retain cohesion. A face... porcelain framed by ebony, it beauty serene came to him in flickers. The flood of emotions both bitter and wonderful was too much to process. He curled himself into a ball on the cavern floor and slept, the soft green glow bathing him in its nourishing light.

A full beard was the only indication of the passing of time when he awoke again. His bloodied fingers provided the only clue as to how he had arrived. He should have been famished and dehydrated, yet he felt neither hunger nor thirst. Once again, he attempted to take in his surroundings. The underground chamber was near identical to those he frequented beneath the kingdom save for a garish metal tube which churned water from the stream that coursed through it. Jadestone was predominant amongst the various mineral deposits about him, and once again this seemed to glow as though possessed with an internal fire. He was lying next to a hot spring, this much was certain, for mist clung to the air, wafting about him, infused with the green light that emanated from the cavern walls, lending a sparkling pallor to the room which denied the existence of any other color. His thoughts stumbled into cohesion. His ribs screamed in protest as he laughed.

Above him was a bath house where wealthy nobles no doubt enjoyed the water drawn from the cave, their fat lecherous bodies scrubbed by nubile servant girls. He knew that the wives of such nobles cared not a whit, for such activity kept said lecherous bodies off of them. The irony was delicious. He continued to laugh. He laughed until the pangs in his ribs strangled the breath in his lungs. In so doing, he found new purchase on life. Even in death, he remained a thief to the last, for the elite paid in gold what he enjoyed for free.

Fox could not fault the enterprising man or woman who had discovered the hot spring and tapped its resources in order to cater to travelers eager to relax and refresh from the weariness of the road. Indeed, the call to succor was one he himself had heeded, though he knew not how. The green mist seemed to float about the innards of his mind as readily as they did the chamber so that even his thoughts were filtered through a dense fog.

For the span of an eternity, or perhaps a few days, Fox remained in Balthazar's womb, bathing in the relaxing waters. The ambient green light penetrated his being with a surreal infusion of vigor and health. He had not yet the strength nor the inclination to leave, for a dim cognition told that he only clung to life due to the mysterious properties of the cave, and that should he distance himself from it, his strength would fail him once more. He had partaken in neither food nor drink, yet his strength slowly returned. The cavern afforded him a clarity of vision and purpose which grew in direct proportion to his returning health. He found that his limbs, once feeble and weak, gained new strength by performing the swordplay exercises taught to him as a child, this time using the root of a tree in place of his sword. Fang was lost to him now, yet he came to believe that this was for the best, for against a normal foe, he could manipulate the weighted short-sword deftly, yet against his most recent adversary, his movements had been like those of a man underwater, fighting with the current.

With clarity of thought came clarity of purpose. He felt as though he could linger here forever, yet the face he saw during his nightmares taunted him relentlessly. Despite the shroud of comfort he was swathed in, he knew he would not know peace until he confronted it. There too were the dreams he had during his waking hours, haunted by the beauty of one who beckoned his return. Though he now saw the world about him through a green lens, the visions of darkness and light both taunted and tantalized him incessantly.

Never before had the game he made of life held any true stakes. With a mind now unencumbered by distractions came the sobering realization that he had wasted his gifts. He had taken for granted his many talents, perverted them in frivolous pursuit of hedonistic joy and debauchery. Only through the potent combination of love and hate was he reborn here in the nurturing womb of Balthazar itself. He knew not whether his newfound strength and single-mindedness of purpose would fail him if he left the cave. He only knew that he had unfinished business in the world above that demanded resoluteness.

On the day Fox had chosen to leave the cavern, he had not the slightest inclination how long he had spent there. Time had seemingly stood still in the mysterious, secret hollow, allowing him to heal, yet he knew that the outside world existed on another plane of reality which refused to wait for him. Had Sariss and her family moved on? Were they now in Damaas? And if so, how would he find them again?

Though he had scant memory of his descent into the cave, he found his path easy to re-trace. Amidst the plethora of roots which snaked their way towards the underground stream was a split just large enough to admit him. Perhaps this was the very same shaft the patron of the bathhouse above discovered in days past when they stumbled upon the hidden fountain and chose to capitalize on its resources. How he himself, during his feverish, weakened state, discovered it could not be explained lest his mind was somehow susceptible to the calling of the cavern itself. To further explore this thought led to madness. He concentrated instead on the task at hand. The shaft was narrow and winding. Due to his uncanny ability to see in near total darkness, he was able to negotiate the passage until it opened to a small room above. He blinked several times in attempt to return his vision to normal. No longer was his environment seen through a pane of green. The bloodied claw marks on the floorboards slowly became infused with red where he had, in what must have been a desperate display of strength and frenzied determination, torn them to splinters.

He exited the room and ambled down a slight corridor carved into the rock. The corridor came to an end with no apparent doorway in sight, merely a stark wall of solid rock which had been rendered smooth and planed flat. He ran his hand along its surface; feeling for the secret latch he knew must be there. His sensitive fingers, trained from a lifetime of picking locks and snatching coin from out of purses, traced a line across the surface until they settled upon a loose stone, invisible from sight. He pressed upon it and was greeted with the familiar grinding of internal clockwork mechanisms as the entire rock face slid aside on a track, revealing the interior of the bath house on the other side. All thieves were familiar with such mechanisms, remnants of a bygone age scattered throughout the secret world of the guild. He knew the location of each within the capitol and had oft used them to slip through its outer wall in order to affect his escape from many a daring raid. That he had discovered this one here in Serdia, half-dead and delirious, was impossible. It caused him to wonder about the state of reality and what he once thought he understood of it.

He did not know what time of day it was, for the sun's rays did not reach into his most recent lair, despite its infusion of mysterious light. He hoped that it had long since set, that the bath house would have been closed for the night. Unfortunately, the room was full to teeming with naked politicians, nobles and lords who were stunned into silence by the sudden appearance of the most ragged and disheveled man they had perhaps ever seen materializing suddenly into their midst.

Many a jaw dropped over the rounded bellies of the bloated, wrinkled, and decidedly naked men assembled as he nonchalantly walked past, whilst the eyes of the servant girls who were working said bodies with sponges and vulgar caresses screamed at the sight of blood which soaked his clothing. The soothing melody of the harpsichords screeched, the result of plucking fingers struggling to find strings before themselves falling silent. The very ambiance of the room itself seemed offended as he strode confidently through and made his way to the front door. Fox merely waved and smiled at each in turn as though this were a daily occurrence. The door was latched from the inside, yet thankfully unguarded. Fox slid the bar aside and strode out onto the street, leaving a manic collection of shocked and incredulous lords behind him whose fragile sensibilities would likely never recover.

The overhead sky told that it was midday and the shocked expressions of those about were only slightly less vexed as he strolled about the streets. He set himself to canvassing the neighborhood in search of Sariss, his single-mindedness of purpose perhaps greater in this endeavor than when he had discovered his most recent lair. He had last seen her at the Golden Tower and decided to begin his search there. Fellow travelers gave him a wide berth and the path forward parted before him.

He wasted no time in leisurely appreciation of the garden and made his way directly to the front gate. Such was his determination that the gasps of shock and awe of those about were lost on him. He arrived at the gate only to have his passage hindered as before by the shaft of a spear placed lengthwise against his chest.

"Whither do you think you are going peasant?" the guard sneered. He took in Fox's appearance with decidedly non-sympathetic candor. "You'll find no clerics within."

Fox lacked the habitual humor and patience he had so often availed himself of when dealing with this type, yet thankfully the sentry was spared his temper by the sudden interjection of a familiar voice.

"My lord!"

Fox spun about to see the same sentry he had entrusted with the security of Sariss upon his last visit as he raced towards him.

"Mind your tongue man!" he scolded the guard whom Fox confronted. "Know you not that you now address a Lord of the highest caste?" he turned to look at Fox and lowered himself into a bow "My sincerest apologies my Lord. I shall see to it personally that this one is reprimanded for his insolence."

He raised his eyes from where he had been staring in reverence at the ground. His concern did not appear to be forced.

"My Lord! Are you well? What has happened? Shall I alert the guard?"

Fox's erstwhile opponent lowered his spear and took a step back, still stinging from his rebuke.

"I am well, thank-you. As I feared, some local bandits recognized me despite my peasant's costume and ambushed me near the western wall. I have been waylaid at the local Temple of Light where I was treated for my wounds, yet I fear that my lady must fear the worst during my absence."

"Indeed my Lord. When you did not return, the lady instructed me to tell you that she would be staying..." he hesitated

"Out with it man!" Fox demanded

"That is to say sir; that she would be staying at the Pilgrim's Oasis. It is an inn of very ill repute, my lord."

"Understandable." replied Fox "As our fortune resides with my own personal banker; my lady has not had access to any funds. I shall make my way there forthwith that she might be spared further indignity. Where can I find this inn?"

"You shall find it south of the eastern gate my lord, near to the wall, in the district known as Beggar's Basin- It is the quarter of the city where most residents reside. As such, there are few inns. What little there are are mostly frequented for their taverns. You should have little trouble finding it, though I would suggest that you do not linger, as those filthy creatures are just as like to rob you as they are to look at you."

Fox thanked the sentry, his fellow guardsman having fully retreated back to his post in fear of what reprisals awaited him, and exited the garden. He made his way in the direction thus indicated, ignoring the hawkers in the central marketplace, though his stride; once measured and sure, became noticeably weaker as he continued his search.

The afternoon had transitioned to evening by the time Fox came to Beggar's Basin, his stamina decreasing in marked measurement to the distance he travelled, so that by the time he arrived, he felt every bit as decrepit as his appearance suggested. It took little effort to ascertain the location of the Pilgrim's Oasis, for those about, though still somewhat shocked at his appearance, shared none of the disdain characteristic of the upper class when it came to conversing with him, and the tavern in the inn proved to be a popular one.

The inn was indeed rustic, yet well-maintained from the outside. It was only upon entering that he realized why it was so regularly frequented by travelers, for it had a homey charm reminiscent of the many farmsteads and smaller villages which dotted the landscape along the route from the capitol. All about him, humble men and women of the working classes greeted each other with frothy pints of ale in wooden tankards, and there was an air of warmth and comfort that spoke of a place of safety and security for those who had learned to enjoy the simpler things in life.

A small fire blazed upon the hearth at the center of the room where people feasted on legs of mutton, spiced potatoes, warm bread, and other hearty foods that may have been common in their fare, yet whose aromas were as inviting as any of the exotic foods served at the Golden Tower. Indeed the decor of the establishment echoed that of the people who patroned it, for the men seemed as solidly built as the unadorned wooden tables they sat at, and the women diced and sang bawdy songs along with their husbands.

There were no paintings or tapestries on the walls, yet wooden carvings of local wildlife from the skilled hands of hunters, trappers and fishermen, dotted the room, heavily lacquered, and expertly wrought by those whose very survival rested upon their deftness with their tools. The floorboards, like the rest of the inn, were made from the wood of the mighty oaks which grew in the nearby forest that rimmed the desert sea, and were as meticulously kept as the rest of the tavern, whose plain copper candlesticks and brass copings were lovingly polished with care.

A geriatric couple, each clad in aprons and far too advanced in years to be running such an establishment approached him as he entered, their silver hair and wrinkles testament to a lifetime invested in the place. The woman was short and plump, her rosy cheeks lending added warmth to her smile, while the man was tall and lean, with skin like leather and a wiry physique that was nonetheless impressive for one who was bent over with age. His warm blue eyes shone amicably over his near-skeletal features beneath a shock of un-kept hair. There were no other servants to be seen, and Fox marveled that the man was still capable of chopping wood for the hearth, while the old woman's rotund figure told that she enjoyed her own cooking as much as the patrons about her. They greeted him enthusiastically, not bothering to question him, nor even to notice his garish attire.

"Welcome!" the old woman bellowed. Hospitality may have been the stock and trade of such folk, yet Fox found that they came about it naturally. Though they no doubt lacked the means to retire from their professions at any age, given that the guests in the tavern did not seem to have coin in abundance, the pride they took in its maintenance indicated that these would never do so willingly.

"Good evening" Fox said in return. His smile was not forced, for he warmed to the old couple immediately. "I am expected by a farmer named Aron and his two children"

"Wonderful people!" ejaculated the old woman "Why, did you know that Aron's youngest daughter is to be wed? It's so exciting is it not?"

"Indeed." replied Fox.

"You must be Custard!" she cried, still beaming at him lovingly

"Costa!" corrected her husband

"Yes, Costa!" said the wife, seemingly now quite irritated "They left a message for you, ah.... It seems that they...."

The woman's husband interjected –"They have delayed their travels in order to await your arrival. They have rented quarters upstairs."

The old woman frowned at her husband "There you go finishing my sentences again!"

"The man looks to be in a hurry woman! We can't wait all day for you to remember your own name!"

"Oh really!" she responded. "And who was it who forgot our anniversary last month hmm!? Certainly there was nothing wrong with MY memory on that day!"

"Thank-you." interrupted Fox "I believe that I shall search for my friends upstairs."

Without waiting for a reply, Fox left the couple to what he assumed was their familiar routine of bickering and made his way to the stairwell. He stumbled slightly upon the first few steps, but righted himself again by placing his hand on the solid brass railing. With much effort, he ascended to the top and came face to face with a startled Erik, who was ambling down the hallway in the direction of the tavern.

"Costa!" he shouted.

Briefly, Erik took in his friend's horrific appearance, his blood-stained clothes and full, un-kept beard which hung drably about his pale features. Panic tugged upon his scalp, widening his eyes and mouth into an expression of shock and horror.

"Good evening lad." Fox mumbled; his breath decidedly strained "Forgive my tardiness."

Having arrived at last at his destination, Fox fainted into his arms.

Consciousness returned sporadically. He was lying on a bed. Aron was hastily administering to him somehow. For a moment, he did not recognize him, for, like himself, the large man had grown a full beard since last he saw him. Erik and Sariss shuffled about nervously. They were near enough to touch, yet far in the distance, as though seen through a lens speckled with fog. Their faces were wrought with panic and worry. He could hear Aron speaking, yet the voice seemed as distant as his kin.

"These wounds! He should have been dead ten times over! Fetch me my satchel!"

Fox felt the big man place a handful of leafy herbs on his forehead. It burned like ice to the touch. The fever he had not even known he was suffering from abated slightly. With the clarity this afforded him, he recoiled in shock, for the image of the herbs he had spied the farmer selling to the white lotus dealer sprung immediately to his mind.

Aron placed one mighty arm on his chest and, try as he might, he could struggle no further.

"Easy lad!" he said

"What is this?" Fox managed to cry out

"Desert sage; 'tis an ancient remedy. The waters within the plant are drawn from deep beneath the soil. They contain healing properties. Try and relax."

"Then, it is not white lotus?"

"White lotus!" Aron cried "You must be mad with fever! Why would I administer white lotus to a man in such a state?"

The potent herb had done its work, and Fox was able to ease himself into a seated position on the bed. Sweat ran down his face in beads and formed rivulets in his beard. Suddenly, what little restraint he possessed was lost to him.

"I saw you Aron!" he managed to cry, despite his weakened state "I was there on our first day in Serdia! I saw you peddling white lotus to the wretches in that alley!"

The words that Fox had not meant to say came of their own volition, fueled by his own inner anger and confusion- they denied any refusal to be spoken aloud.

The words cut deep. Aron staggered back from the blow. He seated himself on the simple chair next to the mantle, which were the only other items of furniture in the sparse room. He took a long, deep breath before he spoke again, his brow furrowed in consternation and hurt. For the moment, the images of Erik and Sariss dissolved into nothingness, so affixed was Fox's attention on the man.

"No lad." he said in a soft voice "I am no white lotus pusher. The man you saw me speaking with is called Samara. He is a cleric of the Temple of Light sent to administer to the lotus addicts in Serdia. Desert sage is a difficult item to come by and one which clerics are willing to pay well."

"Father!" interjected Sariss, making her presence known and seemingly hearing the news for the first time. Her voice was riddled with betrayal. "How is it that you had the plant at all? How do you know this man and why have you kept this from us?!"

Aron looked at his daughter pensively before replying. When he did, his reluctance was evident.

"He is an old friend of your mother's. It was she who nurtured a crop of the flower before her death. I have preserved it these many years and often sold the leaf at market in Gemmen. Had you known, your life, and that of your brother's would have been in great peril."

"Why?!" Sariss protested, not willing to let the matter drop. Her concern for Fox was momentarily forgotten, washed away in waves of anger and frustration. "Is it illegal?"

"Not illegal." responded Aron "There would be many questions asked as to how I knew of the flower's properties; or indeed how to maintain an entire crop in Gemmen's climate... that is all."

"And how did you?" This time it was Erik who spoke. The words were meant as a barb as much as they were a question.

"Enough of this!" Aron shouted "We have more pressing concerns at hand! Our comrade lies half dead. Costa, what has happened? We were rife with worry."

"Don't try and change the subject!" Sariss cried again, refusing to be denied. Fox remained quiet, for he thought it wise not to place himself afore Sariss's anger.

Exasperated, the giant man took a deep breath and steepled his fingers.

"I suppose now is as good a time as any." he sighed "I had intended to tell you all at some point during our journey- why I was so reluctant to allow Veronica to join the Temple of Light, why I was so willing to sell our farm in order to see to her safety. You believed it was because of my inherent distrust of noblemen, the like she is set to wed. That is only part of the reason."

Sariss and Erik sat on the foot of the bed next to Fox as Aron spoke, the look in their eyes begging him to continue. Stories of their mother, Fox knew, were a rarity.

"Your mother." he began "My beautiful wife Esmera... was once a cleric at the Temple of Light in Damaas."

"What?!" shouted Sariss and Erik in unison

"Why were we never told of this?!" Sariss cried

"Peace!" Aron cried, resuming his air of paternal authority. "Should you keep interrupting me, then I shall never complete the tale! It is one which pains me greatly to tell and one I'll likely not repeat!"

The words had the desired effect, and the twins continued to listen attentively.

"I was a young man when I met your mother, near in age to you son." he nodded at Erik before continuing "Even then, I stood a head taller than most and could handle a broadsword as well as any trained soldier. I had chosen to seek my fortune in Damaas, and left my parent's farm in Gemmen at an early age. After a night of drunken revelry, I had nearly cleared an entire tavern by myself during a particularly bloody brawl which caught the attention of the King's guard. Rather than place me in stocks, I was convinced to enlist. Damaas is very unlike Gemmen. There, a soldier is an honored, even revered position; one which men take vey seriously indeed, and something as banal as a simple bar fight is met with the harshest of penalties. I was rash, daring, strong and stupid... all of the necessary ingredients for a guardsman. I climbed the ranks quickly, besting all of my peers in swordplay. Soon, I was posted as guard to the palace itself." he paused momentarily to stare at Erik once more before continuing "Yes son; I too was a brash young man eager to conquer the world. Perhaps when you have children of your own, you will understand why I was so strict with you."

Aron's lungs took in air like a bellows before continuing. The slight pause appeared to last an eternity. "On nights when I was not on duty, I would frequent the local taverns with my comrades, and it was there I met Esmera. She was the most beautiful woman I had ever seen, with hair so dark it was as though the sun had never kissed her forehead."

He stared at the ceiling before continuing. Fox knew that visions of his love played through his mind.

"I loved her the moment I saw her. She was then an acolyte at the Temple, much in the same way your sister is now."

"Then..." Sariss began

"Exactly" Aron continued "Veronica received her gift from her. We tried to conceal it, for if any knew it would have brought great sorrow upon our house. After many trips to market however, despite our warnings, Veronica continued to help those in need, and news that a young peasant girl was curing the headaches and various ailments of the locals with hands that seemingly glowed reached the Temple in Gemmen. We could hide her no longer."

"But why hide it at all?" interrupted Erik "Being a cleric is a noble calling."

"Indeed." replied Aron. "And it was for this reason I had to allow her to study in Damaas, lest I betray myself with my own reticence. When the monks from the temple in Gemmen offered to take her with them on their pilgrimage to the golden city, I knew that, had I refused, the all-seeing eye of the Temple would have descended on our homestead. Any investigation would have likely ended in my summary execution as well. Before long- Veronica would have been taken by force.

"Execution!" Sariss cried "I thought that the ways of the Temple were peaceful above all else."

It all stems from our time there." Aron continued "Your mother was a native Damaascian, last in a long line of healers from a noble house. We would meet each other secretly in the night. It was forbidden for a future cleric to dally with a soldier. We were trained to slay- they to heal. Neither of our masters would have condoned the affair."

"One night, I was posted at the front gate of the palace when Esmera came to see me. She was frantic, panicked. I had never before seen her in such a state. She had inadvertently stumbled upon the one secret the Temple would do anything to hide, and barely escaped with her life."

Fox leaned in closer as Aron spoke, for above all else in the room, he knew when foul play was afoot.

"Despite my rank, I had become disillusioned with life in Damaas. The strict conduct demanded of soldiers there and the means with which we were meant to enforce the rule of law had begun to taste bitter. Far from protecting the people, my duties were of subjugation. I abandoned my post and deserted on the spot. Together we ran from the Kingdom and made our way westward as fugitives. We were both young. I had not been stationed at the golden city for long and had told no one that I had come thither from Gemmen. We made our way west. We believed no one would ever find us. Eventually, we were wed and took over the farm from your grandparents. After the two of you were born, we had all but forgotten about our time in Damaas... Yet Khimotai does not take kindly to deserters, and the temple would never stop hunting her. We were forced to keep our past a secret, even from our children."

He placed a reassuring arm on Sariss's shoulder. "Fear not, for the records then were not kept overly well. Many young soldiers came to Damaas and joined the King's guard, and just as many were slain in one of Khimotai's many raids of the bandit villages within the outlying forest. Doubtful there is anyone in the golden city whom I knew, and even those would never recognize me over the passage of time, especially now that I have allowed my beard to grow over the lifetime's worth of wrinkles you and your brother gifted me with."

"But what did she discover?" Sariss cried

"All in good time lass; I'll not so readily place your life in danger. Well enough for you to know that what your mother and I did, we did for the safety of our future lives together. All will be known soon- I promise."

"But father!" she continued to protest

"Enough!" Aron shot back curtly. "You are still my daughter and will do as I say!"

"No father."

This time, the voice came from Erik. He had risen from his seated position at the foot of the bed and crossed the room to where his father sat. The look of intensity he gave the big man was matched only by his voice. Fox did not know if the boy had so openly defied his father before, yet had he done so; it likely would have paled next to this moment. He spoke with cool confidence, calm and assertive... fearless.

"The time for protecting us is over."

Shifting tack, he placed a hand lovingly on the patron's shoulder.

Perhaps in that moment, knowing that the man who raised him was once as reckless and irresponsible as he had been, he shared a kinship with Aron greater than the bond of father and son. But a change had come over Erik in recent times, and he addressed his father as one would a peer.

"I know that everything you have ever done has been to protect us. I am not angered that you have kept this secret from us these many years. Only know that we are children no longer, and if we are to continue to Damaas, if my sister Veronica is embroiled in some danger, then I would know of it."

Aron stared at his son with a mixture of wonder, incredulity and amazement, followed closely by a look of unrestrained pride. No longer did a petulant child stand before him, but a man whose strength of character and devotion to his family demanded respect.

"The Temple of Light is a sham." he said "A pale imitation of its true self."

"Ages ago, before the great war which defined Damaas as a Kingdom, it was little more than a village which sprouted around the original temple, only the temple lay underneath the ground- the only way to access it was through a series of tunnels and caves. The great healers who lived there never came to the surface, but gave aid to any who would brave the darkness to seek them. They were revered as gods and many were the men and women who made the pilgrimage to seek them out. Thus, Damaas itself was formed as a collection of travelers who came eastward in reverence. Deep within Balthazar, the caves were rife with gold. This was gifted to the people, a reward for their devotion; their allegiance. It is thus the city arrived at its name. It was a time of great prosperity… or so the legends claim. Yet such abundance bears a heavy cost."

Fox's mind reeled. The pieces of the puzzle all began to fit. The caves beneath Gemmen, so well protected by the supernatural monsters that dwelt there, the healing chamber he had himself so recently visited- it all had to be connected somehow. He listened intently to Aron's every word, hoping for a further clue to the mystery.

"Many of the great healers became enamored with their treatment as gods and came to live upon the surface that they might bask in worship. A great temple was built for them, the temple now known as the Temple of Light. Gifts and concubines were laid at their feet. In time, their descendents, having inherited the gift of healing, spread out all across Balthazar, erecting many other temples, yet their powers faded with the passage of time and they began to become jealous of those who still resided beneath, for the surface temples fell to neglect as the people sought out the more powerful healers who dwelt within. Eventually, the clerics of the many temples scattered about Balthazar sealed off all points of entry to the underground. Any who dared speak of them were systematically slain. Any records were burned to ash. In time, none lived who possessed any knowledge of the original temple at all. It was then that the Kingdom of Damaas adopted the standard of the eagle, a creature of the sky, ever a reminder that, despite the gold mined beneath their feet, ones destiny was writ in the air above."

"Then how have you come to know of it?" questioned Sariss

"The temple in Damaas still maintains ancient scrolls which tell the story of their inception. None know of the existence of these, save for a scant few leaders of their order, the elder monks whose duty it is to protect and preserve the illusion of their sovereignty. They are kept safely hidden in a secret library in the temple. Your mother, ever a curious one, was exploring the forbidden passageways late at night when she stumbled across the library and read the forbidden scrolls. Luckily, none of the guards protecting these secrets were allowed weapons of any kind, lest she never would have made it out alive when they discovered her."

There was a long pause before Aron continued to speak. "I have no doubt that the scrolls are more closely guarded now and I am sure that Veronica will never learn of them. Only Samara, himself a young acolyte at the time who had befriended Esmera, knows of our secret, and I doubt very much that your sister's life is in any danger; yet I did not sell our farm to King Alric just so that I could give her hand in marriage to some prancing bard, nor did I flee that accursed temple with Esmera in tow just so that our daughter could become entangled in the web of deceit the thrice accursed monks weave! I need... I must see to her safety myself!"

It was Fox's turn to speak, and he did so with great humility. "I am sorry Aron." he bowed his head, burdened with the weight of sorrow "Sorry that I ever doubted you. I was convinced that the herbs you were selling were naught but white lotus you grew on your farm. I believed you had betrayed your family. I know now that you have done everything for them."

"Easy lad" Aron responded consolingly "all is well. Though it seems as though the turn in yours to tell a tale. Did you run afoul of the war 'tween the guilds? We have been told that the streets are not safe after dark. How did you survive? It looks as though you faced a thousand swords and lived to tell of it."

Fox's mind was in turmoil. He longed to confide in his new friends. He nearly did. How could he reward such candor with deceit? Yet how could he tell these that the man who killed Esmera, the mother of Erik and Sariss, the great love of Aron's life, was once again a threat and that it was all his fault? They had suffered enough. He did not know how long he spent in the cave, yet he was sure that the time could be measured in weeks. By all rights, they should have abandoned him, yet Aron had placed his welfare on par with that of his own children. Though he longed to, he would not add to their burden. Sariss bore the weight of his secret. He would not add condemn another. Krillian was his problem to solve. Should any place themselves afore the assassin's sword, they would be cut asunder, as he himself was. Cammarran had already paid for his hubris, he would not add to the price of perfidy.

His teeth gritted in determination and hate as he pondered these thoughts. If Krillian was to cast his dark shadow over the lives of this family once again, then he would kill him. He had failed to do so before- he would not fail a second time. His life upon Balthazar had, for the first time, come to an impasse. Were he to move forward, he must put Krillian to the blade. To do so, he would have to become strong. He once believed that he was stronger than any. Though he was never wont to learn any new lesson, this new threat had taught him that he must be stronger.

"Indeed. I was simply in the wrong place at the wrong time. I became enmeshed in a fierce battle between assassins and thieves." The words tasted like poison. They coursed through him, infecting him with self-loathing. Like Aron before him, he knew then the lengths one must go in order to protect those whom he loved.

"You look pale." The voice came from Sariss and had the effect of breaking his reverie. "Father is right. You should rest."

Fox stared at her in shame. He felt dizzy and weak. He had indeed brought much misfortune to this family. In times past, he would have simply abandoned them rather than face any accountability. Responsibility was a burden that crippled most men, one which he had done everything in his power to avoid. The cost was suffering; one which he now paid.

"Perhaps you are right." he managed to say "I will need all of my strength for what lies ahead."

CHAPTER EIGHTEEN - FORGED

Fox had never required much rest in order to perform at optimal efficiency, regardless of how many libations he had partaken in the night before. This morning however, the sun had risen and cast its invasive rays into the room long before his eyes opened to allow them the privilege.

He momentarily forgot where he was- further evidence as to how weak recent events left him, for, since that day, so long ago, that he was ambushed by Cammarran's elite, he had been a light sleeper who was always braced for imminent danger.

He noticed that he had spent the night as the small bed's sole occupant and deduced that his comrades must have slept on the floor. Clearly they thought that he needed the opportunity to regain his strength, yet the sacrifices Aron and his family continually made for him, including delaying their trip out of worry for his safety, both impressed and humbled him.

Aron and son were nowhere to be seen, yet Sariss, seeing that he was awake, moved to his bedside and sat next to him smiling. She placed a package atop of the bed, wrapped in cloth and twine.

"What's this?" he asked

"You slept most of the morning." she replied, placing her soft lips on his forehead "I had the chance to visit the market. Father and Erik are making preparations for our departure downstairs."

Fox sat upright and opened the package. Aside from his sword Fang, he could not recall having ever received a gift. The twine came loose under his nimble fingers and the cloth fell aside to reveal a leather jerkin and tough deerskin trousers.

"The ones you wear now have been cut to shreds and blooded." she replied

Fox looked at her and smiled. The jerkin no doubt, had none of the hidden pouches his trade necessitated, yet the tough material would suit his needs well. He suddenly found the strength to place an arm about her, and this he did, their embrace ending in a passionate kiss.

"Do not let me interrupt you." came the voice of Aron in the distance

Fox jumped back as though physically struck by the words. Never had anyone succeeded in startling him before! Aron merely laughed.

"Relax lad. I am perhaps not quite as stupid as you have believed me to be. If I can stomach my youngest daughter set to wed some prancing fop, then I am sure I can reconcile your relationship with Sariss."

"Father!" Sariss cried "How long have you known?"

"Since before the two of you I'd wager." he replied, still smiling as though thoroughly amused by the entire scenario "Come. We have lingered long enough. Erik has finished packing the wagon and has just retrieved your horse from the local stables. I am told that they kept excellent care of her."

"Bolt!" Fox cried "I had nearly forgotten about her. You must allow me to repay you the stabling fees."

"Think nothing of it. The desert sage provided for her and this inn, though we have spent far more time in Serdia than I care for. Can you walk?"

Fox moved his legs beneath the soft cotton of his bed sheet. They responded, though slowly and with no small amount of effort. "I believe so." he said

"Then change out of those rags and let's be off! Your boots are about all that was left of you. You'll find them on the floor next to the bed."

Aron succeeded in surprising him once again, as the look Fox gave the big man could readily attest. For his part, Aron laughed once more before replying. "Come now. It's not as though we haven't seen you in your breeches before. Very well; come daughter, we'll wait outside while Costa prepares himself."

Sariss echoed her father's laughter and made her way to the door. She turned about and stroked her cheeks over a wicked smile, wincing as she did so.

"Oh and Costa? Do see to it that you give yourself a shave. That is, of course, if you ever expect to kiss me again."

With laborious effort, Fox put on his new costume. He found a razor on the crude mantle next to the bed along with an earthen bowl full to brimming with fresh water. Aron had left his hunting knife behind as well, its blade polished to a smooth sheen which allowed him to see his reflection in the steel. When he had finished, despite his mighty wounds, he felt refreshed and invigorated. He had partaken in many a bath in the days he spent within the green chamber of mysterious healing. With fresh clothes, unsullied by the dust of the road, he decided that his appearance and odor were decidedly less obnoxious. Though his movements were not infused with vigor, his steps felt as though they were guiding him in this direction. He splashed the cool water on his face and left to rejoin his comrades.

Aron and Sariss were at the foot of the stairs speaking to the elderly couple Fox had met earlier. He found the simple act of descending the stairwell to be as challenging as scaling the steepest ramparts in Gemmen, for his limbs screamed at him in protest with every grueling step he took. Finally, he came to stand next to his friends, though despite himself, he could not fully conceal his efforts and winced openly in pain.

"We are loathe to see you go!" said the old woman. The comment could have been meant for any of them. "It's rare we have ever had such a beauty in this place!" This comment was meant for Sariss alone, for eyes beset with wrinkles yet sparkled with youthful playfulness as they stared her up and down. The gaze turned to Fox and became buried in said wrinkles as she smiled. "Fine marriage stock this one!" Fox merely winced again in reply.

"And how is that any of your affair?!" chided her husband who emerged suddenly by her side

"Just because you don't remember what it is to fall in love, oaf!" she shot back, punctuating her words by striking him on his shoulder.

"We thank you for the courtesy!" interrupted Aron, who was clearly familiar with the routine

They made their way out onto the street, the bickering voices trailing behind them.

Erik stood next to the wagon when they emerged from the tavern. Luthor and Lola were bridled, and seemed, as ever, utterly uninterested. Bolt stood alongside them and neighed joyfully at seeing her master once more. Fox ambled to her side and pressed his face against hers, himself overjoyed at the reunion.

"You have been well taken care of!" he whispered to her lovingly. He placed one foot in the stirrup only to have a halting arm placed across his chest.

"Not quite yet Costa!" came the voice of Erik who had thus barred his path. "I shall ride your mount. Father will take the reins of the wagon. You and Sariss will ride atop of it until you recover your strength."

Reluctantly, Fox agreed and allowed the boy to help him aboard.

It was a short jaunt to the eastern gate from Beggar's Basin, and as ever, the process of leaving proved to be far less extraneous than entering. Soon, the party was upon the King's highway and set towards the golden city once more. For a time, they made slow progress along the busy thoroughfare, and Aron had to shout to be heard over the braying of the many pack animals.

"We are now within the province of Damaas. Our hosts at the Pilgrim's Oasis spoke of a trail a few leagues hence that will take us off of this accursed highway. Damaascian law is far from palatable to outlaws and I have little doubt the war between assassins and thieves has cleared most of the many bandit villages along the trail, as they have all likely been invited hither to serve as reinforcements; glad for the opportunity I'd expect. We should have an uneventful journey."

This was the second time that Aron had spoken of the harsh penalties those who ran afoul of the King's guard in Damaas could expect. It was the same in Gemmen of course, yet there, King Alric had maintained an unspoken alliance with Cammarran. He wondered if the same could be said for King Khimotai and Ciella, the Queen on the thieves' guild within whose province they had now entered.

"You will find that the golden city is but a couple weeks ride hence." Aron continued, breaking Fox's chain of thought "Our most recent hostess informed me that her cousin Orin maintains an inn there much the same as her own. Though it is a fair distance from the Temple of Light, we can at least rest assured that we will be given a fair price for our lodging."

“So short a span?” Sariss replied “We have only just entered the province.”

“Aye” Aron replied “Though the province here is smaller than Gemmen, you’ll find that Damaas is the most powerful empire on Balthazar for a reason, in both land and wealth, for the capitol city expands across near the entire region and makes up the brunt of the entire eastern realm. There are no outlying villages past Serdia in fact, next to those occupied by bandits who have fled Khimotai’s harsh regime. The city itself takes days to cross on foot from the western gate to the palace itself. Once we enter it, we still have yet a good distance ahead of us before we reach the temple, and your sister.”

“A city so large that it takes days to cross...” Sariss replied to no one in particular, her doe eyes sparkling with imagination “It must be a wondrous sight.”

Aron’s constant allusions to the fate of thieves made it difficult for Fox to reciprocate. The patron farmer kept his eyes fixed on the horizon. There, visions once faded to the realm of obscurity pulled themselves back into focus.

“Wondrous and terrifying...”

As Aron had predicted, the travelers soon found the trail they had been anticipating. It was well hidden behind the overgrown foliage which struggled vainly to reclaim the king’s highway, yet Erik, acting as scout, was able to spy it. Fox did not know if King Khimotai charged the same exorbitant taxes for the usage of his thoroughfare as did Alric, yet if Damaas was as large as Aron claimed, with no ports to speak of, he suspected that the tolls might be even greater. The wagon wheel tracks on the old, beaten path were jagged and ill-kept, and the going was rough, yet there was no traffic to impede them and they were soon swallowed by the tree-line as they followed it.

The afternoon wore on with Sariss continuing to ply the potent desert sage to Fox. Each time he began to feel warm and flustered, the cool waters trapped within the veins of the leaf fought back his fever. He knew that she was suspicious of his story as to how he had obtained the wounds, yet with her family nearby she had thus far avoided any such discussion. The trail was serviceable, for even amongst the stretches where it was overgrown with foliage from lack of regular usage, Bolt was nimble and agile enough not to be encumbered, and Luther and Lola pressed on as though they didn't notice. His strength slowly returned under the peasant girl's tender ministrations, just as the aches and pains in his limbs seemingly faded as well. She marveled at the healing properties of the plant, though Fox knew that his physiology possessed healing properties nearly as miraculous as that of the herb. By the end of that afternoon, he felt as though his own body was capable of healing itself without need of the sage whatsoever, yet Aron insisted that the plant continue to be applied until their reserves were depleted. Fox was certain that it possessed no addictive properties, and he had come to trust Aron completely, yet was perplexed as to why he was so unnecessarily adamant.

By nightfall, Erik chanced upon a small stream which coursed between the tall trees and they made camp. Sariss had been so busy tending to Fox that the party had not the opportunity to avail themselves of her hunting skills, yet the stores of food their most recent hostess had provided them with were ample and they enjoyed a hearty repast by the firelight.

The twins spent the evening plying their father for stories about the wonder and majesty of the golden city, yet Aron seemed reticent to comply. Fox, who had become weary of being nursed and coddled, chose to retire early in order to regain his strength for the morning. As before, Erik had constructed a shelter for them whilst his father attended the fire, though as the weather was mild, this one was not quite the fortress he had built outside of Serdia. Fox spread apart the pine boughs of the enclosure and was fast asleep on the leaf-strewn floor before the sun had well and truly set.

He awoke well before the others the following morning. Sariss had spent the night pressed tightly against him, whilst Erik and Aron still snored loudly next to her. He gazed at her lovingly, for she seemed even more beautiful in sleep than she did during her waking hours. Slowly, so as not to disturb the still and serene state of her slumber, he pushed aside the arm she had draped about his chest and crawled out of the shelter.

The fire was still smoldering and the coals were perfect for toasting the flax bread the old woman had provided them with, but Fox had a better idea concerning breakfast. Feeling much refreshed and invigorated under the waning moonlight, he retrieved Sariss's longbow and Aron's hunting knife from the wagon. His own daggers he had stored there as well, for the jerkin he now wore possessed none of the hidden pockets he once used to conceal them, though these he chose to leave behind, preferring instead to acquaint himself with the bow. He strung the weapon, dimly lit by the morning's feud 'tween moon and sun. Like Bolt, he took no joy in being pent up, and he knew the animal was as eager as he to run free. Even if his hunting trip provided him with no game, he was certain that they would both benefit from the exercise.

He slung the bow across his shoulder and swung himself onto her back, foregoing the saddle; then they set along the path of the river. They travelled but a short distance before they came upon the wide plains of a leafy dale hidden by the tree-line. There, the modest river flowed into a small pool, the fresh water completely hidden by morning mist, where a herd of horned beasts he did not recognize were slaking their thirst. Larger and sturdier than the deer native to his homeland, the meat and hide would provide a much needed boon for the weary travelers. Fox smiled at his good fortune. Never before had he relied on anyone to tend to his needs, and had spent a lifetime being fiercely self-reliant. Such a gift could only help to alleviate his debt to Aron, for the inn and stabling costs the farmer had to absorb in Serdia for his benefit alone was a burden he did not bear lightly.

Outside of the line of trees which concealed Fox and his mount, there was no cover in the small valley for a stealthy kill, which suited him fine, for he had not taken the time to secure the fastest steed in all of Gemmen in order that she might serve as a pack mule. There was no need to press his heels into the animal's flanks, for both man and steed relished the opportunity which had here availed itself. Acting as one, Fox and Bolt shot out of the trees and raced across the grassy veldt with speed unmatched in all of the four Kingdoms. The animals scattered in frenzied panic as the sudden threat charged into their midst, shattering the fragile serenity of the valley. The primal instincts of the beasts endowed them with unnatural speed fueled by their own instincts for survival. Despite carrying the burden of his weight however, Bolt closed the distance between them effortlessly and Fox slung the bow from his shoulder and notched an arrow to the string with speed and grace that matched her own. The herd stampeded in all directions, each heading for the safety of the outlying forest of the perimeter where the ancient trees would render a bowshot impossible. For a moment, Fox entertained the idea of racing up to the largest buck, leaping onto its back and pitting his powerful muscles against its own in a desperate battle of survival between man and beast, but he dismissed the idea. He was yet in no fit state for such a contest, and the pack leader was so large and corded with muscle that he had not the means to transport it back to the camp had he managed to fell it. His attention fixed instead on a smaller stag, plump, yet not so large that the meat would be overly laced with fat and thus impossible to carry.

The longbow he now availed himself of was a hunter's tool, and thus never employed by soldiers or thieves in the close quarters of Gemmen, as such, Fox was unfamiliar with its usage. Its tensile strength was strong, for it was designed to fire over long distances, and Fox mused that no lady of the court could have drawn the weapon, much less fired it. He was reminded as to how deftly Sariss had wielded it the day of their first meeting and smiled.

Not wishing to slow Bolt to a canter and thus deprive her of her much anticipated run, he steered her away from his intended prey until there was a good distance between them. The hickory creaked as he pulled the bow taut and brought the fletching of the arrow to his eye. He aligned the shaft perfectly with his target to ensure a proper angle before pointing the arrow upwards to compensate for distance. Whilst on horseback, and with his prey momentarily out of his sight of vision, he had to be careful lest the shaft vary in direction by even the slightest degree. Even the most accomplished of archers would never have attempted such a shot while mounted, much less at full gallop, but Fox was certain he could compensate. When he was sure that he gauged the distance accurately, he released his grip. The missile flew through the air with power unmatched by a standard reflex or crossbow, completely unaffected by the soft breeze which wafted off the lake, and descended in an arc along the path of the racing stag.

The beast's own speed in trying to escape proved to be its undoing, for it ran straight into the path of the descending arrow. The barbed shaft buried itself deep into the back of its neck, sending mighty tremors through the ground as it fell. A victim of its own momentum, the animal careened through the air, its limbs splayed about unnaturally, yet by the time it struck the ground a second time, it was dead.

Fox raced to the side of his kill and dismounted. He allowed Bolt to continue to run about freely. She had been well tended to in Serdia, yet the stabling yards of that port were not ample enough for the exercise a racing horse required. He had no doubt that she would return to his side when he had need of her. He pulled Aron's hunting knife from his belt and began to slice carefully into the animal's quarters so as not to stain his new clothes with blood.

That Fox had been rewarded with such a prize so soon after setting out left ample time before his comrades roused themselves. He cut the game into sections to make it easier for transport and placed them upon a make-shift platform he constructed by weaving together the branches of an evergreen. His labor completed, he decided that he would make the most of his excursion. Despite his recent performance, he knew that he was not yet fully recuperated from his encounter with Krillian. Then, he was strong and healthy, yet the assassin had made short work of him. He had much to do were he to survive a second encounter.

As before in the underground chamber beneath Serdia, he availed himself of a sliver of wood and resumed his rigorous training exercises. He spun the branch about him in complicated maneuvers that would have put any swordsman to shame, yet he knew it was not enough. Visions of his enemy, dressed head to toe in strange black armor danced through his head as he repeated the maneuvers, adding to his fury and hate. He knew that if he abandoned the family now, that Krillian would strike at them in order to draw him out.

His focus narrowed upon an image of Esmera, a woman he had never seen yet was somehow conjured effortlessly by his imagination, being struck down by Krillian's rapier. Try as he might, the image transformed into the familiar visage of Sariss. Ignoring the stress he put on his still-recovering body, he continued to train.

CHAPTER NINETEEN - TEMPERED

The days passed quickly. As Aron had predicted, they encountered neither foul weather nor bandit. Fox's superhuman recuperative abilities saw him back to full health long ere their stores of desert sage were depleted. He continued to rise early every morning in order to go off hunting alone. Sometimes he returned with larger game, sometimes he was rewarded with merely a pheasant or a squirrel, but always he set aside time to continue his training, which he had now come to take very seriously indeed.

Occasionally, Erik insisted on joining him during his morning hunt, and on such days when the boy rose early enough, the two would fence with sticks in order to pass the time. Fox had alluded to having no skill at swordplay, and thus feigned defeat at every turn, though the lad was in fact a swordsman of immense skill and he relished the opportunity to spar with such a worthy opponent, even if it meant having to play at being a student. Though his defense was somewhat lacking, the boy was particularly gifted when it came to breaking through his opponents own defenses. He proved exceptional at capitalizing on openings he created with powerful lunges that never fell short of their mark. Despite Fox's own lackluster performance during these duels, Erik continued to improve, for all displays of reckless arrogance faded day by day, replaced by strategems calculated to precise efficiency.

Sariss continued to keep his secret, and the two of them would avail themselves of any opportunity to sneak off for a nightly swim whenever they happened to chance upon the small river which periodically snaked across their path, though by now even Erik had guessed as to the nature of their relationship and allowed them their privacy.

It was during one of these excursions when Sariss broached the subject that Fox had been futilely hoping to avoid. The narrow stream which emanated from the nearest of the lakes they last passed had grown to a river which was now deep and wide enough to water the oxen. Sariss had been wading waist deep and as ever, Fox was admiring her silhouette in the moonlight. She made her way towards where he sat, stripped to his loincloth, and the expression on her face seemed to register the newly acquired scars which now decorated his body, for these seemed ever more stark where they were illuminated by a thin veneer of moisture. She pressed her firm body against his and her hands traced a line across a particularly vicious mark left by Krillian's sword which now stood in relief upon his side. As she gazed into his eyes, the loving expression laced with worry, intermingled with a slight tinge of anger told him that she would not be denied.

"Fox." she demanded "A change has come over you. What really happened? I saw your skill with a blade in the oasis, and I am not fool enough to believe that you were simply accosted on the streets of Serdia as you claim. I am content to refer to you as Costa in the company of my family, yet if I am to keep one secret, then I would know them all."

Fox stared at Sariss's perfect features briefly, for shame would not allow him to linger. She placed a delicate hand on his cheek and refused him the luxury.

"I have no right to unburden myself upon you."

"You have my heart." she replied smiling "Yet I have never told you why. I love you because I have never met any man who loves life as you do; a man unburdened by the cares and whims of others. Never have I known such a man, yet you now wear your troubles about you, and the burden weighs heavily. If I might alleviate this, then I would do so."

It was in this moment Fox realized that should he gaze upon that smile every day than he would be happy. The thought was thrilling and terrifying; to be so dependent upon another. Should she remain, then he would truly love life, yet should she not, he would know only despair. It was a power he had never granted to one, nor did he believe he ever would. The girl could wield such power to make him weak just as she could to make him strong... yet he trusted her. He must trust her now.

"I am indeed a fortunate man." he replied "Fortunate to have found you. I have little time for pity. Balthazar is cruel to those who resign themselves to it. All have the power to love life, to live it fully, it is they and no other who resign themselves to misery, they who allow themselves to be caged by that which they lament. My problems are no worse than any, yet I find myself caught in the sway of that which I have so often scorned in others."

"Then unburden yourself to me now. I do not question your strength, yet pain festers in the strongest of men when it is seeded. You must cut it free."

Fox placed his hand on her cheek, returning the caress. "Do not ask this of me. I have never had so much as I do now, yet if I tell you what tortures me, I risk losing it all."

"No my love... you do not. To love someone is to share in both pain and joy. There can be no other way. If you deny me this, than you deny me your true self, and I cannot love a shadow."

Fox lowered his eyes. What emerged from his lips was a torrent of pain. He knew that he would hurt her with his words, yet he could not do otherwise.

The knowledge that Krillian, the man who had killed her own mother had now re-entered her life- that he himself was responsible- he had expected any reaction save for the one he received. When he finished the tale, Sariss removed her arm from his side and placed both around him. Then she wept. She wept for some time before she spoke again.

"That monster killed one whom I loved." she whispered "I will not stand by and watch him kill another."

"No. You shall not."

The river continued to mark their path, sometimes receding to the slightest of streams, other times growing so large as to accommodate a morning bath for the entire party as well as their beasts. In places, the old road was so overgrown that low-hanging branches shredded the wagon's tarpaulin, yet the skins of Fox's many trophies provided patchworks that only made the canvass stronger. Bolt enjoyed a steady diet of carrots and wild radishes to supplement their stores of oatcakes, and Luther and Lola continued to devour whatever was fed to them. Oft times Sariss filled their slop bags with gruel as they marched simply to keep them from devouring stones, though Fox suspected that such a diet would perfectly suit their palate. The stamina of all had greatly increased from the journey, due in no small part to the easing of their road-wearinhess in Serdia, and they continued to make swift progress. They had not come upon any other travelers whatsoever until late into their trek, when Aron assured them that the golden city loomed near.

The old road led them down a winding path within a small mountain range, though these paled in comparison to the great bluffs in the west, consisting of little more than rising swells of rocky land. As ever, Erik had been scouting ahead, now mounted upon Bolt, for the mare had come to warm to him nearly as much as her own master- when he returned to inform them that riders in the distance approached. They were within a small clearing in the hills, dotted with caves, and Aron indicated they halt here and prepare for the imminent arrival. The presence of a fire-pit in the center of the clearing, fallen logs which acted as benches, as well as scraps of cloth which lined the cave openings proper, told that the area had recently been an encampment of some kind.

"Probably just fellow travelers wishing to avoid the clutter upon the King's highway." Aron said in attempt to mitigate concerns and uneasiness "Nevertheless, t'would be wise to be on our guard, for this place looks to be a bandit hideout, and from my days as soldier, I can well remember those lot not taking kindly to any invasion upon their territory."

The small infantry of soldiers who crested the rise could not possibly have announced themselves in louder fashion had they trumpeted a war-horn. Each was clad in gold-plated armor from head to toe which shone like a beacon under the mid-afternoon sun. There were five of them in total and Fox ascertained that, save one, they were all veteran soldiers. The four men who made up the rear rode their war horses with practiced skill. Their squinted eyes branched into several lines at the edges, etched into their skin from staring too long at the sun, darted about for any sign of danger. Their swords were not attached to their saddles so as to spare them their added weight, but on their belts, near to hand should they need them. Such was not the case with their apparent leader. At the head of the horsemen rode a man whose young eyes and fair features had not a trace of premature wrinkles. His shaven face, and indeed his armor as well, seemed not to have the faintest trace of road dust upon it. Unlike the others, he wore no helmet, yet his perfectly coifed blond locks flit about his high-born features, chiseled cheekbones and pointed nose, which seemed every bit as bird-like as the eagle crested headwear his fellow soldiers wore. The plates and chainmail of his armor seemed lightweight, despite its gold ornamentation, which, though Fox merely assumed the alias of smithy, he knew to be the most impractical substance for armor of any kind. His sword, nestled in its jewel encrusted scabbard, was strapped to his war horse's saddle. He alone bore the standard of the golden eagle upon his breastplate, and this was polished so as to render any attempt at stealth impossible. The sword arms of the calvary men twitched as he rode in abrasively, unarmed, and spoke in loud, condescending manner.

"Identify yourselves and state your business!" he yelled in a high pitched, well manicured accent.

"We are travelers on our way to Damaas." responded Aron "We avoided the highway so as to make better time."

"A likely story!" the soldier shrieked "Know that you now face Lord Fabian, nephew to King Khimotai himself! I have been instructed to ferret out any thieves who may still be lingering nearby. With princess Asteria to be wed, the King does not want to risk the type of uprising we have heard tell is currently taking place in Serdia! We have even heard rumors that the fearsome Fox of Gemmen himself, most notorious of all thieves, is said to be travelling east. Tell me, why are you camped here at this known bandit hideout?"

Fox winced at the lordling's speech. Had they indeed been bandits, this one had just identified himself as a valuable hostage whose ransom would likely be more than a lifetimes worth of coin any bandit could net pilfering from caravan trains. The jewels on his scabbard alone simply begged to be stolen from any such bandit he might run across in his attempt to apprehend. Likewise, the gold plating he bore could be melted and sold in the more unscrupulous quarters of Serdia as easily as freshly minted coin with Alric's own seal. It was not difficult to deduce that Khimotai, having been made aware that the local bandit villages had been cleared and sent to aid in the fight in Serdia, had sent his nephew on a mission of no real danger, yet rife with the illusion of import. He nearly felt sorry for the guards who were assigned to protect him, lest they accidentally happen to come across any real danger this one was so convinced they had been seeking.

"Clearly my lord" Aron continued "we have not set up camp as our wagon is still packed, and you can see from our recent tracks that we have made swift passage hither since early this morn. We are but farmers, here to visit my youngest daughter in yonder Damaas."

Fox had to suppress his laughter, for Aron stood nearly as high as the noble seated atop his mount, and the entire scene gave the impression of a perched sparrow scolding a buffalo for its audacity at disturbing its roost. The speech seemed to confuse Fabian momentarily. Perhaps feeling as though he were being tricked somehow, she shook aside Aron's words with a turn of his head as he faced his men.

"Search the wagon! I will have nothing interrupt my cousin's wedding!"

Fox watched as the soldiers dismounted and feigned rummaging through their belongings. Such a chore was clearly beneath them, yet accosting innocent peasants in swelteringly hot armor was still a better fate than having one's head charred on a pike. Bolt alone echoed what all were feeling, for she snorted in open derision at their efforts. Fox in particular bristled. Had he been the man he was when he had begun this adventure he would have abandoned his pose there and then that he might teach the whelp a lesson. The guardsmen did such a poor job searching however that his temper cooled. Had he supervised their efforts, even a fop such as Fabian would likely have chastised them for their laziness, yet his his attention was fixed upon Sariss. He dismounted with a flourish and walked to where she stood; his smile so wide that his polished teeth competed with the loudness of his breastplate. For a moment, he paced about her in a circle, one hand cupping his chin appreciatively as his eyes drank in every inch of her figure. Sariss stiffened, clearly accustomed to such attention from nobles, yet said nothing. Fox's blood boiled. Visions of snapping the whelp like a twig over his knee danced through his mind. Despite his time in the presence of Aron and his family, he had not yet developed the restraint most peasants displayed when dealing with such men.

Fabian continued to ogle Sariss openly, lingering on the swell of her hips and taut, rigid midsection, before gazing upwards at her heaving chest and long, raven black hair which framed her pale features. His thin lips curved into a smile.

"Farmers you say?" the lordling grinned in open avarice, pausing momentarily for emphasis "Well farmer, I must congratulate you on such fine stock!" He had not taken his eyes off of Sariss as he spoke, and it was she whom he now addressed. "Tell me my beauty; have you seen any thieves upon your journey that I might dispatch for you?"

"None, my lord." Sariss replied diplomatically "Though I do wish you much luck on your quest."

"Luck!" ejaculated Fabian "I can assure you that my men and I represent the finest soldiers in Damaas. I hardly need luck to know a thief when I see one."

By this time Fox had taken a few steps towards Fabian, his unrestrained anger writ explicitly on his features. Despite the nobleman's lustful attentions towards Sariss, his outright hostility did not go unnoticed.

"And who are you?" he said, swiveling his head about dispassionately

Out of the corner of his eye, Fox could see that Erik's fingers tapped upon the pommel of his sword. In front of him, Aron was knotting his massive hands into fists and seemed ready to brain the young whelp for his audacity. The entire situation drew the attention of the guardsmen, who clearly did not relish their fates if they failed to protect their charge, for, like Erik, their hands drifted to their hilts.

Fox closed the distance between them, placed his arm across Sariss's shoulders and planted a kiss firmly on her lips.

"Come my love. You need not fear to trust these men, clearly they are the best hunters in the realm!" he affixed his gaze on Fabian "We were accosted by thieves some leagues back. If you follow our trail and hurry, you might still be able to catch them!"

"Truly?!" Fabian shouted. He stood erect and straightened his armor.

"Come men, clearly these farmers and their stable boy have nothing to hide. Mount up! The game is now well and truly afoot!"

The soldiers left the wagon, which seemed completely unmolested, and mounted their horses. Fabian swung himself into the saddle ahead of them and bowed low towards Sariss. "If our paths ever cross in Damaas my pretty, I should be honored to give you a personal tour of my quarters in the palace."

He attempted to draw his sword. Realizing that it was out of reach, he simply thrust his hand in the direction Fox and his friends had come and yelled. "Onward! For honor and victory!"

He charged off into the distance, his soldiers following him. Remembering that Aron was once a soldier in Damaas himself, Fox wondered if he felt sorry for their lot and turned his gaze to look at him. Their eyes met briefly, and Aron began to laugh. He continued laughing, and soon all were infected. The entire party doubled over in laughter, past the point that the situation warranted. Soon they were laughing merely because they could not stop laughing.

In no time all four were lying upon the ground, laughing hysterically. At regular intervals, one of their number regained control of themselves, only to look upon the other and the entire routine commenced again.

It was the release each of them needed. By the time they were able to stop themselves; even the overly stern Aron could not cease smiling and his face was stained with tears.

"Come." he said "We yet have much distance to travel, yet can feel secure in the knowledge that our path has been cleared."

By late that afternoon they had crested the hills and the winding path they were following opened up into wide plains as far as the eye could see. Before them, the King's highway snaked its way to the horizon where the sun glowed unnaturally strong.

"I must warn you." came the voice of Aron "The ways of Damaas will seem strange to you. You must follow my example if we are to find your sister without drawing too much attention to ourselves, and ending up in the dungeon for our trouble."

"Dungeon?" Erik replied quizzically "Do you believe that Sariss and I intend to slay a nobleman in the streets?"

Aron did not laugh at the jest, but merely sighed. "There is a reason boy, that my rank as soldier here was a position of high honor. The city guard are fanatical. Be wary, and still any insolence when we arrive."

Their conversation was brought to an end by Sariss whose attention was fixed on the horizon. "Father. I see a line of mountains yonder, yet I have been told that there is little but plains between Serdia and the eastern sea, and why do they shimmer so?"

"Those are not mountains you spy my daughter," Aron replied "though you can be easily forgiven for thinking such. What you see before you is the skyline of the golden city itself. Damaas. Its towers reach as high at the loftiest mountaintop."

Erik, Aron and Fox joined Sariss in staring in open wonder and awe at the sheer size and soft golden glow of the Kingdom in the distance. For a long while, they stood motionless, utterly consumed by the moment. It was Aron himself who broke the silence. "Come." he said "Though it has been an age, I'll warrant I still know of a few taverns where they do not bleed a man of the entirety of his coin for a decent flagon of ale. I have no doubt that I am not alone in my desire to wash the trail dust from my throat."

CHAPTER TWENTY - THE GOLDEN CITY

From their earlier vantage point Damaas had seemed near, yet such was merely an illusion due to the sheer size of the Kingdom, for 'twas late the following day by the time they arrived at its outer perimeter. Aron had insisted that they break camp before entering the plains, avering that little sleep would be had amidst the chaos of those vying for entry. They retired afore the sun went down and were upon the trail again long afore it crested the sky. No lamplight was required for this leg of their journey, for the land before them was bathed in the golden glow of the city beyond, just as the moon itself seemed as a shiny golden orb in the night sky. They had not merged with the King's highway as Fox had expected, for there seemed to be no single entry point to and fro the city. Each and every roadway from every direction simply dissolved into the enormous valley that surrounded the shining realm where it abutted the great eastern sea. Warriors from the northlands spilled into the valley from their home atop the great mountains. Pilgrims from the west as well as dignitaries from the south who followed the path of their own respected highways found that all such ended here, the final destination before the infinite sea beyond. There was no vegetation in sight. Even the grass had long since been trampled underfoot. It was as though the forest which once, long ago, must have lived here, had to retreat beyond the borders of the valley in order for the civilization within to thrive.

Without a single tree or outlying building to provide cover, the feeling of claustrophobia was stifling. By midday Fox felt as though he was drowning in a sea of wayfarers, and he had to keep his hands on Bolt's reigns where he and Erik walked astride her to keep her from panicking. Aron and Sariss rode atop the wagon. All were stunned to silence by the sheer majesty of the futuristic architecture which could now be seen in all its splendor. Golden spires stretched so high that their balconies seemed to be crafted of clouds. He recalled, as a child, having seen the palace in Gemmen for the first time. Now, as a man, he was brought back to that moment, a gleeful regression, for the same youthful exuberance coursed through him now at the sight of palisades which soared above even the grandest towers of that majestic abode. Afore now, Fox believed that the title 'golden city' was but a reference to the Kingdom's vaunted wealth, yet it appeared as though the city itself was chiseled out of a mountain of gold. The construction seemed beyond the skill of men, and Fox was reminded again of Aron's story. Truly, this was the domain of gods; yet as all about him craned their necks in wonder and amazement, he began to feel the chill of the unnatural upon his spine- that which always warned him of danger.

There was no outer wall to protect it. No stone, nor masonry nor battlements; as though none would dare stand in defiance before it. His growing sense of unease increased with each step, for the image of an open sore upon Balthazar- a poisonous blemish on the land which would only continue to spread lest it were lanced, grew incrementally in his belly. He was familiar with the feeling, for he oft felt disillusioned with life in Gemmen for similar reasons, yet there at least he could retreat to the outlying woods to find succor. Here there was no escaping that all-too familiar sensation that, despite the stunning accomplishments and innovations of civilization- there was something obscene and vulgar in its utter defiance of nature. A feeling of self-loathing began to affect his pallor. Each moment of awe he experienced; that which eclipsed such emotions known to him previously during his encounters with the beauty of nature, were accompanied by surges of guilt and betrayal. Throughout his life, such repressed revulsion followed his every step, bubbling to the surface with every new discovery, every new adventure; yet never before had it carried with it such potency. He stared about him only to discover that he alone felt this way. Whilst all eyes stared upwards in astonishment, he alone lowered his gaze. Were he to continue, he would somehow need to reconcile, to atone somehow, though he knew not how or why. It remained only to bury the sensation. He had a mission to fulfill. Somewhere within this impossible domain was Ciella, Queen of thieves. It was Cammarran's wish that he find her. He understood now that the machinations of his mentor were never as they appeared. She was a clue to the ever expanding riddle the path Cammarran set him towards had become. Despite all, he would not fail.

As there was no outer wall, there was no single entrance point, no funneling of traffic through any sort of gate. The entire kingdom was exposed, as though, in their vanity, even the smaller buildings which seemed to act as bracers for the countless golden towers about them wished to display themselves proudly for all to see. The spires and parapets of the tallest of these towers seemed to be woven from real gold, and not the polished brass he was expecting, which had the effect of drawing the sun from their mirrored surfaces and casting its glow down to the base of the kingdom- which in turn shone outwards, bathing the entire valley and the people about him in blinding golden hues. The effect was nauseating to the point that traffic was slow despite the lack of impediments as every traveler needed time to adjust to the overwhelming assault to their senses.

The letter he had been given from Cammarran which identified him to Ciella as a young thief named Barnabas was still hidden in the weave of his saddle bag safely tucked within the wagon, yet he could not imagine how any city with a guild the likes of which operated in every other district on Balthazar could contain such indescribable wealth without having been stripped to its core long since. Despite its enormous scale, the Kingdom seemed imminently vulnerable to a raid, both from without, and from within. The danger was so apparent, that he did not believe he would betray his lineage as a thief, nor his gnawing sense of unease if he commented on it.

"How is it that such an undefended Kingdom of riches has not yet been razed to the ground?" he addressed Aron, shouting to be heard above the crowd "Such an abundance of gold so ripe for plunder must be a tempting target for conquest. And what of the citizens, surely these would have turned to thievery with such wealth so near to hand?"

The farmer was busy trying to steer the oxen through the thong, for the traffic became even more congested as their proximity to Damaas narrowed.

"The Damaascian army." he replied "I did not jest when I said that a position as soldier is the highest honor one can attain in Damaas. Their army is yet larger than any two of the four powers of Balthazar combined. At all hours, legions of soldier march about the streets, monitoring the behavior of all. The golden city, as you can see, is surrounded by plains, and any who would attempt to conquer Khimotai's forces would have to face them in open warfare. Even distant Raimia is not foolish enough to attempt it. Also, the eastern ocean lies many leagues in the distance, making it impossible to mount any assault by sea. Were these not times of peace between the four realms, I would hazard that it be they who should fear the might of Damaas."

Try as he might, Fox could not let the matter drop. He knew that a thieves' guild operated out of a secret headquarters called the Tarot deep within the heart of the city. He could not imagine such a guild existing in tandem with a plethora of unparalleled wealth and not having availed themselves of it.

"It hardly seems conceivable." he pressed on "Should a well-coordinated team of insurgents pilfer the gold from just one of yonder towers, they could escape to Gemmen and live like Lords."

"Aye." Aron replied "The forest is rife with bandits who would like nothing less; yet there is a reason these stick to robbing caravans. You have only to look about you."

Aron's point was well-made, for in every direction soldiers clad in golden armor outnumbered the very travelers who attempted migration. There were so many of them in fact, each performing their duties with precise military efficiency, that not a single skirmish had broken out upon the valley floor- the result of fraying tempers of road-weary travelers pressed too tightly together.

Soon, they warranted the attention of five of these who approached them with lances held upright in perfect symmetry, each clad in polished armor which gleamed impeccably despite the trail dust about them. Aron and Sariss both disembarked from the wagon to greet them.

There was no fop such as Fabian at their head, which Fox did not find the least bit surprising, for only the most competent of soldiers could have maintained order in such chaos. Their lieutenant, his rank indicated by the golden eagle on his breastplate the others lacked, whose wings ended in claps that held his flowing red cape in place, addressed them.

"Welcome weary travelers, to Damaas!" he said smiling, his arms outstretched for emphasis, his voice bombastic and prideful. There was not the slightest trace of the sort of condescension Fox had become accustomed to when dealing with this type, yet the manner in which he greeted them seemed so amicable as to be unworthy of trust. All five of the guardsmen were young, yet conducted themselves as veteran soldiers. They marched in tight formation, as though they were prepared for battle at a moment's notice. Each had close-cropped dark hair, barely visible under their helmets, save for the one who addressed them, whose red hair and mustache seemed to glow under the ambient light.

"Welcome and well met." Aron responded diplomatically "We are farmers on sabbatical who have travelled the long road from distant Gemmen that we might visit my youngest daughter who resides within. This represents our first visit to your Kingdom, though regrettably we shall be staying but a short while, that my family may meet her future husband who intends to ask my permission for her hand."

"Many are the people from distant lands who come to Damaas." the lieutenant responded proudly "You are indeed fortunate that your daughter intends to unite your house with one of our own. There is no toll for entry, as all are welcome here, though we must inspect your belongings and secure your weapons before allowing you entry."

"No toll?" responded Fox

"Our weapons?" responded Erik

“Why yes.” The guardsman continued “None but the King’s guard are permitted to carry weapons of any kind within Damaas, and as you can see...” he pointed to the city behind him “We have no shortage of gold.”

“But what if we have need to defend ourselves?” Erik pressed on. He would have continued to protest, but a stern look from his father stilled his tongue.

“Protect yourselves from what?” the guard continued “It is the job of the guardsmen to protect all. I can assure you, that unlike from whence you came, there is no criminal element of any kind within our Kingdom.”

As the soldier spoke, and without waiting to be granted permission, the four soldiers who accompanied him began to search the wagon. Feeling somewhat territorial, Bolt once again snorted and reared up on her hind legs in response to their poking and prodding, yet the men continued to rummage through the belongings as though completely unaffected by her outburst. As she herself was unadorned save for her bridle, they let her be, and Fox was grateful, for one was likely to receive an iron-shod hoof in the face for their efforts.

Unlike the lackluster job Fabian’s men had conducted earlier, the wagon was searched thoroughly, yet all was returned exactly as they had left it when they completed. Fox was grateful for Cammarran’s instruction that he should hide his letter well, for despite the efficiency of their search, they did not discover it.

Fox was alarmed to note that they had confiscated Sariss’s longbow, his own daggers, Erik's rapier, and even Aron's hunting knife from their stores. Immediately he understood why Aron had been so adamant that they use the entirety of their stock of the desert sage, for he clearly did not want the plant to be discovered lest these have unwanted questions which might reach the ears of the monks at the Temple of Light.

Having completed their search of the wagon, the men now turned their attention to them. The lieutenant pointed to one of the nearest buildings. It was small, square set, yet nonetheless beautifully constructed, and was mirrored by the many such buildings which lined the entire outer rim of the Kingdom.

"Your weapons will be stored here at this armory. You may obtain them when you leave."

"But..." Erik began, refusing to let the matter drop "You must have countless such weapons stored, from countless travelers who have passed this way, what is to stop anyone from claiming our weapons as their own and absconding with them?"

The lieutenant laughed openly before he spoke.

"Clearly you are accustomed to troubles which simply do not exist here in Damaas. What you are describing would be an act of theft, and I have already assured you that such acts are not tolerated. I have no doubt that once you experience the way of life here, you may never care to leave."

Erik opened his mouth to protest further, yet Aron's firm arm came down on his shoulder and pulled him away.

"We thank you for your service." he said

Feeling utterly bewildered, Fox followed him as Aron led his family towards the street which abutted the armory. The farmer kept his hands on the bridle of the oxen just as Fox held firm to Bolt's reigns, for the mare seemed to share his utter distaste for the civilization they were about to enter and he feared that she might turn about at any moment and race at full gallop back towards Gemmen. As he laid his boot upon the cobblestone which separated the valley floor from the new world which loomed menacingly before them, he mused that with one simple step he would exchange one reality for another. He stared up, his vision tracing a line from the armory to the dizzying heights of the nearest of the towers. Each of them stood taller than the Golden Tower in Serdia, which proved to be but a precursor to what lie in wait for him here.

"Come." said Aron "The old woman gave precise directions on how to reach her cousin Orin's inn. I am told that he has done well here in Damaas. The inn has a stable where we can keep our beasts, and our recent matron has promised us fair treatment if we but mention that we were are friends of the Pilgrim's Oasis in Serdia. We must hurry if we are to arrive there before curfew."

"Curfew!" ejaculated Erik "Are we children to be treated in such a manner? I have had no curfew since long before there was stubble upon my chin!"

"Aye, and little heed did you ever pay it then!" Aron replied sourly "I like it not either boy. Long ago did I become disillusioned with the way of life here in the east. There was a reason why I chose to settle once again in Gemmen, where you and your sisters might know the taste of freedom, and if you ever intend to enjoy such privilege again than I suggest that you curb your discontent and do as I say. Upon the morrow, we shall see Veronica. Until then, we shall govern ourselves in accordance with Khimotai's laws."

Aron's words resonated deeply with Fox. He had always prided himself as being above the laws of men. The thieves guild existed, above all else, for this reason. He was no stock to be shepherded. Having taken his first few steps into Damaas, he looked about him. Guards were everywhere, each carrying their spears like cattle prods, culling the herd. There were no beggars, no vagabonds, wastrels or wantons. No drunkards could be seen leaning upon the trowels for support. No scantily clad women cast doe eyes in the direction of any with a jingle in their purse. None greeted each other. There was no conversation to be had, no bawdy gestures of good will. The people shuffled about the streets without ever once looking up at the majestic towers overhead. Their healthy gaits appeared free of sickness and blight, yet Fox could not shake the overwhelming sense of horror their appearance garnered.

His mind was in turmoil. Had Cammarran sent him here as some kind of test- a means to demonstrate to him that there were other ways of life besides that of a thief? Did the Tarot, the secret location of the thieves' guild even exist? Did Ciella? He made up his mind to find out on the spot. Wordlessly, he approached the wagon. His fingers darted about until he retrieved his map from its hidden location within. His sudden, peculiar behavior caused his companions to turn about and stare at him perplexedly.

"I have a pressing errand." was his response to their questioning stares. He felt as though he had neither the time nor the means to excuse himself with a clever explanation. The sudden need for escape pulled at him. "I shall meet you at Orin's tavern. Aron, will you kindly see to Bolt for me? I have little coin."

The big man's expression shifted from befuddlement to one of understanding, as though he himself understood what Fox did not. He nodded. "Think nothing of it Costa; though I'll warrant you'll never make it there before nightfall."

"I'll see to my own lodgings. In the morning, I will purchase breakfast. Have no fear!"

He tucked Cammarran's letter into his jerkin and raced off, leaving the twins decidedly puzzled in his absence.

CHAPTER TWENTY-ONE - THE QUEEN OF THIEVES

Fox rounded the corner, racing. Despite the towering buildings around him, there were no shadows to retreat to, no privacy. The accursed golden light found its way everywhere. Eventually, he was forced to slow his gait lest such aberrant behavior be slowed by the weight of shackles, though even these were doubtless gold-plated. He retrieved the map from inside his jerkin and began to study it as though it were a shopping list in his attempt to maintain the illusion that the errand he was set to was one of pure innocence. The crowd of citizens he immersed himself in shuffled about in restrained haste themselves, their eyes permanently affixed to the ground and to the business at hand. The silence was deafening, unnatural; it turned his stomach. There was no joy to be found; no pain, no laughter or lament. He squinted his eyes and grimaced, swallowing his unease as though forcing the sourest drink into his gullet. He was perhaps the best there was when it came to maintaining anonymity-in Gemmen, his presence was always felt yet never seen, like an itch no amount of scratching could erase. He never fully appreciated the perfect camouflage found in squalor; never understood how much he depended upon areas where one's eyes refused to probe. An entire world existed in Gemmen where the footpads of undesirables tread alongside the recognition of those with whom they shared the streets, a reality juxtaposed with their own, their existence dimly recognized yet beyond the periphery of what was near to hand. Such a luxury was ne'er to be had in an environment so perfectly engineered. Here, whatever cog in the great machinework that became corroded was removed and replaced rather than built around. There was no old world; no character. All was shiny and new, streamlined, as though nothing withered and broken yet adamant in its defiance lay beneath the plating, polished to a sheen. The constant patrols of guards monitored the movements of all, as though he and the entire populace about him presented an imminent threat to the carefully cultivated order of their own existence. For the first time in memory, his unparalleled talents at dissolving into a crowd failed him. He was forced to rely solely on his generic appearance to avoid suspicion. He felt violated; exposed. The creeping sense of unease which followed him since first having spied Damaas in the distance, like a cluster of emeralds on a rocky escarpment, grew to such intensity that the need for escape now pulled at every fiber of him.

He walked for some time, yet never did he feel as though he covered any distance, for his environment stubbornly refused to change from one gold plated edifice to the next. There were no neighborhoods; no distinct burrows or districts with their own unique personalities and flavors. The few kiosks he passed which sold bread and meat offered little in the way of aromas which might have stimulated his appetite, and he had no doubt that even the food itself was here prepared by pre-approved standards which allotted no room for deviation. The bodies of those whom he passed, completely consumed by the roles assigned to them, were seemingly healthy, yet their spirits, as evidenced by their hollow, lifeless eyes, were in desperate need of nutrition.

All was uniformity. There were no landmarks to speak of- no way to gauge the terrain aside from marking one's environment by the height of the nearest of the many lofty towers, and any pause he might have taken in order to get his bearings threatened to upset the monotonous flow of traffic. The legendary navigators who stories told had eyes which could see further than any predator of the skies, they who plied the many sailing vessels on the western sea near the edge of the world, would likely have fared no better, for the highest steeples shone so brilliantly as to hurt ones eyes if they dared to look at them, making north, east, south and west abstract concepts. No shadows dragged themselves across the terrain that they might indicate the time of day. There were no recesses where a man might find relief, no trees to greet him in welcome with their outstretched branches.

His body continued to recoil, refusing to become sterilized in a sterile environment. Desperation drove him onwards- the search for escape. It was a testament to Cammarran's thoroughness that the map he had given him provided him with directions that were possible to follow. He could not trust asking any of the ever-looming guardsmen for directions, lest they suspect him of reading subversive material and confiscate Cammarran's letter and map- which he knew not only identified him as a thief, but the Tarot itself as the secret headquarters of their guild.

The glare of the streets dimmed but a little, the only evidence that the sun had lowered by the time he found the tavern, yet the manner in which it lingered evidenced a fear at bringing about the night lest an invitation be extended to those who prefer the darkness.

From the outside, there was nothing about the Tarot to distinguish it from any other building save its sign above the door frame. Though it was somewhat smaller in scale than the shops which surrounded it, its window frames, trim, and even the sign itself were intricately woven with the now-generic gold leaf. He took a small measure of comfort when he realized that polished brass adorned its other surfaces. Doubless, this was the closest to privation he was likely to encounter.

He made his way through the front door and was rewarded with a flood of relief. For one precious moment, it seemed as though he was back in Gemmen. Despite its camouflaged exterior, the interior of the Tarot was nearly an exact replica of the Bear's Den. There was not a trace of polished gold on any surface, and the dim light was maintained solely by the fire within the hearth. Whatever fears he had that the thieves guild in Damaas was nonexistant dissolved, for naught but a rebellious society comprised of outlaws could possibly have succeeded in maintaining such defiant and subversive decor. He closed his eyes momentarily, allowing them the chance to adjust to the blandness. When he opened them again he was pleased to note that all about him, men and women drank and conversed openly, singing bawdy songs without fear of censorship from the world which existed beyond their front door. Gone were generic uniforms, replaced by scanty wisps of cloth which clung tightly to well-rounded women, and coarse hide which strained the muscles of hard men with hard faces. Barbarians and rangers drained their tankards in single swallows, wiping froth from their stubble and scars, each having found their way here by heeding the call of the primordial. What assassins he could identify did not hide in the darkened corners, but drank openly, with no fear of discovery.

He made his way to a dimly lit table in the back and breathed a contented sigh at being cloaked in shadow once more. A forgotten tankard of ale sat upon it. He blew out the single candle set in an unadorned sconce and drained the glass. He had not yet received permission for any act of thievery of course, but one could not betray their nature. He elicited a broad grin when he realized that it tasted bitter and flat. His eyes closed as the tension sloughed off of his shoulders. His muscles, knit so tightly as to ache, began to ease as the ale flowed through him, adding to the warmth and comfort of the feral stares and dim light. He closed his eyes once more that he might fully probe the room with his senses. He could hear insults being hurled good naturedly. There was no offense meant, nor taken by those who refused to censor their behavior, but rather enjoyed the privilege of shouting expletives and profanity to those who would not pale nor draw swords, but rather meet such words in kind, carried upon a flow of raucous laughter.

If the guild here was truly akin to the Bear's Den in Gemmen, then there was protocol to be considered- one did not confront a thief in their own lair, one waited for them to come to you. Nevertheless, having attained a level of comfort at last, Fox found that he was in no hurry. A serving girl approached him, her heaving breasts, lacking in concealment and yellowed teeth lacking in number flashed him in greeting and he ordered several more tankards of the familiar, sour-tasting ale. He savored every sip as though it were the finest Raimian wine. He was well into his cups when Ciella, Queen of the thieves' guild of Damaas, sat down to join him.

She did not identify herself as such; merely another nameless patron of the establishment looking for an empty table that she might partake in an ale. The ambiance, the foul air, the unspoken demureness of the crowd identified her as brazenly as any snitch. She was older than he, though still in the prime of her beauty. Her hair hung down to her waist where it was tied back with a leather strap and was the darkest crimson he had ever seen. It was nearly ebon in fact, yet where the light from the nearby hearth cascaded across her mane in flickering waves, it glowed like the embers in the fire.

She was dressed much the same as Sariss herself- tight riding leathers and blouse, though her boots rose as high as her knees and Fox was relieved to note that a long rapier hung from her belt. She was tall and lean, with skin the color of tanned leather stretched tightly across her well-toned physique. Her features were angular, with a pointed nose and high cheekbones, her thin lips complimenting the dark red of her hair where they curved wickedly in sarcastic bemusement. Her eyes were doe-shaped, and the deep amber within them played impishly in the firelight. The effect was one of elusive beauty, set beneath a snare of cleverness and guile.

"Welcome." she said "We don't often entertain strangers here at the Tarot. What brings you to our door?" The words were spoken softly- dulcet tones that screamed menace; and Fox had no doubt that they commanded both attention and obeisance from all whom she addressed.

Wordlessly, Fox slid Cammarran's note across the table. "I have here a letter for Ciella."

"I'll read it to her." she replied

She took the parchment in her long fingers without ever shifting her piercing gaze from his until the moment she unfolded it. Here at last, her expression betrayed her, for she clearly recognized Cammarran's seal as she broke it. She scanned the note briefly before reading it aloud.

"Dearest Ciella. The man before you is known as Barnabas. He has proven himself to be a competent member of our order. Please grant him your endorsement to operate within Damaas as I am sure that he will prove to be of value to you. Cammarran."

As Ciella read the note, Fox was suddenly overcome by a wave of sadness. It occurred to him for the first time since having received it that this was likely the last the old man had ever graced any such parchment with his signature.

Ciella crumpled the note into her fist in apparent disgust and threw it onto the sawdust at her feet.

"Ha!" she ejaculated "Our order… same old Cammarran. He still seems to think that we here in Damaas merely content ourselves with fleecing nobles. Were things so simple… he has no idea of the troubles I've inherited. Or perhaps he has merely forgotten."

Catching herself, Ciella resumed her crooked grin before turning her attention to him once again.

"Well." she began, her barbed expression now resuming all of its wickedness "I have heard much about you. It is an honor to finally make your acquaintance Fox."

Fox refused to give her the satisfaction of registering the shock and surprise he felt. When he responded, it was in cool, calculating tones. "It seems as though I am not the only one here present who has discerned the other's identity. Tell me, was it some secret turn of phrase employed by Cammarran?"

"Nothing so elaborate." she replied, her grin now a broad smile "Cammarran has always underestimated his apprentices, but you and I alone would know all about that."

Fox flashed a wicked grin equal to her own. She was thus far a worthy opponent, yet he refused to give any ground. "He did mention that the two of you shared a history together."

Ciella threw her head back in wanton laughter. "Is that all? Cammarran was always frustratingly secretive. As to your first question, news has long since reached me that the fearsome Fox of Gemmen would soon arrive in Damaas. The guild has spies everywhere. We tracked your movements ere you entered the city. Or do you believe that we here in the Tarot are want to wear our weapons openly in full defiance of Khimotai's law when a stanger comes amongst us? Your reputation seems to have fallen somewhat short. You are embarrassingly easy to follow. I'm certain that this would not be the case were this Gemmen, yet here in Damaas, a thief must employ strategems of an altogether different sort in order to preserve anonymity."

Fox did not take the rebuke well. Who could have possibly betrayed him? What spy did she speak of? There were rumors of course that he had left Gemmen, yet he had heard none which indicated that his destination was Damaas. He turned the question around in his mind before he answered. "Darus!" he ejaculated "Captain Darus of Metropolis!"

Ciella reeled back in her chair, fully conceding him the point. "You are clever! I can see why Cammarran speaks so highly of you. Indeed." she leaned in close before she spoke again "There are plots unfolding upon Balthazar the like of which have not unfolded in many an age. Were I to tell you of what dire circumstances have united a Captain of the Raimian army and the leader of the thieves guild of Damaas I hazard you would scant believe it."

"Why inform me at all?" Fox replied

"Cammarran and I have maintained a correspondence for a long time, and like I say, he spoke highly of you." The sudden change to past tense told Fox that Ciella was aware of Cammarran's demise, just as her expression told that it pained her. "As to my relationship with Cammarran, in light of recent events, it is only just that you know of it."

Ciella leaned back in her chair once more. She took a long haul from her tankard. When she set it down, the solemn expression on her face told that their playful bout of verbal jousting had ended.

"I am not prone to Cammarran's ways of cryptic mantras and veiled truths and I haven't the time for riddles. Let us speak plainly. I met Cammarran when I was but a child. As you and I are near to being kin, he would have wished that you know of his life prior to arriving in Gemmen."

Her tone was a testament to her sincerity, and she braced herself for what was clearly going to be an honest, revealing story. Fox had to wonder if he was to be the first to hear it.

Two more flagons were brought to their table upon a tray adorned with moist bread and cheese. No coin was asked for and none was forthcoming. The small table they occupied was now a lone island, separated by a sea of sawdust where all congregated at the bar to afford them their privacy. Fox sipped at his drink modestly whilst Ciella cut into their meal with a mean looking dagger likely plucked from the breast of the last man who dared offer her insult.

"Prior to meeting Cammarran, I had been raised by bandits outside of Damaas." she placed the point of the dagger between her lips and allowed a portion of the cheese to melt beneath the power and veracity of her words. "The bandits who dwell in the forests beyond our borders are legion. Khimotai himself has but an inkling of their true number. Theirs is a heritage; a culture unto itself, one which exists outside the guild; yet as a people, they are disorganized, scattered, their leaders too preoccupied with clan feuds and perceived slights to honor to truly unify. They exist much as the Northmen once did, before the great war which unified them as a people. Our clan never stayed in one place over long, for the many raids by Damaascian soldiers kept us on the move." her eyes raised to the ceiling, yet were glossy, perceiving a cascade of images in her mind's eye alone "Ever running, ever claiming sanctuary in numbers which could quell any threat, eking out a survival chasing paltry caravans with forces that could crush an army, only to be scattered once more like so many leaves falling from the trees.

I never knew who my parents were, only that they had been killed in such a raid long ago. Our clan was loyal, each accountable to the other. I was cared for. We were a strong people- capable. Yet we had gotten greedy. Our ambition outgrew our reach. We set up camp near the river too close to the highway. We were tracked, and finally ambushed by Khimotai's infantry who, with precise military efficiency, cut off any escape and slaughtered us like livestock... We outnumbered them three to one. We had weapons and the wherewithal to use them. We knew the forest- knew the land... yet were uncoordinated, leaderless. I alone survived. I was cornered by four guardsmen in a small cave I had retreated to. Their commander had issued an order that none were to be left alive- only a single soldier recoiled at the idea of murdering a child. He turned on his comrades and slew them. I was able to retreat through a crevice in the cave I alone was small enough to crawl through and made my escape. I wandered about for days until Cammarran found me, half-starved, lost and alone. He was then leader of another bandit clan similar to my own. He raised me like a daughter, taught me everything there was to know about stealth, whilst I trained every day with the finest swordsmen and archers in the band. In time, I was the best amongst them. I was driven by purpose, a dream, a will that was beyond my brethren. I believed Cammarran to be the leader our people needed. It was he who would unify the clans; he who would keep what happened to me from ever happening to another. He alone shared my passion for rebellion... for revolt!

In time, Cammarran assumed control of the guild here in Damaas. He had taken me into the city many times under the guise of paupers. I still know not what machinations he employed in order to ascend to the head of the order. Cammarran was young then; his charisma overpowering to any caught within it. Our goal was first to assimilate the forest bandits into our order, then any who would join us. A new world order was ours for the taking! He worked within the Kingdom- my task was one of ambassador to the clans."

Fox was dumbstruck. It was true that Cammarran was a persuasive leader, yet the notion that he would ever attept to organize a rebellion ran counter-intuitive to what he knew of the man. In all the years he knew him, the thief lord did not attempt to overthrow

King Alric. He was powerful... respected... perhaps he could have accomplished this, yet such was not the nature of the thieves' guild. It had always been their way to offer the people a choice, 'een if they subscribed to the caste system they were born unto. To do otherwise would be a violation of their free will... They had demanded no such revolution. It was wrong to thrust war upon them lest many innocents suffer as a result. It mattered not if one agreed with the ways of the regime or no. To do so would be akin to replacing one tyrant for another. He stilled any questions that Ciella be permitted to tell her tale uninterrupted.

"The work was grueling. There was no single encampment that I might have relayed information to. Each time I left the golden city I was forced to spend nearly an entire season tracking down my nomadic brethren in attempts to enlist them into our cause. Nevertheless... those were good times. We were fighting... building towards something. For years we worked together, helping to create a resistance to Khimotai's regime from the inside... When he left, I believed he betrayed us all. For a time, I cursed his name...." She hung her head pensively. The regret was not feigned.

"I now know what compelled him to travel to the west, and I bear the shame of placing a dagger to his throat when he asked me to accompany him..."

Fox did not know if the thief Queen spoke in metaphor. Once again, he reserved any questions. The tale was painful for her to tell. It was best he allowed her to do so.

"Cammarran has always been insufferably cryptic. If only he had told me... the years I wasted loathing him, when I could have asked for his council.

I stayed with our people, eventually ascending to the head of the order. It now falls to me alone to fulfill our dream. In my time as leader, I have united both assassins and thieves under my banner. It now remains to recruit the forest bandits, then the Hillmen beyond, following that, any who would deign join our number. A war is brewing here in Damaas. I plan to be on the winning side. For that, I need generals. This is why you are here. This is why you must join me."

Fox stared about the room. There was much to digest. In all of the years he had known Cammarran, never had the old thief imparted so much information. Clearly, the thief-Queen was not one who subscribed to subtlety, nor procrastination. The knowledge that she and Cammarran were so different was accompanied by a wave of nausea and disgust. His erstwhile mentor would never have approved of an alliance between assassin and thief. Fox looked about the room once more. He believed the assassins here congregated to be on an errand of naught but frivolity- the chance to enjoy a tankard free from scrutiny. It was much the same at the Bear's Den in Gemmen, long established as neutral territory where assassin and thief alike could drink together in peace despite the tensions which existed outside the tavern doors... the notion that these were now privy to the secrets of his guild- that such a union was even contemplated much yet realized filled him with revulsion.

"This is wrong." he snarled through teeth clenched into a grimace

"It flies in the face of everything Cammarran stood for. You know this."

"Does it?" Ciella replied calmly "And here I though you knew the man."

Fox was unable to contain the rising tide of emotions within him as they bubbled over into anger; nor did he care to. His thoughts immediately turned to Krillian. A unity between thieves and any guild which could breed such a monster was vile, unspeakable.

"Trust that I will never join your order!" he cried, punctuating his words by slamming his fist upon the hard oak of the table. The candle flame flickered irritably at the outburst, yet Ciella remained placid. "I have been in Damaas merely a day and already I am sickened by what I have seen! Cammarran would never have allowed our guild to descend into such a state!"

"And what have you seen?" Ciella's voice was but a whisper, though she had traded her candor for authority

"I have seen freedom exchanged for servitude! I have seen individuality, ambition, creativity; the need to struggle, to learn, the thirst for adventure, mirth and mischief, all that our guild stands for- sterilized!"

The many patrons of the Tarot, those who had, until now, respected their privacy, turned to stare at the escalating conversation. Many a hand traced circles about the pommels of their swords. Fox raised his voice even higher- purposefully commanding the attention of all.

"We are not assassins! We are not killers, nor soldiers! We do not fight wars! We do not trade in pain and mysery, but in pilfered goods! We take back what is rightfully ours! We serve as a reminder to those who would subdue us that we are free!"

Ciella rose from her seat, her temper flared, her fevered pitch now matching his in ferocity. "And what do you know of the responsibilities of leadership? You who have shirked it? Who are you to stand in judgement of me? I know all about you- how you have wasted your talents in frivolous pursuits! I know now why Cammarran was forced to leave me! Years have I wasted cursing his name! It is you who took him from me! It is you who disgrace his memory! You who have wasted the gifts he gave to you! You who have wasted your purpose! You are but a child! A puppet now mimicking his master's voice! It is such oppression you speak of we have united to fight against! What you lament in the very impetus which drives me! What you callously criticize is the very fire of defiance Cammarran instilled in me before you were dropped on a doorstep, unfit to wipe your own arse you impudent whelp!!"

"Beware." Fox replied, his icy tone betraying the green fire in his eyes "Remember to whom you speak."

Ciella stared into his smoldering gaze. Never afore had anyone who did so not recoiled. Wordlessly, she lashed out. Fox saw the blow coming, yet made no move to stop her. He countered with a smile laced through with venom as blood pooled within the crevices of his exposed canines. Suddenly, the sound of dozens of swords escaping their scabbards rang in his ears and he was surrounded by pointed steel. He ignored them, never taking his eyes from Ciella's.

A long pause followed whilst the air about the room became heavy with tension. With a wave of her hand, Ciella dismissed the assembly. Each sword was placed back into its scabbard as the throng retreated to the firelight. The Queen of thieves resumed her seat before speaking again. With visible effort, she regained her composure.

"You have entered into a world which you cannot possibly understand, therefore in honor of Cammarran, I shall forgive you your insolence. There is intrigue aplenty afoot in the golden city. It is beyond your ken."

"Let it ever remain there." Fox replied scathingly "Such is an unwelcome guest."

Ignoring him, she continued. "With the Temple of Light at the center of Damaas, there is little in the way of sickness, though these have long since turned to the healing properties of herbs to replace their waning powers. With so much gold about, there is little in the way of poverty, despite the fact that there is nothing to spend it on which is not prohibited. You will find that the only price men balk at is the price of freedom. They must be shown a better way. Think beyond yourself for a moment. Do you believe that it was easy for Cammarran to have sent you hither? Perhaps a lifetime of aquiring whatever you wish has caused you to underestimate the true value of things, and people. Perhaps you maintain a nobleman's notion that the world is simply entitled to you- a toy to play with or discard upon a whim whilst the rest of us fight for something grand."

"Nobleman? Nobleman!" Fox cried. This time it was he who rose from his seat. "How dare you! I am more thief than any of you! I take what I want from those around me! I live my life above the laws of men!”

“And noblemen do not?” she replied coolly. Ciella did not rise. Nor did any rush to her side as before.

The words hit him like a cudgel. He struggled for a smart reply, yet was left wanting. After a moment, he spun about and headed towards the door.

“I would not recommend that.” Ciella replied, once again placing her dagger into the brick of cheese. “Curfew is in effect and guardsmen patrol the streets in force. Perhaps you would find another ale more to your liking.”

“I have yet to pay for the first.” Fox replied, affixing her with his gaze “I am a thief still and do not require, nor care for your permission. Perhaps you intend to stop me?”

He allowed his eyes to burn for a moment. When he saw that, once again, Ciella did not recoil nor show fear at the sight, he spun about once more, slamming the door loudly as he left.

He had walked but a short distance before he was accosted. Though it was now nightfall, the streets were aglow with thrice-accursed golden hues, and he had seen the guardsmen well before they had seen him. Perhaps it was because there was no dark alleyway for him to sneak into, or perhaps it was because he felt like doing something stupid, for he walked directly into their midst. They were six in number, and it was their leader, identified once again by the golden eagle crest on his chest plate who addressed him.

"Hold citizen! What business have you on the streets of Damaas after curfew?"

"It seemed like a pleasant evening for a stroll." Fox replied, his cool demeanor concealing the fire within

"Insolence! Your stroll will take you directly to the dungeon!" he shrieked

"Dungeon?" Fox replied, seemingly aghast by the suggestion "Come now. 'Tis but a slight infraction. I suggest that you leave me in peace, for I am in no humor."

"Ha! You must be new to Damaas. All infractions result in a visit to the dungeon."

"Then the executioners axe!" cried another of the soldiers

"Executioner?!" Fox replied "My, you have upped the ante."

"'Tis cheaper than feeding you lot!" the lieutenant cried "Cheaper still if we take care of you here!"

He lunged at Fox with his spear. With blinding speed, Fox side-stepped the attack; gripping the haft of the weapon in his hands as he did so. He drove the spearhead into the walkway and thrust with his shoulder. The result was that the guard flew through the air and collapsed into a heap behind him. Without releasing his grip on the weapon, Fox swung it about like a quarterstaff, spinning and striking like a whirling dervish. It was his first true battle since his defeat at the hands of Krillian. He was pleased to note that his speed was now twice what it was since last humbled. Only when the last of the guardsmen fell to the ground, blooded and broken, did he realize that none of the aggression he had been feeling had been relieved.

He stripped the guard closest in size to himself of his armor and donned it. He had a long night ahead of him before he joined Aron and his family for breakfast, and yet had much aggression to relieve himself of.

CHAPTER TWENTY-TWO - THE TEMPLE OF LIGHT

It was dawn by the time Fox relieved himself of the golden armor. This was not all he relieved himself of, as he had taken recent opportunities which availed themselves to deface many a golden tower. The last of the guardsmen he had encountered lay face-down in the street, and as curfew had not yet expired, there were no eyes on him as he made the transformation from soldier to humble steel merchant. In days past, he would have slain the guardsmen he had encountered, yet remembering that Aron himself was once one of their number, he had done them the courtesy of merely beating them senseless.

He left a bloody swath of insensate soldiers from the Tarot near to Orin's inn, for he learned much of the geography of Damaas during his nocturnal recreation and did not wish to waste daylight hours searching for it. Despite not having slept since arriving, he felt refreshed and invigorated from his recent exercise as he made his way thither. The knowledge that Khimotai awoke this morn upon his bed of nubile concubines he had become too old and decepit to please, only to be told that there was still one amongst his populace who would piss on his perfect sense of order, had succeeded in bringing a smile to Fox's face since first he arrived in the Kingdom.

The joyless commuters of the golden city began flooding the streets once more by the time he arrived at the inn, yet their dulled senses and broken wills evidenced the slightest spark which threatened the monotony of the daily grind. Something of interest was afoot, and the increased presence of guardsmen amongst their number confirmed Fox's suspicions that the palace did not share his sense of humor. He himself had been accosted and interrogated twice in the little time between when curfew ended and his arrival at the inn, yet as he had no contraband on his person, and seeing as how they had no description of him beyond the armor they themselves wore, he was permitted to continue about his business. Perhaps the citizens themselves cared little for the heightened level of scrutiny they faced on this day, yet Fox consoled himself that this was of their own doing. Every thief knew that if one allowed a firm grip to be placed on one's life, it was to be expected that such a grip would ne'er release, but tighten 'til all were choked by it.

The exterior of Orin's paralleled every other inn in Damaas, the

Tarot included, yet Fox had by now become accustomed to such conformity. It was only upon entering the tavern situated on its lower level that he realized why Orin himself had been as successful an entrepreneur as he was rumored to be. As the Tarot was reminiscent of the Bear's Den in Gemmen, so too was Orin's reminiscent of the Pilgrim's Oasis in Serdia. There were no skillfully carved sculptures of wildlife, and this did not surprise him, for inspiration and passion were always key ingredients to revolution, thus the first to be expunged by any militant regime- yet the gold trim had been kept to the bare minimum, and the entire layout and ambiance mimicked its sister inn. The stew which simmered on the hearth smelled flavorful, and Fox had to wonder if Orin himself had not smuggled some of his cousin's recipes to Damaas in order to add to the ambiance. Clearly this was a refuge for those who shared his own distaste for life in the golden city. He could only hope that his vigilante activities in the neighborhood did not result in any guardsman inspection, for such a welcoming environment had to be in violation of the carefully constructed rigidity of Khimotai's dominion and he was loathe to see such a refuge suffer because of his own lack of restraint.

He had just set foot in the tavern when a short, fat man advanced in years greeted him at the door with arms outstretched. "Welcome!" he announced with great jubilation. His rosy cheeks and cheerful disposition lent evidence to the fact that this one clearly enjoyed his own supply of ale. He wore an apron stretched tightly across his ample frame, which barely concealed his humble, peasant's clothing underneath. What little hair he yet had was thin and silver and Fox suspected that this was Orin himself.

"Thank you. I am expected by a man named Aron and his family."

"Ah! Beautiful girl!" he approached Fox closely and jabbed him playfully on the shoulder "Fine marriage stock that one!" he smiled and winked simultaneously as he spoke, which had the effect of sending creases through his already wrinkled face. If there were any doubt that this was indeed Orin, kin to his most recent hosts in Serdia, they were dispelled immediately.

Orin led him to a plain, unadorned wooden table near the hearth, and he was pleased to see his friends waiting there for him.

"I hope I am not late!" Fox announced. "I did promise that I would be buying breakfast."

"Costa!" Sariss cried. She nearly leaped out of her seat and gripped him in a tight embrace. "We have just now left our room upstairs. This city is simply impossible to navigate; we barely made it here before curfew."

Fox remembered his first encounter with the local guardsmen after said curfew had come into effect and was immediately concerned. "I trust you had no other troubles?"

Sariss had not the time to answer however, for Erik stood from his seat next to his father, his excitement barely contained. "Have you heard the news?!"

"News?" Fox responded nonchalantly

"We have only just heard! It is rumored that the fearsome Fox of Gemmen himself is here in Damaas! Rumor has it he singlehandedly defeated thousands of guardsmen in this very district this night past!"

Fox could only smile. Perhaps the lad was wont to exaggerate, yet for once he was pleased that his charade forbade him from telling him so. Let the populace talk, he mused. Let their cries be echoed in the halls of the thieves' guild, that they might know that a true thief has at last arrived in Damaas; one who does not hide in darkened rooms plotting with the likes of assassins.

"Seat yourself boy!" came the voice of Aron. His anger seemed more excessive than the situation warranted. Clearly he was in bad humor. "We have yet half a day's journey through this thrice-accursed maze of gold before we arrive at the Temple of Light. Though your sister expects us, she does not know that it will be on this day, and I want no talk of thieves or guardsmen, nor anything else to mar the occasion!"

Despite the negativity Aron had suddenly infused the atmosphere with, Sariss smiled at him warmly from across the table and Fox immediately understood why she was so jubilant at his arrival. He had never before had anyone worry that he would somehow not return from one of his many adventures. He found the idea both irksome and warming. The notion that she was so concerned about his safety with no one to confide in brought pangs of guilt to the surface, accompanied immediately by feelings of resentment that he should be accountable to anyone. Thankfully his thoughts were interrupted by Orin himself who had by then waddled to their table and placed a hearty meal before them. The inviting aroma reminded him that he had not eaten. Suddenly his attention was fixed solely on food. In this moment, despite the man's slovenly appearance, Fox was convinced he was a culinary genius.

"Nothing but the finest for friends of my cousin!" the rotund man said as he set down the tray heavily laden with stew and bread. "May I interest you in some of our fine ale? Nothing like the bland stock you will find in any other inn, I assure you! I brew it myself from the finest herbs smuggled in from Serdia!" he accompanied the statement with a knowing wink to Aron

"It is yet a bit early for such libations for us, but we thank you." Aron replied

Orin merely shrugged and returned to the bar.

Erik, Aron and Fox dove into the meal, foregoing their cutlery entirely and using the fresh bread itself to scoop up mouthfuls of the thick and hearty stew. Only Sariss restrained herself.

"I am so excited I've lost my appetite!" she said through a small mouthful of bread. "I see now why 'tis said that when the sun sets, it does so in Damaas. 'Twas so bright in our room this night past I was scarecely able to keep my eyes shut. Though in truth, I doubt I might have slept had I been in my own bed back in Gemmen, my belly full of mead, exhausted from a day spent in the fields. You will be joining us Costa, wont you? Costa?"

Fox was once again lost in his own thoughts. His adrenaline had only now left him, in its stead; he was faced with the staggering reality of what he had done. He had sworn to protect this family from Krillian, yet if his nocturnal proclivities were now the subject of widespread rumor, then the arch-assassin knew of them as well. He had been angry and stupid; impulsive and careless. He had behaved exactly how Ciella had characterized him, that which he resented her for- with no thought for any but he alone; intent on venting his frustrations free of consequence. He cursed himself for a fool. He was not accustomed to carrying such burdens. Always he had deigned never to get involved in the complicated dramas which embroiled the lives of others, his role ever that of a spectator, a thief in the night- one whose fleeting embrace left its mark on those whom it touched yet never lingered.

Orin's was the single comfortable environment he had found since entering the golden city. Had he any desire to leave, it was to return to Gemmen, to where life was simpler, free of politics, intrigue or complications of any kind; yet he could not, for any reason, allow his friends to leave his sight. Krillian had used his connection to this family to track him once before. He would do so again. In allowing himself the luxury of their company, he had created a weakness to be exploited. He would not run lest it be they who suffer the repercussions of such wanton cowardice.

The notion of spending the day in the company of servile monks and an overly excited girl swooning over a nobleman bard was low on the list of activities the master thief cared to engage in. He winced visibly before he replied.

"Certainly." he said, forcing a smile

As they ate, Fox entertained different theories as to why Orin's had not yet been investigated by guardsmen looking for any suspicious stranger who may have booked a room that morning. It was possible of course that Orin himself had come to some kind of arrangement with them, but years spent observing the world from the outside had afforded him the ability to judge a man's character and mien with unerring accuracy, and he did not suspect the amicable fellow of being in possession of such a duplicitous nature. Likely, the guardsmen themselves enjoyed the escape from their own structured lives the inn afforded them when they were not on duty and thus chose to remain in Orin's graces. It was even possible that many seated about him were members of the city guard, now off-duty and enjoying the one establishment in Damaas where one could shrug off the weight of constant discipline.

Fox had but a pittance of coin remaining from his time in Serdia, but it proved to be enough to pay for breakfast as he promised. Aron had, after all, stabled Bolt out of coin from his own purse for the second time since he met the man, and this was but the least of the services the farmer had rendered him. He sprinkled his remaining coin across the table, feeling silly as he did so, for of what worth a few coppers in a city of gold, yet a monetary system was a means of controling the populace, and Fox no longer doubted that few dared to avail themselves of the abundance of wealth which lay about. He lamented that such wealth must seem a prison to commoners forced to labor every-day for their coin, a constant reminder of the hold Khimotai held over them. In this strange place, metaphor meshed with reality, for he had always viewed those who lived in squalor as being too blind or cowardly to simply reach out and avail themselves of the riches about them. In Gemmen, he had seen noblemen parade about in expensive attire as a means to lord it over the peasants as a daily occurence. It was difficult to comprehend an entire kingdom being guilty of the same demeaning sense of vanity. 'Twas yet another reminder of his resentment towards Ciella, for were it he who were lord of the thieves guild, he would have pilfered Damaas to its core and redistributed the wealth to the people. 'Twas true that he had seen no beggars or vagabonds in his short time here, yet though the peasants themselves seemed healthy and well-fed, he had no doubt that many of them in days past, haven been driven mad by their surroundings, must have attempted to avail themselves of the bounty of gold which surrounded them day after day. He was reminded of one particular soldier's comment about the fate of peasants and the executioners axe. Many must have been the men and women who met that axe, forever sealing their fates in grim fashion- their price fully paid for being livestock so well tended to.

The hearty meal was devoured with nary a scrap of bread left upon their plates and Fox and his companions made their way to the door only to be met by their host once again. "Will you be needing a carriage?" he asked them "Tis half a day's walk to the temple."

Fox did not recall mentioning the temple as their destination. 'Twas possible his friends had done so prior to his arrival, yet Fox suspected that Orin himself was privy to more than he alluded to.

"I believe we shall save our coin for another of your delicious meals." Aron replied

The compliment was well-taken by their jovial host. "Ah!" he cried "Then you shall not be permitted to leave without taking a loaf of sweet bread for the journey! I would be remiss as host should I allow you to partake in any of the bland fare offered in any other tavern! Make no mention of coin!" he handed a small basket to Sariss who smiled her acceptance of the gift. Orin blushed openly before addressing Fox directly, "Shall I fetch your mare from the stables? As fine a beast we have had in an age if I may say so!"

"I believe I shall walk as well." Fox replied "If you take care of your horses as well as you do all of your charges, then I am sure that she is in good hands."

Orin bowed low over his short, unsteady legs as they made their way past him and out onto the street once more. The sudden shift from the interior of the inn to the city of gold was blinding, and they were forced to take a moment to allow their eyes to adjust before setting out in the direction of the temple. Aron was the only member of their party who knew where the temple lie and it was he who led them through the streets, now bustling with an insurgence of guardsmen who continually harassed the locals in their haste to reinstate the order Fox had so upset the night before.

"The Temple of Light sits at the centermost point of the kingdom." Aron said as they made their way through the throng "We have but to travel inwards. Further east lies the palace which is best to be avoided at all costs. We shall meet this bard of Veronica's and after I have seen to her safety to my satisfaction we shall return to Orin's immediately. If we make haste and keep our heads down, we should have little trouble from the guards and will hopefully make it back before curfew. Simply behave as I do and our progress should remain unhindered."

The plan suited Fox's palette well and they wasted no time in executing it. Following his lead, they travelled in silence; heads bowed low, their meekness lending no evidence to any apparent subterfuge. The stratagem had thus far proven to be effective, but for differing reasons than perhaps Aron had expected, for a new life and excitement seemed to permeate the air from the chatter of the otherwise tamed populace, one which diverted attention from wayfarers- much to the agitation of the soldiery who busied themselves in frustrating attempts at reinstating the customary banality. All about them conversation permeated the air as to how the fearsome Fox of Gemmen had dared to challenge Khimotai's rule. This was purely speculation of course, for aside from Ciella and Sariss, none could know for certain that he was indeed in Damaas, yet there had been rumors that he was headed east, and the story of a daring rogue who struck at the King's guard in the night aligned with his notoriety enough to awaken flames of imagination long quagmired in drudgery. As such, swift progress was made, and Fox was impressed with Aron's memory, for though all seemed uniform in design; he led them onwards quickly, taking no pause whatsoever in order to readjust their heading. Clearly, the act of sneaking to and fro the temple during his youth in order to visit his love left the location of the temple fully ingrained in his memory which the passing of so many years could not diminish.

Things were going so well in fact, that Sariss took it upon herself to raise spirits by attempting conversation.

"Our host is certainly a pleasant man." she said smiling

"Aye." responded Aron "A lively sort. He informs me that he laments not being able to send more gold to his cousin and her husband in Serdia, yet all are inspected thoroughly upon leaving Damaas, and Khimotai will not allow for any of his wealth to leave his Kingdom. What little contraband he manages involves naught but ingredients for his brewery. These he keeps well hidden in a storage room in the basement where none but he is permitted entry. Upon emerging from it, his portly cheeks are rosy, his stout legs wobble and his belly jiggles with mirth." Despite himself, Aron had to suppress his laughter

"Khimotai sounds to me a worse tyrant than Alric!" Erik said, completely ruining his sister's efforts at ambience

"Quiet boy!" Aron chided him. "Such talk will likely see you in the dungeon if any guards about hear!"

"I for one am absolutely teeming with excitement to see Veronica again!" interjected Sariss, refusing to allow Erik to spoil her humor "Three seasons have past in the fields since last I laid eyes on her. In her last letter, she seemed deeply in love!"

Aron merely grunted in reply. Clearly this latest attempt at introducing a subject which might better his mood had utterly failed. Sariss accepted defeat and they travelled in silence once more. Aron's inexplicable gloom hovered above all and the rest of their journey was marked by the uneasy tension.

It was midday by the time they spied the Temple of Light in the distance. 'Twas not difficult to miss, for next to the palace itself, it was the largest citadel in the kingdom, spanning several city blocks. It was also the only structure Fox had seen not inlaid with gold, likely the only such in the whole of Damaas. It consisted of three ivory towers which stood prominent above all, so tall and narrow one feared they might topple. These were interconnected by smaller buildings and arcades, themselves topped by several domes and spires. The dichotomy was staggering, for such awe-inspiring architecture yet remained completely unadorned, an effect pronounced when contrasted with the rest of the city. The effect was one of humble and pious vanity. The entire structure was so white and pure that its porcelain surface seemed to swallow the golden light about it, refusing to reflect it outwards. The imposing structure was malicing, yet despite himself, Fox could not help but find the ambience refreshing, for he had long since grown tired of appearing as though he himself were a golden statue come to life.

"It's beautiful!" Sariss cried, echoing her own statement from the day before when she had first spied Damaas itself from a distance. "I believe it is larger than our entire farmstead back in Gemmen!"

"Aye." responded Fox "Never have I seen a Kingdom so... monochromatic."

Despite himself, Aron threw his head back in laughter. Fox could not be certain if his jest had succeeded where all other efforts had failed in cheering up the old farmer, or if he were simply overjoyed at the notion that he would soon be reunited with his daughter. He did not care which was true, so long as the rest of the day passed quickly.

As they approached the temple, Fox was quick to note that the courtyard which surrounded it was similar to the one which surrounded the Golden Tower in Serdia, only much larger. It seemed as though every type of flower on Balthazar, even ones not native to the soil, grew here. It occurred to him then that that tower existed for those who actually enjoyed the way of life offered in Damaas, and much like Orin's inn was a refuge here for those from Serdia, the tower was a refuge to those who called the golden city home.

The west entrance to the garden was manned by guardsmen in the familiar golden armor, yet there the resemblances ended, for these greeted the party with warm and inviting smiles. They were waved through immediately only to find that the guardsmen within were much the same in demeanor. These walked about pleasantly, their lances held upright, yet could be seen smelling the flowers and admiring the sculpted fountainheads, each wearing broad smiles in place of wrinkled brows. Clearly, it was the monks who ran things here, and though Khimotai had succeeded in infiltrating the temple with his security forces, he had little sway or dominion beyond this meager accomplishment. All about them monks draped in sparse white robes ambled about, tending to the garden. Upon every knoll sat a young acolyte, either reading from a scroll, or writing upon one with quill and ink. Many of these made music by blowing into lutes and other instruments made of pipes and reeds, or were engaged in amicable conversations with the guardsmen themselves, who were caught in the sway of the relaxed atmosphere to such an extent as to prove unsettling.

"Welcome to the heart of Balthazar!" The nearest of the guardsmen bellowed. He was so affable that Fox nearly felt guilty about beating so many of his comrades to a bloody pulp the previous night.

"Well met." Aron replied, somewhat taken aback by the abrasiveness "I am father to a young acolyte who resides within. I believe she is expecting us."

"Ah!" the guardsman shouted gleefully "Likely you refer to Veronica! A vision of beauty and grace! Why, I never thought that my station here could have possibly been more pleasant until your daughter began bringing us baskets of fresh elderberries she so lovingly picked from the garden!"

"Err... yes." replied Aron "I have no doubt that she has."

Fox and Erik cast glances in each others direction, laced through with sarcastic wit they dared not express whilst Sariss beamed with joy.

"Please! Come and seat yourselves!" he gestured to a small patch of grass surrounded by flowering bushes. "Her morning rituals are likely completed at this hour. I should consider it an honor to fetch her for you!"

"I see no chairs." Aron replied

"Nonsense!'" the guard retorted "The grass brings one closer to Balthazar!"

Aron merely grimaced in response. Sariss laced her arm through his and laughed.

"Come father. We have had picnics before."

"I shall see to it that you are served the finest herbal hibiscus whilst

I fetch her!" said the guardsman, smiling from ear to ear. He ran off towards the temple, his excitement barely contained.

"This place certainly has an effect on people." Erik commented

"You have the right of it." replied Aron, rolling his eyes in response "I feel as though should I prick my thumb upon a thorn that half of this temple's monks would descend upon me proffering succor."

Erik looked about the garden with darting eyes, when he was content none were close enough to hear, he whispered to his father. "Was this place as strange when mother studied here?"

"Aye." responded Aron "Though she was of a more adventurous sort. She snuck away from the temple at every opportunity to visit me and consistently bristled at what she referred to as the choking isolation of the place. She had the gift, and her family believed the life of a cleric to be a noble calling, though she never took to the temple. I am thankful that it was my son who inherited her rebellious streak, lest Veronica find herself in similar straits."

Erik took in the environment once more before responding. "I shall take it as a compliment." he sighed

They seated themselves squat-legged upon the ground as instructed. Aron's demeanor did not change and Sariss laughed openly at his discomfort. The weather, once mild and pleasant, seemed to operate under different principles here, for the garden was bathed in such magnificent light that the heat was stifling. It was clearly a place of study and quiet meditation. The temple itself radiated a tranquil feeling of peace which strived to affect all, though Sariss alone of their party was smiling, perhaps less due to the effects of the garden and more so in reaction to the dour expressions of her companions.

"I wish I had brought my sword." Erik announced bitterly

"Aye." responded Aron

"Come now!" Sariss interjected, laughing "I for one am glad that Veronica has found her calling! With Erik constantly off wandering, fencing with imaginary adversaries upon the knoll, and her tending to every wounded starling she found, it's a wonder father and I were able to till the fields!"

Erik joined in the laughter. "Remember when father intended to slaughter our pig for solstice? What did she call him? Lord Oink?"

"Sir Oinkers!" Sariss threw her head back in laughter

"Aye." said Aron "I was forced to tell her that I had found a pack of wild boars in the forest who adopted the squealing thing after I sold it at market in Gemmen, else she likely would have never spoken to me again!"

Their reminiscing was interrupted by the presence of an elderly monk who laid down a platter of herbal tea and miniature disks of toasted bread before them. Fox was not the least bit surprised to notice that the cups and tray were of white porcelain, as indeed the monk's wispy hair and beard seemed to be. "Our finest flax wafers and hibiscus for our honored guests." he said smiling. "Wonderful diuretic."

Aron took the tray and set it before them, his forced smile betraying his disgust.

"Our thanks."

"I do hope you find the temple as calming an influence on troubled spirits as we." the monk continued, clearly noticing the expression

"Aye." responded Erik in the most affable tone he had displayed thus far "The tower of porcelain is very... serene... As though t'would shatter like glass if one threw a rock at it." He squinted as the words escaped his lips, his efforts at flattery failing him utterly.

The monk registered confusion as he bowed low and ambled off. Fox could contain himself no longer and burst into laughter. It wasn't long before all joined him.

Acknowledgments

Darren would like to thank...

First and foremost, my parents for nursing me back to sobriety and making this book possible- my sister, niece and extended family for always being there- the AA community of Sault Ste. Marie- comic-book mentors, particularly Geof Isherwood, Yannick Paquette, David Finch, Marco Rudy, Leonard Kirk, Lee Weeks, Ty Templeton, Alphonso Espinos, Ramon Perez, Zachariah Campbell, Mike Rooth, James O'Barr, and too many more to list- my friends who modeled for characters in the book,Rudolf Gjios in particular who brought the character of Fox to life, and to Fox himself, who taught me that a real, grown up life can be properly balanced with shenanigans. Shenanigans is my favorite word in the English language and I look for any opportunity to use it in a sentence. Shenanigans.

About the Author

Darren Emond was born one Halloween morning in the frigid northern wastelands of a little mining town called Wawa in Northern Ontario, Canada. The day will forever be commemorated in the annals of history, for elsewhere in the world a two-headed calf and a rutabaga shaped like the head of Alastair Crowley were also discovered somewhere in the Mediterranean. His parents forgot to keep the receipt and thus began their long ordeal raising the peculiar child who had few interests outside of comic-books, drawing, and chicanery. With a penchant for the creepy and the absurd, he broke his restraints and crashed around like a mad fiend calling many places home, finding a particular fondness for Montreal, before rampant alcohol abuse caused him to move to Sault Ste. Marie Ontario where he continues to terrorize the local populace from his headquarters near the central bus terminal.

Wherever he went, Darren wrote and drew stories. The guy can draw, he can write, and is a talented magician, pool, and chess player, who, unfortunately, tends to fail miserably at every other endeavor, particularly when pertaining to social graces. Perhaps this is why he shelters himself in a cocoon of fantasy, having no applicable skills in the real world. He is tolerated by his cat Conan, (as no woman could possibly want him) who does not care that Darren spends all of his time painting and drawing, so long as he is fed.

Darren plans on writing and illustrating the Fantabulous Tales of the Frivolous Fox as an ongoing series of graphic novels. Look out for them!

Made in the USA
Monee, IL
27 March 2023

30339744R00268